PENGUIN

A PILLAR OF

Julia Hamilton is also the author of *The Idle Hill*, and her new novel, *The Good Catholic*, is shortly to be published by Michael Joseph. She is currently writing a biography of Mary Queen of Scots. She lives in London with her two daughters and a black Labrador.

A Pillar of Society

JULIA HAMILTON

PENGUIN BOOKS

PENGUIN BOOKS

Published by the Penguin Group
Penguin Books Ltd, 27 Wrights Lane, London W8 5TZ, England
Penguin Books USA Inc., 375 Hudson Street, New York, New York 10014, USA
Penguin Books Australia Ltd, Ringwood, Victoria, Australia
Penguin Books Canada Ltd, 10 Alcorn Avenue, Toronto, Ontario, Canada M4V 3B2
Penguin Books (NZ) Ltd, 182–190 Wairau Road, Auckland 10, New Zealand

Penguin Books Ltd, Registered Offices: Harmondsworth, Middlesex, England

First published by Michael Joseph 1995
Published in Penguin Books 1996
1 3 5 7 9 10 8 6 4 2

Printed in England by Clays Ltd, St Ives plc

For my mother, Ann Belhaven

PROLOGUE

The letter was a love letter and it was fifty years late. He knew she was still alive because he had seen a programme about her on the television, rather out of date, admittedly, but since the Wall had come down things had begun to get through (he thought of the end of Communism as being like a glacier melting, releasing things in its meltwaters that had been held frozen for half a century) and one of them had been Marjorie, now a famous gardener, in the company of the Prince of Wales in the garden at Highgrove.

Something gave in him when he saw her, like the string of an instrument breaking, and he knew he would have to try and see her again. She was still exceedingly beautiful, almost more so – if such a thing could be – than she was fifty years ago. She was as tall and slender as a willow wand and beautifully dressed. She had been wearing a striped silk skirt and shirt with a coloured sash and a large and exceedingly beautiful straw hat with a piece of the striped material tied around the brim with a flourish. The Prince, grinning and nodding with his hands behind his back (inspecting his plants, Hubert thought, like a general reviewing troops) was plainly rather smitten with her and who could wonder? This image of her in the wild wood amongst the flowers and birdsong remained in Hubert's mind like a Hilliard miniature. There had been a profile of her in one of the English newspapers now taken by the library of his old college which he still used, and Hubert had cut this out and brooded over it. He suspected it was unhealthy but he didn't really care. Love did not die, all the poets knew that, and she had always been his love.

The article gave a potted history of Marjorie's life: the passion for gardening conceived when her husband was a prisoner of war of the Japanese and the castle had been used as a nursing home, how this great interest had helped her survive his absence; the husband's return, the late arrival of a daughter the year of the Hungarian uprising in '56, the husband's development of a complementary interest as a botanist and finder of rare species of plants in odd corners of the world. She was the modern Miss Jekyll, the article suggested, an astonishing and innovative gardener, an English institution.

It was the priest who had encouraged him to write. They had watched the programme together and later, under the auspices of the confessional, Hubert had told him the story, a short, painful fable of love, war and folly, the telling of which made him feel like St Sebastian stuck full of arrows of remorse.

'Don't wait,' Father Ignatius had said, 'do it now while you still can. Life is so short.' He had added. 'Of course, we can see that from this end of it. You should try to make amends for the sake of the child.'

Masses would be said for the soul of the lost one, which had reposed in limbo until they had abolished it.

'Where is it now?' Hubert had asked.

'The souls of the dead are in the hand of God,' said Father Ignatius firmly. 'She must have lost the child after you left, I suppose.'

'Probably.' Hubert nodded sadly.

He waited a further two weeks to write, until the morning of his seventy-fifth birthday. He wrote a short and quite formal letter saying that he knew it would be a surprise to her to hear from him again and that she need not see him if she did not want to, but that he was thinking of coming to England during the next month or so . . . He put his pen down and looked out of his window at the thin line of apricot light travelling up the sky. It was fifty years ago to the day that they had met; half a century ago. He couldn't believe it, the way time had gone. As he got older important events in his early life seemed somehow closer as the mountains do on certain days when the air is clear. He watched the first rays of light break over the gleaming stucco façade of what had once been his family home and had since become a department of records for the Institute of Housing of the former GDR, now no more since Herr Kohl had soldered together the jagged edges of the two Germanies.

Hubert had crawled back here when the whole world was disintegrating in the terrible winter of 1945. The camp he had been in had been liberated by the Americans and he was free to go. (He remembered that strange last-minute reluctance to leave; freedom seemed something too immense, too crushing.) The schloss had belonged to his mother's family and she and her Dutch husband had raised their large brood there between the wars. His sisters were in America and both his brothers had been killed; when Hubert came back from the camp the place was all smashed up and there was nobody to bother about it. It was so odd, so lonely to be the only one left, to come back into the scene of one's former life as both someone who had been there and as a stranger. There had been troops billeted in the schloss at the beginning but they were long gone, leaving chaos in their wake. Windows were smashed, the banisters had been used for firewood, everything was ruined, defiled. The pretty painted panels in the ballroom ceiling had been used for target practice, the faces and limbs of the nymphs blackened and torn, those plump white arms and legs, those billowing draperies, everything was smashed and spat upon and trampled. He had walked through the rooms in despair, nevertheless vowing that he would see the place put to rights again if it killed him in the process. He began the next day with fanatical zeal, boarding up windows, sweeping rooms, clearing out fireplaces full of dead birds. Later on, when he had found a post at the local university teaching English Literature, he had been allowed to stay on at the schloss. He was useful for he knew where everything was and how the boiler worked due, largely, to a misspent youth.

After more time had passed and the schloss had been declared an important cultural landmark (and restored to a state of grandeur it had not known in this century), Hubert would give visitors guided tours when he had the time, not usually letting on that it had once been his own home; that would have been politically inexpedient.

He had married a woman in his department at the university who had died two years ago of cancer of the breast. There had been no children. His only child had been the unborn one he had left behind in Fordingbridge in 1942.

CHAPTER 1

'I should think the best thing would be for you to tell me, step by step as we walk the garden, how the thing began in your mind all those years ago. Our viewers are as fascinated by the personality of the gardener as much as they are by the garden . . .'

'Well, you could hardly have one without the other,' said Marjorie, giving Conway, the producer of the new series *English Gardeners*, her famous Mona Lisa-like half smile.

'Of course not,' said Conway, pushing back the stray lock of hair from his forehead. Everyone said of Marjorie Jessop that she was a bit of a femme fatale, a man-eater, but he found her charming and attractive and still bloody sexy for a woman who must be seventy if she was a day: but then that was her secret, he thought, half ashamed of his feelings; she was powerfully gentle, wise, a touch vulnerable, and took a great and pointed interest in people very quickly: she had already asked him how the baby's cold was and whether Jessica, his wife, was back at work yet. She knew how to manipulate people, but God, was she ever charming!

'That's a good idea,' Marjorie said, consulting a notebook with a dark green cover. 'I've made a list,' she added. 'A plan of how we should proceed. I'm never without a plan, you see; gardening does that to one; you find yourself tracing knot gardens in your sleep or altering something or even discovering new plants.'

'I should have thought that was your husband's province,' said Conway.

'Oh, it is,' she agreed, 'but it's mine too. You spend so much time imagining things you almost begin to think you invented them.'

Looking back over one's life it was sometimes difficult to distinguish between what one had made up and what one hadn't. And then there were the rôles one assigned to people: lover, protector, provider, dependant, entertainer, intellectual combatant: the new vicar, for instance: good-looking, intelligent (for once), intriguingly unhappy. Ah . . .

'All gardeners are thwarted artists, you know,' she said, seeing that Conway was waiting for her to finish. A cliché, of course. Someone had once said to her jestingly at a party that he thought gardening gave middle-aged women a chance to play Charlemagne. So true, so gratifyingly accurate. She had laughed out loud and surprised him. He had thought he had hit home.

'Thwarted?' asked Conway in surprise. 'More fulfilled than thwarted, surely?'

'Gertrude Jekyll trained as a painter, you know. Her eye for colour – knowing what went with what – stemmed from that.'

'What started you off then?' Conway looked round the drawing room as he spoke, relishing the grand family portraits, goitrish Lely women in rust-coloured taffetas with roses in their laps, great masses of flowers on the piano strewing petals over the polished surface and among the photographs (he noted Marjorie by Beaton: satin dress, the pillar, the garden beyond), serried ranks of delicious knick-knacks, faded, wonderful Colefax materials in curtains and chair covers; everything lovely.

'A garden gives you an illusion of control,' she said. 'It makes you think you're in charge: it's a drug, it goes to your head.'

'Something happened that made you feel the need to be in control?' Conway said curiously. There had been a strange look on her face as she spoke, as if she had remembered something painful that had been forgotten or buried.

'My darling boy, there was a war on. We were none of us in control of a thing. I began as a vegetable gardener, growing cabbages and potatoes, carrots, anything that would feed us. Then I began to embellish: I had ornamental cabbages among the real ones, lavender edging my beds. I became obsessed by herbs and their properties . . .'

'Wonderful,' said Conway, turning to his assistant, Carrie, who was sitting quietly beside him taking notes. 'You've got all that, haven't you?'

'Every word,' said Carrie, looking up.

'Let's walk it through,' said Conway, 'and see how we get on. May we?'

'Of course.' Marjorie got up at once. 'I'm longing to show off the garden. We'll go out here,' she said, indicating the long windows that reached from ceiling to floor, 'and make a circular progress downwards to the wild wood and then back through the vegetable garden, the potager – the herb garden – and the orchard.'

'The castle is very old, as you know, although what we call the castle now was actually a house built in the grounds of the original,' said Marjorie, taking Conway's hand as she stepped across the low sill on to the parterre. 'Edward the First was supposed to have stayed in the tower' – she gestured with her arm towards the ruins that were partially visible from the terrace where they now stood beyond an arch of yew – 'and there's always been a garden here, although not laid out as it is now, other than this bit of it.'

She turned back to look at the façade of the house, the long line of windows on the ground floor and above.

'In 1770 Bartholomew Jessop married a Miss Hughes who was an heiress – which was lucky for him – and with her money they changed the whole look of this side of the old house and allowed their landscape gardener to fiddle with the ruins – which meant knocking some of them down to make it seem more romantic. Bartholomew couldn't do much with the layout of the garden because, as you can see, it's set on the side of a hill, falling in a series of terraces towards the road. But he dammed the stream and made a rill, then he made what he called a lake down there, below the ruins – à la Claude – although it's more of a pond, really.' She pointed with one hand, sunlight glinting on her enormous diamond rings. 'And a wood up there.' More glinting rings and arm movements.

'What sort of shape was the garden in when you inherited it in ... 1936, wasn't it?' Conway had his notebook out as he spoke and was turning pages.

'Yes,' said Marjorie. 'February, 1936. Cold as charity, frost every night. I was more interested in hunting then, the garden bored me. I walked round it, of course, but there were several gardeners in those days, including Willmott, the head gardener, and he certainly didn't want a whippersnapper like me getting in his way, but the war changed all that.'

'Your husband was away for a long time, I gather,' said Conway.

'That's right,' said Marjorie, who never answered questions about Guy's absence if she could avoid doing so. Memories from those days ached like old wounds: it was a fact, she thought, that pain (even more than pleasure) was a knife that etched memories as clear as a steel engraving, or as sharp as the blades that cut the yews in their cones and pyramids.

'This parterre is the oldest part of the garden and was laid out in the sixteenth century: the little box hedges were put there to make divisions and to protect flowers, the paths are of sand. The statues are for sheer pleasure. We added the orange trees in tubs – they go indoors in the winter. I adore it because of the symmetry and the shelter and because the rest of the garden is like a mystery: you can't tell from here what to expect.'

'Who is this?' asked Conway, looking up at a statue.

'Demeter,' said Marjorie briefly.

'The yew trees are marvellous,' said Conway, seeing that a change of subject was somehow necessary. 'What is it about yew that makes it so satisfactory?'

'Its density and its obedience,' said Marjorie, 'and the fact that it defies nature instead of humouring it. In the war the men would come out on to the terrace and sit in the sun. The ones in wheelchairs could roll themselves round the paths. We grew vegetables in those flowerbeds then.'

'A series of rooms,' said Conway, following Marjorie down a flight of steps under a yew arch; urns sat in the green/black recesses of the hedge. Everywhere one looked there was something to delight. He thought of his own back garden in London which consisted mainly of mud and plastic toys that the puppy had chewed.

'That is what a garden is, a large garden at any rate,' said Marjorie. 'One room enticing you into another.'

'Heavens,' said Carrie gazing around her, 'it's so lovely. I love the pergola. Is that wisteria? I'm such a nitwit about gardens, I don't know a thing.'

'You can always learn,' said Marjorie. 'People think there's a mystique about gardening, just as they do about cooking, almost as if it's something only certain people can do, but anyone can do it. It's a question of enthusiasm to learn, that's all, and a willingness to experiment, a metaphor for living in a way.'

'Have you lived your own life like that, do you think?' asked Conway, smiling.

'I hope so,' said Marjorie, 'I hope so . . .'

The sunlight on the wisteria made it seem so extraordinarily silvery, so luminous; as she looked it all went black. Time stopped. Then started again. Conway was finishing the word she had heard him begin – he wanted to talk about the Prince of Wales (they all did, in the end) – and she wondered if she had imagined it. Everything blotted out by night, a black and encompassing silence that frightened her. It had happened twice before, but it was nothing. She walked on easily, fluently. Just anno domini. She was seventy-five. 'Seventy-Five Years Young' the caption had said about her in *Harpers & Queen* in their most recent interview. She had worn Armani like the Duchess of Kent, only not that ridiculous crochet trouser suit that made one look like an antimacassar . . .

'He's done very well with his garden at Highgrove,' she said. She always said the same thing in different ways. An eager young man with a doomed look about him. His enthusiasm had made her fear for him in a way. People were so cruel.

'And you are his official adviser, aren't you?' Conway asked as they passed through a wrought-iron gate into the most ravishing garden he thought he had ever seen.

'No, no, not at all,' said Marjorie. 'I just go along sometimes when I'm asked and . . .' She didn't finish her sentence. 'This is my palette garden, a kind of homage to Miss Jekyll whom I revere. She was very clear about colours, you see, what you could do and what you couldn't do.'

She began to explain the plants – how each end of the great border was planted in Miss Jekyll's 'grey and glaucous foliage' and how the colours linked with santolina *incana* or yucca began in pure blue, grey, white, palest pink, pale yellow, each colour partly in distinct masses and partly intermixed, moving on into stronger yellows and red, then receding in inverse sequence; how Miss Jekyll had known that an eye saturated with powerful colours will fall with relief on greys and purples.

They walked slowly round the raised borders that lined this ravishing little walled garden. Learning about plants took years of experiment and study and love, but it was one of the most satisfying things in the world. This had always been her favourite part of the garden because a hidden door in the wall with only one key led into her secret garden, and that was a place she never let anyone enter except Guy, and before Guy one other person, long dead, long vanished, but whom she had not forgotten.

CHAPTER 2

In the afternoon of the following day, Sir Guy Jessop Bt, dressed in corduroy trousers of great antiquity and a tweed jacket which a label inside informed him had been made for his father Hugh in 1912, was looking for his wife. She was not in her own sitting room, nor in the book room on the ground floor where they kept all the horticultural books, and so he supposed she had gone to ground in the drawing room with her coffee. When he peered in he could see she was sitting in a winged armchair covered in tattered chintz that had been chosen by his mother at about the same time as his father had ordered the jacket Guy was wearing.

Marjorie had concentrated on changing the garden, not the house, displaying her usual excellent judgement. She had declared the house 'perfect' in 1936 when she had first crossed the threshold as a bride, thereby endearing herself to his mother, Lavinia, until her death in 1939 by allowing her to continue to do everything whilst she, Marjorie, concentrated on her hunting and had a perfectly wonderful time both in London and in this remote corner of Gloucestershire which was still, mercifully, beyond what Marjorie called the Range Rover belt. All those ghastly vulgarians in their new shooting clothes calling him Guy without being asked to and then cornering him to enquire whether he wanted to become a Name at Lloyd's at luncheon afterwards; and those women with blonde streaks who were all called Fiona . . . ugh, he shuddered at the thought of them, noticing as he did so that Marjorie was asleep, which was not entirely like her, but she must have been tired after yesterday, although that young man had seemed polite and intelligent. He had wanted to see if Marjorie was all right and if she needed anything. Harriet, Guy's sister, told Guy that Marjorie treated him like a major-domo.

'You should assert yourself more,' she told him, being used to assert herself on a variety of committees, 'make her look after you for a change. I don't think she knows how lucky she is.'

Harriet had grown awfully like their mother, Guy thought, stout and tweedy and utterly without imagination, absolutely the opposite of Marjorie whose attenuated seven-denier elegance had been the inspiration for a thousand magazine interviews: elegance and strength and determination, that was Marjorie. He didn't *mind* looking after her, in fact it kept him going now he was getting fractionally too old to go the Himalayas hunting plants in the airlessness of the heights or other outlandish spots for months on end. It was Guy who had brought back *thymus Jessopiana* from Madagascar, now one of the most popular alpines and sold in every garden centre in Britain. He considered that as he pottered round the room straightening things and peering into the vases to make sure the flowers had enough water now that the weather had got warmer: those moments, rare, rare moments, when he had known that he had discovered something new, had made up for so much disappointment, the lack of a son, for instance, the fact that his physical relationship with his wife had ceased years and years ago (men flocked to her, but he was not allowed to worship where he should really have liked to): these dissatisfactions that moved like dangerous currents beneath the apparently perfect façade of his life: the title, the castle, the wife, what more could a man want . . . what, indeed?

'Guy', said Marjorie, 'stop fiddling.'

'Did I wake you? I'm sorry.'

'Not really, I was just lying doggo for a moment.'

'What's happening this afternoon?' he asked, sitting down on the sofa and putting his cup on a little table.

'Chloe's coming this evening. You hadn't forgotten that, surely?'

'No, no.' Guy frowned and looked at his hands. 'What else?'

'David's coming up to read and to help me do some things.'

'Oh, I see. Hasn't he anything better to do?'

'He wants to learn,' said Marjorie calmly. 'The vicarage garden is a jungle, as you must have noticed.'

'Ye-es.' Guy thought for a moment. 'Pity his wife won't help.'

'You know as well as I do that she won't.'

'Hmm,' said Guy, and sniffed.

He got up and went to a window, automatically noting that the *azara microphylla* needed cutting back. After the previous incumbent, Canon Jones, had died, the vicarage garden had got the bit between its teeth and romped, Guy remembered, whilst a replacement was found for poor old Canon Jones, a rather handsome and intriguing replacement of considerable charisma called David Doughty (*'Very* Pilgrim's Progress,' Marjorie said on hearing the new appointee's name, which was typical of her worst kind of nonsense ... the way she confused imagination with reality and saw not what was there but what she wanted to see – she had re-cast Doughty already as a cross between Gerard Manley Hopkins and Gilbert White), who had been a slum priest in Notting Hill, building up a practically derelict church from nothing much, but in the Anglo-Catholic tradition rather than as one of those ghastly creatures in grey suits with microphones who now ruled in the C. of E. He had been worn out, the bishop said, by this appointment, and although reluctant to leave had accepted that a country living might be a good thing for all of them.

There were two daughters of indeterminate age. Doughty's wife was an academic of some kind, a teacher and a committed feminist, a rather odd companion for such a traditional kind of priest: one of those slightly mannish-looking women with short spiky hair, round gold glasses with wire rims and dangly earrings, a species which roamed the streets of Islington, Hampstead and Notting Hill, or so Guy was led to believe. She had ordered the *Guardian* from the newsagent's in Bridge Street, as well as some feminist magazine with no pictures in it, causing eyebrows to raise, and was already running a discussion group on Tuesdays which was causing tongues to wag: 'Removing the gag – women and the priesthood'; 'Aids, drugs, your children and you'; 'If your son is gay'; 'The bloodied sheet – the stigma of menstruation' ... Fordingbridge was a farming town, conservative, suspicious, and more concerned with milk quotas and barley subsidies than the stigma of menstruation or whether their sons were poofs or not.

Doughty was good-looking (not a good thing in a priest) and intelligent, and keen to fraternize, Guy imagined. He also supposed that Marjorie was using him as a sounding board about Chloe's problems, which, if Guy thought about it, he did not like, although he did not question himself closely as to why this should be so. Chloe, who had had everything going for her, had made rather a mess of things one way and another. Of course, Doughty was the physical type Marjorie liked: tall, dark-haired, loose-limbed, with a beaky nose and a twinkle in his eye. She had always gone for that kind of aristocratic angularity. Once upon a time he had been rather like that himself, Guy thought, before he had been a prisoner of war: those years had ruined his stomach and reduced his stature, buggered up what remained of his youth and beauty. There had been plenty of that here in the war when he had been away for so long; then the place had been a convalescent home for officers run by Marjorie, who had worn and made her assistants wear a little uniform of her own devising, rather too short and very sexy; he remembered a photograph of them lined up outside the long windows on the parterre, chaps seated on dining room chairs or in wheelchairs brandishing rakes and trowels, and the nurses in between, all nipped waists, padded shoulders and watches on their prominent bosoms. In that particular photograph Marjorie was standing next to a black-haired fellow who rather resembled the vicar, now he came to think of it, a lean, beaky-looking chap who had been with the Free French or something, anyway a tearing good-looker. Even the length of time and the rather poor quality of the photograph could not disguise the fact that *she* had looked radiantly happy, although she had no business to. What had become of him? Guy wondered, returning across the hall and through the green baize door into the passageway that led to the kitchens. Probably dead, he thought, putting the coffee cup down on the draining board in the scullery which was lined with oak cupboards built in situ at least a century before at roughly the same time the great table was assembled in the kitchen. Guy opened one of the cupboards without being entirely sure why he was doing so and gazed at the vast heaps of plates inside: so many objects accrued for the sake of it, more than one could ever need, there to be passed on to one's son and heir, except in his case he didn't have one, the first Jessop since God only knew when who hadn't had a son. As a family they had always been proud of the purity of their blood line. James, Chloe's son, would inherit these plates; marvellous little chap, but it was anxious-making not to know how the boy would turn out, particularly if he were now to be brought up solely by his mother without the restraining influence of a father. However hopeless the father it was undoubtedly better to have one. Guy shut the cupboard door firmly upon these disquieting thoughts and returned aimlessly to the kitchen.

Mrs Bosworth, the help, had cleaned up and gone early, as it was the back clinic at the local health centre on Fridays. She had left supper in the larder and a note for Chloe about what the children were to eat, something about lasagne in the fridge. Lasagne! When he was their age he had meat and two veg with pudding if he was lucky. Without being able to say why, he felt that this (to him) exotic nursery food somehow represented a decline in standards. Children were supposed to suffer, it was good for them. The two black Labradors wagged enthusiastically from their bean bags by the Aga as Guy muttered to himself. One of them, Nero, rose to his feet expectantly, seeing in Guy's presence a chance to suggest a walk, preferably down to the pond for a swim amongst the water lilies.

'Nothing's doing in that department,' said Guy. 'Lie down, sir, lie down, dogs.' He emphasized the last word deliberately, for it always made them wag even harder. They knew they were dogs, which seemed to Guy to be philosophically rather advanced. In fact he was certain that his dogs had a larger vocabulary than most *Sun* readers.

'*Dogito ergo sum*,' he murmured under his breath.

'Hello,' called a voice from the back door beyond the scullery. 'Anyone there?'

It was the parson. The dogs, thrilled to have something to bark at, rose in a tidal wave of wrath and indignation and rushed out.

'Come back, you blighters!' shouted Guy without conviction. 'It's only the padre,' he added, but the dogs paid not the slightest attention. They enjoyed barking at people. Guy sympathized.

'Sorry about that,' he said, raising a hand in greeting as the dogs came slinking in behind Doughty, noticing at the same time that the padre had exchanged his collar for a shirt and tie in an attempt, he presumed, to be more like an ordinary chap and less like a priest. Guy distrusted that. Priests should be priests or who knew where it would lead, and why should this chap come smarming along creaming off his wife's confidences?

'Marjorie was asleep when I went in just now,' Guy said; it was not a lie if it prevented the lower orders from availing themselves of one's household secrets. 'Have some coffee, there's some in the pot.' He added off-handedly, 'Cups on the shelf. I'll be back in a tick.'

'Thank you,' said David, helping himself and looking round the vast kitchen with interest tinged, he would be the first to admit, by envy. The other half, as his sister Tessa had once said to him, really did do itself awfully well. The oak table on which he was leaning had been built in this room in the last century, so Marjorie had said, together with the oak dressers that dominated two walls and the countless other cupboards in this marvellous welter of old back rooms: still rooms, where the jam had once stood to gel, sculleries full of vast stone sinks, a butler's room where the butler had slept every night over the silver chest, larders the size of bathrooms, boot rooms, a servants' dining room where a toy train was now laid out on the old table for the young grandson. The walls of the kitchen were hung with water-colours of the Italian lakes painted by Guy's grandmother and the whole place, from the old stone flags on the floor to the contents of the dressers, was agreeably tidy and gleaming, rather the opposite of the vicarage kitchen which was in a state of perpetual chaos verging on the slummy. It had been like that in London, but there had been reasons for it in London which no longer existed here. His London ministry had been organized chaos and sometimes merely neat chaos. The kitchen had been his headquarters, particularly after the parish room had been damaged by fire and groups had had to meet there for house masses, discussions and the hundred and one other appointments that were the substance of his endless days at St Anselm's where, towards the end of his time there, he had begun to feel he would collapse if the phone rang just once more, which of course it always did.

'You take too much on yourself,' Frances had said, which was true, but then so did she with her teaching and lecturing. Her commitment to feminism and his exhaustion and endless busyness meant that the housework did not get done and the cooking was skimped. Washing and ironing were a bit of a joke. Kitty and Tanya were supposed to do the ironing but they were always behind and never without a good excuse: 'My maths homework . . . my project . . . I have to get this done by the morning . . .'

'Iron your own shirt,' said Frances at breakfast one morning, which meant standing up eating a piece of toast before rushing off with the girls to school on her way to the college where she was teaching.

'I don't have time,' he said, trying to be calm.

'Well, neither do I.'

He heard himself shouting, almost with surprise: 'You don't have time for any bloody thing that doesn't serve your own end.'

Both the girls stared at him in shock. He never shouted. He was always calm.

'I'm sorry you feel that way,' said Frances, 'but I can't discuss it now. We have to go. Come on, girls, hurry or we'll be late.'

Was it only then that he realized – could he have been so stupid? – what a pretty pass things had come to between him and Frances?

They had met when David was an ordinand at theological college in Oxford and Frances was an undergraduate reading English. Her hair had been long in those days, like Kitty's was now, long and dark and curling; she wore it loose or in a wonderful bun with curls escaping, showing off her slender neck that had looked like the delicate stem of a plant from behind. He remembered that he had been moved by her appearance when he first saw her in Blackwell's. She had dropped a pile of books and he had helped her pick them up and had then asked her out to tea on the spur of the moment. She had been very thin in those days and wore the most amazing clothes from the Oxfam shop or jumble sales. He remembered noticing the hole in her dress by the zip at the back – the brown skin showing through – and the fact that her hair was tied back with what looked like a piece of a man's tie (and which had turned out to belong to her current boyfriend). At tea she told him that her father was an architect and her mother a sculptress and that they lived in Richmond in a house designed by her father, that she, Frances, disliked intensely. She loathed anything concrete, open-plan, or avant-garde in the way of houses, and had always longed to live in a cottage with cosy rooms and small windows or something *old*. That made him laugh.

'Now I inhabit my dream,' Frances said, spooning three sugars into her tea. 'Panelling, ordinary windows, a fireplace that looks like a fireplace instead of a plinth for burnt offerings.'

He had loved her sense of humour and the air she had about her of being ready for anything, plus the fact that she was exceedingly bright. They had married as soon as he had finished his training. David's father, who was a country solicitor near Cirencester, had taken to her at once, and so had his mother; but it was his mother, so acute in such matters, who had said about Frances: 'She has a passionate enthusiasm for things, you'll have to make sure she doesn't go off at a tangent. Women can, you know, especially clever ones like Frances if they get bored at home with small children and too many domestic tasks they're ill suited to.'

In those early days she had been curious about, but at the same time detached from, David's vocation. Her parents had had her baptized and she had got herself confirmed at boarding school in order, she said, that she could attend the early communion service in the local church and avoid the boredom of matins. This detachment had persisted until she began a teacher-training refresher course after Kitty was born. On this course she had met Jenny Benn, who was a member of a Christian feminist group. Frances started to go to meetings on a regular basis. She and David began first to discuss and then to argue about the ordination of women as priests. Frances joined a further group whose aim was to achieve the ordination of women. The years went by. When at last David moved from his suburban parish in Twickenham to St Anselm's, Notting Hill their growing differences of opinion were swamped by the astonishing busyness of their lives and the excitement of being needed, the satisfaction of knowing they were the hub of the community.

After he had shouted at Frances that morning, David began to think carefully, for the first time in a long time, about their marriage. Two things, in particular, worried him: he couldn't remember when they had last made love, and he couldn't remember when they had last finished a discussion in which they disagreed with one another without one of them getting angry and leaving the room.

CHAPTER 3

When he had first married Frances, David couldn't quite believe his luck. He had work that made him feel useful and he was deeply in love with his wife. Her cleverness delighted him and he used to enjoy discussing things with her; she could always surprise him by coming up with an angle he hadn't thought of or devising some novel way of dealing with a problem. They would lie in bed at night and talk – it amazed him to find this kind of companionship with a woman. That she couldn't cook and wasn't much good as a housekeeper hadn't bothered him in those days. They had no children, they both worked. He regarded her as his equal and was more than happy to do the cooking. A woman came in twice a week to clean and do the ironing. But once Tanya was born, three years after their marriage, things began to change. Frances went back to work when Tanya was six months or so, but the advent of the baby meant there was three times as much to be organized. David's vicar was ill and he had to do everything in the parish, but he liked it in a way because he knew he was a good priest. He had a good voice and convincing delivery, and regarded it as his purpose in life to be a converter of souls. His tutor had once told him that his danger was that he would grow vain because everything came easily to him, but David did not regard a realistic assessment of his abilities as vanity. He loved the Church and he wanted to bring people into it. He was busier than he ever had been, although he continued to do the cooking. Tanya was an amazingly sleepless and fretful baby. They didn't have a single unbroken night with her until she was almost two, and by then (by some miracle or other) Frances was pregnant again with Kitty. After she was born, Frances was so busy that the house grew dirtier and dirtier. A succession of dreadful girls looked after the children, each more feckless than the last: one got pregnant, one stole, one went out and left the children on their own, on and on it went.

When the girls were seven and four, David went to St Anselm's.

It was a huge challenge: his task was to awaken and sustain an inner-city parish with a very ethnically mixed population containing extremes of poverty and riches. The excitement and the challenge were intense. Both he and Frances were busier than they had ever been in their lives. There was no time to notice that they found it hard to talk. David was out all day in the parish seeing people and taking services and when he got in the telephone claimed him or people banged on the door. There was the day's work and then the night's work: counselling, house masses, discussion groups, Bible study. Family life fitted around all this somehow. Frances and David no longer argued about women and the priesthood together with the countless other subjects that had once been currency between them because there was no time.

One day she cut her hair off, her lovely long hair. David and the girls were appalled, but even then he did not recognize the danger signals; that such an act was a bid for attention, for a sympathetic ear, for support.

'Why did you do it?' he asked, in between phone calls, as he stirred the sauce for the pasta. Frances was marking essays at the kitchen table.

'It's my hair', she said, without looking up.

'You might have told me'.

'Why?'

'I always loved your hair.'

'You mean you thought of it as your property.'

'I didn't say that.'

Frances turned a page and began ticking again.

'Am I not allowed to admire you?' he said.

'Do you admire me?'

'Of course I do. I respect you enormously.'

'Except when I do something you don't like.'

The telephone rang, putting an end to further discussion, and when that call was finished the girls came in wanting supper.

'Tanya, lay the table, Kitty get the plates out.'

'I always lay the table', said Tanya. 'She always get off lightly.'

'Why did you cut your hair, Mum?' said Kitty. 'It was so pretty.'

'It's my hair', repeated Frances, still ticking.

'I hate it', said Kitty.

'That's enough', said David.

'She can say what she thinks', said Frances. 'I want to know what she thinks.'

'I think it's weird', said Tanya, who was cross with Frances for reasons she couldn't quite put her finger on. It would be nice to have a mother who was more normal.

We'll have to talk about it later, David thought, draining the spaghetti. Perhaps chat in bed like we used to. But even as he thought this, he knew it was hopeless. As soon as he lay down he went to sleep, which was why he had taken to saying his prayers standing up in his study before going to bed, and even that was becoming harder. The source of grace seemed to be drying up. One morning recently, in the limbo-land of a waking dream, he had discovered that a part of his mind was thinking it was all a sham, all mumbo-jumbo, mouthing prayers into a kind of mocking emptiness, just a mental trick. Faith, after a pause, had flooded in again, but the memory of this lapse haunted him.

Some weeks after this, Mary Chandos asked David, after the Thursday morning mass, whether he would bring the sacraments to her husband Bobbie Chandos, the painter, who was ill at home. David knew something about Bobbie Chandos because there had been items in the newspaper about him and also because they lived two doors down from his sister Tessa in Cumberland Grove off Ledbury Road. Tessa and her composer husband occasionally dined with Bobbie and Mary Chandos, but it was the newspapers that had told him Bobbie was dying of Aids. Bobbie, it was said, was anxious that people should know what he was dying of in order to make it easier for other sufferers. He was not ashamed, he said, of having Aids, he was only ashamed to be a member of a society that could treat victims of the disease in such an unChristian way. Where, David wondered, did that leave Mary Chandos? He had noticed her in the congregation although he had never spoken to her other than to shake her hand at the door. She was a handsome-looking dark-haired woman in her mid- to late- thirties, also a painter, who often came to his Thursday mornings.

'When would you like me to come?' he asked.

'When can you come? Today? Or are you too busy? We know how busy you are.'

'I'll come now,' he said, 'if that would suit.'

'I'm very grateful,' she said, pulling her camel-coloured coat around her. 'You know he has Aids,' she said. 'I suppose Tessa must have told you. I hope you don't mind.'

'Tessa didn't tell me,' he said. 'I read it in the newspapers. And I don't mind a bit. Give me a minute or two to get my things, then we'll be off.'

'Thanks,' said Mary. 'I'll wait for you outside.'

When he came out wearing his cloak, but not his biretta, she was smoking a cigarette which she continued to do as they walked along the road together.

'Sorry,' she said, noticing him looking, 'do you want one?'

'I'd love one,' he said, surprising himself. They stopped while she found the packet in her bag and then hunted for her lighter. Standing close to her, he saw that she was older than he had thought, perhaps in her early forties. It was quite a shock to him to realize that he found her very attractive. He couldn't remember when he had last thought that about a woman – other than Frances, of course.

'There you are,' she said. 'I wish I could stop this, but I like it too much. I feel I need it too at the moment.'

'How long has your husband been ill?'

'On and off for ages.' She began to walk on, picking her way round an old sofa someone had left out on the pavement. 'He's always had boys. I knew it when I married him. I thought I was the one who would save him. So stupid of me, so, so stupid.

'People mind my frankness,' she said, glancing at David. 'They say: "Oh Mary, you can't mean that," or, "Oh Mary, you mustn't say that . . ." So you end up never saying what you mean because it doesn't accord with what they want to hear and, in the case of AIDS, it isn't politically correct. Your straight friends think it serves you right and the gay ones feel sorry for Bobbie, but the thing is,' she went on, 'when he got this foul disease I began to be angry with him for spoiling everything. I couldn't speak to him for a bit. Then I began to be angry with myself because . . . because I was scared I might get it myself.'

22

'And have you?' asked David as they turned past Tessa's house up Cumberland Grove.

'I don't know,' she said, going up a flight of steps between two pillars and hunting in her bag again for her keys. 'I don't dare go and find out, but I find I watch myself all the time for symptoms. It's pathetic.'

'It's perfectly understandable,' said David, following her into a large hall with yellow walls and a black and white tiled floor.

'You are nice,' she said, smiling at him before taking off her coat and flinging it on to a chest. 'Now I see why people rave about you. Just let me go and tell Bobbie you're here. Do you want to leave your cloak on? I think Bobbie would rather like it. I wish you'd worn your hat too, he'd have adored that.'

She went up the stairs, two at a time.

When she came back, she said, 'He'd like to see you alone. He needs confession and absolution. I mean you do do that, don't you?' She didn't comment on the fact that he had taken off his cloak.

'Of course,' he said, picking up his bag. Clever tricks, said a voice in his head, and then fell silent.

'Well, then,' she said, after a pause. 'It's up here, follow me.'

When David came down again, Mary came out of the drawing room and stood in the doorway.

'Would you like a drink?' she asked.

'I ought to get back.'

'Just a quick one,' she said.

'I don't drink when I'm working.'

'You sound like a policeman,' she said.

'It's just a guideline,' he said, seeing her need. 'I'll have a very small whisky.'

'Thank you for doing that,' said Mary, from the drinks tray behind a large sofa covered in dark red brocade and littered with enormous tasselled cushions, pouring him, against instructions, a rather large whisky. 'He needed shriving. He tells me things I'd rather not know. Sometimes I can't bear it, and I can't bear him being so sorry . . . Do you understand?'

'Yes,' he said, taking a glass as heavy as a cannonball from her and sinking into a matching sofa which faced the other one across a kelim-covered stool strewn with books. 'I think so. Obtaining forgiveness is sometimes a way of not feeling guilty, I think, a way of passing the burden back again.'

'Which can't be wrong,' said Mary. 'I mean I suppose we should share these things, shouldn't we? That would be Christian, wouldn't it? Trouble is, it's all so difficult.' She sighed.

David admired her honesty. 'This is a very Christian act,' he said, raising his glass to her.

'Don't mention it. I'm glad you're here.'

'Do you have children?' he asked.

'One, a boy. He's at prep school learning how to be a merchant banker or whatever it is they teach them.'

'What sort of things does your husband paint?'

'Haven't you seen his work?'

'I don't think so.'

'He does portraits of people, naked boys mostly. They're very good.'

'And you?'

'I'm just a dauber,' said Mary looking into her glass. 'I'm not serious, or at least not any more. I used to be,' she added, 'but living with Bobbie sort of crushed it. He's so much better, you see, and then I had Nick and it all ground to a halt, although I do have a studio.'

'Here?'

'No. Elsewhere.'

'The pictures here are very good,' said David, gazing at something over the fireplace that looked awfully like a Claude.

'Chandos things,' said Mary dismissively. 'Bobbie got a job lot when we got married, that – Claude – a couple of Orpens, a Hubert Robert, a clutch of other stuff too that's on loan.'

'How lucky,' said David, unable to think of anything else to say.

'Depends on what you think of as luck,' said Mary. 'Personally, I don't think getting Aids is much luck.'

'I'm sorry,' he said.

'Don't be. I'm a pig.' She lit a cigarette without offering him one. 'Will you come back next week?' she asked.

After that he began to see Bobbie regularly, always staying afterwards to have a drink with Mary. He liked sitting in Mary's beautiful drawing room and he liked talking to Mary because she was so outrageously frank. He had never met anyone quite like her. She said what she thought without editing it first. And it was so peaceful there, so civilized, such an escape from the pressures of his life, so different to home. One day, however, when, sitting side by side with her one of the brocade sofas, he took her hand to demonstrate a point and she made no effort to remove it, he realized with a sudden shock that he was practically in love with her. After what can only have been a second but which felt like a very long, very charged second, David reluctantly took his hand away and got up.

'What is it?' she asked, looking at him anxiously.

'I must go.' He glanced at his watch.

'Is it something I've said?'

'No, no it's not. I have to get on.'

'You think I'm trying to trap you,' she burst out. 'That's it, isn't it? Well, I'm not.'

'I don't think that, Mary.'

'You're lying,' she said sadly. 'Can't we be honest with one another? You've been so good to us all these months, so kind to Bobbie, so sweet to me. The fact of the matter is I am lonely and I do like talking to you.'

'I like talking to you too,' he said, knowing he was being a coward but unable to admit his own fault. He found her dangerously attractive and he was scared to death. Mary's honesty and generosity shamed him. All he wanted to do was to get out as fast as he could.

'You will come back again, won't you?' she said as he put his coat on. 'Bobbie depends on it now.'

'Of course I will,' he said as calmly as he could manage.

'I depend on it too,' she said.

He tried to pray about it, standing up in his study that night, but all he could see in his mind's eye was Mary's anxious expression as she said, 'You will come back again, won't you?' He prayed for the other people on his list, but with no sense of being heard. It was as if the line had gone dead. He put it down to tiredness and the capriciousness of grace. All clergy had trouble praying at some time or other, and the reception hadn't been good for a while. St Francis had spent two years without any sense of being heard, he remembered; now it was his turn. After several weeks, however, he began to despair. He had continued to see Bobbie on Thursdays but he avoided having a drink with Mary afterwards, pleading lack of time, which was both true and not true.

When Bobbie died a month later David, to his eternal shame, found that he was relieved. A week after the funeral, Mary telephoned him at the rectory and left a message on the answering machine, but he did not return her call. Some days later Tessa, his sister, telephoned him.

'Look,' she said, 'I know how busy you are, but I think you'd better go and see Mary. Mary Chandos,' she added. 'She's in a bit of a state. I had her round here last night until two or three in the morning. She wouldn't go. David, are you listening?'

'Yes.'

'Well, I think you'd better do something.'

'What do you suggest?'

'You're the priest, not I,' said Tessa. 'She's a bit hysterical. She went on and on about what a help you'd been to both of them. She's not in love with you, is she?'

'Why do you ask?'

'Just some of the things she said last night.'

'She's very vulnerable,' said David. 'I don't want to encourage her in any way to think of me as . . .'

'As what?' said Tessa impatiently.

'As a man.'

'Do you find her attractive?'

'Not particularly.'

'I see. You're quite sure you haven't encouraged her in any way?'

'Well . . .' he said uncomfortably.

'Have you talked to Frances about it?'

'We never talk,' said David tiredly. 'Hadn't you noticed?'

'What a mess,' said Tessa, 'but you mustn't be an ostrich, David. You must do something, see someone, you must talk to Frances about it.'

'I told you,' said David, 'we never have the time.'

'Well *make* time,' said Tessa, 'otherwise you'll be in real trouble, not just half trouble which you're in at the moment, failing your flock.'

'Thanks a lot,' said David.

'Don't mention it,' Tessa said, and put the phone down.

The following week, David rang up the Archdeacon and arranged to see him. The Archdeacon, who had trained as a psychiatrist before he turned priest, listened very carefully to what David told him.

'Are you attracted to this woman?' he asked, forgetting for a moment her name. 'And does your wife know about this?'

It was what his wife called one of his multiple-choice questions.

'My wife doesn't know anything about it,' said David, dodging the first part of the question and hoping the Archdeacon wouldn't notice.

'How are things between you and your wife?' asked the Archdeacon gently.

David looked at him before he replied.

'Pretty bloody awful,' he said.

'Can you tell me why?'

'We never talk any more,' said David. 'We live side by side in the same house but that's about where it ends.'

'She's a teacher isn't she? What does she teach?'

'Women's studies,' said David, looking away.

The Archdeacon closely resembled a friendly vulture, with his bald pate and wild grey corkscrews of hair that stuck out almost at right angles from the side of his head. He had beady, almost black eyes that fixed one with gimlet intensity, but he was not an unkind man. In the old days when people were not embarrassed by such talk he would have been described as a man who could read souls.

'What are "Women's studies" specifically?' he asked. 'Are they subjects that can only be studied by women?'

'It means re designing history and literature from a feminist perspective,' said David.

'Sounds exceedingly tiresome,' said the Archdeacon, making a note on this pad, 'but to get back to this woman for a moment. Are you attracted to her? I don't think you answered my original question.'

27

'Yes,' said David. 'I'm ashamed to say that I am.'

'Right,' said the Archdeacon, 'now we can begin. Why are you attracted to her?'

'Because we can talk, she listens to what I say, we discuss things. I never talk to Frances these days. We're both so busy, you see, and on the rare occasions we do exchange a few words we argue.'

'What do you argue about?'

'She opposes me in everything, large or small.'

'I hear she's keen on the idea of women being priests,' said the Archdeacon, making another note.

'Very keen.'

'Do you think your attraction to this other woman is a way of getting at your wife, tapping her on the shoulder, as it were, and saying, "Look, my dear, I am searching for a woman who is a real woman, not a half man, not someone who challenges me."'

'It might be,' said David uncomfortably.

'You love your wife, of course?'

'Yes,' said David, 'I do, very much. But I feel I love her less than I used to.'

'That is probably because you're angry with her.'

'My prayer life's a mess, too. Do I put that down to anger as well?' asked David, suddenly impatient with all this sweet reasonableness.

'I wanted to get on to that,' said the Archdeacon soothingly, 'You've done marvels at St Anselm's, you know, single-handed, but it sounds as if you're overstretched.'

'Priests should be overstretched,' said David, 'I'm not complaining about that. I'm just saying I can't pray any more. I know that's normal, but I feel as if I've been abandoned when I need help most.'

'You have to keep on bashing away,' said the Archdeacon, 'and remember that Our Lord also felt that he had been abandoned.'

'Yes,' said David wearily, thinking of the prayer that went; 'Do not pray for tasks equal to your powers, pray for powers equal to your tasks.'

'What I want you to do,' said the Archdeacon, 'is to talk to your wife about this and then come back and see me. Can you make time to do that, do you think?'

'I can,' said David, 'but I don't know whether she can.'

'I'm sure she can,' said the Archdeacon, rising. 'Come back and see me, say, in ten days' time and we'll decide what's to be done next.'

The next night, David, who got in first in the evenings, went to meet Frances as she opened the front door. She hardly seemed to notice him as she came in holding carrier bags and her brief case.

'Could we have a word?' he said quietly.

'Why? What is it? Has something happened?'

'Nothing's happened,' he said, leading the way into his study, 'but I need a few minutes of your time.'

'I have a MOW meeting,' she said, 'at seven, and I've got to make some calls before then.'

'It's important, Frances.'

'I wish you'd tell me what this is about,' she said, taking off her raincoat.

'I want to talk about us. Do I have to make an appointment? Should I ring your secretary?'

'Don't be ridiculous, David, and besides, I don't have a secretary. Chance would be a fine thing,' she said crossly.

'Well then?' He waited.

'Tonight's impossible,' Frances said, 'but tomorrow evening's free. The reading group has cancelled. Margo rang me at work.'

'Do you have to go to this meeting tonight?'

'Yes, of course I do. Why?'

'Because I have to talk to you.'

'You keep saying that.'

'Don't you want to talk to me?'

'Of course I want to talk to you,' she said, turning away. 'It's just that I'm short of time. As if you didn't know, and I don't want to be lectured.'

'Tomorrow, then,' he said, ignoring this. 'I better go and drain the spaghetti.'

'Let Tanya do it,' she said on her way out. 'You mollycoddle those two. I'll tell her to in a second.'

The following evening, Frances came to David's study. The girls had been told to answer the phone and to say that the rector or

29

Mrs Doughty – whoever was being requested – would ring back shortly.

'Well,' said Frances, sitting down in a chair opposite David, 'fire away.'

She was wearing an old black skirt and a yellow jersey with a hole at the neck, a jumble-sale purchase by the looks of it, David thought. The line between her nose and mouth had deepened. She seemed much older. He wondered that he hadn't noticed this before.

'A couple of days ago,' he said, suddenly longing for a cigarette, 'I went to see the Archdeacon because I was worried that Mary Chandos was becoming too dependent on me.'

'What do you mean "too dependent"?' she asked incredulously. 'Has she got a crush on you or something? I mean, that's nothing new, is it?'

'I meant that I was also attracted to her,' he said reluctantly. In the old days, Frances had teased David about his looks and the effect they had on his parishioners. The old ladies in hats were dazzled by his good looks, his splendid voice, his undeniable sex appeal.

'Oh, I see.' She stared at him. 'I'm amazed you have the energy to fancy anyone. I know I don't.'

'I'm sorry,' he said. 'She was just there. I used to have a drink with her after I'd seen Bobbie. She listened to me. It was so peaceful in that house.'

'Was it high jinks or just comfort you were after, someone who would agree with you the whole time?'

'Please, Frances,' he said. 'I didn't sleep with her.'

'You might as well have done,' she said, turning her mug round and round. 'Did you kiss her?'

'I held her hand once.'

'Is that all?' said Frances, half laughing. 'All this soul-searching about holding someone's hand?'

'It's the intention, not the act,' he said.

'Oh, and what was your intention? Rape and pillage?' She put her mug down on the table with a bang.

'We're drifting apart,' he said, trying to hang on to his temper. 'Mary's a symptom.'

'I can't give up my life to bolster yours,' said Frances, shaking her head, 'and that's what this is about, this so-called "drifting apart". You always knew I wouldn't. I know you resent my working and having views of my own, not being a good rector's wife, but it's too –'

The door opened and Kitty put her head round. She was so like Frances, David thought, when she was younger, same expressions, same gestures, same lovely hair.

'You two look serious,' said Kitty. 'What's up? It's Joyce Boyle, Mum. Says it's urgent.'

'She'll ring back,' said David.

'No, I'll take it,' said Frances, rising.

'She'll ring back,' David said to Kitty, 'now off you go.'

Kitty stared at her parents. 'OK,' she said and went out, closing the door softly behind her.

'You shouldn't have done that,' said Frances. 'It is urgent, I know. Joyce –'

'What's more important to you?' asked David. 'Joyce Boyle's marriage or ours?'

'Right,' said Frances, sitting down in her chair. 'What else do you have to say?'

'We are drifting apart,' said David, 'and I think we should try together' – he emphasized this word – 'to do something about it.'

'What do you suggest?' asked Frances acidly.

'That we should try and talk, make more time for each other – to be together, I mean. Our sex life's in ruins, but you know that.'

'Sex life,' said Frances. 'What a joke. OK. How are we going to manage this?'

'We won't get anywhere if you take that approach.'

'But you don't listen to what I'm really saying,' said Frances, 'so what's the point in our spending more time together if I'm just to let you have your say?'

'What are you trying to tell me?'

'That's exactly my point,' said Frances in irritation. 'You don't know, do you?'

'Stop being so bloody clever,' said David. 'This is serious. We won't have a marriage if you go on like this.'

'You put it all on to me,' said Frances. 'What about your part? You're the one who fancied someone else.'

'I know,' he said, 'and I'm trying to tell you I'm sorry.'

'Are you really?' She looked at him sharply.

'Of course I am,' he said more calmly.

'Well,' she said in a slightly gentler voice, 'what do you think we can do?'

'The Archdeacon wants to see me again soon. I suppose I'll have to abide by what he tells me.'

Frances thought about this for a moment. 'What about Mary? Have you seen her?'

'No.'

'Perhaps you better not. But someone should. Maybe Tessa could have a word with her.'

'She already has.'

'She does love to interfere, our Tessa,' said Frances.

'In fact, Mary went to her.'

'Then that solves the problem. Tessa can sort Mary out. I think it would be best that way.'

'Poor Mary,' said David.

'Rather rich Mary, from what I can gather.'

'Money isn't everything.'

'No, but it helps,' said Frances. 'I sometimes wonder if it is everything and we're all deluding ourselves.'

'What do you mean?'

'Oh, nothing.' She shrugged. 'I'm worn out, I'm going to go to bed. I've got a big lecture tomorrow and I'm not properly prepared. I'll have to get up early.'

'You should slow up a bit,' he said.

'I'd love to,' came the unexpected reply, 'but I can't think how I can do it, other than leaving.'

'Leaving?'

'Going somewhere else,' she said, and laughed when she saw his expression. 'Not without you, you dimwit.'

'Frances,' he said.

'What?' She had bent over to pick up her mug and was not looking at him. He wanted to tell her that he loved her as much as he ever did, but somehow or other he couldn't get the words out.

'I'll put the cat out,' he said.

In bed, he said, 'Frances?', and put his hand on her shoulder, the old signal between them, but she didn't stir so he left it. He was tired, so very, very tired, that it was probably a joke to think he was capable of making love. He lay on his back and thought for a second of Mary alone in that large, empty, luxurious house, and his heart ached.

CHAPTER 4

'Well, and how are things?' asked the Archdeacon when David returned two weeks later. 'Have you talked to your wife?'

'Yes, I have as a matter of fact,' said David, thinking how well these servants of the Church did themselves. The Archdeacon's study – more of a library – was a handsome room with a fine ceiling and a marvellously peaceful view out over a large communal garden, not unlike the view from Mary's drawing room, or the kind of room a Harley Street consultant might have, minus the bed in the corner of course.

'And did you manage to make some sense out of it?'

'A little,' said David, 'I told her what had happened.'

'You came clean with her, you mean?'

'As clean as I could.'

'"What is truth?" said Jesting Pilate,"' quoted the Archdeacon with a smile. 'I've thought about you a good deal,' he continued, 'and there are two suggestions I would like to make.'

'Go on,' said David.

'First is therapy for you and your wife. I have a feeling it would be good for you both to go and talk to a third party about the tangle that has arisen between you. The second is that I think it may be time for a change of foot, by which I mean a different parish. Something in the country, say,' he added, in a manner which suggested to David that the whole thing had already been arranged. 'Now, tell me what you think.'

David was silent.

'The suggestion of therapy makes me feel I've already failed,' he said, after some seconds had passed.

'That is a very English approach,' said the Archdeacon, as David had known he would, 'There's no suggestion of failure. Marriage is a very difficult institution, far more difficult than the priesthood.'

'In that case, I suspect I'm a double failure.'

'Stuff and nonsense. The Bishop was saying only yesterday

what a success you've made of St Anselm's. "A beacon of faith" he said.'

Another Anglican cliché, thought David, who was feeling uncomfortably anxious as well as irritated.

'Now what do you say to this idea of therapy?'

'Do I have to accept?'

'My dear fellow, I feel it would be very much in your best interests to accept.'

'I see.'

'Clergy marriages are notoriously difficult, as we all know.'

'Yes,' said David, meeting the gimlet eye of the Archdeacon. Aren't they just? he thought to himself.

'After my wife lost our third child – a miscarriage – we underwent therapy together. It was a great help. Helen was able to express her anger in safety, I was able to express my sorrow and my need for her. We went on after that much the better for it. My faith was sorely tested during that time, as yours is being at present, but the great thing to remember is that everything changes. It won't be like this for ever or even, I suspect, for very much longer. Are you finding things any easier?'

'Not really, but I'm managing to blunder along on automatic pilot for the present. It's like being terribly ill. No one writes about it. People write about success, but not enough about failure.'

'Because failure is, I suppose, so debilitating, it drains one of energy. When one is in that condition it seems as if there is nothing to say. But don't forget our dear old friend Thomas à Kempis. I always think there's something in him for everyone. The advice is so straightforward and invariably appropriate, don't you find?'

'I'll get out my copy,' said David. His mother had given him the book when he was confirmed, he seemed to remember. What a long time ago that was. Another life.

'Now,' said the Archdeacon briskly, 'this business of change. How would you feel about leaving St Anselm's, and how do you think your wife would take to it?'

'You mentioned the country,' said David cautiously.

'Indeed I did. I've been talking to my old friend the Bishop of Hartchester. He has something up his sleeve at Fordingbridge, the part of Gloucestershire nearest to Wales, charming place. It's where Marjorie Jessop lives, the gardener. The living's in her gift, as a matter of fact, or, rather, that of her husband, Guy Jessop, but the Bishop tells me if Lady Jessop approves that'll be that. She wants somebody young and high church; apparently, the last incumbent was old and depressingly low. So there you are. There's an art college in Wayemouth, apparently, a nest of the most advanced feminist ideas − you know what students are like, prey to anything new-fangled − where your wife will be able to teach. I believe they're advertising for a lecturer there, so it'll be just the job. There are good local schools, state and private, for your children.'

'The idea of a fresh start is very tempting,' said David, 'I must say, although I can't imagine not being at St Anselm's. I love that place. I think of it as my life's work.'

'You're overstretched here, dangerously so in my view,' said the Archdeacon gently. 'You've done excellent work as a slum priest, but now I think you'd do better in the country, I do really. Parishes like St Anselm's are wonderful places because the challenge to us in terms of outreach is so very great, but one can only stay in the front line for so long and I think you've reached the point where it's time for you to move on.'

'Into the support trenches, you mean?' said David wryly.

'Nothing wrong with that, my dear. Now what do you think your wife will say to this?'

'I think she might be glad,' said David, remembering what Frances had said the night they had talked.

Frances was astonished. 'Just like that − to the country! How amazing! What do you think?'

They were in David's study again with the telephone switched off. Outside the window the chestnut tree that was one of the glories of their garden was in bud, the yellow-green of spring, of vitality. It seemed to be a metaphor for something, David thought vaguely, half observing it. He suddenly felt an unexpected sense of hope rising in him like sap.

'A mixture of things,' he said. 'Sorrow, hope.' He looked at her to see what she was thinking. 'Excitement at the prospect of the country, anxiety about whether you would be happy.'

Frances sat back in her chair slightly and folded her hands.

She was smiling. He had not seen her in such a relaxed pose for months, years.

'We should do it,' she said. 'I like the idea of change, not only for myself but for you and for the girls. It's a fresh start for us.'

'The Archdeacon also wants us to go to a therapist together,' said David, wondering what she would say to this.

'This is the outcome of the confessional, is it?'

'I suppose it is.'

'I don't know,' she said. Perhaps it's better to let sleeping dogs lie.' Her sense of dissatisfaction frightened her. David's indiscretion and his obvious sense of guilt had not hurt her so much as irritated her. At least that was what she said to herself. Why make such a fuss? she had wondered at first, but now the idea of change – growing out of the seedbed of David's foolishness – had taken root in her imagination and was already flourishing there. This cloud certainly had a silver lining, but therapy . . . The idea rattled her.

'He said it helped him when he did it with his wife. "Clergy marriages are notoriously difficult." I quote.'

'I thought they always sent ailing clergy marriages to a friendly nun,' Frances said. 'Why therapy?'

'Because he trained as a shrink before he took the cloth. I thought you'd jump at the chance.'

'Did you? Why?' She gave him a look he could not interpret. 'Because it's the sort of stuff I'm usually interested in and you aren't?'

'I didn't say that.'

'No,' she said, 'you didn't have to.'

David sighed. The shared enthusiasm had plainly worn off. It was back to treading on broken glass again. He wondered where he'd gone wrong.

'Think about it,' he said.

The therapist was a dumpy, brisk middle-aged woman called Laura Leaver. She wore a jersey suit and sensible shoes and her glasses hung round her neck on a chain. She practised from her own sitting room in St Petersburg Place, Notting Hill Gate, a quiet backwater not far from St Anselm's. She had been at university with the Archdeacon 'rather longer ago than I care to remember,' as she said to David and Frances when they went for a first session.

'When couples come to me,' she said after they were seated in carefully arranged armchairs, 'I let one half speak − I do sometimes ask questions − and I then refer what has been said to the other half, acting as an interpreter where necessary. Healthy relationships contain this function inherently. Sometimes, when people are worn out or over-stretched, the interpreter gets overlaid or wiped out completely. I hope this doesn't sound too rigid. Human nature, as you both know, is enormously flexible and serpentine. All sessions are different, all take their own individual shape. So, who's going to begin?'

'You start, David,' said Frances. 'It's because of you we're here.'

David glanced at Laura Leaver, who seemed, he thought, dangerously alert. like a highly trained terrier ready to pounce, she was watching and waiting, pad to the ready. He hated people who took notes as it made everything feel so unbalanced: the performer and the observer. He made a habit of never doing it himself. His palms began to sweat; in his heart he felt fear and loathing of the Archdeacon for plunging them into this acid bath.

'We've been married for a long time,' he said lamely. 'We're both busy, we both work − too hard, probably − we have two children aged thirteen and ten, two girls, Tanya and Kitty. Recently I ministered to a man who was dying of Aids and whose wife came to rely on me rather too much, perhaps. I only realized too late what was happening −'

'What was happening?' interrupted Laura Leaver.

'Well, I . . .' He didn't see how he could say it. They would tear him limb from limb. He felt as if he was sitting in a room with the Eumenides.

'She was attracted to me . . . I was attracted to her.'

'Did you tell Frances about this?'

'Not at once.' David looked at Frances who was looking at Mrs Leaver.

'I see. What made you tell her?'

Again David looked at Frances.

'I went to see the Archdeacon because I was alarmed by what was happening, and he told me I had to tell Frances.'

'He wouldn't have bothered otherwise,' said Frances, trying to smile.

'I hope I would have done.'

'And how did you feel?' Mrs Leaver asked Frances, making a note on her pad.

'I really couldn't see what the fuss was about,' said Frances, hoping that her relaxed tone of voice would lull Mrs Leaver into believing her. 'David has always been attractive to women; the old ladies in hats have always had a crush on him.'

'Is that true, David, do you think?'

David frowned. 'I hope not. I never really notice that sort of thing.'

'I see.'

Mrs Leaver paused for a moment in thought. It was very difficult to manage this kind of meeting when both parties were lying. It was quite clear to her that they were a couple who were in the habit of lying to one another and no longer knew they were doing it. His desire was, ostensibly, to come clean, to spare his wife, to say sorry, but really, she suspected, he felt none of these things. It was inexpedient, it was difficult, but what had happened to him had gone deeper than self-discipline. He had met serious temptation, probably for the first time in his life, and he had not managed to deal with it. It would undoubtedly happen again. The wife's reaction was complex. She wanted to pretend she didn't really care − although she undoubtedly did − presumably in order to punish him, but possibly, also, in order to disguise her own ambivalent feelings about their relationship and how much mileage it had left. There was also, according to the Archdeacon, a serious imbalance in their marriage: the wife was hard-working and tough, not feminine enough for the husband. 'He can't worship her, you see,' the Archdeacon had said, 'so he automatically attracts the more helpless kind of woman who relies on him and whom he can put on a pedestal. I don't know what the answer is.'

'Neither do I,' Mrs Leaver had said.

'Frances,' she said, 'tell me how you met David, what attracted you to him in the first place.'

Sometimes, if one encouraged a couple to look back into past happiness, they could begin to connect again.

'It was in the High,' said Frances.

'No, it wasn't, it was in Blackwell's.'

Frances shrugged as if to say, See what I'm up against?

'I dropped something and David retrieved it. Classic pick-up stuff.'

'Did you want him to do that?'

'What? Pick up my book? Certainly not. I don't think I'd even noticed him. I was waiting for my then-boyfriend.'

Mrs Leaver resigned herself to a wasted thirty minutes, which was what remained of the therapeutic hour. She would tell her friend the Archdeacon that this couple's best hope was that they could, somehow or other, in different surroundings with rather less to do, find out what it was that had originally drawn them together. They would need a good deal of praying for.

'What a waste of time,' said Frances when they came out, blinking slightly, into the street.

'I didn't think it was,' said David, 'but I don't see why you had to be so difficult.'

'I wasn't being difficult, I was telling her how it really was.'

'You made me sound like some kind of Don Juan.'

'Don't be so sensitive,' said Frances, glancing at her watch. 'I better go, I think. I'll see you later.'

'I had a letter from Lady Jessop this morning,' said David, 'asking me to go down there next week. If you agree, I'm going to write and accept.'

'Go ahead,' said Frances, 'with my blessing.'

CHAPTER 5

When Guy failed to come back, David walked through the house and out into the garden which was where he supposed Marjorie was. It was where she was usually to be found. When he had first come here last spring, she had suggested they walk outside together and talk.

'Easier,' she said, 'than me grilling you across a desk. Do you like gardening?'

'I hardly know a plane tree from a chestnut,' he said, 'but I love walking round gardens.'

'It's very simple, really. Just a matter of knowing what's what and where to put it. And when you see things growing, a most tremendous feeling of omnipotence sets in. One starts to feel like God commanding the universe, or perhaps I shouldn't talk to you in those terms.'

'Why not?' David asked, amused, following his tweed-clad hostess out through the tall drawing room window, and thinking how nimble she was for a woman who must be seventy if she was a day.

'Well, that's your province, isn't it?'

'Not just mine,' said David, looking at the parterre with pleasure and amazement, 'yours too.'

'Tell me about your work in London. Billy Hartchester was full of praise for you. Won't you find it rather quiet here, if you were to come?'

'Do you mean would I be bored?'

Marjorie laughed. 'Well, you might be. The church isn't exactly bursting at the seams on a Sunday morning.'

'That can be changed.'

'I wouldn't bet on it,' said Marjorie. 'People here are resistant to change, they don't approve of it. I hear you're very high and this is non-conformist country, or at least the edge of it. The ethnic minority here are the Welsh, just over the hedge, rather dour, you know. I'm afraid it's catching. I like sacramental religion myself, it's like gardening, a visible sign of the invisible kingdom, but I couldn't get Canon Jones to budge. He thought *rosa mystica* was something I had in my border. This garden is divided into boxes,' she said, scarcely drawing breath, leading David down another flight of steps and into a herb garden, with beds divided into shapes by box hedges and brick paths. There was a sundial in the middle and a little cluster of beehives looking like laundry baskets tucked under the yew hedge. 'In the eighteenth century,' she said, 'an awful lot of herb gardens like this one were swept away by the passion for landscaping everything. Luckily this house and garden weren't important enough to be completely changed. Bartholomew Jessop had a go, but the site of the castle doesn't readily lend itself to change – too steep, you see – so things survived here that were swept away elsewhere.'

'What is this?' asked David, bending down.

'Lovage,' she said. 'Fennel you know, rosemary.'

'Does your daughter garden?' David asked.

'Oh, you knew I had a daughter,' said Marjorie. 'That was clever of you.'

'It was mentioned in the articles I read about you.'

'How old are you?'

'Forty-five.'

'She's younger than you, then,' said Marjorie, 'Chloe's thirty-eight. She's got two children of her own, James and Miranda. I'm terribly worried about her, as a matter of fact,' she added, pausing by the sundial, 'but I can't talk to Guy – my husband – because he's not a person one can talk to, if you know what I mean. She's having terrible trouble with her husband, Rupert. She rings me up sometimes in tears and I find I don't know what to say. You see he's had a lot of girlfriends, extra-curricular entertainment, and he doesn't have the decency to disguise his activities. He has no idea how to behave about it. He's always coming back late without telling her, or inventing excuses as to why he can't come home, or going on business trips with these creatures in tow. Chloe had a friend in Rome, of all places, who saw Rupert having dinner with a girl she didn't recognize.'

'And told her about it.'

'And told her.' Marjorie nodded. 'But what are one's friends to do? Sometimes it is better to know things, to know where one stands, don't you think?'

Before his induction he had taken a service in St Mary's, (there was a clutch of other churches as well: St Nicholas at Sweffling, St Bede's, Little Neville, All Saints, Marston) robing up in the damp, unfamiliar vestry. The chasuble had smelt, he remembered, overpoweringly of mothballs. The Jessops had sat in their own box at the front, Marjorie and Guy and their daughter Chloe, and although it was early May it had been intolerably cold. His feet had been like blocks of ice. According to Major Hewlett, the church warden, the boiler had given up the ghost and would have to be replaced. Afterwards, he had stood at the door shaking hands with the congregation, most of whom said something polite and then bolted off for their gin or their pint of Badger. He sympathised. Later, when he had returned to London, Marjorie had rung him up to tell him what a success he had been.

'They all liked you' she said, 'I think they could see they had nothing to fear. I've trumpeted you as ultra-conservative which of course they adore. What they dread is a wolf in sheep's clothing, someone who'll come along and introduce guitars and all that ghastly hugging some churches go in for at the offertory. Promise me, you won't do that.'

'I promise' he had replied, smiling to himself.

David thought both of this and of the first conversation he had had with Marjorie as he went down to the lake where Anna, one of the gardeners, had told him he would find her. Since that time a year ago he knew that things had gone from bad to worse for Chloe. Her husband had begun an affair with a close friend of Chloe's and had moved out by Christmas (just at the moment when David and Frances arrived in Fordingbridge), leaving Chloe to cope with the children on her own. He had heard more about this from her mother than he had from Chloe herself. Their acquaintance had been limited to shaking hands after the ten-thirty Mass on Sundays. She was a younger version of her mother in looks: fair-haired, a little thin for his taste, with the same knack her mother displayed for looking elegant in anything she wore. When he had happened to glance at her during the sermon on Sunday, he thought she had a sad, slightly distracted air.

'Hello,' called Marjorie, waving from behind a clump of arum

43

lilies – one of the few plants David had known when he first arrived at Fordingbridge. 'I was going to come and look for you,' she said, as he drew closer. 'You're late.'

'Guy said you were asleep when I arrived. I've been sitting in the kitchen.'

'Oh, he is naughty,' said Marjorie. 'Here, hold this.' She handed him a roll of twine. 'Something's crashed through here. I've had to tie these up. Probably one of those damn dogs. Guy will throw sticks for them into the water, although I've asked him not to. Dogs always get their own way, I find. I was resting actually, earlier, I was tired after yesterday and that filming and fooling about. I think Guy's cross because I get all the attention. Chloe's coming later. How are you?' she asked and put out her hand which David took, feeling the bumps of her enormous rings in his palm.

'I'm all right.' He smiled as she got nimbly to her feet. 'What is the plan? I'll read, if you like, or help you, whichever you want.'

'I don't think I'm on for reading today, although it's kind of you to offer. I'm more in the mood to sit in the shade and look at the water, or just to potter about checking things.'

'The lilies are looking beautiful.'

'I'm mad about them, always have been. Miss Jekyll said anything with large leaves looks good in or near water. How right she was. The children like to come here with me to watch the fish feed. I've always found this a terribly tranquil place. In the war I used to come and sit here on this bench. The pond wasn't good for anything much so it was left alone, although the fountain got blocked up and I couldn't fix it.' She pointed at the nymph holding a shell in the middle of the pond.

'How are the children?'

Marjorie lit a cigarette. 'They seem all right, I suppose. Miranda is being very naughty, Chloe says, James is disguising his feelings. He's always been a bit of a stoic.'

'And Chloe?'

'Not good. She's very depressed. Drinking rather a lot, as one does.'

'What will she do now?'

'I don't know,' said Marjorie, 'and I can't understand from

talking to her whether she's going to divorce Rupert or is waiting for him to return. I was wondering if you would have a chat with her.' She put her hand on his arm and he noticed that her pink nail varnish had chipped.

'I will if you think it'll help. What sort of a fellow is Rupert?'

'Well,' said Marjorie, blowing smoke out through her nostrils, 'he's older than she is, quite good-looking, rather well-off. When you first meet him he seems terribly steady and at the same time eager to please, but the real Ru is clearly someone quite different. I must say it all came as rather a shock. And it's the cruelty that I can't fathom. When he met her she was the one and only. Now he seems to do everything to wound her. I think she should divorce him but Guy thinks she should overlook it, says he'll come back in good time, but I think that's a rather demeaning position for Chloe, don't you?'

'It sounds very difficult,' said David diplomatically. 'Does she want him to come back?'

'I simply can't fathom what she wants. She's started going to a therapist, but she seems worse not better. I thought it was meant to help.'

'It's like anything else. Sometimes it does, sometimes it doesn't.'

'Have you tried it?'

'Yes.'

'And did it?'

'Not really.'

Marjorie laughed and threw her cigarette end into the bamboos behind her. 'Well, I never have, thank God. I prefer the solace of friends, although when you're my age your friends start to die off and your husband is cantankerous because of his arthritis or, in Guy's case, because his guts ache, poor darling. How is your Frances getting on with the bloodied sheet or whatever it is?'

David raised his eyebrows. These discussion groups of Frances's were a sore point with him. He had made a point of not attending the two so far.

'She's all right,' he said. 'Enjoying her job at the art college. People go to the groups but I don't know what they make of them. Miss Ames asked me if the lecture about Aids was going to include the work of Oxfam. I think they're all in a bit of a daze.'

'It won't do them any harm to have a bit of a shake-up,' said Marjorie. 'News from the great world. As long as it makes Frances happy.'

'She's busy enough,' said David. 'I hardly see her. I hoped things were going to change in that respect. We left London in order to have more time for ourselves and for our family. Fat chance.'

'It's this business of being always on tap,' said Marjorie, 'always available. I can hide when I want to behind my secretary or the answering machine, but you can't.'

'I don't really mean to grumble,' said David. 'I think priests should be available to their flock, as much of the time as they can reasonably manage, sometimes more. One of the things about therapy that concerns me is this business of the caring fifty-minute hour. Therapists aren't generally available when they're needed, unless you're paying, of course.'

'I've always shied away from the whole thing in horror,' said Marjorie. 'There are some stones it's better not to look under. How's your compost heap coming along?'

CHAPTER 6

Chloe went round the house in Caithness Road, off Brook Green, looking into all the rooms. She had taken to doing this lately in an obsessive way, as if by stealing up on her rooms – taking them by surprise, so to speak – she might find out something about herself that she had not previously known. Everything *looked* lovely, but she knew that somehow it was meaningless. She lacked for nothing and yet she lacked everything. Sometimes she seemed completely hollow inside. Part of the reason for this exercise, at this moment, was that she was about to go and see her therapist, which made her nervous and at the same time hungrily curious about why she felt so ghastly most of the time. Then she would pick up her children from their schools and drive down to Fordingbridge for the weekend. It was quite a long way and she found it tiring trying to keep the peace with the children in the back and do the driving. She lingered in James's room, looking at his books and the fossils he had found last year in Suffolk. She picked up Jack, his one-eyed bear, and put him down again, then she lay on the bed and closed her eyes. Ever since Ru had left, taking his squash racket, some suits and a handful of shirts, she had felt this enormous oppressive loneliness, a kind of emptiness that made her feel as if, in some way, she had ceased to exist. She slept badly at nights, usually waking at three or so and being unable to go back to sleep again without the help of a large glass of whisky. Then she would oversleep in the mornings and feel tired for the rest of the day.

One of the things she found most difficult to deal with was why she should mind so much. It wasn't as if Ru's philandering had been exactly a secret. It had begun after James was born when she had changed – so Fanny, the therapist, said – from being the lovely princess captured by the handsome prince into a mother (Ru had passed out in the delivery room), and that could mean, apparently, this business of being perceived as a punishing, persecuting goddess, an image a man like Rupert would resist with might and main, as indeed he had done before in his first marriage. For years Chloe had sat on the sofa in the drawing room downstairs, growing sadder and sadder the angrier she got (according to Fanny she was unable to acknowledge anger and felt sad instead, depressed, victimized), in her beautiful pink room that she had grown to hate, waiting for Ru to come home, wondering where he was, lying to the children about it: Daddy's having a business dinner, Daddy's working late, Daddy's . . . busy. Lying to herself: Oh, he'll be back in a minute, oh, he doesn't know what the time is . . . Knowing full well there was a girl, girls, several, maybe hundreds, she didn't know. By the end, she half longed for there to be a call from the police, what she thought she had always dreaded, saying, 'Mrs Durrell? I'm afraid there's been a fatal accident, your husband has been killed.' Then at least she would have been free of the awful tyranny Ru exercised over her, a tyranny she had been warned about by Marcia, Ru's first wife, described by him as 'potty' or 'demented', who had rung up periodically over the years to tell Chloe that Rupert was incapable of feeling anything except for himself, that he used people, that he was mostly dead inside and so on. But what amazed Chloe was how reasonable, how sane Marcia seemed; a far cry from the Mrs Rochester figure painted by Ru.

But it was the last girl who had been the worst: when she thought (wrongly as it turned out) that Ru was changing, he suddenly went off at a tangent again. And this time it was with Lucy, her so-called best and oldest friend. Some friend. She had met Lucy when they had arrived at the same boarding school aged twelve and they had shared a hymn book. After that they had become best friends, like sisters really. They had shared everything, told one another everything. They were both only children, which increased the strength of the bond between them. When Lucy's mother's new husband, the German prince, Heinrich, had made a pass at Lucy the summer after he married her mother, Lucy had rung Chloe at Fordingbridge from the yacht's phone and begged her to ask her mother if she could come and stay.

'He tried to kiss me,' Lucy had confessed to Chloe in their bedroom on the nursery floor. 'And then he unzipped his flies and his thing just sort of fell out. He told me – get this – that he wanted me to take it in my mouth; then he put his hand on the back of my neck and I screamed and ran for it. Told Mummy.'

48

'What did she say?' asked Chloe, agog.

'She told me not to be so silly,' said Lucy, 'and to stop making a fuss about nothing.'

'Ugh,' said Chloe, torn between disgust and laughter, remembering Heinrich's puffy debauched face and his red mouth.

But it had been during that visit that Lucy had confided to Chloe that Guy himself had made a pass at her; nothing much more than a creeping hand on her knee at dinner and a quick squeeze of her breast on the landing as he was coming past, but enough to make Lucy exceedingly wary of him.

'It's only because he's fond of you,' Chloe had said. 'He doesn't really mean anything by it. He does it to me, too, sometimes.'

'I know, I know,' said Lucy, wishing she had not mentioned it, and wondering why she had.

Lucy did not go to university. Her father was dead and her mother said it was unnecessary for a girl to be educated. She was to do the season and find a rich husband. But when Chloe came back from Bristol to share her flat with her, she had not done so. She was incredibly pretty with thick, fair hair that swung in a bob around her face, blue, blue eyes and long slim legs, but experience had taught her that men were best kept at arm's length. However it was Lucy, an enthusiastic attender of lectures at the Royal Geographical Society, who had taken Chloe to the lecture where she had been introduced to Rupert (whom Lucy had already met at a drinks party somewhere, although she claimed not to remember this); Lucy (of all people) who had warned Chloe early on that she was getting in too deep with a man whose life was already very complicated.

'I don't trust him, Chloe, I don't think he's good for you. He wants you as a prop. And he likes Fordingbridge too much. He's dazzled by your mother and all that glamour. He wants to join your mother's team. And I hear that he was rotten to his wife.'

'That's not what I heard,' said Chloe hotly. 'I know what you're thinking,' she said, seeing Lucy's expression. 'I would say that, wouldn't I? But I do believe him. He's not a bastard, Lucy, he just wants another chance.'

'Be careful,' said Lucy maddeningly. 'Don't buy into his

49

version too much. One never knows about people's marriages, it's mostly a mystery except to the two people involved and probably even to them. I'm sure he had some right on his side too, but I'm your friend, I want to defend your interests, and I think you should consider these things. Remember, Ru's giving you one side of the story – his.'

Had she been jealous even then, or was she truly being a good friend? Chloe could not decide.

'How come you've suddenly become the world expert on marriage?' said Chloe crossly.

'He's older than you,' Lucy went on, 'and you're probably in search of an older man, a father figure. Your relationship with your real father hasn't been too great, has it?'

'I simply don't believe this,' said Chloe.

'Listen,' said Lucy, 'I'm speaking from experience. My father was even worse than yours. He wasn't any good at anything other than being my begetter, but these men, useless as they are, are our role models, our only role models. I'm just saying watch out.'

'Thanks all the same,' said Chloe, 'but I'm old enough to know what I'm doing.'

'And he drinks too much,' said Lucy. 'You should think about that, too. What is he trying to escape?'

'Oh shut up!' said Chloe. 'I can't bear it when you play psychiatrist.'

After this, Chloe had been even more determined to make her relationship with Ru work. She thought about what Lucy said on and off but rejected most of it. So what if he did drink? Everyone she knew drank too much. Besides, she was in love for what felt like the first time. Her previous boyfriends rather paled beside Ru. They seemed like boys, not men, or were busy establishing themselves in a career. Ru was already well established and successful. And he needed her. He did a lot of business entertaining and needed a clever and attractive woman on his arm to help him. He also needed support in the battle with Marcia over money, property and children which was reaching white-hot intensity and looked as if it would end in court. They would go for long walks in the hills above Fordingbridge at the

50

weekend or take the dogs down to the river for a swim. Ru made Chloe feel easier at home than she had done before. Marjorie enjoyed flirting with him and Guy liked having an extra pair of hands around the place to help him with the heavy stuff. Ru was eager to help: he liked mowing, chopping and slashing things. Chloe occasionally watched him at work and wondered what was going through his mind. Sometimes she thought he might be mowing Marcia down again and again and again.

In London they liked doing the same things. Ru took culture seriously. Marcia hated concerts, was bored by the theatre and never set foot in an art gallery if she could help it. Their two children, Tom and Piers, were encouraged to be sporting. Ru liked Satie and Picasso and certain pieces of Bach. He admired modern architecture and professed to find the Pompidou Centre 'fascinating' and 'different' and was an enthusiastic supporter of Richard Rogers. He was interested in Chloe's job as an editor at Hull & Sang, the publishers, and would read his way through everything new, although it was difficult to know what he made of certain authors – Salman Rushdie, for instance, or Martin Amis. But he enjoyed his job as a merchant banker and would talk to Chloe in bed about new bridges for devastated zones where the flood waters of the river had swept away the old one, or the natives had blown it up for some reason best known to themselves. For months he was obsessed by the idea of a new sewage system for Mexico City. Chloe did get a little tired of hearing about projected quotas of shit per head in the year two thousand.

Ru and Chloe went to take the younger boy, Piers, out from his prep school, which was somewhere amongst the manicured woodlands of Surrey. They drove through village after village of brick and flint cottages with cricket pitches and pubs with names like 'The Jolly Wheatsheaf' and stopped off in one for a drink.

'Have you warned him I'm coming?' Chloe asked, returning from the ladies'.

'No, actually.' Ru was counting his change and didn't look at her.

'But don't you think it'll be a bit of a shock?'

'Children take you as they find you,' said Ru confidently. 'He's a dear little chap, you'll like him.'

But will he like me? wondered Chloe nervously. She knew nothing about children, being an only child.

'What if he doesn't like me?' she asked.

'Darling, he'll adore you. Stop fussing.'

They turned into a drive past a brick and flint lodge with gothic windows and a sign which said 'BRAMFIELD LODGE' in white letters and underneath 'PREPARATORY SCHOOL FOR BOYS'. A large Victorian house swung into view surrounded by playing fields and nets and Portakabins. Chloe waited in the car while Rupert went inside. She wondered what Piers would look like and whether he would resent her. A man and a woman came down the steps with a small boy between them and got into a large, new Daimler. The woman had dyed blonde hair and wore a fur coat over a pair of jeans. The man was in sports clothes and Chloe caught a glint of gold from the chain around his neck.

After what seemed like an age, Rupert came down the steps holding the hand of a leggy, fair-haired boy dressed in grey shorts and a matching grey blazer. Instantly, Chloe was horribly jealous.

'This is Chloe,' said Rupert, holding open the door of the car for the boy.

The child glanced at Chloe but said nothing.

'Say hello,' said Rupert, giving him a gentle push.

'Hello,' said Piers tonelessly. He climbed into the back and sat down. Chloe looked round to smile, but Piers stared at his lap and then, in a mannered way, gazed out of the window as they went through one village after another, past more cricket pitches.

'Mitchell Minor is in the San,' Piers volunteered eventually.

'What with?' asked Chloe, eager to interact.

'Toe fug,' said Piers stonily.

'Hope you haven't got it,' Ru said heartily.

'I've had nits.'

'How do you know?' asked Chloe.

'You can feel them crawling about in your hair.'

'How horrible.'

'The cleaner the hair the better, Miss Lindsell said.'

'Who's she?'

'We won the interhouse cricket match,' said Piers, ignoring Chloe.

'Jolly good, old fellow. How many runs did you score?'

'Half a century,' said Piers. 'Dad, can I have a new cricket bat?'

'Of course you can, darling. Can you get one through the school?'

'Mr Watts said I should. He said he could get me one.'

'Do you love cricket?' asked Chloe.

'He's still got the bat he had when he was my age.'

'He played for his county, didn't he?' asked Ru.

'Yup,' said Piers. 'He scored a century for Surrey once. In the dawn of time.'

'That's good,' said Ru, laughing. 'Where did you learn that expression?'

'It's what Mr Watts calls it,' said Piers, leaning forwards so he could rest his hands on the back of his father's seat. 'He's always saying it. It's because he's so old.'

'How old is he?' Chloe asked.

'Not much older than you, darling,' said Ru. 'Is he, Piers?'

But Piers sat back in his seat and said nothing. He was doing his best, Chloe realized, to pretend that she was not there at all.

They went to a hotel called the White Hart, which had mullioned windows and flock wallpaper, and ordered tea.

'Indian or China?' Ru asked Chloe.

'China, please.'

'Mummy says China tea is dishwater,' said Piers.

'What would you like?' asked Ru, ignoring this remark.

'I like tea you can stand your spoon up in,' said Piers. 'Mr Watts has four sugars in his.'

'Goodness,' said Chloe. 'Is he fat?'

'No, he's very thin, like a stick. He's as thin as a knife.'

'A lath, you mean,' Chloe corrected him. 'Thin as a lath.'

'It's not. It's as thin as a knife.'

'It isn't, actually.' Chloe could feel her temper giving.

'You don't know anything,' said Piers quietly.

'Cakes, darling?'

'Everything,' said Piers. 'I want everything.'

He ate and ate and talked to his father. Afterwards, Ru took him for a walk round whatever town they were in. Chloe waited in the hotel and read the promotional literature for Trust House Forte which left her feeling even more depressed than she had been before. What a little brat he was. She would never be able to like him, let alone love him. She had no idea children could be so unpleasant and get away with it.

'Could he go in the front, do you think?' asked Ru as they went out to the car.

'Why?'

'Because he doesn't see much of me, and he always likes a go in the front when his brother's not around.'

'All right,' said Chloe coldly and got into the rear seat of Ru's car which was designed for a dwarf.

'I don't want to go back,' said Piers as they turned into the school drive.

'Of course you do,' said Ru in a jovial, caring, fatherly sort of voice. 'You love it here.'

'I don't, I hate it,' said Piers, beginning to cry.

'I'll take him in,' said Rupert. 'Won't be a minute. He always does this.

'Poor little chap,' he said when he came back. 'He's a bit miserable at the moment.'

'Oh, dear,' said Chloe sarcastically.

'The housemaster says he's having nightmares and sleep-walking.'

'Does Marcia know?'

'She came yesterday, apparently, to see him in a match.'

'It's a long way just for a match.' Chloe couldn't imagine her parents doing such an overindulgent thing. Sending children to boarding school was a way, she had always thought, of avoiding such tedious activities. Marjorie had appeared occasionally in a blaze of glamour . . .

'She always comes. She likes it. She is a very good mother in that way.'

'Bully for her,' said Chloe.

'There's no need to be like that,' said Ru.

'Like what?'

'It's not his fault.'

'I didn't say it was.'

They drove the rest of the way in silence. When they got to South Kensington Rupert said, 'I think I'll stay at my place tonight, if that's all right with you.' He had taken a room in his old friend Andrew Cruickshank's flat, whom he had shared with briefly before his marriage to Marcia.

'It's fine by me,' said Chloe. They were at the traffic lights, so she opened the door and got out.

'Oh don't . . .' said Rupert, but Chloe slammed the door very hard and walked off. She supposed they had had their first row.

'What's up?' asked Lucy, when Chloe came in and threw herself on the sofa, still in her coat.

'We went to see Rupert's boy, Piers, the one who's still at prep school.'

'And?'

'It was a disaster,' said Chloe sniffing. 'We had a row. I left him at the lights and came home.'

'It's a hell of thing taking on someone's children,' said Lucy reasonably. 'What's he like?'

'Who? Piers? What one might expect, I suppose. Spoilt little brat.'

She wanted to be number one with Ru and she felt in competition with Piers. So stupid.

'For heaven's sake, Chloe,' said Lucy, 'it must be hard for him too, you know, having a strange woman arrive with his father. Children take years to make sense out of their parents splitting up. I think it was very selfish of Rupert to take you. He should have known better.'

'He thought it was for the best,' said Chloe, springing to Ru's defence.

'You're going awfully fast with Ru,' Lucy said. 'Why don't you cool it a bit?'

'You don't like him, do you?' Chloe said suddenly.

She remembered the way Lucy had looked at her when she said this: a long stare before she spoke as if she were formulating something complex.

'I don't think he's good for you,' said Lucy carefully, 'and he's got a lot of problems with his wife and kids. Those things don't unravel easily.'

'But I love him,' said Chloe. 'I can't give him up. It's not so simple.'

She felt, but could not express, a deep need for Rupert. He had something she wanted and had always wanted, although she could not have said quite what this something was. But he seemed solid and dependable. She felt secure with him. In bed at night, after they had made love, he would hold her very tight and she would wake in the night hot and cramped and safe.

Chloe and Ru's visit to Piers' school had provoked an almighty row with Marcia. She had written to Rupert afterwards accusing him of upsetting Piers, who had been found sleep-walking again, and forbidding him to take his tart girlfriend there. The same edict applied to Tom at his public school in Dorset. Over the years Ru's contact with his sons declined, almost as if he had decided to withdraw from the contest with their mother for their affection, although strangely Chloe grew rather fond of them, particularly of Piers. As Ru grew more distant with his sons he grew harsher with them, and Chloe sometimes found herself defending them. They came to stay from time to time, after Rupert had married Chloe, two tall gawky fair-haired boys who hung around awkwardly and ate a lot. Piers adored babies and would take James out in his pram then spend hours talking to him and tickling him, holding toys up so he could see them.

Marcia, whom Chloe had never met, went on ringing up periodically for years to denounce Rupert to Chloe in her down-to-earth way.

'You'll see,' she would say, 'he's never grown up. You wait. He'll ruin your life too, if you don't look out. He turns against people who challenge him or make him feel threatened. He'll begin to insinuate you're not quite sane. He'll ruin your life, if you let him, just as he tried to ruin mine.'

Fanny, Chloe's therapist, practised from rooms in Devonshire Street. Chloe had liked her at once. She terribly wanted to be like Fanny, who seemed to her to be a superior being, so extraordinarily beautiful and cool and detached, so very much (Chloe felt) the opposite of Chloe. She was also warm and intelligent and she listened in a way Chloe had not known one could be listened to. She combined the patience and affection of a friend with the extra ear of her professionalism. Since she had stopped seeing Lucy, Chloe had found herself short of someone whom she felt could really understand her. She had plenty of friends and acquaintances – superficially her life was full of talk and bustle – but she was shy of boring on about her unhappiness. She had heard too many tales of others who did not know when to stop in her situation, exhausting the patience of family and friends.

'Oh, so and so,' she would hear at dinner parties. 'I felt sorry for her to start with, but *really* . . . actually, I'm not surprised he left . . .' Chloe had determined not to be that person, the dinner-party bore, the bereft wife, but it left her feeling isolated and desperate. People were so incredibly cruel on the whole, and so insecure that the problems of other people made them feel threatened. Chloe, who was sensitive and sympathetic, realized this very quickly. And Fanny seemed, in the beginning, to be the perfect answer to this problem. Except that Chloe found it impossible to really trust her with her problems. She had thought it would be simple to hand over emotional baggage, but things had to be drawn out of one slowly and painstakingly, with the risk of a dependence along the way that scared the wits out of her. She sometimes had a feeling that if she did let go she would drown, pulled out to sea by those dark currents of fear that troubled her dreams. She could talk to her mother, but it always had to be talk of success. Marjorie didn't care for failure and didn't know what to do when she was confronted with it. As for Guy, Chloe felt she had been the ultimate disappointment. He had wanted a son and he had got her instead. They had never been close and Chloe had never felt she could please him. For a brief period after James was born she felt she had, but as James grew older Chloe realized the pleasure she had basked in had been for the child, not for her. Now they were as distant as they had ever been, particularly since her marriage had begun to give. And of course her parents had been so awfully good at marriage. 'Amazing' people had said when they celebrated their fortieth wedding anniversary in '76. 'Absolutely amazing – such devotion . . . a tour de force . . . and the garden . . . monument to their life together . . . wonderful couple . . .'

57

CHAPTER 7

What would you like to talk about today?' Fanny asked.

'Um,' said Chloe. She never knew how to start or what to say to make the transition between the casual friendliness of greeting Fanny and the kind of deep talk which was her reason for coming. She felt like a swimmer sliding without preparation towards the deep.

'Would you like to talk about Rupert?' asked Fanny. 'Last week you said you wanted to look back at the beginning of your marriage and into the time before you were married.' She paused and waited for Chloe.

'I suppose I do,' said Chloe slowly. 'I'm awfully tired of thinking about Rupert. He seems omnipresent at the moment, but I suppose that will pass.'

Fanny smiled, but said nothing.

'We had such high hopes about ourselves, our marriage. At least I did and I think he did too. It was as if we had reinvented love and marriage. All lovers feel that, I expect.'

Again, she looked at Fanny for corroboration.

'Which isn't to say,' said Fanny, 'that it is any less true for being universally felt.'

'No. What's so odd is that the whole situation is repeating itself. Now it's Lucy and Ru with me as the villainess. I'm playing Marcia's part.' She paused for a second, then said: 'I felt we would never break up. It was as if we had so many problems to solve that we couldn't, that we had to stick together.'

'*Had* to?' said Fanny softly.

'Yes. At the back of my mind was the idea that I couldn't ever leave him, that Marcia had been wrong for him and I was right. I had to make it right.'

'Make it right?'

'Paper over the cracks,' said Chloe, 'support him, be dutiful, obedient. Marcia was so awful over the divorce. Rupert tried to be good to her but it fell apart and then it got very acrimonious. We spent days in the High Court sorting it out.'

'How did you feel about that?'

'Terrible,' said Chloe. 'Absolutely terrible. Dickens was right about the law. It grinds you into the dust, pulverizes you, takes your life and digests some bits and spits out others.'

'How awful,' said Fanny, passing Chloe some coloured paper handkerchiefs. 'How did Rupert feel about all that?'

'He seemed to pass a lot of it to me. It was as if I had to deal with his problems,' said Chloe, rather surprised by her answer.

'Do you think he did that at other times in your marriage?'

'What do you mean exactly?'

'I mean, do you think Rupert gets – got you – to bear the burden of the problems, not only the problems you faced as a couple before you developed some of your own, but then made you feel responsible when things went wrong between you?'

'You mean does he blame me?'

Fanny waited.

'Yes,' said Chloe. 'Yes, I think he does . . . did. He always makes me feel as if it's my fault.'

'As if he had nothing to do with it,' put in Fanny. 'That's something we could talk about if you like. Why you feel you're always at fault.'

'I've always felt everything was my fault,' said Chloe.

'Always?'

'Yes.' Chloe nodded. 'It's definitely something Rupert knows about me. That I do tend to take the blame, to feel guilty. I think he's played on it a lot. Ever since I've known him there have been things I felt very badly about that were *his* problems, not mine, but somehow they seemed to have become mine.'

'Such as?'

'His children. When they began to come to us, Ru would never put himself out for them after a bit. I had to do it. Look after them, play with them.'

'And did you mind?'

'Yes, I did. Then, after I'd had James, I began to get on with them better because they were so sweet to him, particularly Piers, the younger boy. He was always playing with him and taking him for walks in his pram, like a proud father. He was so nice.'

'Do you see them now?'

'Sometimes. They ring me up to chat.'

'What do they think about Rupert's behaviour?'

'They think he's mad. They can't understand it.'

Fanny made a note.

'Do you think we go on repeating our parents' mistakes,' said Chloe, 'like Oedipus? Bound to dreadful things before we have a choice, and unable to change them?'

'No, I don't,' said Fanny. 'Being aware of things is to have the power to resist a pattern, the power to change things. Did you have any particular mistake in mind?'

'Oh, I wasn't really thinking of my own parents,' said Chloe defensively. 'They're practically perfect. I was thinking more of Ru and his boys.'

'Perfect?'

'Well, you know . . .' said Chloe, groping for something to justify her remark. 'I mean not exactly perfect – she's a flirt, he has eye for the girls, so I'm told; he used to make passes at my friends when I was younger – but perfect so far as the outside world is concerned.'

Fanny raised her eyebrows. 'The outside world?' she repeated, feeling that they were in a rather circuitous way getting nearer the true centre of Chloe's preoccupations.

'They've always been keen on appearances,' said Chloe. 'Building things up. God knows what really goes on between them. It's impossible to tell. But they always seemed terribly wrapped up in themselves when I was young. I always felt left out. Being an only child is not an ideal thing.'

'Is Rupert an only child?'

'Yes, he is. We're two onlies together. Or apart should I say,' she added bitterly.

Fanny looked at her sympathetically and then glanced at her watch. The therapeutic hour was drawing to a close.

Rupert Durrell's secretary, Sharon brought him a cup of coffee and put it down on his desk without slopping it. She had been with Rupert for fifteen years and often said to her friend Sheryl when they had a drink in the Ship and Biscuit that she knew more about Mr Durrell than either of his wives, and it wasn't a pretty picture.

Rupert, who was on the telephone, raised a hand in thanks

then swivelled his chair towards the window behind his desk where he could look out over the City of London, like a king surveying his kingdom.

'You know why . . . it just isn't a good idea at the moment. Soon, perhaps. Chloe's being difficult and I don't want to give her the chance of a stick to beat me with,' he said into the receiver in his patient, client-soothing voice, only it wasn't a client he was talking to but Lucy, his mistress, or 'his new squeeze' as his friend Andrew Cruickshank put it, a girl at any rate whom he had known a long, long time and always fancied, never mind the fact that she was practically his wife's sister. He had taken her out once or twice around the time he had started to date Chloe, but she had been funny about sex (being an RC) and he had begun to chase her friend as a kind of tease.

The slightly taboo aspects of the affair made her, in a way, all the more alluring to Ru.

'It wouldn't be right for them to come to your flat yet,' he continued, meaning James and Miranda whom Lucy wanted him to bring round. 'Give it time, OK? They'd find it strange, especially as they've been there with Chloe so much.'

Lucy wanted him to move into her flat in Campden Hill Mansions, but he wouldn't. He wasn't even quite sure why he wouldn't, he just didn't think it was the right thing to do. The children were a convenient excuse. Instead, he had moved back in with Andrew, his old friend, still a bachelor, still living in the same flat in Pembroke Road. At Andrew's place his options were open. He could (if he wanted to) either return to Chloe or move in with Lucy. He liked the peace and quiet Andrew's flat afforded at night when he and Andrew would sometimes sit over a bottle of whisky and chew the cud about business. He felt safe there and the freedom exhilarated him. It was comfortable and he could do more or less what he wanted. He missed the children, of course. He was sentimental about his children in their absence and liked to talk about the patter of little footsteps, but in fact the presence of children irritated him after a while, particularly if they were disobedient. Chloe had seen him at his very, very best with Piers all those years before.

*

When he had met Chloe she had been such a sweet girl, so compliant, so tender, and such a good listener – although she had her moments, but who didn't? – but she had changed and it had become noticeable, he supposed, after James was born. (It had taken him some time to get over the sight of all that blood in the delivery room.) At any rate, from being more of a mistress or a girlfriend whom he happened to be married to, she had become a wife and mother. She began to nag him and lay down the law about how much he should drink and smoke. She had wanted him to give up cigarettes, having given them up herself (temporarily, as it turned out) when she was pregnant with James. She had also wanted him to come home earlier and help her with James, as they had had no nanny in those days. She had put on lot of weight with her pregnancy and Rupert suddenly found he didn't fancy her so much. The birth had been difficult and she found making love painful. Rupert looked around and noticed that one of the new graduate trainees was a particularly attractive Swiss girl. He began an affair with her, the first of many.

'I'll take you out to dinner tonight,' he said to Lucy, towards the end of their conversation. 'Would you like that?' It was a sop, he knew, but he hoped it would do.

'I don't know,' Lucy said. 'I'm not feeling too brilliant as a matter of fact. I think I might have an early night.'

'Go on,' he said, 'don't be a spoil sport.'

'I really don't feel great, Ru.'

'I'll call you later,' he said. 'You might feel better by then.'

'OK,' said Lucy, adding, 'love you' before putting the phone down. She had learned better than to wait for Rupert to reply to that one. He was in love with her, she was sure of it, but being English he found it difficult to say so. Or at least this was how Lucy reasoned with herself.

CHAPTER 8

'Ah Chloe,' said Guy, coming out of the front door with the dogs in tow as Chloe turned her engine off. 'Good journey?'

'So, so,' said Chloe, slamming her door and opening the back for the children to jump out. 'Took longer than it should.' She kissed her father, noticing that, as usual, he suffered the gesture and did not attempt to return it. He smelled familiarly of essence of limes and pipe tobacco. All her life he had smelled the same. It was amazing how certain smells took one straight back into the distant past and made one's heart ache.

'Nero's going grey under his chin,' said Miranda, kissing his nose.

'He's been like that for a long time, silly,' said James, who was stroking Gus. 'Go and find a stick,' he said. 'Good boy, Gussie.'

'No, he hasn't,' said Miranda.

'Yes, he has.'

'Oh, stop *arguing*,' said Chloe. 'Put a sock in it. They've been at it since we turned out of Brook Green,' she said to Guy.

'It's a long way for them in the car,' he said.

'It's a bloody long way for me, too,' said Chloe. 'Keeping control *and* doing the driving.'

'No need to snap,' said Guy.

'Where's Mamma?' Chloe asked her father, going inside.

'Having a rest before changing, I think. We had a film crew all day yesterday, doing whatever series it is. I can't remember.'

'*English Gardeners*,' said Chloe.

'And then this afternoon the vicar came. He's only just gone.'

'She likes him, doesn't she?'

'Seems to,' said Guy dismissively.

'I think he's rather dishy,' said Chloe, hoping to annoy.

'Men of the cloth aren't supposed to have SA,' said Guy.

'This one does. Mamma obviously thinks so.'

'He's learning about gardening,' said Guy. 'He's her new disciple.'

'I see,' said Chloe. 'Well, the vicarage garden could certainly do with someone paying attention to it. His wife's the one who's running those hilarious discussion groups, isn't she?'

'That's the one. Here's your mother now,' said Guy, making his escape.

Conversations with his daughter made him increasingly uncomfortable; there was a double-edged, bitter kind of tinge to everything she said now. He felt obscurely that he was being got at.

'Hello, darling,' said Marjorie, coming downstairs. 'Everything all right? Good journey?'

'Ghastly,' said Chloe, making a face in the direction of the children. 'They fought the whole way.'

'Beasts,' said Marjorie, kissing them both. 'You must look after your Mama.'

'She shouts at us,' said Miranda.

'She wouldn't if you behaved yourselves.'

'Yes, she would. She shouts all the time.'

'Mrs Bosworth will bath Miranda,' said Marjorie. 'I asked her to stay. I knew you'd be tired.'

'That was kind,' said Chloe gratefully.

'I want Mum to bath me,' said Miranda.

'Well, you can't have her,' said Marjorie. 'Run along and find Mrs Bosworth, darling, there's a good girl.'

Miranda, reluctantly, did as she was told. Marjorie had that sort of effect on children.

'Can I go out for a bit?' asked James. King James the dreamer, Marjorie called him. 'I want to walk about in the garden.' This was diplomatic and designed to flatter his grandmother.

'OK,' said Chloe, knowing he really wanted to clamber about in the ruins. 'Don't fall off anything,' she said.

'I won't,' said James. 'Come on, Gus.'

'How are those two?' asked Marjorie, leading the way into the drawing room. 'They seem fine.'

'James is all right, although he's been having bad dreams, and Miranda is completely impossible. I don't know what to do with her.'

'She'll get over it,' said Marjorie. 'Children always try to divide and rule. She's probably missing Rupert.'

'Yes,' said Chloe.

64

'Drink, darling?'

'Whisky, please, lots of soda.'

'Now, darling, about *you*,' said Marjorie. 'How are things? Have you been to Digard yet?'

'Not yet,' said Chloe, taking her glass.

'He's a very good lawyer. He'll know how to manage Ru if he gets up to any monkey tricks, which, on present form, seems highly likely.'

'Yes, it does rather,' said Chloe.

'Have you seen him?'

'He comes to put the children to bed every now and again. It's absolute hell. I try to avoid him, otherwise we just row.'

'Why are you delaying seeing Digard then?'

'I don't know,' said Chloe hopelessly. 'It's lawyers, you know . . . how awful they are. They make everything worse, everyone says so.'

'They're also there to protect you and take care of your interests,' said Marjorie sharply. She found Chloe very difficult to deal with when she went floppy like this, like a dog that wouldn't get to its feet for a brisk walk. She couldn't think where this apathy came from. Both she and Guy were doers with bags of get up and go. They'd had to be. No good waiting for life to come to you, as Chloe seemed to be doing.

'Are you hoping Rupert will come back?' asked Marjorie when Chloe didn't seem inclined to reply.

'I don't think I am,' said Chloe, lighting a cigarette. 'I can hardly bear to look at him at the moment, so it can't be that.'

'He's behaved so badly,' said Marjorie. 'I don't see why he should get away with it.'

'Please, Mamma,' said Chloe. 'I'm exhausted, I've just got here after a hell of a journey. Tell me what you've been doing. How did the filming go and how's the vicar? Dad said he'd been up this afternoon.' Getting her mother off the subject of Rupert was like trying to get a dog to drop a bone.

'The filming was splendid,' said Marjorie, disguising her irritation. 'The maker of the series is a young man called Conway, very bright, very easy to deal with.'

'When's it going to be shown?'

'I'm not sure yet,' said Marjorie. 'They never seem to know themselves.'

'Did they film all of the garden?' asked Chloe. 'Did you allow them into the secret garden?' Chloe had spent much of her early childhood pretending she was Mary Lennox and trying to find the way into this sacred grove of her mother's.

'No, I didn't,' said Marjorie. 'And he didn't ask.' The old roses that flowered there now had been planted when Hubert was here, so long ago, roses with a sweet scent and the most beautiful stripey petals; on one wall the thornless climbing rose, 'Zéphirine Drouhin', and over the pergola, like a dream, a great white cascade of 'Aimée Vibert'.

'And the vicar? Dad said he was here.'

'He was, this afternoon. He really is a dear, so sympathetic.'

'To what?'

'Why to one, of course,' said Marjorie in surprise. 'I can really talk to him and he's taking such an interest in the garden.'

'Jolly good,' said Chloe.

'Don't be like that, darling. You could talk to him if you wanted to. I told him you might.'

'About what?' asked Chloe. 'My spiritual difficulties?'

'Anything,' said Marjorie, 'anything at all. He's unshockable.'

'Have you tried?'

'Darling, what is the matter with you?'

'Nothing,' said Chloe. 'I'm sorry.'

'He's coming to dinner tomorrow night with his wife.'

'His spouse,' said Chloe. 'That's what they're called in the church.'

'Quite,' said Marjorie. 'Such a ghastly word. She's rather ghastly too. Tough and aggressively feminist. Another dreadful word. But can't keep house properly. The vicarage is a shambles.'

'Feminists don't keep house, Mamma, that's the whole point. Someone else has to do it. Anyway, how do you know all this?'

'Mrs Bos. gets it from Mrs Dacre. It had all been tidied up when I was there last.'

'How depressing,' said Chloe, who was mildly curious in spite of herself. The vicar was handsome and gave good sermons which one could listen to without falling asleep, but most of the vicars Chloe had ever met seemed to be fantastic drips. This one was very probably no exception, but he was her mother's new enthusiasm. There had been a good many 'enthusiasms' over the years; Chloe's childhood had been peppered with handsome young men come as pupils to sit at the foot of the great muse of gardening, following Marjorie round like lovelorn swains carrying the spare secateurs, the extra kneeling mat, the trug, and sometimes even the hat if they were very honoured. Chloe had always thought of it as a lot of nonsense.

'Who else is coming to dinner?' she asked.

'I'm going to put David next to you,' said Marjorie, 'and then you can have a chat.'

'I hope he won't lecture me,' said Chloe. 'Give me advice about how to solder my marriage back together again. I mean he has to take the party line, surely?'

'David's not a fool. He's quite an original thinker in his own way.'

'Surely vicars aren't meant to think, they're meant to listen to the Holy Ghost, aren't they?'

'I don't see why the Holy Ghost shouldn't be a thinker.'

'Touché,' said Chloe. 'Who else then?'

'Simon and Richard.'

'And?'

'Marion.'

'Is that a good idea?' Marion MacBeth was a writer of crime stories who lived in Fordingbridge and had a tendency to drink more than was good for her at dinner parties.

'Poor darling has to go out sometimes,' said Marjorie.

'But does she have to come here?'

'Your father wants her to come, if you must know.'

'I see,' said Chloe. 'And you don't mind?'

'Why should I mind, darling?' asked Marjorie blandly. 'I like Marion.'

'Well, I don't.'

'All right, all right,' said Marjorie.

'I think I'll go and change,' Chloe said, getting to her feet. 'Could Mrs B. give my little darlings something for their supper? I'd love to lie down for a bit.'

'It's all arranged,' said Marjorie. 'You go and rest.'

Chloe went slowly up the front stairs under the assortment of portraits of former Jessops. She paused when she got to the painting of her mother by Birley, done just after she had come to Fordingbridge as a young bride. Marjorie was seated in a gilt chair which was now in the drawing room with her hand on one arm. She wore a white open-necked shirt and a little tweed suit by some Paris dressmaker. Her beautiful hair was pinned up and her expression as she looked out of the portrait past the painter was both bland and yet expressively full of life and energy. It made Chloe feel tired just to contemplate her. As a child she always tried to dodge that penetrating gaze which seemed to follow her as she came up or down the stairs.

In her room, Chloe went to the window and looked out towards the ruins of the old castle where Edward the First was supposed to have stayed, very uncomfortably, she imagined. The garden was always at its best at this time of year. Later, after dinner, she would walk round it under the full moon, by herself. She searched for signs of James but he was nowhere to be seen – perhaps he was in the kitchen by now having his supper and feeding the dogs surreptitiously under the table. She saw her father come up the steps on to the parterre from the direction of the kitchen garden. He stopped to examine something in one of the beds, a sample of something rare or new, no doubt, some exquisite little snipping from somewhere rich and strange. It certainly had all his attention, Chloe thought, surprised by how bitter she felt as she turned away.

CHAPTER 9

'That looks interesting,' said a voice with a strong American accent at Frances's elbow as she pinned up the notice about her forthcoming series of lectures at Wayemouth College of Art on the main college noticeboard.

'Thanks,' said Frances, looking round. The woman who had addressed her was tall and slender and was wearing an Afghan skirt with mirrors round the hem and a startlingly pink teeshirt. Her long black hair was piled into an untidy bun and she had a pencil stuck behind her ear.

'I'm Maria Weill – hi – I teach textile design.'

'Frances Doughty,' said Frances, taking Maria's outstretched hand. 'I'm new here. They've taken me on to the women's studies programme, I'm really excited by that. These lectures are just for starters. There's so much I want to have a go at. How long have you been here?'

'Five years,' said Maria. 'Seems a lot longer in some ways. Got time for a coffee?' She began to walk slowly across the acres of rubber flooring to the staff canteen which was located in the new wing, opened the previous year by Nicholas Serota. 'I was on my way. I'm gasping.'

'Well,' began Frances doubtfully, looking at her watch, 'I have to get my daughter Kitty at a quarter to four.'

'Plenty of time,' said Maria. 'How many kids do you have?'

'Just the two,' said Frances. 'They're enough. How about you?'

'One girl, Tashie. She's ten – but Viva, who I live with, she's an artist, Viva gets her from school every day. Are yours both girls?' she asked, holding open the door of the canteen for Frances.

'Yes. Kitty's ten, like yours, and Tanya is thirteen.'

She had known at once that Maria was a lesbian. It was not the first time she had been chatted up by a woman, but it was the first time she acknowledged to herself that it gave her the tiniest frisson of excitement.

'Do you live with the father?' Maria asked.

'Oh, yes,' said Frances. 'He's a vicar, the new vicar of Fording-bridge. We arrived at Christmas, but I only took up this post at the beginning of term. I don't know why we haven't met before.'

'I've been away,' said Maria. 'My mother died and I had to go and sort out her stuff in New York, deal with the apartment, all that crap. It takes so long.' She looked at Frances and grinned. 'You'll be a rarity here,' she said. 'Hardly any of us are married, let alone living with the father of our children.'

'Where's the father of yours?' asked Frances cautiously, helping herself to a doughnut.

'He lives in London,' said Maria. 'He's a really nice gay guy, and he was willing to do the necessary. You know, the turkey baster, it's really simple.'

'Turkey baster?' said Frances, staring slightly.

'Artificial insemination . . . a friend helped me. It was so easy.'

'I see,' said Frances. 'Does he see . . . Tasha?'

'Tashie,' corrected Maria. 'No,' she said, shaking her head. 'I didn't want it that way. I mean he's a great guy but he's a man, even if he is gay, and I didn't want all that crap about patriarchal attitudes. It comes out even when they don't mean it to.'

'Try being married to a vicar,' said Frances, stirring her coffee.

'It must be amazing,' said Maria. 'Don't you find all that stuff really *difficult*, I mean God the Father . . . The Church is so male it's brimming over with testosterone. The Church needs oestro-gen, goddesses, the feminine principle.'

'I couldn't agree more,' said Frances. 'In London I was a member of the movement for the ordination of women − I still am, but moving out of London hasn't helped − which caused me a great deal of trouble at home. David is absolutely opposed to the idea, whatever I say. We've given up talking about it now. I find the whole thing too painful. Look, I must go,' she added, 'it's been great meeting you, hope to see you around.'

'Me too,' said Maria, 'come by sometime. We're the pink cottage by the bakery at the back of St Luke's.'

Kitty was waiting outside the school when Frances finally arrived to collect her.

'You're late,' she said crossly, 'everyone else has gone home.

Helen's mum offered to drop me off in Fordingbridge – even though it's *miles* out of her way – but I said, no, I'd wait. You're always late,' she said, stumping off to the car.

'Sorry, sweetie,' said Frances, 'I got delayed in the college. I'm really sorry. Here, let me take your violin.'

'No, it's all right,' said Kitty, who wanted to let off steam and was not ready to be deprived of her crossness. 'Other people's mothers aren't late. Helen's mother's always on time. She's there five minutes before Helen comes out, without fail, Helen says.'

'Well, I'm only human,' said Frances mildly, 'and I am late sometimes, you know that. Helen's mother doesn't have a job like I do.'

'I wish you didn't,' said Kitty.

'I have to work, Kitty. Dad doesn't earn enough if I don't. And anyway, you and Tanya aren't going to need me so much soon. What am I supposed to do then?'

'We will need you,' said Kitty, who was still sulking and not prepared to give an inch. Her home life seemed to her imperfect in almost every way. Her mother worked, her father was a slave to the parish, her sister was horrible and a vegetarian (Kitty disapproved wildly of vegetarianism), they didn't even have a dog to cuddle. Helen had a dog and a Nintendo *and* a new bike. Her family were going to France in their new Volvo for three weeks in August whilst she, Kitty, might get a week with each set of grandparents if she was lucky, or unlucky more like. She positively hated going to her mother's parents: the house was even colder than the vicarage, they ate funny food – they were vegetarians too (which was where Tanya had got it from) – and it was all so somehow *cheerless* and sad. Her grandfather wore sandals with socks – the final straw – and didn't seem to know that he looked like a nerd.

'I wish we were going on holiday somewhere,' said Kitty, climbing into Frances's banana yellow Renault 4 and shutting the door which creaked embarrassingly in protest. The back right-hand wing of this car was stoved in where Frances had reversed into a skip in London ages ago. There never seemed to be enough money to get it fixed and, besides, the rest of the car was so rusted up there probably wasn't any point. Kitty was secretly ashamed of her mother's car. It was the only good thing about her being late: car shame was reduced.

'We can't afford it,' said Frances wearily, glancing at Kitty who was brimming. 'Sorry, darling, but we can't. Being in the country is holiday enough for me anyway.'

'Well, it isn't for me.'

'Cheer up, Kitty Kat,' said Frances, patting her knee.

'I hate being poor,' said Kitty.

'We're not poor,' said Frances reasonably, 'we're very well off in comparison to some people.'

'Who? Tramps, you mean?'

'No, I didn't mean that.'

'What's for supper?' asked Kitty as they turned into the vicarage driveway and bumped towards the house, avoiding the potholes.

'I'm not quite sure,' said Frances vaguely. 'I hoped Mrs D. might rustle something up.'

But Mrs D. had clearly forgotten when they went into the kitchen. She was sitting at the table in her blue nylon overall smoking and reading the *Wayemouth Chronicle*.

'Potter girl's had her baby very premature,' she said. 'Message from the hospital for your husband. Said it won't last, poor little thing. He'd just got back from the castle when the call came through.'

'Oh dear,' said Frances. 'She's that girl from the garage, isn't she, the one behind the till?'

'That's the one,' said Mrs Dacre, stubbing out her cigarette. 'She was in the family way when she went up the aisle. Canon Jones would have spun in his grave.'

'Come on,' said Frances, 'it happens all the time.'

'Well, I suppose so,' said Mrs Dacre disdainfully, putting a hand to her helmet of home-permed curls. 'Perhaps you'll be doing a lecture on it next,' she said.

'I might well,' said Frances, who sometimes wondered quite how she had managed to lumber herself with Mrs Dacre; but she had done for Canon Jones and so she would have to do for the Doughtys.

'How's Kitty today?' asked Mrs Dacre.

'All right,' said Kitty ungraciously. 'What's for supper?'

'Oh, my Lord, it went clean out of my head. I was going to do you some chips. There's fish fingers in the freezer. Where's Tanya then?'

'With Jenny,' said Kitty, 'lucky thing. I hate fish fingers.'

'They used to be a novelty,' said Mrs Dacre. 'Kids used to clamour for them.'

'I ought to have vegetables,' said Kitty. 'Shall I go and see what there is? Dad might have some beans or something.'

'Quite the market gardener now, your dad isn't he? Canon Jones would be glad to know someone's taking an interest.'

'Yes, I'm sure,' said Frances abstractedly, looking through her letters. She was thinking for some reason of Maria, and of the colour of her skin against the shocking pink of her teeshirt. 'I must go and make some calls. You'll do the fish fingers then, Mrs D?'

'Yes, yes,' said Mrs Dacre, in her most put-upon voice.

Maria walked briskly home up the High Street, taking the short cut through the graveyard of St Luke's Church, to arrive at the pink cottage by the bakery which was closing as she came by. Some girls from the high school were hanging about in groups eating things out of bags and giggling. It occurred to her that Frances's girls must go to this school if she had had to collect one by a quarter of four and she wondered where a vicar would find the cash; vicars, as everyone knew, were famously poor, but most likely the school, which was an ancient one, would make some provision for clergy children. Tashie went to St Luke's Church of England Primary School just around the corner, but the time was coming when she would have to go by bus to Hartchester every day. Perhaps, thought Maria, one way and another the time was also coming when she would have to return to NY.

Maria went into the kitchen and slung her bag in the Windsor chair that was hers.

'Hi,' she said to Viva who was kneading pastry. 'How's tricks?'

'OK,' said Viva carefully. 'How're you?'

'Good, I'm good.' Maria opened the fridge and then closed it again. She was hungry but she didn't know what for. 'I met our new lecturer today,' she said.

'What's he like?'

'She. He's a she. Interesting looking. You might like to get her to sit for you. Why don't I ask her?' said Maria provocatively.

'She might not want to,' said Viva, getting out the rolling pin. Maria was always saying these kinds of things to her nowadays. It went with the restlessness that seemed to have afflicted her since her mother's death and which worried Viva, for it was a small but potent symptom of the malaise between them. For some reason they could no longer communicate without irritating one another. They were like a see-saw: Maria angry and independent, Viva hurt and passive. It was the same in bed. Maria was bored and would turn away. Sometimes, like an angry or disillusioned husband, she even slept in the spare room under the Shaker quilt.

'Where's Tash? Is she home yet?'

'In her room,' said Viva.

'What's she doing?'

'I don't know,' said Viva. 'Why don't you give her a shout?'

'How long will the quiche take?'

'I don't know,' said Viva impatiently. 'Half an hour, forty-five minutes.'

'I think I'll go out for a walk then.'

'Take Tash with you.'

'I'll go on my own,' said Maria. 'I need some space.'

When Maria had gone Viva got out the quiche dish, greased it, lined it with her pastry, poured in the mixture, placed it in the warmed oven and then sat down with her head in her hands. She was very, very scared by what was happening to her. She had met Maria at a conference two years ago on 'Women and the Inner Goddess' at Wayemouth College of Art, a conference organized by this new woman's predecessor. The attraction between them had been instant (Maria was an instant sort of person) and she had very soon invited Viva to move into Pink Cottage where there was even a studio. Viva, who was younger and who had been struggling in London, had accepted with alacrity. It seemed like something made in heaven. And, of course, from the moment she had set eyes on her, she had adored Tashie.

The first year in Wayemouth had been absolutely perfect. It was a beautiful old market town with a plethora of Georgian houses (of which Pink Cottage was a minor example) which had somehow or other escaped the attention of the developers. There was a museum and a good library and plenty of mysterious corners and little dark alleyways where time seemed to have stood still. Best of all was the river itself, which wound round the edge of the town through marvellous lush water meadows where cows stood and gazed into the distance as they had done in the eighteenth century. Viva felt that her heart might break if she had to leave this place she had grown to love.

'Hi,' said Tash from the doorway, sounding exactly like her mother. 'What is it? Why are you crying? Where's Maria?' She called her mother by her first name, which Viva secretly disliked. It seemed to disparage the sacred bond between mother and child.

'I'm not crying really,' said Viva, sniffing.

'Yes, you are,' said Tash, coming over and putting her arms round Viva. 'Is she being horrible again?'

'No,' said Viva. 'It's me, I think. I'm tired.'

'Poor V.,' said Tash, who was dark and thin and sloe-eyed like her mother. 'It is Maria, I know it is.' She paused for a moment. 'Has she said anything to you about going back to New York?'

'No.' Viva looked up in alarm. 'Why? What's she said to you?'

'Oh nothin' really,' said Tashie, perceiving she had made an error by mentioning it. 'It's just . . .'

'She's very restless,' said Viva. 'It's since your grandmother died. That upset her a lot.'

'Yeah, you're right. What's that cooking?'

'Quiche. Give me a hug, Tashie.' When Tashie did, she said, 'I love you so much, I couldn't bear to be parted from you.'

'You're not going away, are you?' said Tashie, alarmed in her turn.

'I hope not,' said Viva, 'but everything I say irritates Maria. And she hasn't said anything to *me* about New York.'

'If you go, I'm going with you,' said Tashie, dragging a chair along so she could stand on it to reach a wine glass from the dresser.

'Don't be silly,' said Viva smiling. 'Anyway, I'm not going anywhere.'

'I mean it,' said Tashie, looking down from where she stood on the chair. 'I hate Maria sometimes.'

'No, you don't,' said Viva.

'I do,' insisted Tashie, banging the glass down on the table, reminding Viva painfully exactly how much she resembled her mother.

David had come down the hill from the castle, pausing at a certain point to enjoy looking over the irregular rooftops of this old and agreeable town towards the church, his church as he now thought of it. Once upon a time it had been both a priory and a parish church. The core of the building was its fantastically ancient and beautiful early Norman tower, which he had already grown to love. The interior of the church bore witness to the tides of history: porches and screens had been added and then burnt, the chancel and transepts had been demolished in the Dissolution of the Monasteries, but later rebuilt; the conventual buildings had been razed to the ground and the poor nuns scattered. They, of course, had not returned. It had a Norman font, a Jacobean pulpit, a fifteenth-century screen, a Jacobean communion rail and some medieval glass that had somehow survived Cromwell's merry men. Sometimes, when David was in the church by himself, he noticed that the quality of the silence felt different to what he had known at St Anselm's, which had been a red-brick Victorian church built in 1897. The silence in St Mary's was an ancient silence, dark and watchful. He would kneel at the altar rail in the east transept gazing at the tabernacle where the Blessed Sacrament was now reserved (for the first time in this church since the Reformation), trying to keep his mind empty so that he would be able to hear God when He spoke, knowing that He was there but unable, somehow, to feel this knowledge in his heart. He was a priest who believed in a God who no longer spoke to him.

The Potter girl had been rushed by ambulance to Wayemouth General. The cottage hospital at Fordingbridge did not have facilities for emergency births. It was more of a twilight home for the elderly, where David had taken to holding a communion service once a week for the poor old things, most of them not much older than Marjorie. He tried to imagine Marjorie with a zimmer frame and dentures and failed. She had such stamina, such energy, and yet he frequently felt when he spoke to her that, other than the obvious problems her daughter was going through, there were things that troubled her which she could not express, or did not wish to express. And there were the rumours about Guy that he could not help hearing. That he had a mistress in the village, the writer, Marion MacBeth, that she was the last of many, that the marriage was a sham marriage, one of mutual convenience. But what marriage was not a bit of a sham? David had wondered, filing these pieces of information and opinion without comment. His own marriage could easily be termed a sham. The move had produced an improvement in his relationship with Frances which was now, as they both settled in, falling away in the ceaseless and seemingly ever-increasing round of commitments they were both bound to.

David parked his old Volvo in the car park of Wayemouth General and made his way towards the maternity wing carrying his black bag of tricks. Margaret Potter was one of a number of much younger people who had begun to come back into the church at Fordingbridge over the last few months, most of them women. Frances said it was the old charm working its magic, but David knew perfectly well that this was a subtle disparagement of the real reason, which was that sacramental religion, vigorously conducted, worked.

At the nurses' station he paused to enquire for her, and a young nurse, who looked scarcely older than Tanya, told him that she was in a room on her own, and that her husband was with her.

'And the baby?'

'The baby's in intensive care, in an incubator, poor little fellow.'

'How much did he weigh?'

'Three pounds. Quite a good weight for a prem, but he's having trouble with his breathing.'

'I see. Well, I'll put my head round the door anyway,' David said, relieved by the information. He had somehow, without realizing it, expected to find a sad little corpse. He had quite frequently been telephoned in London by local undertakers requesting that he should come and say some prayers over babies that the parents didn't want to know, still births, or babies with dreadful deformities. People thought these things scarcely ever happened, but they happened all the time.

David looked through the glass window in the door and saw Margaret lying back on her pillows with her husband Jason holding her hand. He knocked and entered.

'Hello,' he said, advancing to the bedside. 'How are you?'

'All right,' said Margaret. 'Not brilliant. They've taken the baby away,' she said, and a large tear rolled out of her eye and down her neck.

'The nurse said he was a good weight for a premature baby,' said David. 'He'll be all right, you'll see. Rest now, if you can.'

'She's fretting,' said Jason. 'I've told her the same.' David glanced at him with his crew cut and his earring and saw that he was almost as upset as his wife. One sometimes wondered about a God that imposed such suffering on people. As a vicar he wondered about it all a great deal.

'Shall we go together and have a look at him?' suggested David to Jason. 'What's his name?'

'Paul,' said Margaret. 'You won't christen him yet, will you, Vicar?'

'Not without you,' said David.

'He's doing really well, Paul is,' said the nurse in intensive care. 'I don't think he'll be in here for too long. A real fighter. You go in there' – she indicated a waiting room – 'and I'll wheel him up so you can see him.'

David and Jason went in and stood by the glass wall. When the nurse wheeled up a tiny scrap in a clear-sided cot, his miniature body studded with drips and plasters and tubes, Jason said, his voice breaking,

'I can't believe he'll live through this. He's so little.'

'I know,' said David, who secretly agreed, 'but he will. You wait.'

'I thought you was going to lecture me,' Jason said in the corridor outside.

'What about?'

'Not comin' to church, God and Jesus and that.'

'I tell you what,' said David. 'When Paul's gone home with you and you're settled in, I'll buy you a pint, OK?'

'OK,' said Jason, pumping his hand. He grinned suddenly and the effect was as if the sun had come out from behind a cloud.

'I could do with one now, as a matter of fact,' he said.

CHAPTER 10

Chloe slept badly as usual. She was in the habit of it now, it seemed. She fell asleep easily but woke up again after two or three hours and that was when the torments began. She would lie wide-eyed in the dark like a terrified child, worrying about her own future and that of her children until she summoned the energy to turn on the light and get out of bed. In London she went downstairs into the kitchen and sat at the table drinking tea or whisky, or both, and read magazines or back copies of the *Spectator*. Since Rupert had left she had become very well informed about the world. At Fordingbridge she got out of bed quite quickly. She knew she had to beat this tormenting wakefulness at its own game and not let it take her over. She went as softly as she could along her own creaking corridor and up to the nursery floor with its cracked old lino and the bookcases full of the same books that had been there when she was a child. Miranda lay neatly on her side with her thumb firmly in her mouth, her bears lined up against the wall on her elderdown. James, however, lay spreadeagled on top of his bedclothes with his pyjama jacket buttoned askew and his book face down on the floor with pages crushed. Chloe covered him, picked up his book, stroked his cheek and crept out.

At night, she thought, going down the main stairs, this was a very haunted house; things creaked and stirred and fluttered. The faces in the portraits gazed out upon her in judgement as she went by, as if to say, What have you done with your life? Made rather a mess of things. Even in the half-light of summer dark she could feel her mother's glance following her. In the drawing room Chloe stood for a moment listening to the clock ticking, and the roses shedding petals on to the polished surface of the piano. She let herself out very quietly into the ordered darkness of the parterre and stood for a moment in the curious deathly unlight of a full moon. She went softly along the paths and under the yew arch that led down a flight of steps into the garden where the great borders were, their colours blanched into grisaille in this light. These borders had been the subjects of hundreds of articles and photographs over the years: their colour schemes, vibrant or pastel, the use of colour to offset one thing and encourage another, the rare plants picked and plucked from peaks and bogs, seeds found in caves and in tombs on Turkish hillsides, she had heard it all. This garden led through another arch into her mother's palette garden where the plants were also the subject of constant discussion and change depending on whether her mother was in an abstract or a realist mood.

Beyond that lay the garden which her mother had begun during the war and had always been very secretive about. When she was a child, Chloe sometimes wondered if her mother had buried something in that garden that she didn't want anyone else to find, treasure of some kind, but when she asked Marjorie about this Marjorie shook her head and laughed and said, no, it was just that the rest of the place was so gone-over, so written about, so photographed, she wanted to keep a corner to herself, that was all.

The key, Chloe knew, was kept on a nail under a cascade of ivy, but when she put up her hand to find it it had gone. She searched the ground, but in spite of the moonlight it was impossible to see if it had fallen off. The shadows were immensely deep, like black pools. Chloe looked at her watch and decided, as it was after three, that it was time to go to bed.

The next morning she slept late, and woke feeling refreshed, for once. The children, she decided, must be outside somewhere. In the dining room, breakfast had been cleared away, so she went into the kitchen for some coffee and found Mrs Bos. cooking lunch in a bad mood.

'Someone slept well,' she said, wiping her eyes with her apron. The kitchen smelled deliciously of onions and garlic.

'Not really,' said Chloe. 'I wake in the night and then over-sleep.'

'Like that, is it? You should get some sleeping pills to help you through.'

'I've tried some,' said Chloe, 'but I kept waking up with a hangover.'

'There's lots of different kinds,' said Mrs Bos. 'I should know, I have to take them for my back.'

'How is your back?' asked Chloe, realizing she had been outmanoeuvred.

'Dreadful, Chloe, just dreadful. Hilda Bowen's running this back clinic now on Fridays, showing us exercises and that . . .'

After half an hour of this, and two cups of coffee, Chloe escaped. James was out and about somewhere or other with the dogs and Miranda had been secconded by her grandmother into being chief carrier of the secateurs, which she rather liked as she was allowed to snip things off with them as a reward.

'We're doing the flowers for tonight,' said Miranda importantly, when Chloe came upon them amongst the cascades of roses in the palette garden, 'and Granny's going to let me do my own vase.'

'That's generous,' said Chloe, smiling.

'She's being immensely helpful,' said Marjorie, coming along the path with her trug full of white roses. She was wearing a large flattish straw hat, a very dark blue linen skirt and a white shirt with large covered buttons.

'You look marvellous,' Chloe said.

'Thank you, darling. So do you, but tired, I think?'

'A little. I'm going to wander off for a bit, do some shopping in the town, and be back at about midday.'

'Can I come?' Miranda asked.

'No, darling, you're helping me,' said Marjorie. 'I need you too much. You're so useful.'

'All right,' said Miranda. 'Will you get me a Mars bar, Mum, one of the king-size ones?'

'If you're good,' said Chloe.

Chloe went her favourite way into the town, through the kitchen garden, past the greenhouses where her father was deep in conclave with McCormack, the head gardener, and out into the flower meadow which her mother so loved, wading her way waist-deep through ox-eye daisies and hawkweed and buttercups. She went through the gate at the bottom on to the road and walked round behind the church, seeing the tower looming up. In the churchyard she wandered about amongst the graves for a few minutes until she found her favourite one, the poor Jesuit priest implicated in the Titus Oates Plot, who had been hanged in Fordingbridge in 1679.

The church itself smelled strangely of incense. It gave Chloe quite a jolt to realize what that familiar and yet alien smell was. It almost but not quite overlaid the other smells in this place of must and dusty old hymn books and mice and stone, ancient, cold stone. In the crypt of the church lay the coffins of previous Jessops. She would lie here herself one day in this ancient quietness, rotting gently away. The thought seemed not so much macabre as relieving. There were moments, Chloe thought, when it was good to know one would not live for ever.

'Chloe, dear,' said a voice from nowhere, making her jump, 'what a surprise! Are you here on your own?'

Chloe looked round but saw nobody.

'Up here,' said the voice. 'In the gallery.'

'Mrs Hewlett,' said Chloe. 'I didn't see you or hear you. I'm sorry. I thought I was alone.'

Mrs Hewlett was married to Major Hewlett, who was one of the churchwardens.

'My dear, I don't expect you to have X-ray vision. I was polishing the brass bits up here. I'll come down.'

'No, don't do that,' said Chloe, 'I'll come up.'

The gallery was dusty and smelled of sun and hymnbooks and, faintly, of damp, where the roof leaked.

'Nice to see you,' said Joanna Hewlett, brushing cobwebs off her tweed skirt. 'Are you down for the weekend?'

'Yes, that's right,' said Chloe. 'It's quite a long drive but it's worth it to wake up here on Saturday morning, especially when the weather's like this.'

'I'm sorry to hear things aren't too easy for you at the moment,' said Joanna Hewlett tactfully. Chloe was such a nice girl, everyone liked her. She had grown up here, of course, and knew everybody. She was less hooked on her own self-image than her famous mother (whom, people said, had always been as she was now, even when she first came here) and more approachable than her cantankerous father who was not greatly popular although he was the squire. It was also said that the female writer, Marion MacBeth, knew him better than she should. Donald, her husband, who was a charitable soul said the war had twisted Guy Jessop. He had been a prisoner of the Japs for years, which was enough to twist anyone. 'Never forget,' Donald was fond of saying, 'that the Japanese are a naturally cruel race.' Privately, Joanna Hewlett thought Guy Jessop had always been a bit of a b***, but she wouldn't have dreamed of saying so. It was also known that he was devoted to his wife.

'That's life,' said Chloe, who knew better than to dwell on such a topic.

'How are the children?'

'All right,' said Chloe. 'James is being very good and Miranda is being very bad, so everything is normal.'

They both laughed at this.

'What do you think of the vicar?' asked Chloe.

'I like him,' said Joanna. 'Most people do, but he's very high. Donald isn't entirely happy, but he's agreeable and *frightfully* good-looking, my dear.' She put her hand on Chloe's arm. 'You must have noticed how we all go weak at the knees on Sundays.'

'Oh, do you?' said Chloe.

'Us old things,' said Joanna, 'not you young perhaps. We have a thurifer these days, a man from Wayemouth – you've seen him, haven't you? – as well as reservation of the Sacrament which Donald says hasn't happened in this church since the Reformation. He's having some success, too. Young people like him, you see. There are new faces in the church on a Sunday now, local people. The Sunday School's beginning to take off and it's really rather exciting. He was in London before this in a poor district with a rickety old church which he built up from nothing – but you must know all this, since your mother practically chose him single-handed.'

'Yes, Mamma does go on about him,' said Chloe. 'He's her new passion. She's teaching him how to become a great gardener at the moment.'

'Well,' said Joanna, 'between you and me, nobody else is going to do it. The vicarage garden is still half jungle, but have you seen his wife?' Her voice sank to a whisper. 'She's the complete opposite of him: a *feminist*,' she said, 'very radical, a member of the Movement for the Ordination of Women, a lecturer in women's studies, if you please, and she teaches at that ghastly place in Wayemouth. She has the most extraordinary discussion groups – topics are listed in the porch, you'll see them on your way out – which he doesn't go to, I might add, and with good reason. None of us can understand how they came to be married in the first place.'

'I'll have to go to one of these famous groups,' said Chloe, 'just to see what the fuss is about.'

'I shouldn't bother if I were you,' said Joanna. 'Anyway, I'd better be getting on. Bring the children to see me one day, Chloe. You're always welcome, you know that.'

'Perhaps in the holidays,' said Chloe, 'when there's more time. That would be lovely, thank you.'

In the porch, Chloe paused to look for the notice about the discussion groups, but before she had time to read it properly she saw the vicar coming along the path between the cherry trees in his cassock; it was a curious sight, like something out of a French novel, she thought. Priests in England were more associated in the public mind with billowing surplices than cassocks. He *was* good-looking, Joanna Hewlett was right. No wonder the old ladies were doing jigs.

'All you need is a biretta,' she said when he came within earshot.

'Funny you should say that,' said David. 'I used to wear one in Notting Hill to keep up with the ethnic minorities, what with saris and batik robes and one thing and another, but I suspect in Fordingbridge they'd accuse me of being pretentious.'

'Yes, they would,' said Chloe. 'You know how hypocritical people are, secretly they'd rather like it.'

'Your mother warned me about the nonconformists hereabouts,' said David. 'I translated that information as a warning not to be too flamboyant.'

'But you're being wildly flamboyant in other ways,' said Chloe. 'Incense, thurifers, sanctus bells, practically turning the church into a bastion of Roman Catholicism.'

'Do you disapprove?'

'Not in the least,' said Chloe, noticing that his cassock was missing a button. One more thing his wife didn't do for him, she supposed. 'I like it. If I'm ever in London I go to All Saints, Margaret Street,' she said. 'That's more like twelfth-century Portugal than an Anglican church.'

'I know it is,' said David laughing.

'You can hardly see for the clouds of incense' said Chloe, thinking that he was much too attractive to be a priest. Priests were not meant to have a sexual presence. She always assumed it was stamped out of them in theological college on the basis that father figures weren't meant to be glamorous or attractive to too many women, but this one had *it*. What her father in his antedeluvian way called SA. No wonder her mother had taken him on as the equivalent of an acolyte.

'Have you seen my favourite tomb here?' asked David.

'Adam Williams?' This was the name of the Jesuit priest whose tomb Chloe had visited earlier.

'The very one,' he said, leading the way. 'Hanged and then burned. A real martyr,' he said, stopping in front of the mossy stone which lay practically concealed in the grass.

'You sound envious,' said Chloe, looking at him.

'Do I?'

'Are you?'

'I don't know,' he said, turning to her, gripped suddenly by some presentiment whose source he couldn't fathom.

'Wasn't it Donne who said, "Other men's crosses are not mine" or something like that?' said Chloe. 'That makes us all martyrs, doesn't it, in our various ways, nailed to our various crosses?'

'I supposed it does.' He glanced at her and then away. 'I mean to clear this grave up, cut the grass, plant something to grow over it decoratively.'

'Bring him out of his obscurity, you mean.'

'Yes.'

'I really must go,' said Chloe, looking at her watch, 'otherwise I'll be late for lunch and Mamma will be cross. You're coming to dinner, Mamma says, so I'll see you later. By the way, thank you for being so kind to her, but don't let her bully you. She's an awful old man-eater is my mother.'

'She's been very good to me,' said David. 'Now I know an aconite from a ranunculus, which is more than I did before.'

'She's a brilliant teacher,' said Chloe, 'but don't let her try to remodel your soul.'

'I think she'd find that rather hard work,' said David. 'I know I do.'

On Saturday night, Rupert rang Chloe from Andrew's flat, having fortified himself with a couple of extremely strong whiskies. He was rather put out to find that now she was no longer there he missed her. Towards the end their rows had become so bitter and Chloe's distaste and dislike of him had become so palpable that he had judged it best to go; in doing so, he had managed to convince a fairly large portion of himself that it was because she was so impossible that he had to go, not because his own behaviour was in any way out of order. Chloe was a harridan. He had been forced out.

In contrast with his wife's ungovernable behaviour Lucy's sweet reasonableness and her open adoration had been balm to his soul to start with, but now he had to admit that he occasionally (if he was honest more and more frequently) found her approach too anodyne. He was used to sharper treatment, and like a man who was used to a good drubbing from time to time he craved it. Lucy was *boring*. The affair which he had begun as a refuge was running out of steam, even though she seemed to have shed a few inhibitions over the years about sex. He missed Chloe and the children, particularly at weekends, and he missed going down to Fordingbridge and enjoying the privileges of being associated with the grandest family in the county, even if he had found Guy irritating and sometimes patronizing and Marjorie maddeningly vain and overbearing, fancying herself as the queen bee of the gardening world. Poor old Chloe really hadn't stood much chance with those parents and she certainly hadn't managed to grow up and away from them. Every weekend she went home like a child going back to Mamma (as she would infuriatingly insist on addressing her mother) and Papa. Before they were married she was still taking her washing home. Rupert had found this pitiable and endearing. He had married Chloe in order to give her a chance to grow up and look what had happened. She was like an animal in a cage with the door open who couldn't summon the courage to leave, poor darling. Poor little Chloe. She still needed him. Rupert picked up the receiver and dialled.

'Hello,' said Marjorie in that offhand way of hers. 'Oh, Rupert. It's you. Haaryou?' She put her hand over the receiver. 'It's Rupert,' she said in a loud voice to Chloe, who must have been beside her, 'do you want to speak to him?'

Bitch, thought Rupert.

'I can tell him you're in the bath if you like.'

Cunt.

'No,' said Chloe's voice, lighter than her mother's but with the same offhand edge to it, 'I'll speak to him.

'Hello, Rupert.'

'I was just ringing to see if you were all right.'

'That was kind.'

'And the children?'

'They're fine.'

Silence.

'Can I come and see them on Sunday night?'

'If you want to.'

'I do want to. Chloe . . .'

'What time?'

'Sevenish.'

'OK'

More silence.

'Chloe?'

'What, Rupert? Do hurry. There are people coming in a minute.'

Bitch, bitch, bitch.

'See you Sunday,' he said, and put the phone down without saying goodbye.

Chloe gazed at the receiver in her hand. 'No manners.'

'He never did have any manners.'

'You used to like him.'

Marjorie looked at her. 'So did you, darling.'

'OK,' said Chloe, who was angry with herself as well as with Rupert. 'OK.'

The last thing she needed was a bloody duel with her mother too. She wished she could say no to Rupert, but she couldn't. She could be cool with him, but she couldn't refuse him a thing. It was as if she were in thrall to him, as if she had to accommodate him, to do what he wanted, otherwise . . . but what this 'otherwise' was, she simply couldn't put her finger on. Only when she was very, very angry, sustainedly angry, did she have the power to refuse him anything.

'I still find it hard to believe Lucy has done this. Not her mother's daughter for nothing, I suppose.'

'Please, Mamma,' said Chloe wearily.

'I do hope you'll have the sense to go and see Digard next week.'

'We've been through this,' said Chloe through gritted teeth.

'I just wish you'd see sense.'

Sense. Chloe took a mouthful of whisky, and felt it smoothing its way down inside her. She knew she was drinking too much but she hardly cared. It was the only way she could numb the beastly constant pain inside. Fanny had told her to try and 'stay with it,' whatever that meant, and she did try to let the hurtful thoughts float like scum on the surface of her mind, but most of the time she felt terrible, as if she were lying on a bed of nails. Drink made the nails less sharp, that was all, for a short time. Then she would wake in the night and they would be like skewers again.

'I'm only trying to help you, darling, that's why I go on about it.'

'I know you are,' said Chloe, who was a pleaser at heart. 'I know.'

'I'm sorry you're so unhappy. I know what it's like.'

'Do you? I thought your life had been seamlessly happy except when Daddy was a prisoner of war.'

'Nobody's life is seamlessly happy, darling. That's a child's view. Everyone suffers or is broken in some way.'

She spoke with feeling, remembering with hideous clarity how she had felt after Hubert had gone in '43. He had been her great love, her one and only love. All the rest had been nothing. Just fluff. Foam. She was devoted to Guy, but he had not been a grand passion. They had had the modern equivalent of an arranged marriage. She had had money and breeding, he had had breeding and needed money. But it had not been a grand passion and Marjorie had never wanted it to be. It was better this way: mutual respect, friendship, affection and so on. She wondered sometimes if Guy had not wanted more from her, but when he had come back from the war, broken inside and impossibly needy, she had not been able to help him. After Hubert had gone and for a long time afterwards she had been broken herself; during that long period when she had not heard from him, and yet still hoped to, before she had begun to accept the fact of his death, she had wanted so much to die herself. But she had not had the courage. The ferocious energy of that wanting and her resistance to it had been channelled into the garden. Even now when she thought of him she was aware that it was unsafe territory, rather like the land around Verdun that she had heard couldn't be used for anything because it was still full of explosive.

'How did you suffer?' asked Chloe. 'You never told me . . .' But at this point her father put his head round the door and said, 'Miranda's crying. She wants you. I won't do, apparently.'

'Oh,' said Chloe, 'all right. I better go up.'

She went upstairs thinking of her mother's enigmatic remark. She did not think she had ever heard her mother, in all the time she had known her, talk of suffering. With Marjorie it had always been a stubborn gospel of joy.

CHAPTER 11

'Hello,' said Rupert into Lucy's intercom at about eight o'clock on Saturday night. 'It's me.'

'Right,' said Lucy, pressing the buzzer, 'come on up.' He sounded pissed, she thought, damn. Tonight was so important and he would have to go and get plastered before dinner, especially with Piers, his son, coming for the first time. He was late, too. What was it about this family?

She had given Rupert keys as a gesture of trust, but for some reason she didn't understand he refused to use them, preferring to behave like an acquaintance rather than a lover. Still, she thought, going back into the bathroom where she had been putting on her lipstick for the fourth time, perhaps it was a better indication that he was honourable. There were some men who could hardly wait to get the keys to one's apartment. It was a good argument, but a large part of her remained unconvinced of its validity. Earlier on, she had pleaded with Ru to move in, but he insisted on remaining at Andrew's. He said all the right things: that he loved her, that he wanted to be with her, that he thought about her the whole time, but he had never quite come to the point of saying that they should get married when he was divorced from Chloe. She had no idea what they were doing about that. She knew Ru had a horror of lawyers from his experience with Marcia, and of course it was impossible for her to know what Chloe was up to these days. Chloe. Lucy looked at herself in the glass. She was sorry about Chloe but, as the old saying went, all's fair in love and war; except that she dreamed about her: dreamed they were friends, sisters, companions as they always had been, confidantes. And she would wake every time with a sense of horror at her own behaviour which wore off as she came towards the surface of wakefulness. Better not to think about it. Having resolved not to think about Chloe, she immediately began to do so.

When Chloe had first started going out with Rupert all those years ago Lucy had been enraged, although she hid her feelings cleverly. There were several occasions on which she had felt like saying, 'Look, I *know* what he's like, I've been to bed with him too', but she could never quite bring herself to this point. Instead, she began to gain a greater satisfaction from playing wise woman and sage to Chloe's passion, feeling quite relieved (or so she told herself) that it was not her pigeon when things got so difficult with Marcia. Lucy began to believe that she had always disliked Ru. But later on, when the marriage was looking good and the Durrells had become very prosperous, those original feelings of envy resurfaced. Chloe had always had the luck, or so it seemed to Lucy. Men flocked to her, not only because she was pretty and nice, but because she emitted some indefinable essence of vulnerability. Men, particularly older men, wanted to protect Chloe and care for her. It had always been like that. It was possible, Lucy admitted to herself, to love someone (she did love Chloe) and yet to have mixed feelings about them too. To want to do them harm. It was what she had known when she was very young. Love and hurt dished out in the same bowl. Chloe had real parents, a fantastic house, brains, beauty, charm, and now she even had two divine children whilst she, Lucy, had had an alcoholic father (long deceased) and one of those jaded, jet-set, sex-crazed, silly, slightly druggy mothers who had never provided a steady home (successions of hotel rooms in ski resorts and borrowed flats in Marbella, marble bathrooms, gold taps), no husband until it was too late (and then Heinrich) and, worst of all, when Chloe had her darlings, no child of her own to love. Until now, that was.

She had done the test that morning, waiting in agony for the result although she was fairly certain she was pregnant. Her breasts hurt and her body felt somehow, indefinably, different. She was both scared and elated by the thought of a child, thrilled by the idea of her body's ingenuity, scared, scared, scared about what Ru's reaction might be. He already had four children, would he want a fifth? She hadn't discussed it with him because, underneath, she felt he would not. And if he did not, then her chance would slip from her.

'You're suffering from bio-panic,' Peter, her boss at the agency, had told her. 'Women get it in their late thirties. We're on the wrong side of thirty-five, darling, it's our hormones, they do play us girls up. Resist, resist, with all your might and main. We tell people babies are designer aids in order to sell them cream for their disgusting bottoms, but you and I know that babies are a nightmare: they keep you up at night screaming and throwing up, and then they grow up and get into glue-sniffing. Who needs it?'

'Hello,' said Rupert when Lucy opened the door. 'How are you?'

'I'm fine.'

'Good.' He followed her across the hall, then he said, 'I must have a leak,' and lurched off towards the bathroom.

When he came back into the sitting room, he said, 'How are you, darling?', as if he had not previously greeted her.

'Did you drive here?' asked Lucy.

'Of course I did. Why?'

'I just wondered.'

'Might offer a chap a drink.'

'Help yourself,' said Lucy, but refused when he offered her one.

'You're not going all holier than thou, are you?'

'No,' said Lucy, shaking her head. 'There's the buzzer. It'll be Piers.'

'Ah, Piers, yes.'

He had been such a sweet little boy in his shorts with his Harrods haircut, but it was when he had started to grow up that he had become tricky, like his elder brother before him. Wanting things. Money, time, help. Everybody always wanted something from him. Even Lucy. She wanted marriage, babies, the whole kit and caboodle. Nightmare. No more marriage, no more babies.

Ru poured himself yet another large whisky and paced about Lucy's pretty sitting room, picking things up and putting them down again. Telephoning Chloe had made him feel twitchy. The sound of her voice when she was off-hand like that stirred up all kinds of feelings in him: he felt as if she were the one who had got away rather than he. They would be having drinks now in the drawing room at Fordingbridge with the great windows open on to the terrace and people would be arriving for dinner. There was always a dinner party on Saturdays, which everyone changed for. Must be one of the last places in England where people still changed. It was a bore, but he liked it. It was wrong here somehow, being here like this with Piers coming. Wrong house, wrong wife. In a minute he would wake up and find he was back in Caithness Road with Chloe. He didn't want Piers to come here. He didn't want his past to obtrude in this way into his present, but it had a maddening habit of doing just that.

'Hi, Dad,' said Piers casually, following Lucy into the room and staring around him with open curiosity in the way only the young could get away with. He was very like his father in looks, tall and fair, but his eyes were brown like his mother's and he had inherited her Jewish nose, a real pothook. He was dressed in the uniform of the under-25s: ripped jeans, old leather jacket, teeshirt, Doc Marten boots which left tread-marks in Lucy's deep-pile. He was a student at the Royal College of Art (paid for by Marcia in order to annoy Rupert), learning how to express himself and study the making of installations. Nothing so old-fashioned and ridiculously absurd as drawing or learning how to paint intruded into his working day; he spent a lot of time in a garage workship belonging to the college throwing paint at the walls. If some hit a canvas, well and good.

'Nice place,' he said to Lucy as if, Rupert thought, he had been brought up in a council house.

'Thank you,' said Lucy. 'Would you like a drink?'

'Got any vodka?'

'I've got most things,' said Lucy, looking in the cupboard under the drinks tray. 'Which do you want, Polish or Russian?'

Piers made a face and came to kneel beside her, his jacket creaking as he bent down. 'Give us some of the Polish stuff,' he said. 'We all know the Russian stuff's made in Wigan or Warrington, don't we?'

'Here you are,' said Lucy, handing him the bottle. She stood up and smiled at him. She was wearing a white teeshirt, a short black skirt and high heels and looked good. And she knew he knew it.

'Haven't we met before?' said Piers, putting his head on one side so that his blond hair scraped one shoulder of his jacket.

'We might well have done,' said Lucy, 'over the years.' She turned away. She desperately didn't want Chloe's name to be mentioned. 'Ice? Lemon?'

94

'Both, thanks.' Piers took the glass from her. 'So here's to you two lovebirds,' he said, raising his glass and swallowing half its contents. 'How's Chloe taking it, Dad?'

'I hardly think,' said Rupert slowly, 'that that is any of your –'

'Oh, quit it, Dad,' said Piers mildly. 'What am I supposed to do? Pretend nothing is happening? You get yourself a nice new piece and we're not allowed to mention it.' He waved his glass in Lucy's direction as he spoke.

'Lucy is not a "piece", as you vulgarly describe it,' said Ru. 'If you can't be civil you'd better leave.'

'Just asking,' said Piers, raising his eyebrows. 'Is he living here, then?' he said to Lucy.

'No, I am not,' said Rupert. 'Please don't speak about me as if I were not in the room.'

'Sorry, Dad,' said Piers, looking anything but. 'How're the kids? How's Jamo-boy?'

'Fine,' said Rupert tersely.

'And you, Dad, how're you? You look fucking awful, if you don't mind my saying so. Too many late nights, perhaps. You're not as young as you were, you know. You've got us hard on your heels now.'

'I think you had better go,' said Rupert, getting to his feet but unable to prevent himself from swaying slightly.

'Whoops,' said Piers, draining his glass and putting it down on a little mahogany table. 'You shouldn't drink so much, Dad.'

'Get out,' said Rupert.

'I'm going,' said Piers. 'Sorry about that,' he addressed Lucy. 'Watch him once he gets on the whisky, he can be quite nasty.'

'Just go,' said Lucy. 'Stop provoking him.'

'Come again?' said Piers, who had picked up some very undesirable expressions, among other things, at art school.

'You heard,' said Lucy.

'Yeah,' said Piers, 'don't worry, I'm going.' He went to the door. 'Just remember this,' he said. 'You're supposed to set an example to your kids, but you don't give a flying fuck for any of them. For Mum, for me and Tom, for Chloe, for the kids. Watch him,' he said to Lucy, who was staring at him in horror. 'He's walking wounded, fucked-up. Mum was right.'

He went out of the sitting room leaving the door open, crossed the hall, opened the front door of the flat and left that open too. Lucy and Rupert could hear his heavy tread as he went down the service stairs two steps at a time in his biker boots.

'Sorry about that,' said Ru, pouring himself more whisky.

'I thought you managed him very well,' said Lucy loyally. She was more rattled by Piers than she wanted to admit.

'What a nightmare,' said Ru. 'To think I've fathered that.'

'He'll improve,' said Lucy. 'It's just late adolescent challenging behaviour.'

'Bloody late,' said Ru. 'He's twenty-one, you know. When I was his age, I had a job. What sort of work is he going to do after being at that place? All he does is make mud pies like some kid, or throw paint at things.'

'I shouldn't have asked him to come,' said Lucy, 'you were right.' She remembered Chloe's reaction to Piers all those years ago, and felt that the wheel had come full circle, although he was infinitely, infinitely worse now. And the way he had looked her, as if she had no clothes on!

After dinner, which they ate at the little table in Lucy's pretty yellow and white kitchen, Lucy poured herself another glass of wine and waited for Rupert to light a cigarette. He was always in a better mood when he was smoking.

'I have something to tell you,' she said.

'What? Got a pay rise?'

'No.'

'Well – what then?'

'I'm pregnant,' she said, holding her breath.

CHAPTER 12

As David tied his bow tie with great difficulty and some muffled swearing, he thought of Chloe and what she had said to him by the grave of the priest, Adam Williams. He must look up that quotation of hers in his Donne. The idea of every life, however ordinary, as a martyrdom was an interesting one, a profound one. For there were always things upon which one foundered, things one couldn't manage or that one was too weak to achieve because of some inherent flaw. For a brief moment he remembered Mary Chandos with regret. Unfinished business, said a voice in his mind and then went silent again. He had wondered lately where that voice came from or who it was speaking. Had God capriciously adopted a new method of addressing him, David Doughty, whispering uncomfortable phrases in his ear at inconvenient moments in car parks, or in his bedroom as he hurried his dressing?

Having finished grappling with his clothes, he looked at his watch and wondered where Frances had got to. She hadn't particularly wanted to go to this dinner at the castle as it smacked to her too much of a kind of patronage that she particularly disliked. She saw no reason why Lady Jessop should feel superior to her.

'She doesn't,' said David. 'She asked us to dinner, that's all.'

'You're her new protégé, her new lap-dog,' said Frances. 'She likes people to adore her, I hear, and you're certainly obliging in that department.'

'Do you mind my going to see her?' David asked.

'It doesn't matter if I mind or not,' said Frances typically. One of her argumentative gambits was to attack him and then pretend she hadn't. It was very feminine, David thought, and exceedingly tedious.

'But I'm asking you . . . Does my going to see her upset you?'

'Why should it?' said Frances. 'It's your life.'

'I wish you'd answer the question,' he said.

'I have.'

'Frances,' said David, putting his head round her study door, 'we're supposed to be there in twenty-five minutes.'

'Yes, yes,' she replied, without looking round. 'I'm coming.'
She was sitting at her desk typing very fast.

'What are you doing?' he asked.

'Some rough notes for my class at the college next week. We're looking at the role of women in the Reformed Church.'

'I didn't think they had one.'

'That's the whole point,' said Frances, over her shoulder. 'They didn't. Luther says, "The woman, on the other hand, is like a nail driven into the wall . . . the wife should stay at home and look after the household."'

'It would be a lot better if they did,' said David, 'instead of trying to become imitation men which is all the women's movement has succeeded in doing.' He was still smarting from her earlier jeers.

'That's not true,' said Frances. 'Luther's fear of sexuality made him Augustinian in his theology: dark and light, women and men. Surely you can see that?'

'You haven't answered my point.'

'What point?'

'About feminists being imitation men. It's not as simple as you'd like to think.'

Frances, however, did not reply to this. She stopped typing, pressed a button and the text on the screen vanished and then reappeared again. David, who wrote by hand, was always amused at these technicalities.

'If you don't hurry,' he said, 'we'll be late.'

'My word,' said Frances, surveying her husband in his dinner jacket. 'Very smart. I'm sure Lady Jessop will enjoy looking at you in that outfit.'

'Hope so,' said David cheerfully, in order to conceal his irritation.

'I'll be back in a minute,' said Frances. 'Let Mrs D. in when she comes, will you?'

In their bedroom she opened her wardrobe and ran her hand down the line of hangers as if hoping to surprise some hitherto undiscovered perfect dress for dinner at the castle. She knew she had nothing that would really do: a part of her minded and another part thought it was funny. She didn't want to go anyway. It was so *feudal* this hobnobbing. Marjorie Jessop had gone to David's head like strong drink, but at least she was old even if she was exceedingly glamorous, and it gave David an object, someone he could fantasize about, someone he could set on a pedestal and worship.

Since they had come to Fordingbridge their relationship had improved marginally, she thought. It had been good for them to get away from the city. He was less tense and she found herself intrigued by the possibilities for change in rural life. There was so much to do here. The first of her discussion groups had been well attended by quite a mixed bag of ages and occupations: there had been what she called the jam-making, flower-arranging element, a handful of young mothers from the new estate (all of whom when she asked for their opinions were greatly in favour of a female priesthood) and quite a lot of others. It was very encouraging. The town itself was also undeniably charming and was always winning a best-kept something award. A Victorian high street led up to an ancient stone bridge spanning the River Waye, and there were several really beautiful Georgian streets behind leading back to the church of St Mary's and the vicarage itself, set in an acre of garden next to the church, with hills and woods in the background and the ruins of the old castle next to the new above.

Sometimes Frances thought it was rather like one of those early Italian pictures with the castle towering over the little streets that clustered about the foot of the hill, with everyone in their place and a place for everything, even, perhaps, the serpent wound round the roots of a tree, waiting for somebody to tempt.

She selected a dark red crushed velvet skirt which she had found in a charity shop and a green cotton shirt with a drawstring neck that someone had given her in London. She added mascara, earrings and some lipstick called 'Talked About Pink' that seemed to have been in her make-up bag for ever. When she had done she thought she didn't look too bad. A bit like an old hippy, perhaps, but it was the best she could do.

'There you are,' said David, coming in. 'We should go.'

He had long ago learned not to say anything about her appearance as feminists, apparently, found it patronizing to be praised for looking nice or having made an effort.

'We're collecting Marion,' he said on the stairs. 'She rang to ask if we would.'

Frances sighed. 'Damn,' she said. 'I could have done without that.'

She went into the kitchen. Kitty was in a knitting phase and Mrs Dacre was helping her to do moss stitch.

'Where's Tanya?'

'Upstairs,' said Kitty.

'We're going,' said Frances, 'but we won't be late.'

'They always say that,' said Kitty to Mrs Dacre.

'Up at the castle?' said Mrs Dacre. 'That right?'

'That's right,' said Frances. 'No later than ten,' she said to Kitty.

'No, Mum,' said Kitty in a bored voice.

Miranda was being impossible. Every time Chloe tried to leave she would cry and bang her legs up and down under the sheets like a baby, arching her back with rage. Chloe had tried to find out what the matter was, but when Miranda said she wanted Daddy Chloe had determined not to get cross and then promptly did so.

'You can't have him,' she said. 'Now stop this nonsense at once. He's in London and we're here.'

'What's the matter with her?' James poked his face round the door. 'Just leave her, Mum. She's a pain.'

'I am not a pain!' shouted Miranda, sitting up.

'Yes, you are,' said James. 'You're a nightmare.'

'That's enough,' said Chloe. 'James, go to bed. I'll come and see you in a minute. Miranda, you can get into my bed but when I want to go down you'll have to come back at once. Do you understand?'

'You shouldn't let her have her own way,' said James as they followed Miranda down the corridor. 'It's bad for her. Why do you?'

'You piss off,' said Miranda.

'Miranda! If you say that again,' said Chloe, 'that's *it*!'

Why, oh why, did children always do this to one? When one was least able to cope the little buggers played up. There must some law for it, some female one. Bernadette's Law, perhaps.

'Sorry,' said Miranda before scuttling through the swing door at the end of the passage.

'Are you and Dad going to get divorced?' asked James when he was in bed.

'I don't know yet,' said Chloe, 'but we might.' She touched his cheek. 'I'm so sorry, darling.'

'It's OK,' said James. 'Stirling's parents are divorced. He says it's better.'

'Does he?'

'His father buys him amazing presents when he sees him at weekends. He's even got an air rifle.'

'You know what Stirling's father's doing, though, don't you?'

'Yes,' said James. 'He's trying to buy his love, but it must still be nice to have an air rifle. Perhaps it works,' he added, looking at Chloe hopefully.

She laughed. 'Buying love? It might for a bit, I suppose, but then you'd get bored with an air rifle and want something else. I don't know what, an aeroplane, perhaps, then when I couldn't buy it for you, you might not love me so much.'

'I'll always love you,' said James, 'even if you don't buy me an air rifle.'

Chloe kissed him, sniffing a bit. It was quite the nicest thing anyone had said to her in ages.

Miranda was in bed when Chloe went in, pretending to read *Phantom Horse Goes to Scotland*.

'Better?' enquired Chloe, sitting on the bed.

'Yes.' Miranda laid the book face down on her knees.

'I find it very difficult when you carry on like that,' said Chloe. 'I can't talk to you sensibly when I lose my temper, so please don't do it.'

'Sorry. Sorry, Mum.' Miranda put her smooth little arms around Chloe's neck and hugged her. 'Who's coming tonight?' she asked.

'The vicar and Mrs Vicar, Simon and Richard, Marion, me. That's it.'

'I hate it when Marion kisses me,' said Miranda. 'She stinks.'

'Oh, darling,' said Chloe, 'I'm sure I do, too. She stinks of drink, doesn't she?'

'She does, but you don't,' said Miranda.

'Are you sure?'

'Sure. You won't smoke tonight, will you, Mum?'

'I don't know,' said Chloe. 'I can't promise. I might.'

'But then you'll get cancer and die.'

'No, I won't,' said Chloe.

'The doctor said you might.'

'Shall I put my hair up?'

Chloe sat at her dressing table with its chintz flounce of overblown roses and ribbons.

'Half up, maybe.'

In the mirror Chloe watched Miranda pick up her book again and begin to read. She put on some more foundation and then with great sweeping gestures added colour to her cheekbones and generally to the rest of her face. Then she added lipstick, which she promptly removed thinking it made her look altogether too much like a death's head. When she was depressed she always felt she looked dreadful, whatever the reality was. There was a terrible hole where her heart should be, a kind of wrenched-out space into which she bled and hurt. She tried not to think of Rupert and Lucy having a cosy Saturday evening together in Luce's so-familiar flat, but the pain of everything was so great that it seemed like something outside herself that moved when she did like a shadow.

'Can I stay, Mum?' asked Miranda.

'Yes, all right,' said Chloe with resignation. Miranda was a genius at timing. 'But don't kick me in the night, OK?'

'I won't,' said Miranda, looking sleepily angelic. 'I promise.'

'Coming,' Marion banged her front door and tottered down the path in high satin heels and a black chiffon tube of a dress that inhibited her progress. From a distance she seemed elegant, but close to, David thought, it was possible to see that there was something adrift: her lipstick was clumsily applied and slightly smeared and her eye make-up was applied to one eye but not the other. Nevertheless, she was what Guy Jessop would no doubt call a fine figure of a woman. She was elegant because her clothes were good and she knew how to wear them. She had the right sort of willowy figure for a dress like that. Her well-cut hair swung and shone and she smelled of something expensively delicious and subtle. No wonder, David found himself thinking, no wonder Guy Jessop . . . and then pulled himself up short. No way for a priest to be thinking.

'So sweet of you to get me,' she said, collapsing into the back seat of David's ancient Volvo. 'I can't walk in these shoes, and I don't want to drive, a) because of the ruddy breathalyzer and b) because I can never negotiate those damn gateposts at the castle. Guy's always getting at me about it.'

'You shouldn't let him,' said Frances.

'But I adore Guy.' said Marion. 'He's sweetness itself, sweetness and light. He's been wonderful to me,' she rattled on. 'When I was having that dispute with my neighbour over the drains, Guy lent me his lawyer, James Tunnicliffe, what a dish, my dear, you've never met such a handsome man, apart from darling David, of course, taking Fordingbridge by storm. The old ladies are speculating about you *like mad*.'

'I wish you wouldn't say that,' said David mildly in order to conceal his irritation. 'It makes me think they don't listen to anything I say.'

'Oh, no,' said Marion, 'they do listen, darling, honestly. They hang on your every word. I keep expecting to see them take out their notebooks once you've begun on a Sunday.'

'"The hats" we call them,' said Frances naughtily, for she could see David was put out. 'David had loads of them in London admiring him and wanting to make him toasted teacakes.'

'Nonsense,' said David, 'absolute rubbish.'

'You should be grateful,' said Marion, 'that God saw fit to give you the means to mesmerize your congregation. I love "the hats", it's too sweet for words. If you see it in my next book, don't be cross, it's too wonderful to be lost, truly a Barbara Pymism . . . Posterity must benefit . . . Of course,' she added, changing tack, 'you've met Chloe, haven't you? Now there's a romantic figure, if you like.'

'Why romantic?' asked Frances. 'She seems very ordinary to me. Just having a spot of bad luck by the sounds of it.'

'Oh, you know,' said Marion dizzily. 'Beautiful woman abandoned by handsome husband for another already known to her.' She often advanced conversation by making experimental statements about people that she knew weren't necessarily true, but it was always interesting to see how people reacted. Mrs Vicar clearly didn't much like Chloe, which was rather intriguing although the reasons weren't hard to guess at. He was a charmer with a bit of a roving eye, Marion would guess, and she didn't like it and had taken refuge in her feminism. Marion always described herself as 'too intelligent to be a feminist,' which invariably got the butch lobby jumping up and down in protest, but too bad.

'Was she?' asked Frances. 'You're well informed, I must say.'

'It's my job, darling, to be well informed,' said Marion. 'It's how I make my living.'

'Preying off people's misfortunes, you mean?'

'No, no,' said Marion amiably. Gotcha, you silly cow, she said to herself.

'I'm exhausted already,' Frances whispered to David as they went into the hall. 'Doesn't she ever draw breath?' In spite of herself, she felt nervous coming into this grand, smooth atmosphere, full of fantastic flower arrangements and daunting arrays of ancestral strength lining the stairs. A flunkey stood by the drawing room door with glasses of champagne on a vast silver tray.

'Hello, Jim,' said David, recognizing the mechanic who serviced his car.

'Evening,' said Jim, grinning. 'Champagne, buck's fizz or just orange juice?' he said to Frances.

'Oh,' said Frances, and took a glass of champagne without meaning to.

In the drawing room Simon and Richard, elderly grand gays, were kissing Marjorie and exclaiming over the beauty of the flowers, the marvellous room, Marjorie's dress − black, belted crepe and pearls − the sweet-scented evening air wafting in, and what was it that smelled so delicious − ah yes, of course, *Azara microphylla* − and where was darling Chloe and Guy, how are you, Marion, as gorgeous as ever, ah the vicarage, so glad, how wonderful to have some decent ritual again, we might start coming back to church, Canon Jones was so drearily low . . .

Chloe came down the stairs listening to the sound of voices and paused. Almost every Saturday night of her childhood there had been a dinner and she had sat peering through the banisters at the people coming and going (as doubtless her own two would do the minute she vanished) until she had got too old and was packed off to boarding school. As a child, she had wondered what people talked about so endlessly, so incessantly, and now she was an adult she knew. They talked about nothing at all.

She took a glass, walked in and saw David Doughty looking absurdly like a sort of matinée idol in his dinner jacket. It shouldn't be allowed.

'Hello,' she said at his shoulder.

'Chloe!' He turned and smiled at her and his heart turned over like a fish flipping in the deeps, startling him. 'We were wondering,' he said, stumbling a little as he registered his reaction to her, 'where you were.'

'Putting my children to bed,' she said. 'Miranda was being tiresome. She's an absolute specialist at that at the best of times, and she's got even worse lately. I think the situation I'm in – you know about that, I know – is making things worse.' She made a face and took a sip of her drink.

'Children have an unfortunate habit of reacting to their parents like litmus paper, which makes it difficult if one wants to protect them from a situation that's difficult, or which won't resolve itself easily or quickly,' he said, and thought how pompous he sounded. This poor girl.

'I don't want them to get hurt,' she said, feeling the catch in her throat that invariably signalled she had stumbled into her own minefield.

'Of course you don't,' he said kindly, 'but you can't protect your children from everything, although you can try and shield them from the worst of it.'

'I don't feel I'm even succeeding in doing that,' she said. 'I feel all the time that I'm failing them.'

'I'm sure you aren't,' he said, looking at her gravely, 'but, as I said, we can't protect them from everything. We can't,' he added. 'I should know. We all fail our children. Sometimes, very often I think, they develop out of that failure.'

'Our failure is their opportunity,' said Chloe. 'I do so hope you're right.' She looked round for an ashtray.

'This is my wife, Frances,' said David. 'I don't think you've met.'

'I've seen you,' said Chloe, 'in the distance, in church and round and about. We were just talking – *I* was just talking,' she corrected herself, 'about failing my children.' She had got a grip of this now and it seemed a suitable topic for the vicar's beady-looking wife. Lady Bountiful enquiries were definitely out of place here – Mothers' Union, WI the annual bazaar – and anyway that was Marjorie's province rather than hers.

'We all do it,' said Frances briskly. She did not enjoy discussing her children with other women because, in her experience, it invariably led on to further discussions about schools or washing powder. 'My daughter tells me I've failed her because she hasn't got a Nintendo.'

'That's a sign of privilege,' said Chloe, 'elitism almost. Soon the most privileged children will be the ones without televisions and all that electronic rubbish.'

'I must try and explain it like that to her,' said Frances, bristling slightly at the charge of elitism, especially coming from this poor little rich girl in her ever-so excessively simple little black dress that must have cost a fortune.

'You never know,' said Chloe, 'she might believe you. Are you liking it here?' she added, seeing from Frances's expression that she had, entirely without meaning to, got off on the wrong foot.

'We love it,' said Frances, glancing up at her husband. 'There's so much opportunity for change in a community like this. It makes it very exciting.'

'What do you want to change?'

'I want to raise people's consciousness about certain issues,' said Frances.

'Such as?' Issues, thought Chloe, consciousness, community, the ideologically laden jargon of change. Words that made her go numb. That which one held dear must, on account of it, be wrenched from one. *How* could he put up with such nonsense?

'The role of women in our society, our perceptions about ourselves, how we must mobilize to achieve our potential.'

'I see,' said Chloe. 'It all sounds exhausting.' She just couldn't help it, she decided.

'Frances has a huge amount of energy,' said David. 'More than most of us. And she does a great deal.'

'You're being loyal tonight,' said Frances. 'Normally, he gets at me about not doing the ironing, or failing to produce solid, well-cooked meals three times a day.'

'Nonsense,' said David. 'Frances loves to portray herself as put-upon, but in fact we've always shared things. I cook, the girls iron.'

'You cook?' said Chloe. 'How marvellous! I hate it myself.'

'Oh, I don't hate it,' Frances said, 'I just don't see why I should always have to do it.'

'But you never do it,' said David.

'What do you do?' Frances said to Chloe, breaking her own rule. She couldn't think what had got into David. He must have had too much champagne.

'Around the house, or out in the wide world?' asked Chloe.

'As a job,' said Frances. 'I don't count housework.'

'I don't do a damn thing at the moment,' said Chloe. 'My brain's probably gone soft. I used to work at Hull and Sang and I'll probably go back there when the children are bigger.'

'Why not go now? Women should consider fulfilment while they have the chance.'

'I wanted to be around for them,' said Chloe, 'while they're little. It is possible and I believe it's better for them.'

'But what about you? Aren't you bored?'

'I am sometimes, but I've got rather a lot on my plate at the moment.'

'I see,' said Frances.

'How old are your children?' asked David, rather admiring Chloe for standing up for herself, and thinking that her eyes were lion-coloured or like marmalade, and also thinking that he should not be thinking about the colour of anyone's eyes, other than his wife's. He began to wonder if he were ill or entering that particularly unattractive phase known as the male menopause that Frances was always going on about.

'Ten and eight,' said Chloe, who was thinking what an ill-assorted pair they were. He was exceedingly warm and jolly, he made her want to confide in him, he seemed so safe and so decent, but the wife seemed to have made up her mind not to be pleased by anything. Those shibboleths that one must worship or else be cast into outer darkness: working women, knocking women who stayed home, denigrating family life. They were definitely, Chloe thought, a two-husband household. She also suffered from inverted snobbery. People who looked like that often did. It was quite all right to come and hang around in someone's beautiful rooms, sit on their Chippendale chairs, eat their food, drink their drink, but you mustn't in any way appear to be pleased or grateful.

'We have a ten-year-old,' said David. 'A girl, Kitty. Perhaps' – he glanced at Frances – 'they could get together, she and . . .?'

'James,' said Chloe, catching her mother's eye and looking away.

'That would be nice,' said Frances unenthusiastically, covering her glass with her hand as Bobby approached with Marion in tow, sent by Marjorie to break up the vicar and his wife.

'If there's anything I can do to help,' said David to Chloe quietly, 'you know where I am. And I'm often up here seeing your mother, as you know,' he added.

'The confessional, you mean?'

'If you want to call it that,' he said, remembering Frances had used the same word in the same slightly derogatory way when she had referred to the outcome of his first meeting with the Archdeacon. 'I don't myself. People want to have a bit of a jaw about things sometimes and find out what they're really thinking. "How do I know what I think until I see what I say?"'

'Mmm,' said Chloe, feeling it might be almost too much of a temptation to go and tell this sympathetic, kindly, handsome priest her troubles, and yet she trusted him. He made her feel strangely safe and comfortable, too. She thought of Fanny briefly, but decided not to mention her.

'One of my jobs,' he said, 'perhaps my main one is to lend an ear. People think they have to justify God's love, to have done something to earn it, but that's not the case at all. God loves us because he loves us, no more, no less than that.'

'Or hates us because he hates us,' said Chloe. 'I'm not feeling sure about God at the moment. I doubt His good intentions, put it like that.'

'That's quite –.'

'You two!' squawked Marion, waving her glass around. 'Don't hide in corners, Chloe, David. Come on, Richard darling, do the honours.'

CHAPTER 13

'You're what?' said Rupert, hoping he hadn't heard properly. He put out his hand for his glass, missed and knocked it over.

'Bugger!' he said, springing to his feet.

'I'll get a cloth,' said Lucy competently, determined to keep calm.

When she had finished clearing up the bits of broken glass with Ru fussing and saying, 'Careful, don't cut yourself' and getting in the way, she sat down again and looked at him.

'I'm pregnant,' she said once more.

'I thought that was what you said.' In his mind's eye he could see and hear Piers thumping down the stairs. That was one matter, one scene ringing and stinging in his ears – that eternal business of children accusing their parents and biting the hand that fed them (he chose to forget it was Marcia's hand, not his, in this case), blaming their parents for all their woes – and now, by some fantastic piece of bad luck, Lucy was presenting him with the unborn version of the same thing. He had to admit her timing was rotten. Children grew up to torment you, either by direct accusation or loss of them – the thought of James and Miranda brought tears to his eyes – and he didn't want to go through it again, he didn't think he could face it. All that love and all that disappointment. All those bills.

'I did the test this morning,' she said, biting her lip but trying to be matter of fact, 'and it was positive.'

'Jesus! I thought you were taking precautions.'

'I . . . was,' said Lucy.

'Then how has it . . . this thing happened?'

'It's not fail-safe,' said Lucy, keeping her hands under the table so Ru could not see how much they were shaking. His coldness frightened her, although she knew she should have expected it. But she wanted to say to him, 'I'm thirty-nine, I don't want to miss my chance of motherhood.' It was as if she had been asleep for years and then woken up to find her time had almost run out. But the expression on his face prevented her from saying what was in her heart. He looked so . . . what was the word? . . . so *stricken*, as if someone had told him he had terminal cancer instead of this news of joy.

'I need a whisky,' he said, getting up.

'I thought you'd be glad.' She had followed him into the sitting room.

'I don't know what on earth made you think that,' said Rupert, pouring whisky. It was one of those evenings when the more he drank the soberer he became. 'We should have discussed something so serious.'

'I told you it was a mistake.'

'They all say that,' Rupert shook his head wearily.

'What do you mean?'

'The women who get pregnant accidentally on purpose say that. Marcia said it, Chloe said it.'

'Chloe said it? What do you mean?'

'She got pregnant when I was still married to Marcia. Accidentally, of course.'

'What happened to it?'

'She had an abortion.'

'Why? You knew you were going to marry.'

'There was enough of a mess already.'

'Mess! You made her have an abortion to keep everything tidy?'

'You don't understand, Lucy. It wouldn't have done. Her parents would have blown a gasket. The timing was lousy. She knew she shouldn't have done it, but you know what Chloe's like. She's determined.' His voice had grown coldly defensive.

'But you destroyed a child, a life, both of you. How could you?'

'We're not Roman Catholics,' he said. We. 'We believe women have the right to choose.'

'Or to have chosen for them. I'm sure Chloe wouldn't willingly have agreed to such a thing.'

'You seem very sure of a number of things that you know nothing about,' said Rupert.

'The fact that Chloe never mentioned it to me means she must have known it was a morally indefensible act.'

'To you, yes. Not to Chloe. Women have the right to choose,' he repeated.

'To choose what? Life or death, to murder or not to murder? I don't think you know what you're saying. What right is this?'

'You are becoming hysterical,' said Rupert in a slow adult-to-tiresome-child voice. 'Let me get you a drink.'

'I'm not hysterical,' said Lucy, 'and I don't want a drink. Don't you remember women are supposed to go off drink when they're pregnant?'

'Not in my experience,' said Rupert, lighting a cigarette.

'Of course, you've had so much,' said Lucy. 'I forgot.'

'Look,' he said, 'I know you're upset, it's understandable in your situation, but you've dropped a bombshell on me. I'm not even divorced from Chloe yet. You and I haven't been together very long, we don't know whether things will work out or not.'

'I don't believe I'm hearing this,' said Lucy. 'You left Chloe for me. Are you telling me you're having second thoughts, backing out? What, Rupert?'

She stared at him, hoping somewhere in her being that he would get up, take her in his arms and say, 'There, there, it's all right, don't worry, I'll take care of you.'

But he was silent. Then he looked up and said, 'I do have doubts, don't you?'

'Obviously not,' said Lucy.

'I need time to think through the implications of this. It's not as if it's young love, first love or whatever.'

Whatever. A terrible word, a flabby word, an open-ended escaping word. Lucy watched as Rupert got up.

'Don't go,' she said.

He sighed.

Please don't leave me.'

'I can't stay here.' He had his back to her.

'Do you always run away from your problems?'

'No,' he said, 'but I don't see the point in staying. I must think this over alone.'

'I'm thirty-nine, Ru,' said Lucy, her voice shaking. 'I don't get another chance to have a baby. Don't you understand?' Tears flooded down her cheeks. Her love seemed like a wounded bird flinging itself against the bars of a cage.

'Oh, for Christ's sake!' said Ru savagely. 'Of course I bloody understand. I understand it all. Fucking female hormones playing tricks. Bloody walking wombs. I don't want any more children, why don't *you* understand? This was a unilateral decision on your part. I wasn't consulted, I'm just the dick who'll have to pay, isn't that right, isn't that what you thought?'

He picked up his glass and flung it into the fireplace where it smashed in a thousand tinkling slivers.

'I thought you'd be glad.'

Ru gazed at her for a moment and then went out of the room, picking up his jacket from the hall chair as he passed. She heard the door slam as if the noise came from a long way off.

'Good God, it's you,' said Andrew. 'I thought it was lovers' night. Why are you back so early?'

He had been to theatre and was cooking a late dinner for himself.

'I've had just about the most fucking awful night of my whole life,' said Rupert, searching in the larder for the whisky.

'Have you, old man? What's up?' Andrew sniffed and then sipped. Not enough wine. He sloshed in some Bulgarian red from a bottle by the cooker. He had known Ru Durrell for years and he had always been in trouble with women one way and another; there had been periods of relative calm interspersed with titanic battles and upheavals. Ru's first wife, Marcia, rather a nice woman actually, had told Andrew once in tearful confidence that Ru secretly despised women and thought of them as being simply there for his convenience.

'Piers came and was bloody rude,' said Ru, 'not only to me but to Lucy as well.'

'Ah,' said Andrew. 'Youth, I suppose. Jealous, I don't know.'

'He behaved disgustingly. Are you glad you don't have children?'

'Mostly,' said Andrew, 'although sometimes . . .'

'What?'

'Oh, nothing really. Just a sense of pointlessness.'

'Children don't give life a point,' said Ru. 'That's a myth.'

'Why do people always tell me they do then?' asked Andrew. 'Is it a conspiracy?'

'People with children have to justify their folly,' said Rupert. 'My God, when I think what I spent on that boy's education . . .'

'I shouldn't do that,' said Andrew. 'Do you want some of this?'

'No, thanks, I've eaten.'

'Suit yourself. It'll be good, though. How's Lucy?'

'OK.'

'Good.'

'She's just told me she's pregnant.'

'Bloody heck!' said Andrew. 'You don't half land yourself in it, do you? Do you *want* any more children? Can you *afford* any more children? You've been keeping English private schools afloat as it is.'

'No, I bloody don't,' said Ru. 'Of course I don't. It was her decision.'

'What're you going to do?'

'God knows,' said Ru. 'It's rather out of my hands now. She's an R C,' he added gloomily. 'That means she won't have an abortion.'

'Hmmph,' said Andrew, putting a lid on the saucepan and leaving it to simmer for a few minutes. 'You should go back to Chloe, you know.'

'I've been thinking much the same, as a matter of fact,' said Ru. 'We should have another go, we owe it to the children.'

'Would she have you?'

'What do you mean?' Ru was genuinely astonished at such a question. Of course she would. 'She's not much cop on her own,' he said. 'Hopeless with money, no good at managing her business affairs, always relies on me to do that.'

'You can't teach an old dog new tricks, but I have a feeling you can teach a woman how to look after her accounts,' said Andrew. 'Come on, old chap, you're not as indispensable as you think you are. Chloe's a lovely girl, very attractive and all that, she might have found someone else.'

'I bloody well hope she hasn't,' muttered Ru ominously.

'What will you do? Go after him with a stick?' said Andrew, much amused. 'She's your wife, not your daughter, and you did leave with her best mate, don't forget.'

Rupert didn't reply.

'Of course that would leave Lucy in rather a pickle, wouldn't it, assuming she's going to keep the baby. She might change her mind.' Andrew looked at Ru speculatively. 'Is she absolutely dead set on keeping it, do you think?'

'I told you,' said Ru. 'She's a holy Roman.'

'Have some more whisky,' said Andrew. 'Strikes me you might need it. Rather you than me, old man.'

CHAPTER 14

'I'm to take you in,' Said Simon Ferrars politely to Frances once Marjorie had given the signal.

'In?'

'To dinner,' he said, proffering his arm. 'They always do it here. I think it's a charming custom because it breaks the ice.'

'I thought we were already supposed to have done that,' said Frances, looking round for somewhere to put her glass. She was feeling decidedly ill-at-ease, in spite of the champagne.

'Between dining partners,' he said, smiling. 'Or at least that's the idea.'

'It's like something out of Thackeray,' said Frances. 'I thought this sort of thing went out with the ark.'

'No, no, not at all,' said Simon patiently. 'Would you like it to have done?'

'It just seems archaic, that's all.'

'Do you mind things being archaic? I rather like it myself,' said Simon, standing back to allow Frances to pass in front of him through the doorway. She suffered like so many modern people from a distaste for anything old, anything tried and true. He sometimes wondered where this distaste had come from and whether it might originally have begun as idealism after the war when everything was to be made new and fresh by socialism.

'Feminists,' he said, 'and I know you are one from the way in which you're taking Fordingbridge by storm, seem to me to want to throw out the baby with the bathwater. Good manners, the whole lot.'

'I don't want to,' said Frances, allowing him to pull out her chair for her, 'but there are some things that do need to change. Take women priests, for instance. Everyone agrees the calibre of male priest has fallen tremendously since the war. The women who want to be ordained are usually highly motivated and ambitious, better than their average male counterpart.'

'I'm sure you're right about that,' said Simon, 'but I'm dead set against women priests, I'm afraid.'

'Why?' Frances was puzzled by Simon. Normally, she had no trouble relating to gay men, but Simon baffled her because his opinions seemed so orthodox. She could not understand a gay man who did not define himself as part of a tortured minority group.

'Because we've never had them. I believe in a male priesthood, not a female one.'

Ah, thought Frances. 'But can't things change?'

'Yes, of course they can, but I think change is a slow thing in truth. Two hundred years should be a measure of change, not twenty, or however long it is you've been trying to get the General Synod to rewrite the rules. However,' he added, 'let us not quarrel so early on. Tell me how you're enjoying Fordingbridge.'

'Oh, we like it very much.'

'You're certainly making them sit up,' said Simon. 'Nothing ever happens here – which is one of the reasons we love it, of course.'

'I never believe that,' said Frances. 'It's there, just under the surface.'

'Miss Marple certainly thought so,' said Simon. 'Take any of the people sitting round this table, Guy, for instance, or Marjorie. They've had interesting lives, more than most, but we only see a fraction of it. Guy was a prisoner of the Japs for years, but he never talks about it. Marjorie ran this place single-handed during the war. She didn't know whether he would come back or not. She went months without news of him, not knowing if he was alive or dead. That would mark a person, don't you think? And yet, looking at her, you'd never guess, would you?'

'Oh, I'm not so sure about that,' said Frances. 'I would say hers was a face marked by life, by suffering. I mean nothing is ever perfect or quite what it seems is it? I hear that she's had quite an exciting life one way and another.' *Boyfriends*, old Mrs Madden, had said. *Admirers a-plenty, that one. It wasn't always just the garden, you know. And of course he came back from the war all messed up, unable to . . . you know . . .*

116

'What about Chloe?' said Simon, changing the subject. 'Or your husband? What about them?'

'I can see you're a writer.'

'I'm nosy,' said Simon, 'rivetted by people's lives. Take yourself: you must have had an interesting time being married to the cloth.'

'I have,' said Frances, 'but I've had an interesting time on my own account too. I don't consider myself a traditional clergy wife.'

'Do you ever long to escape?'

'Yes,' said Frances. And smiled.

'What to? You look as if you have a secret, Mrs Doughty.'

'Frances. Don't call me Mrs Doughty.'

'Frances, then.'

'I wouldn't tell you,' she said. 'You might put it in a book like Marion.'

'I would, I'm afraid, but very chopped and blended. You wouldn't recognize it.'

'Is that how writers work?'

'That's how I work, I don't know about anyone else. Now tell me about your husband. Is he happy here? He's popular, you know. He has a broad appeal to different ages and classes. He's far too handsome for a priest, of course.'

'Why shouldn't priests be handsome?'

'It's distracting,' said Simon. 'Priests shouldn't be distracting, or distracted for that matter, but frequently are. His temptations must be greater than the average, I should have thought.'

'Would you now!' said Frances. 'Most priests are too busy to be tempted.'

'Why did you leave London when it was such a success there?'

'How did you know it was a success?'

'My dear Frances, we aren't a million miles from London, even if you do think you're in the sticks. As a matter of fact, Bobbie Chandos was a great friend of mine.'

'I see.'

'He said your husband was very good to him. I used to go and see him a lot at the end. He was very good to Mary, too, I believe, poor girl.'

'Yes,' said Frances. 'How is . . . Mary these days?'

'Not too well. Of course you knew she had a slight problem with illegal substances?'

'I didn't know that. I don't think David did either.' Frances was shocked in spite of herself. 'What substances?'

'Heroin, amongst other things. Very unfortunate.'

'Where is she now?'

'Rehab, or whatever they call it, I believe.'

'Your ministry must be very different here,' said Chloe to David across the other side of the table.

'Totally in some ways, not much in others. Fewer drugs, more people who speak English as a first language.' He ate a slice of whatever delicious something it was on his plate without really noticing. The attention of his senses was fixed elsewhere. She was wearing a black dress with loose chiffon sleeves caught at the wrists, within which her skin glimmered if that was the right word. At Lent in his old church they had wrapped the crucifix in gauze and he was reminded of this now, before he thrust the thought away. He took a sip of wine and recognized that he was drinking something exceptional.

'I had a friend,' said Chloe, 'who used to say there were three sets of problems in life − this was when we were in our twenties − and they were: job, flat, man. If two out of three were all right then you were doing well. Things don't really change too much from that, do they? Although, I have to say . . .' She paused.

'What?'

'My tongue is running away with me,' said Chloe. 'It does when I've had too much to drink.'

'Have you?' He picked up his glass and then put it down again. She was right, he thought, one really ought to try and keep a clear head.

'Go on,' he said.

'I was going to say that I have this thing about burdening people with my troubles. I'm so buttoned up I can't talk most of the time, unless I've had something to drink. I always think people will be bored by my problems. One is brought up now to burden other people.'

'My job is to be burdened,' he said as lightly as he could.

'I've never had any luck with laying my burdens on Jesus or whatever it is one is supposed to do. "Come unto me —" and all that stuff. How *do* you do it?'

'Sometimes I can't either.'

'Can't you? That's honest.'

'A lot of priests have trouble praying. It's one of the best-kept secrets of the Church.'

'Why can't you?' she asked, then added, 'Sorry, it's none of my business.' She rushed on, 'I'm seeing a therapist at the moment and I can't manage. I suffer from what Freud called a resistance to the transference. I tell her some things but not others, I can't be completely honest with her. Not like I am with you.'

'Is it helping?' he asked hastily. 'I mean if you feel like that, why bother with it?'

'If it hurts it must be good for you,' said Chloe. 'It's that kind of thing. I find it terribly painful – I mean I terribly *want* to cooperate, but I can't quite . . . It's like having a knife twisted in your guts.'

'Suffering,' he said.

'Is that what it is?' said Chloe. 'I had wondered. I mean I wasn't sure I could dignify it with the name of suffering. That always seemed to be for saints, or only saints can dignify their pain enough to call it that.'

'Saints weren't . . . aren't . . . necessarily saintly in the way I think you mean,' he said. 'You seem to be saying that if you're perfect, pure and unsullied, only then can you be allowed your pain, only then can you say "this is suffering". We're all martyrs in our own way, as you said yourself this morning. In early Christianity everyone was a saint, all believers, not only the goody-goodies; later on it came to mean what we think of nowadays: people close to God because of their holiness and yet accessible to men whose nature they share.'

'I see Chloe is having her usual effect on the new priest,' said Marion to Richard.

'What effect is that, darling?'

'Bewitchment,' said Marion. 'It's new word, I've just invented it.'

'I should be more careful what you say, darling,' said Richard in his slow American drawl. 'It might not go down too well with the hatchet lady sitting next to Simon.'

'Frances, you mean,' said Marion in her loud voice. 'Oh yes, she's hilarious. Absolutely without humour. You must go to these discussion groups, they're a guinea a minute. I adored "The Bloodied Sheet".'

'The what?'

'It's about menstruation, darling. What us girls call the curse. And the stigma of it.'

'I wouldn't know about that,' said Richard, putting the rest of his venison to one side.

'She's having one on AIDS, too.'

'Thank you, Marion.'

'Oh, don't be like that,' said Marion, draining her glass. 'I only meant to infer that there's something for everyone. Are you going to Frances's discussion group, darling?' she asked Guy.

'I haven't been so far,' said Guy. 'Not my scene. I can't bear the idea of women priests and her other subject matter is of very little interest to me, I'm afraid.'

'But there's no reason why women shouldn't be priests, darling. They played a very important part in the early Church.'

'I think women priests should be rounded up and shot,' said Guy, 'quite apart from the fact that I simply cannot see how a handful of middle-class people in a committee can change the rules of the Universal Church to which I thought I belonged. It won't wash, my dear.'

'But why should it make any difference if you have testicles or not when you celebrate communion? That's what I don't understand.'

'Are you saying you believe that men and women are exactly the same?' enquired Richard, who found Marion both a bore and a lush.

'Of course not, darling. But they won't be able to keep women out, will they, Frances?'

'Will they what?' Frances had to lean sideways to see Marion.

'Out of the Church, darling. Tell us why women should be priests.'

'Not now,' said Frances. 'Come to my discussion group and we'll talk about it afterwards.'

'Spoilsport,' said Marion, pouring herself some more wine. 'Come on, David, defend yourself.'

'From what?'

'From your wife, of course,' said Marion, who clearly thought she was being funny.

'Marion,' said Marjorie from the end of the table, 'I will not have my dinner party turned into an arena for a prize fight.'

'Whatever you say, darling,' said Marion. 'I was only trying to jolly everything up a bit.'

'Marion's plastered,' whispered Chloe. 'She does this every time. I wish Mamma wouldn't keep on asking her. I've told her.'

'Your mother has a rare patience,' said David. 'It's not her most obvious quality but it's certainly there.'

'She needs it in this case,' said Chloe. 'I'm sure you know what I'm talking about.'

'I'd heard rumours,' said David cautiously.

'I can't understand why he's so keen on her.' She put her hand over her mouth. 'God,' she said, 'I must be drunk. I've never discussed this with anyone.'

'You know, then?'

'Of course I bloody do,' she said. 'It's just that it's never, ever mentioned. And I don't want to talk about it now. I don't know why I brought it up.' The pattern round the edge of the plate, an old Spode one given to her great-grandmother as a wedding present, flowered suddenly like one of those Japanese paper trees that unfold under water.

'I'm sorry,' he said. 'I didn't mean to –'

'It's all right,' said Chloe fiercely.

'Listen,' he went on, 'I have a three-day conference in London next week. Perhaps we could have lunch or something, if you wanted to talk.'

Chloe looked at him. She did not feel fully in control of herself. In fact she felt slightly sick, but at the same time she felt a desperate desire to talk, talk, talk to him, tell him everything, cleanse herself of the things that choked her, that prevented her from being honest.

'Yes.' She nodded. 'OK, ring me. I'm in the book. Durrell, R.J. Where do you stay?'

'With my sister, Tessa, in Notting Hill. She's married to a composer.'

Marjorie led the women out of the dining room after the pudding. She was a great believer in the necessity of allowing men to bore one another.

'If you want to powder your nose,' she said to Frances at the bottom of the stairs, 'Marion will show you where to go, won't you, Marion?'

'This way,' said Marion gaily. 'Follow me, darling.'

'I'm fine, thanks,' said Frances, anxious not to be closeted with Marion.

Marion went up the broad stairs holding on tight to the banister. At the top she turned left and went into Marjorie's bedroom where the coats were. Such a lovely, lovely room this: a four-poster bed with a chaise-longue at its foot, madly old-fashioned but so charming; dressing table, photographs, delicious smells lingering faintly in the air, a bathroom beyond where the bath, as Marion knew, was in the middle of the room. She hesitated for a second and then crossed the large room and sat down at the ravishing dressing table which had some silver hairbrushes on it and a silver hand mirror embossed with cherubs. There were one or two pots of very expensive face cream and a book of poetry. Marion picked it up. It was Yeats. Nothing but the best for Marjorie, of course. She read a couple of lines and then put it down carefully. Books were objects of veneration. She examined her reflection, leaning nearer, but could make out nothing new. One looked and looked at one's face through life and yet it remained inscrutable when what one wanted to know was how did other people see one?

'Marion?'

Chloe came into the mirror, framed by the door, and stood watching.

'What is it, darling?'

When Chloe did not reply she said lightly, 'Just doing my face.'

'I wish . . .'

'What, darling? What do you wish?'

'There's powder in the bathroom,' Chloe said.

'Yes, yes, darling. Thanks awfully.'

Marion rose and walked away out of Chloe's gaze, closing the door softly behind her.

'May I come in?' Chloe put her head round her mother's door to see if she was still awake. Seeing her mother sitting cosily in bed wrapped in an enormous fringed silk shawl made her think of that other, alien, polluting presence who had been in this room earlier, sitting at her mother's dressing table as if she owned it.

'Yes, do,' said Marjorie, who had been reading. She put her book down. Her hair was still pinned up, but her face was bare of make-up. She looked incongruously young and vulnerable, Chloe thought, worryingly naive, as if she had shed her image as matriarch with her daytime mask. She was not sure she liked this image of her mother, this vulnerable girl-like creature. She expected her mother to be strong and organizing, an almost elemental force.

'Did you enjoy the dinner?' asked Marjorie, putting her hand, also bare of rings, on top of her daughter's.

'Not much.'

'But you had a good chat to David?'

'Yes. He's very nice. Very sympathetic.'

'Well, darling,' said Marjorie, 'is there something you especially want to say? It's quite late.'

'I want to talk about Marion,' said Chloe.

'What on earth do you want to talk about Marion for?'

'Why do you have her?'

'Darling, we've been through this. We have her because she's a neighbour and we like her: and because we're prepared to overlook a certain amount on account of the fact that she is amusing.'

'We,' said Chloe. 'Why *we*? I'm not entirely stupid. I'm not a child. I know she's his mistress.'

'And?' said Marjorie, betraying her nervousness by touching her cheek quickly with her hand.

'Why do you put up with it?'

'Why do you think?'

'I'm asking you.'

'Because it's part of our status quo. Between Daddy and me,' she said, when Chloe looked stupidly blank. 'I'm prepared to put up with it. I don't want to sleep with him.'

'Why not?' Chloe was astounded that she could even mention such a thing.

'Because that part of our life ended years ago, after you were born, if you must know, and men must sleep with someone.'

'Oh, shit!' said Chloe, getting up.

'I can't understand why you're so upset. It's best like this.'

'Why are you encouraging me to divorce Rupert when you yourself have been living a lie?'

'I hadn't thought of it like that. I'm fond of your father and I'm prepared to accommodate him,' said Marjorie. She did not want to remember the time when she too had been torn asunder, when she could hardly bear to be touched by Guy. To see the flesh of her flesh in agony made that part of her stir again and ache. Chloe could get free, Chloe could go, for there was every chance she would find someone else to love; whilst for Marjorie that chance had gone with Hubert and she had known it.

'I tell you to do that because you're young, you're still lovely, because everyone gets a divorce these days when they don't like the colour of their husband's tie.'

'That's not entirely fair,' said Chloe, sitting down again.

'I know it's not, but hell's bells, darling, you came in here, late, and prodded me with a stick as if I were some sleeping crocodile you could tickle for an effect.'

'I didn't!'

'Actually, you did. And I don't like it.'

'I'm sorry,' said Chloe angrily. 'I wouldn't want to upset your beauty sleep.'

'Chloe,' said Marjorie, 'I am an old woman. I cannot fight you at this time of night. Why don't you go to bed and we'll talk about it in the morning? I think you're overwrought with this Rupert business. Poor darling,' she said, taking Chloe's hand.

'Yes, all right,' said Chloe, snatching her hand away.

'I am not rejecting you,' – said Marjorie. 'I don't want you to go to that therapist of yours and say "Mamma doesn't love me," because I do.'

'I know you do,' said Chloe biting her lip. She couldn't bring herself to say, Stop being so bloody wonderful all the time, stop rationalizing everything. Sometimes everything stinks and all one can do is admit it.

'I wish,' said Marjorie, 'I just wish I'd had the courage to grasp my freedom. I envy you in a way.'

'Why? ... Was there someone you would have wanted to leave for?'

'Absolutely not.'

'Then why did you say that?'

'I don't know.' Marjorie shrugged. 'It doesn't matter,' she said. 'Go to bed, please. Off you go.' She put her hand on the light switch, controlling to the last.

Chloe went to church in the morning, without the children, and sat in a trance throughout. Her mother had stayed in bed and her father had been to the eight o'clock in order to avoid the hoi polloi and noise of the ten-thirty. She had no idea what the sermon had been about or even what hymns they had sung.

'Hello,' said David at the door, shaking her hand. 'Nice to see you. Thanks for dinner.' It was as if he hardly knew her.

After lunch, as soon as she decently could, Chloe packed the car with children and luggage and left. She felt unbelievably rattled by what her mother had said. Of course they hadn't talked, as she had known they wouldn't, and anyway what more was there to say? Her parents' marriage was a sham, declared as such, and connived at by both of them. Not so bloody, bloody wonderful after all. She felt furiously sad and terribly hurt.

Rupert came to see the children in the evening. Chloe looked out of her bedroom window as the car drew up. Ru got out dressed in cords and a tweed jacket she hadn't seen before (presumably chosen by bloody Lucy) and crossed the road. She wanted to hate him and did, but at the same time she thought he seemed tired and old and anxious.

'Hello,' she said, coming downstairs as he let himself in.

'Hi. Are the children around?'

'In the playroom,' said Chloe. 'Go and find them if you like. I'm going out for a bit.'

'I'd like to have a chat to you after I've seen them, if that's all right.'

'What about?'

'Oh, well.' He was crestfallen. 'Just to see how you are.'

'I'm fine.'

'OK. Well. Good.'

But he looked so defeated that she felt, despite everything, terribly sorry for him.

'We can have a drink together when I come back if you like,' she said, 'and then you can say whatever it is you want to say.'

When she came in after her walk, Ru was already in situ in the drawing room with a whisky and the *Sunday Telegraph*. It was as if he had never been away.

'What would you like?' he asked, jumping to his feet.

'A glass of wine,' said Chloe. 'I'll get it, it's in the fridge.'

When she came back, he said heartily, 'How're your parents?'

'OK, thanks.'

'Good weekend?'

'Yes, thanks.'

'The kids seem fine.'

'They are. Fine, I mean.'

Chloe stared into her glass. 'How are things your end?' she asked.

'Oh, OK, thanks.'

'Work?'

'Work's fine.'

'How's Lucy?'

'She's fine,' he said, avoiding her eyes.

'So she bloody well should be,' said Chloe, giving way to temptation. Once she strayed off the narrow path of platitude, she was immediately submerged beneath a boiling wave of rage and jealousy.

'There's no need to be rude,' said Rupert coldly.

It was as if they were dancing partners who only knew two sets of steps.

'I'm not being rude,' said Chloe, 'I'm being honest.' She drank the rest of her glass of wine in one swallow.

'I thought we could have a friendly drink and a chat,' said Rupert.

Chloe sighed. 'There was something you wanted to say, wasn't there?'

'Yes.' Rupert paused, torn between irritation and desperation.

'Well?'

'I don't think it's quite the moment.'

'I see. OK, then.'

'I'll come in the week.'

'Suit yourself.'

CHAPTER 15

The letter from Germany arrived in Fordingbridge on Monday morning and was delivered to the castle by Morton, the postman, together with an electricity bill, two invitations to book launches addressed to Marjorie and a letter from her American publisher in New York. Guy looked at the letter from Germany without curiosity – Marjorie had an endless postbag from all over the world – and put it with the other things on her breakfast tray. He had been bringing Marjorie breakfast in bed ever since he came back from the war.

He remembered that day as if it were yesterday, returning to the place he had sometimes thought he would never see again. The house had been empty of soldiers by then, but it was terribly tatty and unloved. The garden, however, had surprised him by appearing positively kempt. He had imagined gloomily that the parterre would have been ripped up for the war effort so they could grow swedes or potatoes or some other depressing root vegetable, but no. Marjorie had been so damn clever about that: growing veg in the flowerbeds, so the hedges of box (which were very old) could be preserved. Getting those injured chaps to help out had been a master-stroke because it meant they took an interest. Discovering that the garden had been loved and cared for and finding that his wife had become obsessed with it in his absence was an enormous boost, because it was something of hers that he could join her in. Gardening had undoubtedly saved their marriage. When Guy came back he had been married to Marjorie for ten years and away for four of them. She was more strange to him even than his desecrated house; there was nothing of Penelope about her when they were alone together, that was an image for public consumption. He had been a stranger returning to a stranger, and there had been many times in those early years when he thought their marriage might founder or go under; that was where the garden helped. Marjorie's passion for it kindled his own enthusiasm, although he had wondered on occasion whether her passion was not a substitute for something else, something or someone else. Not that she ever said anything, of course – they were very much the kind of people who believed in sticking things out, however ghastly – but the very young headstrong girl he remembered had vanished for ever under the weight of cares those years had brought, to be replaced by a thin, chain-smoking, brittle creature who looked like the Marjorie he knew, but who seemed in need of soothing like a racehorse that had seen something frightening out of the corner of its eye.

They had not shared a room as they had done before he left. He could tell she hadn't wanted it (the way she recoiled from his touch; you couldn't disguise that): also, he suffered from nightmares and preferred to be on his own in the terrible dead hours between one and four in the morning when his memories came crushing back in on him. It was why Chloe had taken so long to get (Oh, the disappointment of not having a son!) and so on and so forth. Marjorie had not been up to much in that department, in spite of the looks, so like any normal gent he had to get his oats elsewhere. But Marjorie had understood that and she didn't blame him, never mentioned it, in fact. If only modern marriages could be as discreet and tolerant as theirs had been. Chloe and that wretched Rupert seemed set fair for an expensive slugging match in the courts, and to what end? It would be far better, in his view, if Chloe just got on with her life and let Rupert have his peccadillos. He'd always come back to her in the end. Perhaps, he thought, as he climbed the back stairs with Marjorie's tray, he should say something the next time she was down. But it was difficult. They weren't close; he had always left the intimacy business to Marjorie where Chloe was concerned. Girls were better with girls, that was his view, but Chloe had been clever enough to have James and James was his heir, his adored and precious grandson, so he must be careful with her. She was a thoroughbred, his daughter, not fully broken either, given to flightiness and fits of temper as a child. The kind of girl who would be a handful for any chap.

'Here, we are' he said, settling the bed tray over Marjorie's lap. 'Postie's been. How are you this morning?'

'Very well,' said Marjorie, who always said the same thing to this enquiry. 'Thank you, darling.'

'Nothing very exciting-looking,' he said, handing her the letters.

129

'I wonder what this is,' said Marjorie, slicing open the one from Germany which had a typewritten address. She read it in silence, half conscious of Guy pouring coffee and going to sit in the armchair under the window with the newspaper. He always did this. It was a part of their morning routine together.

The letter said: '. . . I am aware this will be a shock for you, and you might well doubt the propriety of such an action, but I felt that I must contact you before it is too late and we are both dead. I hope you will forgive me for this and for the long silence that has prevailed between us . . .'

He told her what had happened to him after he returned to France that winter; of how he had been captured by the Germans and sent to the camp and the rest of the sad and terrible story.

Shock . . . doubt . . . forgive. She couldn't really take it in. It was too enormous, too great a piece of cruelty for her to be able to digest.

How could he have not let her know that he had been alive all this time? All these years she had believed in his integrity, believed in his death, believed in her memories. The letter was like the wind that sweeps into the sealed tomb and turns everything to dust; everything cherished, everything beautiful . . . dust . . . ashes and dust. If the past is not what we think it is, she said to herself, then what is it? All one's life based on a lie . . . no . . . this could not be so . . . She might have left her husband for this man, ruined her marriage . . . and in a sense she had done just that. In her mind, she had always compared Guy with Hubert, had always thought that if only she had married Hubert . . . everything was tinged with the conditional, the other, the how-it-might-have-been. She breathed in and out deeply, tried to steady herself.

She looked up from the letter and saw that Guy had noticed nothing. He was reading the obituaries in the *Telegraph*. It was the first page he turned to each morning, and he read it with a kind of triumphant dismay now that his old friends were dying off and he was still here.

'Anyone interesting this morning?' she asked, thinking how extraordinary it was that she could sound so normal. The letter from Hubert had burst over her breakfast tray like a shell and yet, as in a dream, everything remained, outwardly at any rate, mysteriously whole. She now knew that one could be shattered into a thousand fragments inside and no one would know, not even your nearest and dearest.

'Not really,' said Guy. 'Only a chap called Dickie Waysgarth who sounds vaguely familiar. Who was your letter from?'

'Oh, just an old friend whom I haven't seen for a long time,' said Marjorie. 'A Dutchman who convalesced here when you were away. I haven't heard from him in years. He saw me on television and so he wrote. You know how people are.'

There. It was done, it was out. Another small event catalogued, fitted into the day, the week, the year.

'Mmm,' said Guy, who had abandoned Dickie Waysgarth by this time and turned to the murders page. After a few more minutes, he said, 'I must be getting on. Some new bits and bobs are arriving from Flanigan's. I'd better be ready for them. What are your plans, darling?'

'I've got to check the proofs of an article about Hidcote for *Country Life*, then I want to have a think about the autumn borders in the palette garden. Ring the changes slightly. Will you meet me there?'

'All right,' said Guy, dropping a kiss on her forehead. 'See you later, my angel.'

Marjorie lay back on her pillows and closed her eyes. The shock of appearing to be normal had brought on one of those funny faint attacks. Lucky she was in bed. It would pass in a moment.

The young Dutch officer had been sent to Fordingbridge Castle to convalesce. Marjorie remembered it as if it were yesterday. She had been up to London to see the accountant and the late train she had taken back had been crammed to the gunnels with soldiers. There had been no seats until some town after Reading where there was an army camp and a lot of them had got off there. She gave the Waller twins, the doctor's sons, a lift from Wayemouth into Fordingbridge, plus Joe Stokes, the greengrocer's son, also going home on leave, and Simon Ferrars. She had forgotten until now that Simon had been there, but of course he had been. She dropped the Waller twins at their gate; the doctor lived in one of the big, cream stucco Georgian houses running right down to the river on the other side. Tennis at the Wallers still meant balls flying into the river. Some things never changed.

Simon had come in for a drink. His mother, old Mrs Ferrars, wasn't expecting him until the next day, and Marjorie wanted to talk. She had been surrounded by people since Guy had gone, but they were not necessarily people she could talk to since the castle had been taken over as a nursing home for officers. She missed Guy's companionship more than she had thought she would, and she was anxious because she hadn't heard from him for fractionally too long. She felt something was wrong, but then everybody felt like that most of the time. Life had to go on. But it made her wonder how her own mother, now dead, had coped when she received news of her husband's death. Marjorie was too young to remember this. Her father had been killed in action the day after the Great War was officially over. He had rather foolishly walked in full view down a section of road notorious for snipers and had been potted. Nothing to be done about it. The news had spread patchily, and, as his colonel had said in his letter of condolence, there were some on both sides who thought the war should not have ended when it did.

Marjorie had become engaged to Guy during the third ball of her season and they were married in 1936 when Marjorie was eighteen. Their wedding had been completely overshadowed by the Abdication Crisis and Marjorie had never quite forgiven Mrs Simpson for stealing her thunder. The great sadness of their marriage, of course, was no children. Marjorie knew this made Guy unhappy – he so very much wanted an heir, but what was she to do? Dr Waller's opinion that her fallopian tubes were blocked was confirmed by a Harley Street specialist.

'Sometimes they unblock naturally,' he had said, 'otherwise we'll just have to pray for a miracle, my dear. They do happen, you know.'

Miracles, thought Marjorie, some hope. In a way, a terrible sort of way, the war had solved that problem for her by removing Guy. She couldn't be blamed for not conceiving if he wasn't there. And although he had tried his best not to, she could see that he did, to a certain extent, blame her for her barrenness.

With these things revolving in her mind, having Simon to herself for an evening was an unexpected bonus. He was doing something hush-hush in London, but like the good son he was he returned at frequent intervals to visit his ageing parent at Fordingbridge Manor.

'Well done for getting the officers,' he said as they drove up the hill towards the castle. 'At least it means your premises may survive the war.'

'It was Guy,' she said, negotiating the gateposts. 'His last act. Tipped the wink in the right place. At least they don't spit and light their matches on the walls. That's what happened to the Hanburys at Brightwell. There were so many of them in the dining room that the tapestries started to go mouldy.'

'I always did think those tapestries were second-rate,' said Simon. 'Real ones withstand any amount of sweating and spitting and dogs peeing on them. Any news of Guy?'

'No.'

'How long?'

'Two months.' Marjorie stopped the car, and for a very brief moment put her head on Simon's shoulder.

'He was always a hopeless communicator,' he said, squeezing her arm. 'It'll be all right.'

'Got a ciggy?'

'Here.' He fished in his back pocket for his cigarette case as she drove on, got two out, lit them and handed one to her.

'It's pretty awful where Guy is, isn't it?' she said.

'Yes.' Simon puffed on his fag. No good beating about the bloody bush.

'Drink?' said Marjorie, opening her door.

Matron waylaid them in the hall.

'We've had more admissions, my lady,' she said. 'More than we could cope with, I'm afraid. I've had to put one officer in the library.'

'Then you'll have to take him out,' said Marjorie. 'That's my sanctuary, I can't give it up. Can't he go in the red room? I'm sure we could get another bed in there.'

'That's full too,' said Matron, consulting her notebook.

'Look,' said Marjorie to Simon, 'go and get a drink – you know where everything is – and I'll be back in a tick. I must sort things out with Matron . . . What's this chap's name?' she asked halfway up the stairs, stopping under a portrait of Guy's father,

Judge Jessop. Black Judge Jessop as he had been known on account of his propensity for hanging the working classes at any given opportunity.

'Let me see,' said Matron, fumbling for her glasses. She was exhausted. 'Here we are. Captain van der Meulen, Captain Hubert van der Meulen. Dutch,' she added, 'aged twenty-seven. Dutch Army of Exile, fighting with our boys.'

'What's wrong with him?'

'Fractured skull, broken leg, broken arm, punctured lung, you name it.'

'He ought to be in a proper hospital by the sound of it.'

'The lung's better, in fact, and the rest are bones that will mend with time. Dr Waller will do him just as well, and they need the beds in London so badly.'

'I know,' said Marjorie, as they parted at the top of the stairs, 'don't worry. I'm not going to make your life any more difficult than it already is.'

Captain van der Meulen lay on a folding bed beside one of the bookcases. He was reading a book and smoking a cigarette. There was a bandage round his head and his leg and arm were in plaster. He looked, Marjorie thought, like a caricature of a soldier; there should be a caption over his head: 'Our Cheerful Boys Win Through'.

'Hello,' she said, putting her attaché case down on the desk that had once belonged to the Judge. 'I hope you're comfortable?' It was a silly question, she knew, but the sight of him so injured and yet so much at ease had rather disconcerted her.

'Oh, tremendously, thank you.' The Captain threw his cigarette into the fire rather deftly and smiled. 'It's like heaven,' he said. 'I couldn't believe my luck when that old battleaxe said I could be put in here. It reminds me of home.'

'Where's that?' asked Marjorie, slightly irritated by his self-possession and the way he seemed to have taken over her sanctuary.

'In Germany,' he said. 'It belonged to my mother. She was an only child, an heiress, my father was Dutch. Now it's mine,' he said, 'only God knows what is happening there now, God only knows. It's been requisitioned for use by the military, my father said, so it will probably have been devastated. You know what they're like.' He smiled again. His English was perfect, hardly accented.

'Where is your father?'

'In Ireland.'

'And your mother?'

'My mother is dead.'

'I'm sorry.'

'She died five years ago. I'm glad, really. I wouldn't have wanted her to live through this. She would have died of shame; as it was, she was appalled at what the Germans had become. She used to say their collective psyche as a nation was damaged beyond repair. She was a disciple of Carl Jung's and she was very influenced by his view of the Germans.'

'I see,' said Marjorie, not knowing quite how to react to this. Captain van der Meulen was obviously rather keen on himself but he was also, without exception, quite the most divinely attractive man she had ever seen. Her stupid heart was in a kind of flutter. It was rather like one of those myths where the god has assumed human guise, expecting to be taken at face value, not realizing that he has a radiance about him that gives it all away.

'Would you like a drink?' she asked.

'I'd give my eye teeth for one,' he said.

'Are you well enough, or will Matron kill me?'

'I'm always well enough for a whisky and soda. Besides, don't you English need an excuse for your pleasure and like to think of drink as medicinal?'

'Not all of us,' said Marjorie, going to the door. 'I have a friend downstairs who's come from London. Do you mind if he joins us?'

'Of course not.' But he looked just faintly, flatteringly, disappointed.

'What are you reading?' asked Marjorie.

'Creasy.'

'Guy is fond of Creasy.'

'Guy?'

'My husband.'

Captain van der Meulen nodded. 'Is he here?'

'No. He's away.'

'Away,' he repeated. 'Fighting?'

'Of course.'

'Where?'

'Far East.'

'Ah.' Again he nodded.

She had fallen in love so violently it had seemed like an affliction, a disease. Love hurt. She had not known that before. From the very beginning she was terrified of the time when he would get better and go back. Everything between them was measured by this fear of loss. During this time the news that Guy had been taken prisoner arrived, and that made everything a hundred times worse. Sometimes she would think of Guy when Hubert was making love to her so that guilt and ecstasy (she had not known that love-making could be like that) would become mingled: she would wake in the night from dreams she could not remember in detail, aware only of terrible danger, as if her whole life might at any second go up in her face like a land mine. Guy was a prisoner, kept like an animal, tortured, starved, broken, humiliated, and she was betraying him night after night, and she would go on doing so. She didn't think much of herself but she couldn't stop.

When she began to put on weight, she put it down to happiness. Her bosom grew larger, which was a bore as it meant spending valuable clothing coupons on underwear, her skin glowed. She felt wonderful, until she started to be sick. The awareness that she was pregnant came suddenly.

'Darling,' said Hubert, who was waiting outside the thunder-box on the landing by her bedroom. 'Darling.'

He took her gently by the arm and led her into her bedroom where he placed her on the bed and removed her shoes tenderly, like a lackey. He then sat down by her on a chair and took her hand in his, alternately stroking it and placing his own hand over her large rings, so that she could feel the heat in the palm which she found absurdly comforting.

'So,' he said, 'we are going to have a baby. When will that be, do you think?'

'I suppose we are.' She laughed, more out of shock than amusement. 'I was beginning to wonder what was the matter.'

'You didn't know?' Hubert looked affectionately perplexed. Women were endlessly enigmatic.

'No. Did you?'

'My mother always said she knew at once when she was with child, but then she had plenty of practice. She had eight.'

'Eight goes at this. My God!'

'I'm sorry you feel so awful.'

'What are we going to do?' she clutched at his hand in sudden panic. 'How can I have your child here of all places?'

'We'll find a way,' he said calmly.

'But you might go,' she said tearfully, which was not like her, only nothing she did seemed like her any more.

'There is that,' he said. 'I know.'

'Then what shall I do?'

'I don't know.' He took off his shoes and lay down beside her on the bed, still holding her hand, 'but we'll think of something.'

'February,' said the Harley Street specialist three weeks later, going to the basin in the corner, 'or thereabouts. You may get up now, Lady Jessop, if you wish. I'll fetch your husband in so we can have a chat.'

'Congratulations, Sir Guy,' he said as he led Hubert into the room. 'You must be awfully pleased. It's your first, I believe.'

'I believe it is,' said Hubert, whose lips were twitching. He winked at Marjorie like a schoolboy as Mr Reed sat down and removed his spectacles, revealing large spaniel eyes.

'Your wife is very fit,' said Mr Reed. 'There should be no trouble. Your wife's little – er – problem seems to have resolved itself. These things do sometimes.'

'Oh? What problem was that?' asked Hubert naughtily.

'Her – er – fallopian tubes were blocked.' Reed replaced his spectacles and made a note on the folder in front of him.

'And now they are unblocked,' said Hubert. 'Well, that is very good news, isn't it, darling?'

'Very,' said Marjorie, wanting to laugh and cry.

'Not too much to drink,' said Reed, following them to the top of the stairs, 'and cut down on cigarettes if you can. Otherwise plenty of the usual: green veg, meat – when you can – and so on. Don't hunt.'

'Goodbye,' said Marjorie, waving a gloved hand. 'I'll be back soon.'

'Two months will do,' said Reed, going back into his high-ceilinged room and closing the door.

'I have to go and see someone,' said Hubert in the street. 'I didn't tell you before because I didn't want to worry you.'

'Who?' She knew, even as she asked, that it was bad news.

'Van der Buhl.' He didn't look at her, but kept her hand in his. It was one of his habits.

'I see.'

'You're lunching with Babs at the … Ritz is it, or the Berkeley?'

'Ritz,' said Marjorie, biting her lip.

'I'll put you in a cab and come on later,' said Hubert. 'Try not to worry, darling,' he said, waving his umbrella at a cab. It was a summer's day in England: chilly and wet.

All very well for him, she thought, as the cab moved off. For the first time, since she had fallen in love with Hubert, her initial doubts returned. He *was* vain and complacent. He had behaved from the beginning as if he owned her, basking like a shark in the library that night, helping himself to Guy's books. What on earth was she going to do? She began to cry quietly, sniffing and dabbing with her hanky. Then, knowing she must stop, she got out the gold compact that Guy had given her and dealt with her face. Crying was too relieving altogether. Behind this initial sprinkling of tears lay an ocean waiting to be wept. And it simply would not do. This sniffing and dripping was against her religion. She had been brought up to have backbone and backbone she must have. It was how her mother must have managed after her father had been potted at Gommecourt or one of those God-forsaken places in the trenches: swallow a knitting needle and carry on. She would do the same.

'Darling,' said Babs curiously when they were seated, 'are you *all right*?'

'Perfectly, thank you,' said Marjorie, looking up from toying with whatever it was she had ordered. 'Why do you ask?'

'You just seem . . . a little off-colour,' said Babs. 'You're not eating your lunch.'

'I'm not hungry,' said Marjorie flatly.

'I'll eat it then,' said Babs. 'I'm starving and I can't bear to see waste.'

'You've got awfully Scottish,' said Marjorie. 'Waste used to be your motto.'

'It's living with Archie,' said Babs. 'He lights a lovely fire in the tiniest back sitting room and then spoils it by saying, "That's five bobs' worth of wood there," and I feel guilty.'

'I don't see why you should,' said Marjorie, smiling in spite of herself at this vignette of Highland life.

'Is it Guy?' asked Babs after a minute, putting her fork down.

'Is what Guy?' said Marjorie.

'Is it because you're missing him that you're so gloomy? You do seem terribly down in the dumps, if you don't mind my saying so.'

'I do miss Guy,' said Marjorie, 'just as you must miss Archie.'

'I don't really,' said Babs, bursting out laughing. 'I find it much easier now he's gone. I'm having some fun at last.'

'What *are* you up to?'

Babs smiled and looked mysterious. 'Oh, this and that. But, darling, have you heard from Guy?'

'No. No, I haven't, as a matter of fact.'

'Are you worried?'

'Worried to death,' said Marjorie.

'Oh dear, oh dear,' Babs said. 'This awful war. It does tear one up, doesn't it? I don't know what I should do if Archie were killed. I'd feel it was my fault for having such a good time. I'd feel as I were being punished.'

'*Don't* say that!'

'Well, you know what I mean.'

'I do, but you mustn't say it. I'm feeling superstitious.'

'I wish you'd tell me what's going on.'

'I can't.'

'Yes, you can.'

Marjorie shook her head.

'Who's that divine-looking man?' asked Babs suddenly, staring over Marjorie's shoulder. 'He's smiling at me.'

Marjorie's looked round and saw Hubert making his way towards them across the room.

'Oh, God,' she said, 'it's Hubert.'

'Who's Hubert?'

'A friend,' said Marjorie unconvincingly.

'You're having an affair,' murmured Babs. 'You are a naughty –'

'Hello,' said Hubert. 'He wasn't there, so I'll have to go back later. Bloody rude, I must say, so I thought I'd make up for it by coming to join you and the mysterious Babs.'

He kissed Marjorie and glanced at Babs approvingly.

'Am I mysterious?' said Babs. 'How lovely. How do you two know one another?'

'I am one of Marjorie's patients,' said Hubert, with a little smile, pulling out a chair and sitting down.

'You don't look very ill to me,' said Babs.

'I'm better now,' said Hubert, 'but I was all in bits a few months ago, wasn't I, darling?'

Babs raised her eyebrows at the endearment.

'Is the castle full?' she asked, to tide over the awkwardness of her own response.

'Very,' said Hubert. 'We're making them garden. They seem to like it.'

'Haven't you a girl?' asked Babs.

'We do,' said Marjorie, 'but Hubert has been very helpful to me in planning how on earth to preserve the rest of the garden. It would be such a shame if it went to pot.'

'Do you know about that sort of thing?' asked Babs. 'I can't imagine Marjorie with a trug and a trowel. It's simply not her thing.'

'There's nothing very much to it,' said Hubert. 'You need imagination and an eye for colour, and a great deal of faith in the future. We're planting roses in the little old walled garden at the moment. Marjorie calls it her secret garden, don't you, darling?'

'Oh,' said Babs, clearly astonished at this vision of horticultural bliss. 'I'll have to come and have a look. But surely they're getting you to grow things for the war effort?'

'We are, everywhere we can,' said Marjorie. 'Vegetables in the strangest places.'

As they were getting their things, Babs said, 'Darling, be careful. He's dangerous.'

'What on earth do you mean.'

'Dangerously handsome for one thing and dangerously nice for another. He would quite undo me. But he seems to have taken you over. All those "darlings" and this and that. He's certainly fallen for Fordingbridge. Are you really doing all those unlikely things?'

'Yes, we are,' said Marjorie, catching Babs' eye in the glass. 'I'm not proud of myself.'

Babs said nothing.

'I'm pregnant,' said Marjorie, before she could stop herself.

'I knew you were going to say that. What on earth are you going to do?'

'I don't know.'

'I mean . . . you can't pretend it's Guy's, can you? He's been away too long. You'll have to get rid of it. Here, let me think.' She looked in her bag and scribbled an address on a page of her diary, which she tore out and gave to Marjorie.

'Have you used him?'

'No,' said Babs fiercely, 'but I hear he's good.' She met Marjorie's eye. 'Yes, all right then, I did.'

'But when?'

'Never mind when. Don't lose it. I'll be thinking of you, darling,' she said, hugging Marjorie. 'Keep in touch. Perhaps I'll run down and see you soon at Fordingbridge. I've got to go to Scotland next week to have a look at Port David – *that's* been taken over too – then I'll come back to London. I'll be going back to the far north in about September.' Archie, Babs' husband, had two estates in Scotland, one near Inverness and one in the south-west of Scotland.

'Thank you,' said Marjorie, 'wish me luck.'

In the taxi on the way to the station, Hubert took Marjorie's hand. 'I'm going in a week,' he said. 'I'm sorry, darling. I know it's hard for you.'

'Babs gave me the name of an abortionist,' she said after a minute.

'You can't do that!' He was genuinely appalled.

'How am I going to manage otherwise?' Marjorie lit a cigarette. She felt completely numbed by the events of the day.

'I don't know,' he said. 'Can't you have it in secret and get someone to look after it? Then I'll come back for you and we can –'

'What happens if you don't come back?'

'But I will,' he said. 'I absolutely swear it.'

'You might be . . .' Marjorie looked at him and was unable to finish her sentence.

'When it's over, I'll come for you.'

'I don't think I can bear it,' said Marjorie.

'Yes, yes, you can. There.' He put his arm round her. 'Yes, you can,' he said. 'You are very brave, you have great courage. That's one of the things I love about you, one of the many things. You know I love you, don't you, my darling?'

'Yes.'

'I want you to remember I said it. Before my mother died she told me that she loved me. She said it was important to say it.'

'But you're not going to –'

'No, of course not. But there is always the possibility,' said Hubert, contradicting himself.

'Don't say that,' said Marjorie.

'You must have faith in me,' he said. 'I'm a most tremendous survivor.'

She nodded, unable to speak.

The abortionist practised from a large, gabled, suburban house in East Sheen with a brass plate by the front door: 'Andrew Williams' it said. 'Dental Surgeon'.

'Come in, please,' said the plump, middle-aged woman in a white overall and white shoes (which for some reason struck a sinister note) who answered the door. 'Mr Williams is expecting you, if you will just follow me.'

Marjorie was led through a house smelling of roasting meat and into a room at the back overlooking the garden, an ordinary dentist's surgery, except for the curtained-off cubicle containing a bed and a huge lamp. She shuddered and returned to the window. A child's swing hung from an oak tree. She looked away and then looked back at it again.

'I'd like to take your blood pressure,' said the nurse as she returned. 'If you slip into the gown we can do the preliminaries.' She held out a starched hospital gown with ties at the back.

'I don't think so,' said Marjorie.

'But you have to wear it, otherwise –'

'Does Mr Williams have children?' asked Marjorie, picking up her handbag, although she already knew the answer.

'Yes, he does,' said the nurse, who was baffled by this. 'Two boys and a girl.'

'I'm sorry,' said Marjorie, 'but I can't stay.'

'But,' cried the nurse, 'Mr Williams is expecting –'

'Thank him from me,' said Marjorie. 'For putting his swing where I could see it.'

'I don't follow . . .' The nurse came squeaking after Marjorie. 'You've made an appointment, you can't just –'

'Oh, yes I can,' said Marjorie, opening the front door. 'Goodbye.'

She flew down the path and out of the neatly painted green gate.

Afterwards she could remember nothing of her walk to the bus stop except the sensation of elation and joy such as a prisoner might feel who was suddenly set free.

Months later, Hubert was awoken before dawn by Brigitte. She kneeled beside him and put her face close to his in case he should make a noise. He knew at once that something was wrong because she had not kissed him. Normally, when she came to see him clandestinely, she could not wait but flung herself into his arms without a word.

'They are coming,' she whispered in French, and some of her long, dark hair fell over his face. 'The best thing for you to do is to stay here. Hide yourself under the sacks. They won't see you, but be very calm, very still.'

'Thanks for coming to tell me,' he said, reaching for her. She was a very good, very brave, very beautiful girl, without whom he would never have survived for so long.

'Hurry,' she said, pulling back from his embrace. 'We mustn't waste any time.'

Hubert lay under the sacks and prayed. It was three days after Christmas, Holy Innocents, in the old world into which he had been born. He prayed for Marjorie in England, and for the child, for his father, his brothers and sisters, his mother in Paradise, and for the girl, Brigitte who had risked her life for him over and over again by hiding him, against her parents' wishes, in the apple loft. He had lived up here for two months with the rats and the pigeons and the bol weevils. Now, as he listened, he heard the scrape of a well-made boot on the cobbled yard, and saw the bobbing light of the lantern. He had lived this moment so many times in his dreams that it was almost a relief to know that they had come for him at last.

In the truck on the way to the camp, he managed to scrawl something on a piece of paper: the name of his destination, his own name, her name and address. He squeezed it out through a gap between the boards of the truck and the barred and fastened door, so that it fluttered into a field somewhere near the Polish border.

CHAPTER 16

On Tuesday afternoon, regular as clockwork, Guy would go for a walk down by the river. He always left the dogs behind on these occasions, as they were too easily visible and, besides, had a tendency, in spite of expensive training at a prep school for dogs, to bark at people they didn't like.

Marion's garden ran down to the river and it was therefore possible to enter her grounds without being seen from the street. This particular afternoon she was sitting at a wrought-iron table under an umbrella. 'Hello, darling,' she said, from behind expensive dark glasses, 'Have a glass of wine.'

'Thank you,' said Guy, 'I will. How's it going?'

'Oh, I'm not working, I'm just scribbling some notes for an article. *Women's Journal* is doing a piece on lady novelists for some reason best known to themselves, and they've chosen me.'

'Will they pay you?'

'Of course they'll pay me,' said Marion, pouring herself some more wine. 'Tell me about you, darling. Have you been busy?'

'So, so,' said Guy. 'Some tidying up, nothing very interesting.' He couldn't talk to Marion about gardening. Besides, he was a great believer in not mixing one's incantations. Marion was his mistress. Her function in his life was very clearly defined as far as he was concerned. He took a polite interest in her work for the sake of appearances. He didn't want to *hear* about it, any more than he really expected Marion wanted to *hear* about what he had been doing.

'How's Marjorie?'

'Very well, thank you,' he replied. He always gave the same answer whether it was true or not.

'She seemed to enjoy the party on Saturday. She has such tremendous *energy*, Marjorie, doesn't she? I don't know where she finds it.'

'She's always been like that,' said Guy, noncommittally.

'I thought Chloe looked a looked a little *distrait*.'

'She is. It's Rupert, but you knew that.'

'Our vicar clearly thought she was a bit of all right.'

'Did he?' asked Guy, who couldn't have cared less what the vicar thought.

'Rather too much so, if you ask me,' said Marion. 'Men of the cloth aren't supposed to be attracted to women except in Susan Howatch's novels.'

'Susan who?'

'Howatch. She writes blockbusters about the Church.'

'Good Lord,' said Guy.

'Awfully bloody boring if you ask me,' said Marion.

'Your books don't bore me,' said Guy, putting his hand on her bare arm.

'I should hope not.'

'Shall we go in?'

'Do you want to, darling?'

'You know I do. That's why I'm here.'

Afterwards she said to him, 'Have you always had a mistress?'

'Almost always. Why?'

'Very un-English of you, darling.'

'Is it? I never thought of it like that. My father kept a mistress in Maida Vale.'

Marion shrieked with laughter. 'What! Called Aida or Josie? Oh darling, you are funny.'

'She was called Elsa, actually,' said Guy, who was slightly offended by Marion's hilarity. 'She was Polish. He took me to meet her once. She was plump and pretty and doted on him.'

'What happened to her?'

'I haven't a clue,' said Guy.

'Did he leave her some money?'

'I don't think so. I expect she had other fellows in tow, too. He couldn't have afforded to keep her exclusively.'

'You couldn't afford me, either,' said Marion, lighting a cigarette. 'If I were a tart I'd charge a fortune.'

Guy, sensing a dangerous edge to the conversation, sat up and looked at his watch.

'I mustn't be too long,' he said.

'What, in case M. notices?'

'No. I've got some plants arriving at some point.'

'I wish we could go away somewhere together,' said Marion.

'I hate the way you always rush off.'

'Can't be helped,' he said.

'Does Marjorie have lovers?'

Guy, stepping into his trousers, pretended not to hear this remark.

'Answer me, darling.'

'I can't discuss her with you,' he said. 'You know that's my rule.'

'But what about my rules? What about some honesty for a change?'

'Honesty?' he said, genuinely puzzled. 'What are you talking about?'

'You're a hypocrite,' she said, stubbing out her cigarette. 'Typical English purveyor of the double-standard.'

'The double-standard,' said Guy, buttoning up his shirt, 'is essential to civilization.'

'May I take that down,' she quipped, 'and use it in evidence against you?'

'If you like,' said Guy stiffly.

'Don't be cross, darling,' said Marion. 'I'm only teasing.'

'I must go,' he said. His mind was now firmly fixed on the next objective.

'Do you ever think about changing your life, darling?'

'No. Why should I? I like my life as it is.'

'But nothing stays the same. Surely you know that. Huge mysterious forces are always at work changing things.'

'I don't know what you mean.'

'Don't you?'

'You spend too much time thinking,' said Guy. 'Thinking is dangerous. I avoid it where possible.' He bent over the bed to kiss her.

'I'd like to be with you more.'

'No, you wouldn't. I'm a terrible old bore, only interested in plants.'

'And Marjorie. That's about it, isn't it?'

'Probably.'

'You're hopeless,' she said. 'I don't know why I bother.'

'Because you like it.' He patted her arm.

CHAPTER 17

'Welcome,' said Maria, opening her front door to Frances. 'I'm so glad you could make it. Come right on in.'

She led the way down a passage painted a lemony yellow and lined with splodgy abstracts, each one signed with a red V in the corner. The smell of baking bread wafted from the kitchen where Viva stood defensively by the Aga wrapped in a vast chef's apron which reached her feet. She looked like, Frances thought, a cross between a bride and a sacrificial victim.

'This is Tashie,' said Maria, putting her hand on Tashie's shoulder. 'And this is my friend Viva.'

'Hi,' said Viva, busying herself with the kettle.

'Say hello, Tashie,' said Maria with an edge in her voice.

'Hello,' said Tashie coolly. She was doing her homework at the kitchen table but began to close her books as if preparing to make an escape.

'Don't stop on my account,' said Frances. 'My kids always do their homework in the kitchen.'

'How many do you have?' asked Tashie.

'Two. One your age and an older one.'

'Where are they at school?'

'Wayemouth High.'

'That's private, isn't it?' said Tashie, looking in her pencil case.

'Yes, it is.'

'Maria thinks private education is divisive.'

'Tashie, that's enough,' said Maria. 'Frances has come for tea, not for a harangue.'

'What's a harangue?'

'A lecture, telling you how bad you are,' said Maria. 'Is the tea ready, Viva?'

'Not yet. I'm waiting for the kettle to boil.' Viva turned her back on them whilst she peered into the oven.

'Something smells good,' said Frances, gazing round her with pleasure. 'This is a lovely room.'

'Viva makes it nice,' said Tashie. 'She cooks such lovely things. It always smells of the next meal.'

'Are you a professional cook, Viva?'

'No.' Viva shook her head. 'I'm a struggling artist, but Maria doesn't cook, so someone has to.'

'I see.' Frances caught Maria's eye and looked away. She was trying to figure out the tensions in the room and at the same time to understand why she felt so happy to be there.

'I can't cook either,' she said.

Again, she caught Maria's eye and wanted, this time, to laugh. A shaft of sunlight came through the window behind the sink and caught a particularly buoyant strand of Maria's hair which almost crackled with energy.

'Well, we can't do everything,' Maria said, 'we women. It's so important to resist the superwoman syndrome: that way we become like men. I'm a Mary, really.'

'What do you mean "I'm a Mary"?' asked Tashie crossly, sensing undercurrents.

'I like lying around talking. In the story, Martha cooked and Mary talked to Jesus and Martha blamed Mary for being idle.' She winked at Frances. Behind her, Viva slammed the oven door and stood up.

'You're Martha when you want to be,' she said, and burst into tears.

'You're such a beast,' said Tashie to her mother, getting up and putting her arms round Viva.

'Oh, for Chrissakes!' said Maria, glaring at her. 'What's wrong now, Viva?'

'I'm sick of being treated like a servant,' said Viva, sniffing and wiping her face with her apron. 'I'm going to lie down. The bread is ready if you want it,' she added, and ran out of the room. Tashie followed her, banging the door behind them.

'God Almighty!' said Maria. 'I'm really sorry, Frances. First time you visit and there's a fucking scene. I'm really sorry.'

'It's fine,' said Frances. 'I prefer a scene, really. In my house, everything is submerged, you know.' She shrugged.

'It's marriage,' said Maria. 'Marriage is a fucking nightmare, if you'll pardon the expression.'

She looked at Frances and they both began to laugh.

'Let's eat anyhow,' said Maria. 'Where's the glove, you know, the thing you get things out of an oven with?'

'Here you go.' Frances handed it to her. 'Don't burn yourself.'

'My God, this is good,' said Maria, breaking a bit off and handing it to Frances. 'Butter, jam. Let's go.'

'Do you want to see how she is?' asked Frances, after a minute.

'Nup.' Maria shook her head. 'If I'm honest, I'd say things are winding down between us. She's a sweet kid, but she's young and you know how terrible everything is when you're young. Not like us,' she added. 'Us old troopers.'

She put her hand on Frances's arm.

'No,' said Frances with an effort, looking down at the brown, warm, shapely hand on her bare skin. With a most extraordinary sense of shock she realized she wanted to take that hand and kiss it. A prickle of fear ran down her spine as if someone had stroked her with a thorn.

'Well,' said Maria, suddenly brisk, removing her hand, 'when are you going to ask me out to your place?'

'Whenever you like.'

'I'd like to lay eyes on the famous David.'

'Is he famous?'

'Not really. I mean, I don't know. Just kidding,' said Maria. 'It's a bad habit, I guess.'

'He's in London for three days this week,' said Frances.

'Then maybe I could come out some other time and bring Tashie.'

'That's a great idea,' said Frances. 'What about Viva?'

'Viva will want to paint,' said Maria. 'Besides, we both need a bit of space, as you can see.'

'How long have you been together?'

'Couple of years, too damn long. No, I didn't mean that. My big mouth.'

She clasped a hand to her face, making Frances laugh again. Maria seemed to her so alive; so *zestful*, so unlike . . . so unlike David.

CHAPTER 18

'Charles Digard, how do you do?'

Chloe shook hands with a middle-aged man with iron grey hair wearing a pinstripe suit of great beauty. His office was furnished like an expensive dentist's waiting room with bookcases full of law books and rather sub-standard oil paintings of English landscapes: constipated pheasants flying low over the plough, winter sunsets of rather unappealing sharpness where the tangerine sun sank behind skeletal trees.

'Now, Mrs Durrell, sit down and I'll get us some coffee,' said Charles Digard. 'Then we can discuss how I might be of help.

'Would you like to explain the situation to me,' he asked, sitting back in his chair. Behind his head were photographs of his wife and children, healthy, expensive-looking infants in sailor suits and smocked dresses on a lawn somewhere in expense-account country.

'My husband has a mistress,' began Chloe, 'and I'm not very happy with the situation.'

'I'm not surprised,' said Digard. 'Has he moved out?'

'Sort of,' said Chloe. 'May I smoke?'

'Please do,' he said, pushing a huge cut-glass ashtray towards her. 'Perhaps we had better begin at the beginning,' he said. 'Get the basics down: length of marriage, number of children, husband's income, that sort of thing.

'Well,' he said, when Chloe had told him what he needed to know, 'he's a bit of a player, isn't he? Ex-wife still on alimony?'

'No, she's much richer than he is,' said Chloe.

'That helps.' Charles Digard laughed heartily. 'Do you want the marriage to end?' he asked.

'I'm not sure,' said Chloe, suddenly finding that she wanted to cry, 'but I don't have much choice, it seems.'

'What about reconciliation, counselling, that kind of thing?'

'He won't go to counselling, thinks it's for sissies, and as for reconciliation, well, we've tried, but without much success. The woman he's with now is my best friend.'

'Dear, oh dear,' said Charles Digard. 'Treachery, eh?' He

smiled sympathetically and pushed a box of tissues towards Chloe. 'I still charge when you cry,' he said, 'so try not to. I'm expensive enough as it is.'

When Chloe came out of Digard's office the sun was shining in South Square, tempting her to linger. It was so beautiful and tranquil in the summer air, like an Oxford college, perhaps, or some other dignified and stately institution, and yet it was in places like these, she thought, that human misery and frailty was traded upon. Money was being made behind those Georgian window panes, and painful decisions affecting individual lives for ever. Even now Digard would be dictating a letter to a faithful (and no doubt female) slave in which her whole life would be laid out section by section under a magnifying glass. She was being judged and assessed: hanged, drawn and quartered at £250 per hour.

On the corner of Kingsway stood a Catholic church. Without really knowing why, Chloe went in and sat down. Candles burned peacefully under a statue of the Virgin and the interior smelt strongly of incense. Behind a carved screen more candles, unlit, lined the altar where a tabernacle was placed containing the Blessed Sacrament. Chloe looked at it and then around her, soothed by the gold and the glimmering light of the candles. She did not pray, or even attempt to. What, after all, could God do for this pain of hers? And yet her surroundings made her feel less tormented. She found herself thinking of David and of the conviction that had sprung up somewhere or other in her, in spite of herself, that he could help her. She found that she wanted to see him again, to be in touch, to talk. He had not rung her in London, presumably having thought better of it (which worried her), but she had not been to Fordingbridge for three weeks, which was unheard of, so she had had no opportunity of seeing him to find out why he had let her down. Marjorie had telephoned her to beg her to come, but Chloe had refused. She needed time to think through the implications of what her mother had told her, and she very, very much needed *not* to see her father, whom she felt she hated. Flaunting his mistress at dinner like that! It was insupportable. One of the spin-offs of her mother's revelation was that she had gone to see Digard. *She* would not live the lie her parents had lived. In her present state of mind she could see no virtue in it. Why stay together on that basis? But it made her think how interwoven family relationships were: unravelling her own marriage seemed to mean the unravelling of other assumptions and mysteries within her family; the sins of the fathers being examined under a microscope. She was not sure she believed her mother when she had said there had been no one else, and when she questioned herself as to why this should matter she realized it was to do with her own judgement. She had always thought of her mother as slightly superhuman, but if she was just an ordinary mortal like anyone else then there was no longer a clear point of reference, and the world, her world, based on all her mother's advice, would cave in.

She sat for a long time thinking of her mother and father and how little she knew about them: the long lives they had led before she was even born ... that time her father had been a prisoner of war (a time he never referred to) and her mother alone, running the castle, doing the garden, surviving somehow on her own brand of emotional strength. She thought all of a sudden of Simon Ferrars. He had known her mother in those days, almost the only person she could think of who had done. Perhaps Simon might be able to help her answer some questions about her mother; but, as soon as she had thought of this, she rejected it as absurd. She didn't know him terribly well and she hated the thought of Simon's curiosity turned upon her motives, because she wasn't certain quite what they were herself. She thought about Rupert, too, with a sense of despair mingled with anger; and then, as ever, anxiously of their two childen, wondering what would become of them now that she had taken the first, giant step in officially unravelling their lives.

When Chloe got home from her excursion to Digard's offices, she found, rather to her surprise, that David Doughty had left a message for her, inviting her to supper that night at his sister Tessa's house in Notting Hill. He apologized for not having telephoned her earlier, saying he had got his dates muddled, and also that he kept expecting to see her in Fordingbridge and had not done so. Chloe, touched by this, hastily rang back and left a message on another answering machine saying she would love to come and then, when she had done so, regretted it. She felt she was too excited about seeing him. The thought of him made her heart race which was, as she knew, utterly ridiculous. She was slightly shocked by herself. He is a married man and a priest, for God's sake, she told herself, and he must be terribly used to being besieged by hopeless cases like me. I must not, she said to herself, mistake his kindness and concern for anything else. She was hungry for warmth and sympathy and knew this was a dangerous state in which to find a forbidden man attractive.

But it was too late now, she would have to go.

Tessa Manning's house was in Cumberland Grove, off Ledbury Road, in a row of tall, white stucco houses, some restored, others crumbling. Chloe was early and nervous and decided to go into a wine bar for a drink first to give her courage. She had left home too early because the children were being difficult; Miranda had thrown a tantrum when Chloe had said she was going out and James had been rude to the au pair at tea. Chloe also found going to places on her own rather an ordeal. Notting Hill was all right because at least she knew how to get there, but there had been some other places, south of the river, for instance, where she had arrived at parties practically in tears because she had got lost and panicked.

After two glasses of wine, she returned on foot to Cumberland Grove and stood on the pavement for a moment before she rang the bell, starring down into an uncurtained basement kitchen/dining room were David sat at a long battered-looking table talking to a woman who, Chloe presumed, must be his sister Tessa. They had opened a bottle of wine and Tessa was talking whilst David listened. At one point, she put her hand on his wrist, as if to emphasize a point, then removed it again. David sat back in his chair and poured himself some more wine. He was wearing jeans, a check shirt and a tweed jacket of impeccable antiquity that looked awfully like a cast-off of Chloe's father's, and most likely was. Watching them, Chloe felt that her whole life had been spent looking in at the relationships of others, watching them, analysing them, wondering what they knew that she didn't, and a great sense of loneliness suddenly possessed her. After a minute, she went up the steps and rang the bell.

'Hello, Chloe,' said Tessa, opening the door. 'Come on in.' She was very like her brother, tall and elegant, with the same beaky features and the same dark hair cut in a rather severe bob. She wore a man's striped shirt over a pair of tapering black trousers and was, Chloe thought, both beautiful in her own way and rather formidable. Her heart sank slightly. She had hoped for someone softer and possibly sillier. There was something merciless about Tessa.

'We're downstairs in the kitchen,' Tessa said, leading the way along a passage fashionably carpeted in sisal to the top of the kitchen stairs. 'I hope you don't mind.'

'Of course not,' said Chloe politely, wondering what would have happened if she did mind and glancing, as they passed, into a large pale room with a huge sofa in it and a grand piano, which she assumed must belong to the invisible composer husband.

'My husband is premiering a piece in New York,' said Tessa. 'That's his work room. Have a look, if you like.'

'May I?'

'Minimalist glamour,' said Tessa, 'as you can see.'

'I don't know his name.' Chloe went to the piano and touched it.

'Nicholas Manning,' said Tessa. 'You've probably heard things of his and not known who they were by.'

'I think I have,' said Chloe. 'He's on Radio Three quite a lot.'

'Yes, he's one of their avant-garde darlings,' said Tessa. 'How they do love him.'

Chloe turned away from the piano.

'Do you know David well?' asked Tessa.

'No. Not very.'

'He can be terribly silly sometimes,' said Tessa. 'I think he's vain because he believes he can fix the whole world's problems.'

'He's popular at Fordingbridge,' said Chloe carefully.

'He was popular here, too. A bit too popular.'

Chloe waited, but Tessa was already leading the way out of the room.

'Chloe,' said David, getting up, 'what a pleasure. I'm so glad you could come at such short notice.'

'Pour Chloe some wine,' said Tessa. 'Here's a glass.'

'This house is just inside the boundaries of my old parish,' said

155

David. 'It's funny coming back here and knowing it's none of my business any more.'

'Have you seen anyone you know?'

'I know most people round here,' said David, 'some of them not terribly savoury types. The problem is to dodge them.'

'Who was your successor?'

'Young chap. Very nice, very good at the job.'

'What David means,' said Tessa, 'is that he's carrying on what David began. Don't you, David?'

'I suppose that's what I do mean,' said David, and they all laughed.

'Why did you leave?' asked Chloe. 'That's what everyone wants to know.'

'Time for a change,' said David easily, avoiding Tessa's eyes. Before Chloe had arrived they had been discussing Mary, who was at home again. Tessa had been lecturing David about not interfering.

'We'd been in the front line a long time,' he added.

'Far too long,' said Tessa firmly, 'but the Church is like that. Finds someone good and then wears them to a thread.'

Chloe was aware of Tessa glancing at her, as if she were trying to assess the effect of these remarks.

'Do you miss it?' she asked David.

'In some ways,' said David, 'but not in others. I like Fording-bridge. It's another sort of challenge, and also a privilege to live in such a beautiful place.'

'Have you been down?' Chloe asked Tessa.

'Not yet, but I hope to soon. Your mother is Marjorie Jessop, I gather.'

'Yes,' said Chloe, 'that's right. Are you a gardener?'

'Not like that,' said Tessa. 'But I've seen her on television. She's wonderful.'

'David's her new pupil,' said Chloe. 'Has he told you?'

'He told me he's sorting out the garden at the vicarage, but he didn't tell me where his source of inspiration was coming from.'

'I'm sure I did,' said David. 'But it's Frances who's really attracting attention.'

'Good old Frances,' said Tessa. 'She never gives up, does she, trying to make converts of people?'

156

Chloe, watching her expression as she spoke, wondered whether Tessa liked Frances and decided that she probably didn't.

'Do you go to these discussion groups, Chloe?' asked Tessa. 'Or I suppose you can't really, living in London.'

'I'm here in the week,' said Chloe, 'because of school.'

'Do you work?'

'No, not at the moment. I'm waiting for the children to get a bit older before I go back and, besides, I'm in the process of getting a divorce.'

She stopped suddenly, afraid she was going to cry. Grief could take one unexpectedly, like a rugger tackle from behind.

'Poor you,' said Tessa. 'It's a very upsetting time, I know. You must feel very alone.'

Chloe looked at her. 'That's the worst thing,' she said. 'Sometimes I think I can't stand it.' She felt uncomfortably exposed by Tessa's clearly directed sympathy. Grief made her feel like an animal in some way; she longed to go and lie in a hedge with her pain until it went away; and yet at the same time she wanted to reveal it in order to heal it.

'I'm sure it's better for your children if you're around at the moment,' said Tessa. 'Mine got much more demanding when they grew up a bit. Any idiot can look after a baby, but bringing up older children is really strenuous, if you want to do it well.'

'Tessa's lot are grown up now,' said David, handing Chloe a handkerchief with his initials on in the corner. 'Matty's in Africa doing voluntary work for a year before university, Rachel's a struggling cellist and Flora's a composer like her father.'

'Hopeless way to earn a living on the whole,' said Tessa, draining some pasta at the sink in a cloud of steam. 'Nick's been terribly lucky.'

'Try being a priest,' said David, smiling at Chloe.

'That's next best in terms of fiscal hopelessness, I suppose,' said Tessa. 'What does your husband do, Chloe?'

'Banker,' said Chloe.

'Oh, a fat cat then. Well, I'm sure he doesn't need our sympathy – fiscally speaking, that is.'

'He does very well,' said Chloe.

'Which is lucky for you, I suppose,' said Tessa. 'Make sure you take him to the cleaners, won't you?'

'Tessa!' said David.

'Well, he's got lots of lolly and Chloe has to look after his children, so why not? Let's eat, shall we?'

'I'll go out for more wine,' said David. 'I meant to do it before. Hold on a second.'

'Yes, all right,' said Tessa, 'but hurry. And don't get stopped by one of your old parishioners.'

The front door banged and David's legs walked past the railings.

'I suppose you're one of David's lame ducks,' said Tessa abruptly, pushing plates across to Chloe.

'What do you mean?'

'He likes to help people,' she said, 'but he doesn't know where to stop. He goes too far, he gives too much.'

'I've only just met him,' said Chloe defensively. 'I'm not quite sure what you're getting at.'

'I'm sorry,' said Tessa, 'I'm being tactless. It's a bad habit.'

'What does David do that you don't approve of?'

'He's very good at what he does,' said Tessa, 'because he's sympathetic to people, he listens well, but he exceeds his brief where women are concerned. You're very attractive,' she added, 'and obviously very unhappy, which I'm sorry about, but my dear, dear brother doesn't know the strength of his own unhappiness which in itself draws other unhappinesses to him. He seems to be attracted to unfortunate women, women like you whose marriages are going wrong for various reasons.'

'Is his own marriage going wrong? I don't know him at all,' said Chloe.

'It's been going wrong for years only they pretend not to notice, the pair of them. They've only themselves to blame. Damn,' she said, hearing the front door slam, 'here he is now.'

When Chloe rose to go at eleven-thirty, David got up too.

'I'll walk you to your car,' he said.

'Don't,' said Chloe, shaking her head. 'Please. It's fine. I'm fine.' She turned to Tessa to thank her.

'Come another time,' said Tessa. 'I'll walk Chloe to her car,' she said. 'Be a darling and shove those things in the dishwasher.'

'I need some air,' said David, 'and there's something I want to say to Chloe.'

'Well, don't be too long,' said Tessa, outmanoeuvred. 'Where's your car?'

'At the end of Ledbury Road,' said Chloe. 'Westbourne Grove end. There was nowhere else.'

Outside, the air was balmy and the night sky glittered with stars.

'What did you want to say to me?' Chloe asked, as they went past Tessa's railings.

'To see how you were,' he said. 'You haven't been down for a while. Your mother is saying nothing, but she's rather upset about it. Have you had a row?'

'I suppose we have,' said Chloe.

'Do you want to tell me what about?'

'Daddy and Marion. Why she's put up with it all this time.'

'I see. Shall we walk to my old church? I'd like to show it to you.'

'All right,' she said, torn between reluctance and desire: the thought of Tessa sitting at the table counting the seconds.

'You don't have to,' he said, stopping in the middle of the road.

'I do want to,' she said, 'but Tessa will think I'm deliberately detaining you.'

'Did she say something?'

'Well . . .'

'She did, didn't she?' he said, walking on.

'She asked me if I were one of your lame ducks.'

'My poor dear,' he said. 'You're very unhappy, aren't you?'

'Yes.'

'Poor Chloe.' He took her arm in his.

'Don't,' said Chloe in confusion, withdrawing her arm. 'I'm a liability, dangerous to know.'

'Let me help,' he said.

'You do help, but there are things you can't do. You can advise me, but you can't make the pain go away. Nobody can do that.'

'Only God can.'

'Then don't play God,' said Chloe. 'I'm sorry,' she said, 'I didn't mean that.'

'Is it what I'm doing?' He stopped to look at her under a street lamp.

'Is it what you think I'm doing?'

'I don't know what I think,' said Chloe, unwilling to be dragged further into the quagmire. 'Is this it?' she asked, as they came towards the dark bulk of a church.

'This is it.'

'St Anselm's,' she read on the noticeboard, along with the name of the new rector and the times of the masses.

The windows were covered in wire and the door was locked. But the churchyard, or as much as she could see of it, was full of flowers and the grass was cut. It certainly had an air of hope about it, she thought.

'I'm sorry I've added to your burdens,' David said. 'Everyone burdens you. And now I have too.'

'It's all right,' said Chloe, turning away, 'please. I must go.'

'Don't leave your mother too long,' he said as they got to Chloe's car. 'She is upset, but you know how she disguises things. Sometimes I don't think it's very good for her. She's been looking almost frail lately.'

'You're making me feel guilty.'

'Come and see her,' he said. 'That's all she wants.'

'You've been ages,' said Tessa crossly, opening the front door. 'I was beginning to get quite worried about you.'

She turned away and went along the passage and back down the stairs to the kitchen. David followed her into the big room in the basement. They each sat down on a chair at the table and looked at one another.

'I was not worried about your safety,' she said, 'in a physical sense, but I am worried that you are using this girl and her miseries for some reason of your own. You mustn't do it, David, it's a sin: your besetting sin, perhaps?' she added sternly.

'I know,' he said. 'Don't think I don't.'

'Mary was not an aberration,' said Tessa. 'Mary was the beginning of something, and that was bad enough in itself, but Chloe is a continuation of what was happening with Mary. You must realize that.'

'I'm beginning to,' he said humbly.

'And if that weren't enough, she's also deliciously beautiful, like that mother of hers.'

'Yes,' he said, making a face.

'Somebody has to say it,' she said. 'You're behaving like a bad priest. I say it as your sister and as somebody who loves you. How are things with Frances?'

'Not bad.' He looked at his hands. 'Not good either. Our sex life is nonexistent, the rest of it muddles along: the parish, the school run, the lectures, the discussion groups. Frances is happier, though. She's made friends at the new college and seems absorbed in her work.'

'She always was absorbed in her work,' said Tessa. 'It sounds as if she isn't making the slightest effort.'

David sighed. 'You always could spot a submerged lie or hypocrisy,' he said ruefully.

'Oh, darling,' said Tessa, leaning across the table and taking his hand in hers, 'do, I beg you, be careful. You must pray like mad that things should come right between you. I wish Frances weren't so tiresomely feminist. It's very selfish of her to go round in blinkers like that. I liked Chloe,' she added, for no obvious reason. 'She's rather a dear, isn't she?'

'She's enormously sweet,' said David, hesitating fractionally. 'I'm afraid I might be falling in love with her.'

'But you hardly know her,' said Tessa, who knew her brother's vulnerable heart only too well.

'Since when did that ever prevent one falling for someone?'

Tessa gazed at him sadly. 'I'm not sure I believe in falling in love any more,' she said. 'It seems like something for children or for the carefree. It must be to do with the lack of understanding between you and Frances. Anyway, what is love?' She made a gesture with her hands. 'My God, *I* don't know. How can I say anything, my life being what it is?'

'How is Nick?'

'Bloody. We had a row last night on the phone. I think he's got some girl there with him. He was being so cagey.'

'I am sorry.'

'Don't be,' said Tessa. 'Save your energy. It's business as usual between us. You need to concentrate on yourself. Does Frances have any idea at all what's going on in your mind?'

'She does when she thinks about it, which isn't very often.'

'Mmm. Have you tried talking to her about it?'

'Not enough. I know I should.'

'Not "should",' said Tessa, 'but "must". It's a priority, otherwise you'll be one of those priests in the tabloids who's fallen from grace.'

'I already have, in a sense.'

'Don't be so damn defeatist. It's one of those priestly struggles you read about in devotional books or see in paintings: you must fight with all your might and main.'

'I'll try to,' he said, pouring them more wine.

'Do you have a confessor, or some nice nun you could talk to?'

'There's my old Archdeacon, I suppose, but I feel I can't go back to him. He went to such lengths to help me when I was here. I certainly don't want to see a counsellor or anyone like that. They trade in human misery.'

'But your new Bishop could help you, surely? Even if he's too busy himself, he would know someone — another clergyman — you could go to.'

'You're right, of course. I should do something. But we've really only just got there and there's been so much to do.'

'I know, but that's an excuse. We're all so damnably good at them. What about prayer?'

He sighed. 'Have you ever tried praying when you're really troubled, when you really need help or hope? It's worse than nothing, just deadness.'

'You *are* in trouble, aren't you?' said Tessa. 'Sometimes I think we ask an awful lot of God, though, don't you agree? Instant trouble-shooter, helpmate, nanny, good father and so on. Your patience is being tested for a reason. You must find out what that reason is.'

'You'd make a better priest than me,' said David.

Tessa gave him a look. 'That's rich, coming from you,' she said. 'Promise me you'll talk to Frances when you get back.'

'I promise,' he said.

CHAPTER 19

'Frances? It's Marjorie Jessop. Could I speak to David, please?'

'He's coming back from London tonight,' said Frances. 'He's been on a training course.'

'For what?'

'Oh, they have them the whole time. It's an excuse for a get-together. Essential, so we're told, in the isolated life of a priest. They can all have a good grumble about their problems.'

'You're making me feel guilty,' said Marjorie. 'Would he ring me when he comes back?'

'It might be late,' said Frances. 'How late is acceptable to you?'

'Ten-thirty, I should think. Thank you so much.'

Marjorie put the telephone down and sat staring out of the window. She was in her own room with its window looking out of the side of the house; her view was of a yew arch with the ruins beyond, and the trees of the hill beyond that. So lovely. It had given her so much satisfaction, this garden. It had more than repaid the effort she had put into it. It had soothed her wounds and helped her to find a new kind of pride in herself when she had so badly needed to. And now this. She looked at the letter which she had read umpteen times, and every time her reaction was different. He wanted to come and see her, and she didn't know what to do. Initially she had wanted to repay what she saw as his enormous cruelty by some means or other. Then common sense had reasserted itself and told her to ignore the past, breaking into her present like a knife, but other parts of her clamoured and urged different things still: there was so much that needed to be explained. It was as if, greatly delayed, something would have to be resolved in her life. All her success, in a certain odd way, seemed to have been a stratagem to avoid this central tragedy and its implications. And she had nearly done it, too, although for how much longer she couldn't know. Chloe was already breaking down her defences by her strange behaviour, wanting to know things, disagreeing or distrusting what she was told. Marjorie shook her head. And how, she wondered, would he be? Old and bowed or vigorous as she herself was? She feared the look she would see in his eyes, feared most the sense of regret, of opportunities lost, feared to think of the child she had not seen; feared she would find a meaning in things that cynicism and self-preservation had forced her to abandon. She was too old, she felt, to have her creation smashed, to have it revealed as a sham. After some more minutes of reverie she got up and went out into the garden, hoping to find solace amongst the roses she had planted, together with Hubert, so long ago.

Later David rang, on the dot of ten-twenty.

'Not too late, I hope?' he said. 'I try not to ring after ten, usually, unless it's urgent.'

'This is urgent,' said Marjorie, who was in bed reading. 'Something has happened that I very badly need your advice on. What about tomorrow sometime? Can you manage?'

'I should think so. Let me check.'

She could hear him rustling notes and pieces of paper.

'I saw Chloe,' he said into the silence. 'She'll tell you, I expect. We talked . . . a bit.' He seemed preoccupied with finding his diary.

'Yes? How was she?'

'I told her you wanted to see her.'

'What did she say?'

'She seemed to understand. I think she's trying to make sense out of things and to get a grip, if you know what I mean. But she is courageous.'

'I wonder,' said Marjorie. 'Not a word I would have used to describe my darling daughter.'

'You're too hard on her.'

'Am I?' she asked, taken aback.

'She is courageous because she accepts her weaknesses. To my mind, that is courage; being full of fear and yet going on, going ahead.'

'Did you talk to her for long?'

'She came to supper with my sister, Tessa.'

'Oh, I see.'

164

'What about eleven tomorrow? Will that do?'

'Perfectly,' said Marjorie. 'Is she going to divorce Rupert, do you think? I certainly hope she will.'

'She said she was getting divorced,' said David, 'but she didn't go into any details. She seemed terribly unhappy.'

'I know she is,' said Marjorie, 'but it will pass. I hope you told her that.'

'I wasn't able to do much for her, to be frank,' said David. 'She was angry and sad, and when people are like that there isn't always anything you can do or say.'

'Isn't there?'

'Well . . . no.'

'Good night.'

'David held the receiver, noting the speed with which Marjorie replaced it at the other end, cutting him off mid-word as if he were a tiresome subordinate; or as if a cry for help were regarded as such a weakness that it had to be accompanied by a ritual cuffing.

He looked up as Frances came into his study with a cup of tea.

'For me?' he asked, surprised, taking it from her.

'Why not?' she said. 'I thought we should have a talk. We should, but we don't, at least not enough.'

'I know.' He sipped the tea, which was lukewarm, and then put the cup down.

'How was your con?' she asked, settling herself on the sofa.

'Useful, invigorating in some ways.' He paused, trying to remember something of significance to tell her.

'And Tessa? How was she?'

'Much the same.'

'Come on, I want to know the gossip.'

'Things are difficult with Nick,' he said reluctantly. 'Tess says he's in New York with some girl.'

'Go on,' said Frances. 'What else?'

'Isn't that enough?'

'David!' She smiled at him. 'You make me sound like some kind of monster. I'm sorry for Tessa, naturally, but Nick's been doing this sort of thing on and off for years. I want to know if Tessa said anything about Mary.'

'Why?'

'Just curious.'

'She's back,' he said, getting up to search his desk for something.

'Did you see her?'

'No. Chloe Durrell came to supper, though.'

'You didn't tell me you'd asked her.'

'I didn't think I would. It was a spur of the moment thing.'

'I see,' said Frances. 'Is she your new cause?'

'What do you mean?'

'Do I have to explain it?'

He turned from his desk and looked at her. 'Tessa told me we should talk, everyone tells us that's what we should do, but we don't and this is why: because we cannot agree on one single thing. We have lost the means of communicating with one another. You enjoy riling me. It gives you pleasure to make me uncomfortable. You are extremely hostile to me, for some reason I can't fathom.'

'Really!' she said. 'Is that what you really think?'

'Tell me what you think.'

'I think you keep a certain part of yourself separate from me – I know that is essential in marriage – but I feel you keep your opposition towards me burning over a low flame. You resent most of my views, the way I run my life, my uselessness as a parish wife. You despise things I hold dear, and I don't know why.'

'I've always tried to respect your views,' he said.

'But you don't. In *theory* yes, in practice no. In practice you resent my independence, you always have done.'

She wiped a tear out of the corner of her eye.

'Oh, Frances . . . do you think we'll get anywhere talking like this? I love you, you're my wife, but –' He stopped. He couldn't think what else to say to her. She was unreachable. He wasn't even sure if it was true. He no longer knew if he did love her or not. 'Tell me what I can do,' he said.

'I don't know,' she replied, shaking her head. 'Really, David, if I'm honest, I don't.' She had clearly chosen not to hear his declaration. Perhaps she didn't believe in it any more than he did. 'We seem destined to drift away from one another. If you weren't what you are, I'd say we needed a period apart.'

'A separation, you mean?'

Frances nodded.

'It's quite impossible.' He picked up his cup and put it down again.

'Well, then,' she said, 'we'll just have to rub along somehow.'

'Is there someone else? I have wondered.'

'What do you mean?'

He shrugged. 'What do you think I mean?'

'You're the expert on that, I should have thought. What's Tessa's advice?'

'Talk.'

'Great,' she said sarcastically. 'She's more of a confidante than I am, perhaps that's the trouble.'

'At least she listens to me.'

'And I don't.'

'She listens kindly,' he said.

'We're not getting anywhere, are we?'

'I'm going to bed.' He felt sad and disappointed and somehow treacherous, but, he said to himself, he had nothing to reproach himself with. Tessa was right. He knew he was susceptible to girls, but Chloe needed his help. She was vulnerable too but she knew it, and in that lay safety. It would be all right.

'There are some problems,' she said, 'that can't be solved; they just have to be accommodated. Bleak little word, isn't it? You're so good at solving other people's problems, why can't you solve ours?'

'Good question,' he said from the door. 'I wish I bloody well knew the answer.'

'Hello there,' said Guy as the vicar came past. He was up a ladder outside the drawing room window where he was dealing with a clematis, 'Frances Rivis', a favourite of his. 'Marjorie's expecting you.'

David stopped and looked up, shading his eyes with his hand, and saw Guy perched on his ladder wearing a pair of trousers that were so ancient it was hardly possible to imagine them ever being new, or even to tell what colour they had been originally. His shirt was of similar antiquity and his straw hat had a part of the crown missing. His dress sense was one of the things David did admire in Guy Jessop, and was, in his own small way, trying to emulate. One had to be careful one didn't end up looking like a tramp, or if one did at least one would be a tramp in Lobbs shoes, like Guy.

'As a matter of fact, padre,' said Guy, 'I'm a bit worried about Marjorie. She's been off her grub for two or three weeks now, and I don't think she's sleeping properly. She looks awfully peaky, if you ask me.'

'Have you any idea what might have caused it?'

'No.' Guy was baffled. 'Not really. But why did she ask you to come this morning? It's not your normal time, is it?'

'She said she had something she wanted to discuss with me,' said David, 'but she didn't say what it was.'

'Mmm. Hasn't mentioned a thing to me,' said Guy. 'Well, I don't know,' he went on, scratching his head, 'women are an enigma, don't you think? Never get to the bottom of them.'

David smiled. 'Where is she?'

'Kitchen garden, could be,' said Guy. 'Or you could look for her at the pond. She's been there a lot lately. Keep me posted, padre,' he said, 'there's a good chap. Want to do all I can, don't y'know.'

She was busily picking some broad beans when he found her in the kitchen garden, wearing an old washed-out sprigged cotton dress and, like Guy, an ancient hat of which there were a great many in the boot room.

'Do you want to go on doing this?' he said. 'Or would you like to walk about, or go and sit somewhere?'

'I think I'd find it easier to talk if we were walking.'

He saw how exhausted she was, but her demeanour was the same as ever.

'I don't quite know how to begin,' she said, with uncharacteristic hesitation.

'With very serious matters it's often best just to jump in,' said David, 'never mind feelings of awkwardness or embarrassment.'

'Years ago,' began Marjorie abruptly, as they rounded the beans and set off down a path in the direction of the fruit bushes, 'when Guy was away in the war – as a prisoner of the Japanese – I had a love affair with a Dutch officer called van der Meulen. He was the love of my life – there's usually only one – do you know what I'm talking about?' she looked up suddenly.

'Yes.'

'You do, don't you? I can see it in your face.'

'Go on.'

'Well, he had to go away . . .' She stopped and took a breath. 'I thought he had been killed. I thought so for fifty years. Then, two or three weeks ago, I had a letter from him.'

'Saying?'

'Saying . . .' She shook her head in weary disbelief. 'Saying that he had been captured and sent to a labour camp. When he got out he was in a shocking state. He crawled home to the East, straight into the arms of the Communists. He made a life there, but he never got in touch, never sent a card, a letter, not a single, solitary word. Gradually, I forced myself to forget . . . He wants to come here,' she said, 'and I don't know what to do, whether to say yes or no. I hid it from Guy, naturally. He was away, of course. By the time he came back I was better, not healed, but capable of living . . .'

She blew her nose with a paper handkerchief.

'And you never mentioned it to Guy, in all these years?'

'No. Was that terrible of me?'

'It's perfectly understandable,' he said.

'There's more, David.'

'I thought there might be.'

'I was pregnant when he left. I tried to get rid of it, but in the end I couldn't go through with it.'

'And . . .?'

'My friend Babs arranged it. She had married a laird in the Highlands. He had two estates, one where they lived in Inverness and another by the sea, in the south of Scotland. I went there, to a fishing village in Wigtownshire, to have the baby. It was looked after by the daughter of Babs' husband's old nanny. She had a young family and a husband, and she had just lost a baby. They said it was her sister's, a girl who had gone to the bad, vanished into Glasgow or somewhere like that.'

'Was it a boy or a girl?'

'A boy.'

'And what became of him?'

'I don't know.'

'You didn't keep in touch?'

'Not after a bit. I couldn't bear to. I had to make a life here. Do you see that?'

'Yes.'

'With Hubert gone, I could let him go. He would be all right, the boy, I mean. They were a decent family. I gave them money, quite a lot of money . . . I thought . . . if anyone would get in touch after a long time it would be the boy. I never imagined it would come this way round. I don't want to disturb it, David. I don't want to lift the stone and find the horrors beneath. I can't face it. You see, there's some extra horror in this for me. Guy always wanted a son from me and never had one. He never thought of leaving me to do so, but a son was always the thing for him. Chloe was such a disappointment to him. It's the main reason they don't really get on, which seems absurd when you think about it, but it's true.'

'Rather hard on Chloe,' said David, 'but it's no wonder you haven't been sleeping very well, poor dear.'

'Pathetic, isn't it?'

'No,' he said, putting his hand on her arm, 'not in the least. You loved him. How could it not affect you?'

'But he betrayed me,' she said, 'and that's what sticks in my throat. When I think what I went through. All that time when he was alive and I didn't know.'

'What would you have done?' They paused by the raspberry canes whilst Marjorie examined them.

'Gone to him? Oh, I don't know, I just don't know . . . You can't imagine the relief of telling someone,' she said, moving on again towards the gooseberries.

'That's not surprising,' said David. 'It's a burden you've been carrying round for years and years.'

'But' he added, and hesitated, '. . . didn't you think of the baby?'

'Of course I thought about him' she said savagely, 'how could I not? The years go by, you look at other children of his age and you wonder . . . but I tried not to. What was the point? Our generation' she added, 'don't wallow like the young. We got on with our lives, we had to. I buried my suffering like a dog would deep, deep, deep beneath one of my garden designs. I planted him a garden over and over again. Gradually, you forget. Gradually painful things fade. What should I do? I wish I knew.'

He saw that there were tears in her eyes.

'Does Chloe know any of this?'

'Of course fot. I never told a soul other than Babs, and she's been dead for twenty years.'

'Her husband didn't find out?'

'He was killed in the war. Babs remarried.'

'Perhaps you should tell Chloe. She might help you to decide what to do.'

'What? After the way she behaved the other day, I think that's rather unlikely.'

'She'll come round,' said David, 'especially if she sees that you need her.'

'But I don't want to put any more pressure on her. You know she's having a hell of a time.'

'Sometimes being needed brings out a different part of one,' said David. 'It might develop a part of her that she could then use to help herself.'

'This is very psychological,' said Marjorie. 'It's like playing Mah Jong. Match this and that and then bingo!, a solution. You like her, don't you?' she said sharply.

'Yes. Yes, I do.'

'She's having therapy, I'm sure I told you. I'm awfully dubious about it. They dig and dig and then the patient accuses the parent of never having loved them, which isn't true.'

'I know,' said David soothingly. 'Don't upset yourself. You've enough on your plate as it is.'

'I still don't know what I should do,' she said.

'Do nothing for a few days,' said David. 'I'm a great believer in that. Leave it, and see what comes up.'

'All right,' she said, more cheerfully, 'I will. Why don't you come and get some strawberries for your girls?'

She set off briskly in another direction.

CHAPTER 20

'I'm frightened,' said Chloe into the therapeutic silence of Fanny's consulting room, 'and I want to talk about it.'

Fanny was silent.

'I've met a man,' said Chloe, 'an unobtainable man.'

'Unobtainable?' queried Fanny.

'He's a priest,' said Chloe, with difficulty. She could already feel a terrible reluctance creeping over her. She didn't want to be judged by Fanny. She didn't want to imagine what Fanny must think of her when she said such a thing. How she must despise and loathe her.

'I see,' said Fanny neutrally.

'An unobtainable man who seems to embody everything I'm looking for. He's so kind to me, and so understanding that . . .' She hesitated. 'That I feel absurdly tender about him. I'm sure,' she added, 'that he's only doing his job, but that makes it worse.'

'"Absurdly tender",' said Fanny, quoting her. 'What do you mean by that?'

'Kind in a way . . . that makes me feel grateful, I suppose,' said Chloe. 'I can't think why anyone should bother, and then when they do . . . well, I feel this great rush of gratitude and . . .' She found the word that came to mind was 'lust' but instead she said 'affection', thinking it more suitable for Fanny.

'I think,' said Fanny carefully, 'that when people take an interest in our lives we do feel something akin to love for them. It is, after all, one of the staples of any kind of relationship between man and woman, man and man, woman and woman, adults and children. There is a pointed and delighted interest in the minutiae of other lives. But,' she added, 'you should be very careful of the erotic element.'

'Erotic element?' said Chloe, but she could feel herself blushing.

'I'm trying, with your help, to sort out what you really are feeling,' said Fanny. 'Love. Gratitude. They are not the same thing. You talk of feelings of tenderness towards someone you

172

classify at the same time as being "unobtainable". What we are looking at here is a problem of the transference.'

'Oh,' said Chloe, mortified. She blushed again.

'An interest in one stirs, say, feelings, as in your case, of love and gratitude,' said Fanny. 'Your marriage is foundering, Chloe, think about what that might mean when you meet an attractive, sympathetic, tender man. One assumes that what one is is feeling oneself is being felt by the other person: that is the basis upon which human intercourse works, therefore you might assume that he is also feeling love and gratitude towards you, and that is where you have to be very careful to make distinctions.'

'Distinctions,' said Chloe. 'What? Between gratitude and lust, you mean?'

She was angry and uncomfortable and felt somehow robbed.

'Well done, Chloe,' said Fanny, watching attentively.

'Why "well done"?' asked Chloe crossly.

'Because you've made an important distinction, the one that matters,' said Fanny.

'I suppose,' said Chloe, encouraged by this praise in spite of herself, 'it is possible to love without doing anything. I hadn't thought of that.'

'Go on.'

'Well, sex, I suppose I mean,' said Chloe. 'One thinks that all affection must be rewarded in a physical way.'

'Does one?'

'Well . . . I think I do,' said Chloe. 'If I hold back then he might mistake my feelings.'

'Which are?'

'That I like him and I'm terribly grateful. The thing is, Fanny,' she said, 'he's terribly needy too. I don't think he's very happy.'

'Then he must deal with that himself,' said Fanny firmly. 'It's not up to you to make him better. He may, without knowing it, be looking for someone to do just that: he may be looking for Mummy to soothe his own wounds. You can't do that, Chloe.'

'No,' said Chloe. 'You're right, I can't.'

'People in my profession and the Church, the so-called "caring professions",' said Fanny, 'are very often the walking wounded, you know. They take up pastoral roles of various kinds because it

173

makes them feel powerful. Helping people is tremendously satisfying. And then, of course, everyone is so grateful. All the things one's trying to escape from are soothed by this love, this gratitude.'

'Do you feel like that?' asked Chloe curiously.

'A part of me does, yes,' said Fanny. 'I would be lying if I said it didn't. But I am constantly on my guard against it.'

'I went to see a lawyer,' said Chloe, after a minute.

'How did that go?'

'It was harrowing. He was so amused and complacent, and so . . . competent.'

'Amused?'

'Perhaps I don't mean amused, perhaps I mean he felt superior, listening to the tawdry little mess my life seems to have got into.'

'"Tawdry", "little",' said Fanny, shaking her head. 'You are grappling with a major upheaval in your life. I should hardly describe it as "little" or "tawdry". What have you decided to do?'

'Exchange of letters setting out what information is needed. He knows Rupert's man. They all know one another. It's like a club. The law is a club, a man's club.'

'Perhaps you should find a woman solicitor.'

'Mummy was keen I should use Digard. She knows the firm.'

'Do you always have to do what your mother wants?'

'No,' said Chloe without conviction.

'And Rupert? How is he taking this?'

'I'm to see him tonight or tomorrow,' said Chloe. 'I dread it. He has a way of making me feel guilty about everything.'

'Why do you feel so guilty, Chloe?'

'Because I'm breaking up the happy home . . .' Chloe's voice trailed off.

'"Happy home"? Is it so very happy?'

'No.' Chloe shook her head.

'Then . . .?'

'I know,' said Chloe, sighing. 'But knowing something intellectually isn't the same as knowing it in your heart. I still feel guilty even though I know I shouldn't.'

'What do you want?'

'"What do women want?"' Chloe smiled. 'I want someone to

make up my mind for me and then execute a decision in my name. I want a man on a white charger to come along and take me away from all this.'

'Another Rupert, perhaps?'

'God forbid!' said Chloe automatically, and then she stared at Fanny. 'Are you trying to tell me something?'

'Concentrate, Chloe,' said Fanny, leaning forwards. 'You're so nearly there.'

CHAPTER 21

'Cheer up, darling,' said Pete, Lucy's boss, as he passed by her desk. 'You look like a wet weekend.'

'I feel like one too,' said Lucy despondently.

'How's the bio-panic?' asked Pete, perching on a corner of Lucy's desk.

'The what?'

'Hormones, lover-boy, all that.'

'Frightful,' said Lucy. 'I'm pregnant.'

'Is that good or bad?' asked Pete quietly.

'Both.'

'Shit, darling. How did it happen?'

'You're a grown man – how do you think?'

'Lucien and I are not contemplating having a baby, darling.'

'I thought I could convince him,' said Lucy, 'and then it turned out I couldn't. I've hardly seen him since I broke the news.'

'So what are we going to do?' Pete took Lucy's hand in his. 'Have an abortion, have the baby, what?'

'I loathe the idea of abortion,' said Lucy. 'I'm a Catholic.'

'A Catholic in a mess,' said Pete. 'I thought there was something in the rules about adultery, or did we just forget?'

'Don't rub it in,' said Lucy.

'Well, what *are* we going to do? Either way I support you, darling, you know that.'

'Thanks, Pete.'

'So lover-boy's got in a panic. What shits men are.'

'He says it's happened twice before. Once with his first wife and then again with his second.'

'Sounds like he has a problem.'

'He does. I think he'll end up going back to his wife, if she'll have him.'

'Silly cow should run for it.'

'She used to be my best friend,' said Lucy sadly.

'My God, darling, what a disaster! Have you got a nice quack?'

'Yes.'

'Go and see her. She'll be able to help you make up your mind.'

'I'll do that.'

'Kiss, kiss.' Pete jumped down, dropped a kiss on the top of Lucy's head and went into his office.

Lucy bent her head again to the project in hand, but she couldn't concentrate. Her body seemed to be secreting some new hormone which induced brain death. She found herself thinking of that first heady occasion when she and Ru became lovers.

She had called in with a present for Miranda, who was her goddaughter, and found Ru at home early from a business trip but no Chloe, who had gone with her mother to Paris for a few days leaving the children in the charge of the au pair and a temporary nanny. She had not been particularly pleased to find Rupert there, but he had asked her to stay for a drink and out of politeness she had accepted. She found herself sitting in Chloe's pretty pink drawing room thinking how much she envied Chloe's life: the handsome husband, the house, the two divine children.

When Ru had suggested dinner (after more of his lavish drinks), she had thought, why not? They had known one another for a long time and, besides, it was only dinner she said to herself. In the car he put on a cassette of Bach – he had a wonderful sound system – and suddenly his hand was on her thigh and they were kissing passionately to the blissful sounds of a Brandenburg concerto.

'Lucy,' he whispered in her ear, making her shiver, 'you don't know how much over the years I've wanted to do this.'

'Me too,' she had answered shamelessly (and untruthfully), returning his kiss.

'Shall we go to your place?'

'What about Chloe?'

'Chloe won't know, will she? Unless you tell her.'

'I won't tell her.'

It was a Rupert speciality, she learned this later, always to pass the buck. *Your* decision, *your* friendship.

'Neither will I, although she wouldn't mind. We've more or less agreed we can do what we want.'

'Have you?' She looked at him in amazement. This was not the truth according to Chloe.

'She rather went off it when Miranda was born. She had such a ghastly time.'

'Poor Chloe.' Lucy kissed him again.

'She's a wonderful person,' he said. 'I really admire Chloe. She has courage and endurance and she's incredibly clever.'

'Isn't she just?'

Thus they had neutralized their guilt by admiring the person whom they were harming. After they had made love, Rupert talked of Chloe again, saying how much he admired her free spirit. She was like her mother, he said, in that respect – and Lucy said yes, she was honourable and a wonderful friend who never let her down. She adored her and Miranda and darling James. She must never know, Rupert said, because she had been having such problems lately. She had been so difficult and sad and he had wondered about counselling or some form of help, and what did Lucy think about that? It was why he had thought sending her off to Paris would do her good.

'Sounds like depression,' said Lucy.

'That's right, depression,' Ru agreed, and fell asleep.

In spite of the commendable desire to keep their affair secret, passion, like yeast in a warm cupboard, had grown wildly, sprouting recklessness and cruelty and indifference. Lucy had foolishly started to write letters to Ru, who was really awfully vague. Chloe had found one in his suit pocket when she went to look for some money to pay the cleaning woman with. Ru, who had gone to the office by then in his air-conditioned car with the Bach playing, was astonished and taken aback to get Chloe on the phone threatening him with instant divorce if he didn't come home and explain himself.

Of course he denied it, but she had brandished the letter at him and he had then said it was nothing, that he thought she had said he was free, and she had yelled that that was something he had cooked up himself and was nothing to do with anything she remembered saying. Chloe, according to Rupert, had cried and got drunk and gone to bed. In the meantime, Lucy played the siren: a calm, groomed siren in her immaculate flat. She never yelled, she never cried.

Chloe went round to confront Lucy. When Lucy opened her front door, she had pushed past her into the sitting room.

'You don't know what you've done,' she said coldly. She appeared quite calm, except there was a red flush on her neck.

'I didn't mean to,' said Lucy.

'But you did it.'

'You would have done the same.'

'No, I wouldn't,' said Chloe savagely, 'and I didn't think you would either. Where's all your piety now, I'd like to know?'

'That is none of your business,' said Lucy.

'But it is my business,' said Chloe loudly. 'That's why I'm here. We weren't happy, you knew that, but for you of all people to get involved with Rupert is more than I can bear. I thought you were my friend.'

'I am,' said Lucy.

'You can't be,' said Chloe. 'Not now.' She shook her head. 'Not ever. It's all right,' she said. 'I'll see myself out.'

Rupert's plane touched down at four-thirty and he was through Customs twenty minutes later as he made a point on short trips such as this one never to carry any luggage other than hand luggage. He retrieved his green Daimler from the short-term car park and drove as fast as he dared into London. When he got to Pembroke Road Andrew was out. The flat had a dirty, deserted air. A dinner party had obviously taken place the night before: the kitchen was full of empty bottles and plates encrusted with dried food. Nelly, Andrew's cleaning lady who usually cleared up this sort of thing, quite plainly hadn't come that day. Her money lay on the table with a note. Rupert picked it up, read it and put it down again. He went into his room and saw that Andrew had put his post on his bed. He threw aside several bills and boring-looking circulars and opened a letter from his solicitor, Jonathan Sturt, informing him that his wife had started divorce proceedings. A copy of Digard's letter was enclosed for his information. Rupert read the letters and then tore them both into tiny pieces which he flung in the direction of the wastepaper basket. He went into the sitting room and poured himself a whisky and soda. He felt, unusually for him, depressed, despondent. He didn't want to ring Lucy although he knew he should;

Chloe, he was sure, would be halfway to Fordingbridge by now. In spite of this certainty, he picked up the phone and dialled the house in Brook Green. An answering machine cut in swiftly, followed, surprisingly, by Chloe's voice.

'Hello,' she said uncertainly. 'Who is it?'

'It's me. Rupert.'

'Oh.'

'Were you expecting it to be someone else?'

'No,' she said, sounding offended.

'Why aren't you in the country?'

'I'm going in the morning. I'm tired tonight. Couldn't face the drive.'

'It's a long way for a day and a half.'

'Yes,' she said, 'it is.'

'How are the children?'

'Fine. James has been to Charlie's party and he's exhausted. Miranda is here. Do you want to speak to her?'

'It's you I want to speak to really.'

'What about?'

'I've had a letter from Sturt. Can I come round?'

'I don't think that's a very good idea.'

'Please,' he said. 'I need to talk to you.' Be careful, Sturt had said in his covering note. Digard is famous for getting blood out of a stone.

'I can't face rows,' she said bleakly. 'I'm tired, Rupert.'

'Just for a minute,' he said.

'You always get your own way,' she said. 'All right, but only for half an hour. I'm exhausted.'

When she opened the door, he tried to kiss her but she ducked her head to avoid him.

'That's not very friendly,' he said.

'Miranda's waiting upstairs,' said Chloe over her shoulder. 'She's dying for you to read her a story. Come down and we'll have a drink when you've done.'

She was sitting with her legs curled up under her, a glass by her side on the table under the lamp, when he came in. She looked up and he saw that she was indeed exhausted. There were dark circles under her eyes and something in her expression he couldn't quite put his finger on that made her look both vulnerable and, at the same time, knowing. Seeing that bloody lawyer probably had something to do with it.

'All well?' she asked.

'I read her *Cinderella*,' he said, pouring himself a drink. 'It's still her favourite.'

'I know.' Chloe smiled. 'How was Paris?'

'Fine'

'What were you doing there?'

'The usual.'

Chloe stared into her drink. The usual. Years ago, before she had had children, she used to go to Paris with Ru sometimes. After they had been born she had got into the habit of staying at home when, probably, she ought to have been with him.

'Chloe, there's something I want to say to you,' he said.

'Yes?'

'I think we ought to give it another go.'

'Digard has written to Sturt about that,' she said evasively. 'Anyway, what about Lucy?'

'That's . . .' He hesitated for a second. 'That's over and done with. It hasn't worked out.' He didn't mention the baby. Perhaps she would have had the good sense to get rid of it by now.

'I see.'

'We owe it to one another to have another go,' he said. 'Well, what do you think?' he went on when she said nothing.

'I don't know what I think about anything at the moment,' said Chloe. 'I'm in a state of flux.'

Something about Rupert frightened her. She wanted to be more definite in her rejection of him, but was unable to summon the courage.

'So where does that leave me?' He sounded impatient, as if he was engaged in a business negotiation that was not going the way he planned.

'It leaves you where you put yourself,' said Chloe daringly. 'You were the one, after all, who chose to leave.'

'I know,' he said in a humble voice, but she could see she had made him angry. He was so used to getting his own way with her. He expected her to obey him. He had always treated her like a child. What was it Fanny had said to her? 'Concentrate, Chloe, you're so nearly there . . .'

'It's not just the question of Lucy,' she said, 'although that's obviously important, it's a question of how we relate to one another.'

'That's obvious, isn't it?' he broke in impatiently.

'You won't let me finish.'

'OK,' he said reluctantly, 'say what you have to say.'

'I was going to say,' said Chloe, 'that you're so used to getting your own way. You treat me like a child. I'm not a child.'

He was bored and restless when she was talking, she could see that. He was a child in that sense himself, an imperious, spoilt, adored boy-king who had never been properly disciplined.

'Our relationship needs adjusting if it's to work.'

'What do you suggest?'

'I'm not suggesting anything at the moment, just turning over ideas.'

'I want to come back,' he said, looking round the room. 'I want to be with my children. I don't want those blood-suckers interfering in our life together.'

'I'll have to think about it,' said Chloe. 'I can't give you an answer now.'

'Why not?'

'If you can't see that, then there's no hope for us.'

'Oh, don't be so dramatic, Chloe,' he said. 'You always like to dramatize everything.'

'I'm sorry you feel that,' she said, sniffing.

'Silly sausage.' He got up and went to where she sat and put his arms around her. 'A silly sausage.'

Chloe closed her eyes. It was so lovely to have a pair of strong arms around her that she was almost convinced it would work. She felt she lacked the energy to resist Ru. She was too tired to fight.

'You go away for the weekend,' he said, 'and I'll be here when you come back.'

'No.' She shook her head. 'I need more time than that, Ru. Please give me time.'

'All right, little Chloe,' he said. 'I'll give you time.' He got up, ruffled her hair like one might pat a favourite dog and went to the drinks tray. 'For you?'

'No. I'm going to bed in a minute.'

'Let me stay in the spare room, Chloe, please. I think I've had too much to drink.'

'Have you?' She frowned, wanting space, distance, aware, even in her exhaustion, of how important it was that she keep as clear a head as she could manage.

'I don't want to get stopped, not again.'

'All right,' said Chloe. 'I'm going up now. See you in the morning.'

As she lay in bed, she could hear Rupert moving around, going in and out of the bathroom, then the sound of his door closing reached her and she slept. Her last thought before she went under the waves was that it was good of him not to come and try to kiss her good night. In the night she woke with a jump at the sound of her bedroom door opening. She sat up in bed and said, 'Who is it?'

'It's only me,' said Rupert, coming in and closing the door behind him.

'What do you want?'

'To talk.'

'I'm tired, Ru, so tired. Even when I do sleep I wake up feeling tired.'

'Just let me hold you,' he said.

'I don't want you to hold me.'

'Look,' he said thickly, 'you're my wife.' There was whisky on his breath. He must have woken or been unable to sleep and gone downstairs. He had probably been drinking for hours. She should have locked her door, but then of course there were the children.

'I know I'm your wife,' said Chloe, 'but it's late. Let me take you back to your room.'

'This is my room,' said Rupert with the maddening literalness of drunks, and climbed into bed.

'Please, Rupert!' Chloe could feel a part of herself becoming hysterical.

'Jus' hol' you,' he said, pushing his face into her hair. 'Jus' a li'l cuddle, shat's all. I mish you, Chloe, I'm shorry.'

Chloe allowed him to hold her. After five minutes he fell asleep and began to snore very loudly, so loudly that Chloe slid out of bed and went to the spare room. The bedclothes looked as if he had had a terrible fight with them and there was a cigarette smouldering in an ashtray on the bedside table.

What am I going to do? Chloe asked herself as she pulled the sheets up, but then too tired to even attempt an answer, she fell into a heavy sleep.

The following week, Chloe cancelled her appointment with Fanny, pleading illness. She knew enough about the therapeutic discipline to know damn well what interpretation Fanny would place on this bogus illness, but, somehow, she felt unable to take any more of Fanny's doses for leading a healthy mental life. Perhaps, as she herself had said to him at that first dinner, David was the person she should confide in. She found it so easy to talk to him whereas Fanny made her flush and feel awkward. And she often didn't know what to say to Fanny either. She was fed up with Fanny's superiority, the way she always had to be one jump ahead. Chloe was desperately in need of someone who could *empathize* with her, and David was so good at that. Plus the fact that he knew her mother and father and what they were like. He *understood*. She knew he did.

The same week as she had cancelled Fanny, Chloe rang David in Fordingbridge, reasoning with herself that it was perfectly all right in the cirumstances for her to do so.

The phone rang for ages before it was picked up, and then, to Chloe's displeasure, it turned out to be the dragon wife, the feminist freedom fighter.

'Could I speak to David Doughty, please?'

'I'm afraid he's not here at the moment,' replied the FFF. 'Would you like to leave a message?' She didn't ask who it was, thought Chloe, the bitch. She must know it's me.

'It's Chloe Durrell,' she said.

'Oh yes, hello.' No warmth, nothing.

'When will he be back?'

'Not until seven or so. Is it urgent?'

'No,' said Chloe. 'Could he ring me in London, do you think?'

'It would be better if you tried after seven,' said Frances. 'We have to save money on the phone bill, I'm afraid.'

'I see,' said Chloe, and almost said, 'Tell him to reverse the charges', but then thought better of it.

'I'll ring later, then.'

Fortifying herself with several drinks, Chloe rang David just before eight. This time, he answered the phone.

'Chloe,' he said in his genial way. 'How are you?'

'All right, *just*,' she said.

'What's been happening to you?'

'Rupert wants to come back, he's said so.'

'What do you want?'

'I don't know.'

'But you must have some feelings on the subject.'

'I'm torn,' said Chloe. 'I feel scared on my own. The responsibilities weigh me down, the children . . . making the right decision is crucial for them, but I just don't know . . .'

'You sound tired,' said David kindly. 'The great thing is not to let Rupert rush you into anything. Take your time, go at your own pace. What does your therapist say?'

'I haven't seen her.'

'Have you given up seeing her?'

'Not exactly, it's just . . . I told you . . . I find it all so difficult. It's much easier to talk to you.'

'I want to help you,' he said, but his voice went a shade, a very faint fraction, colder, 'but it's you who is in charge, Chloe, not me, not the therapist.'

There was a pause, and then he said, 'Are you still there?'

'Yes.'

'Are you all right?'

'I'm fine.'

'Your mother needs to see you. She needs a visit. Are you coming down soon?'

'I've just been' she said.

'I think you should come as often as you can,' he said. 'She needs your support. You know how she seems, strong as an ox, but she isn't.'

'What's happened?'

'Come and see her for yourself,' he said.

'Will you be there . . . at the weekend?'

'Of course. Priests don't go away for the weekend, on the whole.'

'Perhaps I could see you then?'

'Absolutely. Give me a ring when you get here.'

'I will,' said Chloe. 'Thanks, David . . .'

She put the phone down and felt herself full of a desire to see him and to talk to him. Saturday, then. She wondered what he was getting at about her mother. Nothing much, probably. Just Marjorie up to her manipulating tricks, as usual.

CHAPTER 22

'I'm going to pull off, you two,' said Chloe. 'I'm shattered and you need lunch. OK?'

'OK,' said James. 'Good idea, Mum. Do you want me to look at the map to see where we are?'

'That would be heaven,' said Chloe, patting his bare knee. He was so adorable the way he wanted to help her. And he knew, from long experience, how she could never find her way properly anywhere, although anything, she thought, was better than south of the river.

'Are we lost?' asked Miranda.

'No, dummy,' said James. 'We're going to have lunch somewhere. Didn't you hear what Mum said?'

'Can I have some crisps?' asked Miranda.

'Of course you can, darling. Let me find somewhere that looks nice first.'

Chloe drove for some time through quiet tree-lined lanes, where the cow parsley grew shoulder high on the verges. In the fields huge cream-coloured cattle grazed contentedly under beech trees.

'It's like France here,' said Chloe, going slower and slower so she could stare at things.

'It's called Great Easton,' said James. 'There's the sign.'

'Oh, yes,' said Chloe, 'never heard of it.'

'Here we are,' said James as they went round a corner. 'Here it is. Look, Mum, there's a pub.'

'It's a hotel,' said Miranda, 'not a pub.'

'It's the same thing, nerd-face,' said James.

'He called me –'

'Be quiet,' said Chloe, 'or I'll crash and it'll be your fault.'

She drove past the hotel, up a deep lane and round the side of an ancient church built out of honey-coloured stone with a square tower which loomed above them. Ahead was a stone bridge of the same colour as the church and a street or houses, one of which was set back behind a high wall. There was another pub called the Great Easton Arms, yet another ancient building with a coat of arms over the doorway.

'Go into the garden,' said Chloe, 'and I'll find out what there is to eat.'

She watched them run outside and then sat down at the bar and lit a cigarette whilst she considered the menu.

'Mum,' said James, coming back in, 'there's a man in the garden who's doing a painting. He's called Patrick. He's got a black Labrador called Poppy who's eating sticks.'

'Oh, really?' said Chloe, watching her gin being poured. 'Well don't be a nuisance. Painters hate people hanging around them interrupting.'

'Miranda's playing with his dog,' said James. 'That's OK, isn't it?'

'Perfectly, I'm sure,' said Chloe. 'I don't mean to sound fierce. Now, darling, what do you want? A baked potato with something in it? Lasagne? Pork chop?'

'Can I have scampi,' asked James, 'and chips? Miranda will have that too.'

'How do you know?'

'She always wants what I have.'

'All right.' Chloe laughed. 'I'll order it. Go outside. I'll join you in a minute.'

She went out of a French window and into the sun. She would never forget the moment: the strongest sensation of déjà vu: smells of box, something herby – rosemary, perhaps, thyme – sun on stone: man in battered panama hat and wrecked, painterly clothes on a canvas stool in front of an easel: dog bounding about as if on springs: children calling. A sentence came into her mind from a Sacred Ritual Chant: 'Give thanks for unknown blessings already on their way.'

She made her way into the garden, and the painter stood and took off his hat, revealing a head of hair which reminded her of Whistler's tumbled locks. The dog ran up and sniffed her hand, wagging so hard that its whole body gyrated like a belly dancer's.

'Hello,' said Chloe, smiling. 'Are they bothering you? I'm sorry we're disturbing your tranquillity. This is a lovely place. I'd no idea it existed.'

'It's all right,' said the man. 'The dog needs friends. She thinks my brushes are sticks: she's always pestering me to throw

188

them for her. I'm Patrick Churchill, by the way. How do you do?'

'Chloe Durrell.'

'Nice boy, that,' said Patrick. 'He came straight up and introduced himself and shook me by the hand.'

'Oh, good,' said Chloe, trying her best not to smirk with pride. 'It's good to know that expensive education is having some effect. I hope Miranda was as polite.'

'She's a menace,' said Patrick, watching her race the dog, 'but a charming one.'

'May I buy you a drink?' asked Chloe.

'I was on my way in to get a pint,' said Patrick, 'but thank you all the same. What about you?'

'I've got one, thank you,' said Chloe, noticing a large streak of blue paint on his arm.

'I'll be out in a minute,' he said, and then, seeing what she was looking at, he said, 'It's amazing, cobalt blue, it gets everywhere.'

Chloe noticed that his shoes were covered in splashes as well as his clothes.

She sat down and thought of nothing in particular, gazing about her at the pretty garden and the ancient back part of the inn. After a minute, she realized that what she was feeling was happiness. She was so unaccustomed to it that she scarcely recognized it.

'Enjoying the sun?'

Patrick sat down opposite her with his drink.

'Yes, it's bliss. I was thinking what a pretty spot this is. We're here quite by accident.'

'Your children told me,' he said, looking at her with interest. She had a face that appealed to him: her bone structure was very good and she would be rewarding to paint.

'Are you here by accident as well?' she said, slightly embarrassed by his scrutiny and wondering what he was looking for.

'Not quite. We're in the district for a few days' – he nodded in the direction of the dog – 'roaming about finding subjects to paint. I'm having a show in London soon, in Cork Street, and I need a few potboilers.'

'Oh, I see.' It amused Chloe to think of items other than books as being potboilers. 'May I come?'

'If you want to,' he said self-deprecatingly. 'Give me your name and address and I'll see you get an invitation.'

'Do you do watercolours too? I'm fond of watercolours.'

'Yes, I do.'

He waited to see if she would say which painters she admired. So many attractive girls fell at the first hurdle. They liked Hockney and Picasso and ghastly dregs like Bonnard and Dufy.

'And portraits?'

'Yes, those too.'

'Sargent is my favourite portrait painter,' she said. 'Of course, that's to be dreadfully reactionary, isn't it? He's always getting biffed about in the newspapers by critics who like installations and piles of bricks. I loathe modern art, or most of it. It seems to have got into a dead end. All it can do is to make snide comments about society and then give itself an Arts Council grant.'

'I couldn't agree more,' he said. 'Have you had your portrait done?'

'Rupert ... my husband ... wanted me to be painted by someone or other, I can't remember his name, but all his clients looked the same: chocolate box poses and streaked hair. Oh, and taffeta, mustn't forget the taffeta.'

Patrick laughed. 'Then,' he said, 'there's Hugo Drane. His sitters look as if they've been fragged, limbs detached from torsos like the aftermath of an explosion.'

Chloe laughed aloud.

'What's funny, Mum?' asked James, coming up. 'Come on, Poppy,' he said, 'I'll throw a stick for you.'

'When's lunch?' asked Miranda. 'Can I have some crisps?'

'Soon,' said Chloe. 'Yes, you can have some crisps as a special treat.'

'Hurray!' said Miranda.

'But you'll have to get them, OK?'

'OK,' said Miranda, taking the money.

'How old is she?' asked Patrick.

'Seven.'

'A handful.'

'She is,' said Chloe. 'James is a dream child and she's the opposite. She's great fun, too,' she added loyally.

'Got an old-fashioned face,' said Patrick. 'She's quite like you, I think.'

'She's really the image of my mother.'

'Where do you live?'

'In London, Brook Green, but we're on our way to Fording-bridge in Gloucestershire.'

'I know it. Lovely stone bridge, and there's a castle with a famous garden. I've painted there.'

'My parents live at the castle,' said Chloe. 'They're the garden-ers, Guy and Marjorie Jessop.'

'Of course!' said Patrick. 'That's who you remind me of. I've seen her on television, haven't I? I only watch it twice a year and one of those times was your mother with the Prince of Wales. She's very beautiful,' he said. 'I remember her well.'

'Yes, she is,' said Chloe. 'She was done by Birley when she was young, but she still looks marvellous, even in her seventies. In some ways more so.'

'Good bones,' said Patrick, 'and a life well spent, I daresay.'

'I sometimes wonder,' said Chloe.

He gave her a startled glance.

'Well,' she added, 'I can't help thinking how much of our parents' lives are a mystery to us. You'd expect to know every-thing about them, and yet you don't.'

'But we only know what people choose us to know,' said Patrick. 'That applies as much to our parents as it does to husbands and wives and to friends.'

'What happens when you find out things you don't want to know?' said Chloe. 'Things that alter the perfect picture?'

'You have to accept them,' he said. 'What else can you do?'

'I'm always putting people on pedestals and then, when they fall off, I get a terrible fright.'

'Lack of confidence,' said Patrick.

'Is that what it is? How do you know that?'

'I've spent a long time thinking about it,' said Patrick. 'No, seriously, I don't know of course, because I don't know you. Are you married?' In spite of the children and the mention of a husband, she didn't seem very married.

'I'm semi-married,' said Chloe. 'It's a new state of being.'

'What does it mean?'

'It means I can't decide whether it's worth going on with or not.'

Patrick raised his eyebrows at this. 'That just sounds like normal to me,' he said. 'Do you live with him?'

'He moved out. Now he wants to move back in. I'm undecided. And garrulous,' she said. 'I can't think why I'm telling you this.'

'Sometimes it's good to talk to strangers,' he said.

'But rather dreary for them.'

'Not necessarily. Did you put the husband on a pedestal?'

'I suppose so.'

'And now *he's* fallen off.'

'I'm afraid he has.'

'Did you nudge him? Were you in any way glad?'

Chloe looked at him in silence. 'Do you know,' she said after a bit, 'I hadn't really thought of it like that. Yes, maybe in some ways I was. It meant I had another chance to start again.'

Afterwards, as they drove on to Fordingbridge, Chloe went over the things they had talked about in her mind. He was intelligent and amusing and seemed to have thought deeply about a number of things. She thought of Rupert's brittle, cultural gloss, so dearly achieved, so carefully burnished (and which had, once upon a time, so greatly impressed her), and saw, with sadness, that civilization had only gone so deep with poor Ru, half an inch, perhaps, into the subsoil and withered, rather as she had read somewhere that plants in Arabia withered when they reached the scorching salt layer just below the surface.

'I liked him,' said Miranda. 'Did you, Mum?'

'Yes, I did.'

'Can we see him again?' asked James. 'He said he would show me how to grind paint and things. And I liked Poppy,' he added.

'Poppy,' said Miranda, drawing the name out. 'I *adored* Poppy. Can we have a dog, Mum?'

'No.'

'Why not?'

'Because . . . you know why not. Anyway you've got Nero and Gus.'

'They're not ours.'

'But you can always see them,' said Chloe firmly.

The day before Chloe made her detour and found Great Easton, the Friday, Dr Waller had been summoned to the castle to see Marjorie Jessop.

'Not sleeping?' said the doctor. 'And what else?'

He followed as Marjorie crossed over from one of her borders to another and stood regarding it.

'Have you any ideas for the autumn?' she said, hand on hip. 'My brain's giving way, I think.'

'I'm the last person you should ask,' said Dr Waller, suppressing his exasperation. 'It all looks the same to me. I'm colour blind.' They were in the palette garden staring at a vast clump of some unknown plant.

'What's that?' he asked.

'Moonshine,' said Marjorie.

Dr Waller glanced at her and then down at his pad. 'I don't feel I'm getting through,' he said.

'My leg hurts a bit,' said Marjorie, 'but I'm used to it. And sometimes I get . . .' She wanted to tell him about her spells of blackness, but decided against it. He would only try and get her to stay in bed and that was the one thing she would not do. She wanted to spend as much of her life as she could in the open air.

'More than it used to?'

'Not really,' said Marjorie, moving along a few feet, thinking how well the hemerocallis had done this year, marvellous choice of colours too these days.

'It's the sleeplessness I can't stand,' she said. 'Forced to confront the abyss of the self night after night. It's intolerable.'

'Is there anything troubling you?'

'I think it's just anno domini,' said Marjorie evasively; a part of her was now thinking of potentilla. 'Can you give me some more of those divine sleeping pills? I can't remember what they're called.'

'I'll give you a few more,' said Dr Waller, 'and then you can tell me how you're getting on.'

'I've told you,' she said. 'I'm getting on badly. That's why you're here.' She pushed up the sleeves of her shirt. 'It only means I have to ring your receptionist and bother her. She's got enough to do.'

'Ten days' supply,' he said, writing something in his impossible doctor's hand.

'I don't see why I should have to haggle with you,' said Marjorie, turning to face him. 'Your darling father never made me jump through a few hoops for a handful of miserable sleeping pills.'

'Times change,' said Dr Waller.

'And not for the better, either. I'll take up pot,' she said, turning back towards the phlox.

'Probably do you good,' he said.

'We don't grow it, as a matter of fact, but it's such a *pretty* plant it's rather a shame really.'

'I want to keep an eye on you,' said the doctor. 'You look peaky. It may mean a few days in hospital.'

'Over my dead body,' said Marjorie. 'I mean it. I know Wayemouth General. Never a moment's peace. There's always somebody coming along wanting to give you something or take your pulse or sell you disposable knickers.'

'I didn't know they sold disposable knickers.'

'You're a man. Of course you don't know.'

'I'll be back on Monday,' he said, 'or Tuesday if I can't. Try and be quiet, don't do too much. No digging.'

'I don't dig, I kneel.'

'Slow down,' he said, 'or I'll have you carted off.'

'How is she?' asked Guy, who had been lying in wait for the doctor at the back of the house where the cars were parked. The dogs were with him, stretched out in the sun.

'Worse than she lets on, I think. She's not sleeping and her leg hurts, which may be the ulcer making a return visit, in itself a general indicator of her state of health. Her heart is slightly dicky, but that's nothing new . . . but I feel there's something else. She's short-tempered, which she isn't normally. Is something bothering her?'

'Well,' said Guy, 'the parson's been to have a chat with her lately about something, but he's up and down the hill like a yo-yo. Marjorie's very fond of him, you see, and he's learning about the plants, or at least that's the story, so that's not unusual in itself. But I told him to keep me posted if there was anything I needed to know, that sort of thing, but he hasn't said a word.'

'Might she possibly have asked him not to?' Sunlight glinted on the doctor's spectacles as he spoke.

'I s'pose so.' Guy stroked his chin meditatively. 'Doughty does rather see himself as an eminence grise, I sometimes think, personal confessor, that sort of thing.'

'Clearly he's obliged to keep his secrets to himself, if asked to,' said the doctor. 'Rather like I am.'

'Yes, but I know you,' said Guy. 'I know you'll tell me what I need to know. I don't altogether trust the padre.'

'Oh, he's quite a good egg,' said the doctor. 'Give him a chance.'

'Perhaps I should ask him myself.'

'What about asking Marjorie direct?'

'Oh, Marjorie can be as close as hell, if you'll forgive my French,' said Guy. 'If she doesn't want to tell you something she won't.'

'Try,' said Dr Waller, glancing at his watch. 'I must be off, but I'll be back on Monday or Tuesday.'

'Good man,' said Guy. 'I'll take your advice and strike while the iron's hot.'

But Guy, having failed to find Marjorie, put off (with considerable relief) having to cross-examine her until the evening.

At half past ten, he put his head round her bedroom door, saw that she was awake and went in. He was wearing his summer pyjams of blue and red stripes and his most comfortable pair of old red leather slippers.

'Hello, m'dear,' he said, 'how's tricks?'

'All right. Why? Has Peter put you on to me?'

'Yes, as a matter of fact.'

Guy hovered at the end of his wife's bed, rather wishing he hadn't come. He loathed difficult chats: so many things better left unsaid. His instinct told him this might be one of them.

'What do you want to say?' asked Marjorie, observing her husband's furtive glances.

'Just wondered how you were doing, that's all.'

'I'm perfectly all right, as you see me.'

'That's not what the quack said.'

'Oh?'

'Thought there might be something on your mind.'

'Such as?'

Phew, thought Guy. She was short-tempered, quack was right. He shrugged like a small boy. 'Didn't really say.' After a minute, he added, 'Is there?'

'I wish you'd stop hovering like that. Why don't you sit down? There is a chair.'

'Don't want to tire you.'

'Do you ever think about the war?' asked Marjorie abruptly.

'Not if I can help it,' lied Guy. 'Why d'you ask?'

'Because I wanted to know.'

He didn't want to ask her why. Feared to know the answer to such a thing. Thoughts of his war surfaced constantly like bubbles from a submerged wreck. Terrible thoughts. Couldn't bear them. Pushed them away. The faces of certain dead hung like masks at the edges of his sleep. Couldn't discuss this sort of thing.

'One of the chaps who was here when you were away has written to me,' said Marjorie. 'Dutchman. He wants to come back and have a look at the place.'

He must have forgotten that she had already mentioned it.

'Oh *him*,' said Guy, with huge relief. 'Is that what you wanted to tell me?'

'I didn't want to tell you anything,' said Marjorie. 'I thought you wanted to tell me something. You seem frightfully anxious. Is everything all right?'

'Everything's fine,' said Guy heartily. 'Bless you, my darling.' He leaned over and kissed her.

'Oh Guy,' said Marjorie, putting her hand to her cheek. 'How sweet you are to me,' she said.

'Better be off,' said Guy. 'Got to get my beauty sleep. Chap from Cassell's is coming tomorrow.'

'So is Chloe.'

'Ah!' He glanced at her. 'How is she?'

'A bit strained.'

'I hope she's not going to be a nuisance.'

'I want to see her.'

'Jolly good, that's excellent then. I don't know why she comes on a Saturday though, it's so short.'

'I don't either,' said Marjorie, 'but I've given up wondering.'

'Absolutely,' said Guy, 'best thing to do. Wondering never got anyone anywhere.'

CHAPTER 23

'Who did you say was coming to lunch?' asked David. It was Saturday morning and he was cooking breakfast while Frances sat at the kitchen table scribbling some notes for another of her earth-shattering lectures.

'Frances?' he said. 'Did you hear me?'

'Yes.' She looked up. 'A friend from the college and her daughter.' She looked down at her pad and began to write again.

'I see.' He prodded the bacon with a fish slice. Since their last attempt at talking, he could practically have counted the exchange of remarks between them of any importance on the fingers of one hand.

'What is her name?'

'Maria.'

'And the child?'

'Natasha.'

'I wish you'd stop doing whatever it is you're doing for a minute and *talk* to me,' he said suddenly.

'What on earth's the matter with you?' Frances slammed her pen down in irritation. 'I'm trying to get something done. Is it a crime?'

'No,' he said, 'no, it's not.'

'You're so tense these days,' she said, 'like a coiled spring. Is there something wrong?'

David looked at her but didn't answer. Then he said, 'Perhaps you'd call the girls. It's ready.' He opened the oven door and got some plates out.

'OK, OK.' Frances pushed her chair back with a screech.

I'll do it,' said Tanya, an hour later, looking up from her maths homework to see her mother struggling with the tin opener. 'You sit down or write your lecture or something. You know how hopeless you are in the kitchen.'

'Are you sure?' asked Frances gratefully.

'Quite sure,' said Tanya, retying her hair and rolling up her sleeves. 'Who are these people anyway?' she said, closing her maths book with relief.

'A friend from the college and her daughter who's Kitty's age.'

'Names?' enquired Tanya.

'Maria and Natasha. Tashie, she's called.'

'Mum?' Tanya turned round from the chopping board as she spoke.

'Yes?'

'What's with you and Dad?'

'Why do you ask?'

'It's just so obvious you can't stand one another.'

'Is it?'

'It is to me,' said Tanya.

'Do you think it is to everyone else?'

'To anyone who knows you, yes.'

'Oh dear.'

'It's not like you to care, surely?'

'To care whether people notice or to care about the relationship?'

'People noticing, dummy,' said Tanya, turning back to peeling garlic cloves with a very sharp knife.

'We can't talk,' said Frances. 'I don't quite know why. But he makes me angry and I make him angry.'

'Then that's why,' said Tanya with remorseless teenage logic. 'Stop being so angry with one another. You're setting us a lousy example. Kitty's beginning to notice too. She's been crying at night.'

'She hasn't!' exclaimed Frances. 'Has she?'

'Yep,' said Tanya. 'I go in and get into bed with her. She likes that.'

'Poor Kitty.'

'You aren't going to split up, are you?' asked Tanya.

'We can't,' said Frances. 'I'm a clergy wife, remember.'

'You don't act like one.'

'Tanya!'

'Well, you don't,' said Tanya. 'You must have known what it was going to be like when you married Dad. You were students together, you knew marriage to a vicar would be for life, didn't you?'

198

'You change as you get older,' said Frances. 'You aren't given a crystal ball when you marry someone, you know.'

'I think you should both try harder,' said Tanya. 'Dad seems miserable and distracted too.'

'He's got those parish ladies to comfort him,' said Frances. 'Lady Jessop and so on. He can go up the hill and cry on her shoulder.'

'You're so mean sometimes,' said Tanya, 'that I'm ashamed of you.'

'What do you want to do?' asked Kitty in a distant voice. She was cross and disliked having this stranger foisted on her. They were seated on the wall which divided the vicarage garden from the graveyard.

'I don't know,' said Tashie. 'Why don't we dance on someone's tomb?'

'That's sacrilegious,' said Kitty.

'What's that?'

'Breaking the peace of anything holy.'

'Graves aren't holy,' said Tashie, jumping down. 'They've just got tons of old bones inside.'

'Why do you want to dance on one then?' said Kitty craftily.

'For kicks,' said Tashie. 'For fun.' She looked up at Kitty. 'You sure know a lot of long words,' she said.

'I like words,' said Kitty, 'I always have.'

'My mother's gay,' said Tashie. 'Bet you didn't know that.'

'What do you mean "gay"? Do you mean she's happy?'

'There's a word you don't know,' said Tashie, crowing. 'She's *gay*, she likes girls,' she added, and upon seeing Kitty's puzzled expression, 'She sleeps with women,' she said. 'Has sex with women.'

'Uuurgh,' said Kitty. 'That makes me feel sick.'

'It doesn't me, I'm used to it.'

'Do you have a father?'

'Everyone has a father, dummy. I just don't know mine, that's all.'

'Where is he?' asked Kitty, also jumping down.

'In London. He sends money, but I don't see him.'

'But why don't you?'

'Maria doesn't want me to. She says I'll get filled up with stuff about how men are superior and all that garbage.'

'Mum thinks women are superior to men,' said Kitty, 'she always has.'

'Does your father help out and stuff?'

They were walking amongst the graves, stopping now and then.

'He does everything,' said Kitty, 'and what he doesn't do, we do. Mum's always busy writing and doing other things. She's hopeless, really. She's always late to get me from school and we never go anywhere and I never have anything that the other girls at school have.'

'Same,' said Tash. 'I never do either. Maria is like that – Viva does the cooking and picks me up from school. I'm afraid Maria's getting tired of Viva.'

'Mum's tired of Dad,' said Kitty. 'They don't speak to one another. Maybe they think we don't notice, but we do. I do.'

'Me too. I'm always having to tell Maria to stop being so horrible to Viva.'

'It's horrible not being grown-up, don't you think? Not being in charge of your life.'

'Maria is talking about going back to New York,' said Tashie, 'and I said I'd like that. I don't want to live in a huge horrible city, but in America kids get to have more control over their own lives. You can divorce your parents in America.'

'Can you really?' Kitty turned her huge blue eyes upon her new friend. 'Would you divorce your mum?'

'I'm thinkin' about it,' said Tashie nonchalantly. 'Look, here's a good one, let's jump about on this and see if the devil pops his head out.'

'This is gorgeous,' said Maria, following Frances into the kitchen where David, in clerical shirt and dog collar, was taking a shepherd's pie out of the oven.

'David, this is Maria Weill.'

'How do you do?' said David. 'I can't shake hands at the moment, as you can see.'

'I do see,' said Maria, looking round her. 'You sure get a lot of space when you're a vicar in the Church of England,' she said. 'This is a palace here.'

'Try living in it in the winter,' said David.

'Oh, is it so much colder here than it is in Wayemouth?'

'We don't have central heating,' said David.

'But you do have an Aga.'

'We do have an Aga, that is correct.'

Frances glanced at her husband. He always became pompous when he was annoyed.

'Shall I lay the table?' she asked.

'No, don't worry your head about that,' he said in a tone heavy with irony. 'I'll do it when I've done this, and everything else.'

'Don't be an early Christian martyr,' she said. 'Maria and I can manage to lay a table between us.' Maria winked at her and Frances began to giggle. She felt like a naughty schoolgirl.

'I'll see if I can find some wine,' she said, going to the larder.

'There isn't any,' said David.

'I brought a bottle,' said Maria. 'Hold on, I'll fetch it. I left it in the lobby someplace.'

'We must have used it up,' said David, whilst Maria was out of the room.

'I guess we must.' Frances folded her arms and stared at her husband with dislike. 'Are you going to behave like this all the way through our meal?'

'Like what?'

'Oh, please,' said Frances, looking away in irritation, setting her earrings swinging. She had been to the hairdresser last week and her short style had become noticeably spikier, like a hedgehog.

'Perhaps you'd be so kind as to inform your daughters and their friend that it is lunchtime.'

'Can't we have a glass of wine first?'

'You can. I'm not drinking today. I have a wedding at four-thirty.'

'Oh, right. I'll call them then.'

In the hall Frances found Maria reading a book, seated on the bottom step of the staircase.

'Is everything OK in there?' she asked. 'David seemed upset about something.'

'Everything's fine,' said Frances gaily. 'I'm going to call the kids in.'

'Give me your hand,' said Maria. 'I was reading about writers and landscape. S'really interesting.'

Frances held out both hands. 'Come on then,' she said.

'Thank you.' Maria stood up, put her hands on Frances' shoulders and looked into her face. Then she kissed her mouth.

'Thank you, darling,' she said.

'I hear you're an opponent of women joining the priesthood,' said Maria to David once they were seated. 'Why is that?' She kicked Frances gently under the table.

'Yes, I am as a matter of fact.'

'Why?'

Kitty and Tanya exchanged a glance; Kitty nudged Tashie who was sitting next to her.

'Because I feel that Synod doesn't have the power to make a change of such magnitude in the way the Church is run.'

'So you're objection is to a technicality then, a dislike of the system?'

'That's not exactly what I meant,' said David. 'I am opposed to the ordination of women because I believe that Christ intended the priesthood to be a male one.'

'Christ had never heard of the priesthood,' said Frances, 'in case you've forgotten.'

'Personally speaking,' said Maria, 'I find the view of God as a male personality unacceptable. The whole thing is incredibly Freudian.'

'By that you mean oppressive, I take it?'

'It's the old father-figure stuff rearing its ugly head all over again, the myth that will keep the world in a permanent state of immaturity.'

'I think we should talk about something else,' said Kitty bravely.

'I suppose you're one of those people who want gender-neutral language in the hymn book and the liturgy,' said David, ignoring her.

'I guess if I ever went to church I might, yeah,' said Maria, nodding her head.

'Who's getting married this afternoon?' asked Tanya in desperation.

'It always puzzles me why people who never go to church have such strong opinions about the way it ought to be run,' said David angrily.

'Am I not allowed an opinion or to ask questions?' enquired Maria, raising her finely marked eyebrows.

'This is intolerable.' David pushed back his chair and stood up. 'I am going,' he said, 'and then you can talk freely about patriarchal domination.' He flung down his table napkin and went out of the room, slamming the door behind him.

'Why do you do it?' asked Tanya, glaring at her mother. 'You knew it would get up his nose.'

'Oh, come on, Kitty Kat,' said Frances, who was in fact more alarmed than she let on by her husband's behaviour. 'Maria asked a question, if you remember ... which she's perfectly entitled to expect an answer to.'

'Oh Mum,' said Kitty reproachfully, 'you're so horrible to him. You ganged up on him, you two,' she said, suddenly shouting. And then burst into tears.

'Come on, K K,' said Tanya, 'I'll come outside with you.' She looked at her mother and then at Maria.

'Now see what you've done,' she said.

CHAPTER 24

As Chloe drew nearer Fordingbridge her spirits began to sink, try as she might to keep them up. She felt that she didn't want to see either of her parents, particularly her father. *He* had rather a large case to answer, as far as Chloe was concerned, but she didn't know how on earth she would ever put it to him. On their way to the castle they came upon him coming out of the undergrowth halfway up the drive carrying a gun. Chloe wasn't going to stop, but he stepped out in front of her so she had to.

'Steady on,' he said. 'This isn't a race track. You were driving like Jehu.'

'Was I?'

'Shouldn't go faster than five miles an hour,' he said. 'That's why we have a sign.'

'All right,' said Chloe impatiently.

'Just pointing it out,' said Guy in rather a miffed voice. 'Hello, chaps,' he said to the children. 'Want to come shooting, James?'

'Yes, please,' said James eagerly. 'Open my door, Grandpa, I can't do it myself because of the stupid child locks. What are you shooting?'

'Squirrels,' said Guy.

'Great!'

'That's not fair,' said Miranda.

'Nothing ever is,' said Chloe. 'Where's Mamma?' she asked her father.

'Search me,' he said, shrugging. 'Could be anywhere. Be nice to her, won't you?'

'Why should I be anything else?' asked Chloe, amazed he should say such a thing.

'She hasn't been herself lately.'

'Oh, right.'

'I'm worried about her.'

'Why?' asked Chloe, feeling rather guilty.

'No particular reason,' Guy said, then turned to James. 'Come on, old man, let's see what we can find.'

*

It was Saturday, but Mrs Bos was in the kitchen making cakes for tea.

'Ah, Miranda,' she said when Chloe came in to say a dutiful hello. 'Just the person. Do you want to help me make a walnut cake?'

'Oh, yes,' said Miranda. 'Can I lick the bowl?'

'You'll have to do a lot more than that,' said Mrs Bos. 'Get yourself an apron and we'll get started. How's Chloe, then?' she said, opening a drawer in the table to look for something.

'Well, thank you,' said Chloe cagily. She didn't want to start a discussion of health with Mrs B. at this stage, otherwise she'd be there all afternoon.

'Your Ma's not so good,' Mrs Bos. said, clashing things about. 'No dinner tonight. I think it's her back myself.'

'Ah,' said Chloe. 'Um, I must just –'

'But she won't listen to me or to Hilda Bowen for that matter, even though Hilda's got this clinic now on Fridays for back sufferers like me at the Health Centre.'

'Where are you going?' shouted Miranda, coming back with an apron.

'Don't you speak to your mother like that,' said Mrs Bos. 'Shouting, indeed!'

'She shouts,' said Miranda cheekily.

'See you later,' said Chloe. 'Save me some cake.'

'She went out on to the parterre and paused for a second. This was one of her favourite parts of the garden. There was something about the yew that always moved her: the blackness of that dark green, coupled with the orange of the fruit on the orange trees and the statues of Demeter and her lost daughter Persephone waiting patiently in their alcoves of yew.

After a minute, Chloe walked down the steps under another arch of yew, wondering if her mother would be somewhere among her great borders, but there was nobody there, not even McCormack in his green gardening apron. The borders were a dream of beauty in the afternoon sunlight, she thought, so, so lovely and so cleverly contrived to look natural when the distance between every petal was planned meticulously by Marjorie. It really was quite something. She walked on into the palette garden and then, seeing the door of the little walled garden was open, she stepped through expecting to find her mother sitting on her pretty wrought-iron bench in her arbour of roses, but although the trug was there and the secateurs, Marjorie's trademarks, Marjorie herself was not to be seen. Again Chloe hovered here, conscious of the beauty of it, wondering why her mother had left the door open. She normally guarded the privacy of this place like Cerberus. She retraced her steps and went out again through the palette garden and down the flight of steps on the far side that led towards the ruins which were on a slight rise. Distantly, she heard a gun go off and wondered if it was James murdering some poor squirrel. But the ruins too were deserted. There was only the sound of the water where the rill ran down towards the pond. Was it her imagination or did she see a figure standing on the bridge? She looked again, but there was nothing. It began to dawn on her that perhaps her mother was trying not to be found.

Chloe walked on up into the woods towards the hermit's hut which had been a charming rustic fancy of Bartholomew Jessop's. Her parents had restored it years ago in the early fifties. As a child, Chloe had gone there to hide or to take her friends. She remembered having her first cigarette in there with Lucy, oh so long ago. She sighed as she remembered this. Memories of happiness associated with Lucy – of which there were a great many – filled her with pain. How could she have jeopardized all that? How could she?

Marjorie was sitting on the stone bench that ran round the inside of the hut. It was cold and shadowy inside compared with the heat and glare of the summer's day outside, but Marjorie did not appear to notice. She was wearing a black linen skirt and a white shirt, a combination she was fond of and which, in spite of its severity, suited her angular looks. Her hat lay on the bench beside her. She was smoking a cigarette, one of a number to judge by the ends that lay round her feet.

'Mamma!' Chloe had to wait for her eyes to adjust to the gloom. 'What are you doing here?'

'Minding my own business.'

'Yes, but . . . why here on such a beautiful day?'

'Why not?' Marjorie looked completely and utterly exhausted. Her skin seemed to have stretched itself tighter over her face like a mask.

'What's the matter?' asked Chloe, suddenly scared.

'Do you really want to know?'

'What do you mean?'

'I'll tell you if you like.'

'Tell me what?'

'The truth. The truth about myself.'

'I don't understand you,' said Chloe in a voice shot with tears. 'I don't know what you mean.'

'Don't be hysterical, Chloe. You always did have a histrionic streak in you. It must come from your father's side. It certainly doesn't come from mine.'

Chloe stared at her mother in dismay. She was like a stranger. Who was this harsh, cold old woman? Where had her mother gone, her real mother, domineering and bossy, but warm?

'You may well look like that,' said Marjorie, still in the same hateful, harsh voice, 'because I am going to tell you the truth about myself. And you won't like it.'

'I don't want to hear,' Chloe, who had been sitting down, jumped up. 'Don't tell me. Why should I have to listen to you?'

'Because somebody has to.'

'Tell David,' said Chloe. 'He can forgive you, I can't.'

'You don't understand,' said Marjorie. 'It's not his forgiveness I want, it's yours. David listens, but he doesn't always understand. To be forgiven, you have first to tell the people you have wronged.'

'You haven't wronged me,' said Chloe wildly. 'You've always been wonderful.'

'Stop gabbling, Chloe. Sit down.'

Chloe did as she was told; there seemed to be no alternative.

'In the war,' said Marjorie, 'I fell in love. *Love*,' she said, stressing the word, 'wildly, passionately, and in the most undignified way, with a man, a Dutchman, who had been wounded and sent here to convalesce.'

'So what?' said Chloe, trying to lighten her sense of dread.

'*Listen!*' said Marjorie fiercely. 'Your father was a prisoner of war by that time, suffering the torments of the damned, and I betrayed him in his own bed time after time, night after night.'

'Shut up,' said Chloe, putting her hands over her ears. 'I don't want to hear this. It's . . . it's disgusting.'

207

'Then I found I was pregnant,' said Marjorie relentlessly. 'Shortly afterwards he was passed fit and sent by his organization back into occupied France. I never heard from him again. I assumed he was dead.'

'What did you do?'

'I thought of having an abortion, but I couldn't go through with it, so . . .' For the first time she faltered.

'You had the baby,' said Chloe, finishing the sentence for her. 'What did you do with it? I mean, is it? . . . Where is −? What was it?' she asked, remembering with sudden pain the time Ru had forced her to have an abortion. She never thought about it, but it was there in her flesh like a piece of broken glass. How, when she had been wheeled into the theatre, she had heard the cries of the new-born babies in the nursery down the corridor. The dreadfulness of it. She had never told her mother.

'A boy.'

'Oh, no!' cried Chloe.

'Does it matter what it was?'

'You always wanted a boy,' said Chloe, 'and you had one. No wonder I was a disappointment.'

'Not to me.'

'Don't lie,' said Chloe angrily. 'You had him adopted, I suppose?'

'Yes.'

'And Daddy never knew?'

'No.'

'But didn't you love him? How could you have done such a thing?'

'I had no choice,' said Marjorie. 'Can't you see that? I tried never to think of him. Better that way.'

'Where is he now?' asked Chloe.

'I'm not sure. He was born in Port David, a fishing village in Wigtownshire.'

'Why there?'

'Because Babs' first husband, Archie, had land and connections there. Babs was the only person who ever knew.'

'Why now?' asked Chloe. 'Why are you telling me this now?' Subtly the balance of the conversation had changed. Chloe felt angry and aggressive. She had a powerful desire to slap her mother's face for her utter, wounding stupidity.

'Because I've heard from him – the baby's father – again.'

'I thought you said he was dead. What do you mean?' In her agitation, Chloe got up and began to pace about.

'I thought he was dead. I told you. I never heard from him. We were going to go away together after the war, when it was over.'

'Oh, wonderful!' said Chloe. 'Wait until Daddy came home and then bugger off.'

Marjorie said nothing for some seconds, then she said, 'These things do happen, you know. Lots of marriages failed after the war when the men came back to women they had forgotten, or who had forgotten them.'

'But not yours. What does he want?'

'To see me. To explain; I suppose.'

'What good could it do? He should have contacted you before. I think it's the most monstrous thing I ever heard.'

'He was in a concentration camp. When it was liberated at the end of the war he went home to his mother's estate in Germany where he had been raised, only to run into the Communist net. There was nothing much he could have done,' she added, stumbling like a runner out of breath.

'I don't believe you can want to make excuses for him,' said Chloe. 'You don't still love him, do you?' Could one take it out, dust it off after all these years and imagine it to be love?

'I don't know.'

'How did you and Daddy manage, then?'

'We had lives to lead,' said Marjorie bleakly. 'We got on with it, we had to.'

'But loving someone else,' said Chloe. 'How could you be with Daddy if you loved someone else?'

'We always got on,' said Marjorie, who was beginning to recover something of her usual form. 'We always liked one another. We had shared interests, shared passions. That's what keeps people together in the end, intellect, not sex.'

'So you let Daddy have his bits on the side. How many were there before Marion?'

'One, two, I'm not sure.'

'Did you know them?'

'One of them. She was a cousin of the Hanburys.'

'But you didn't mind?'

'It wasn't a question of minding. He needed someone to sleep with.'

'Didn't you feel threatened? Didn't you think he might go off with one of these women and have children, the son he always wanted?'

'Your father would never have left me,' said Marjorie.

'But he might if he knew your secret.'

'Never,' said Marjorie.

'Are you going to tell him?'

'Of course not.'

'What are you going to do about this man?'

'I don't know.'

'You're not going to let him come here, surely?'

'I told you,' said Marjorie, 'I haven't decided.'

Chloe left the hut and went down into the town through the woods and then the flower meadows. She could hear the bells ringing, which must mean there was a wedding. She had to catch David before he vanished. She had to speak to him. She felt scorched by the knowledge of her mother's past; it was a corrosive story because it ate away at the foundations of what Chloe had always believed to be true. If her impression of her parents' marriage was false, then who was she? A terrible sense of panic gripped her. There seemed nothing left for her to believe in, as if, like Eve, she had taken the delicious fruit forced on her and eaten, seeing Paradise turn corrupt in an instant.

He was unrobing when she went into the vestry.

'Chloe!' he said in surprise. 'What are you doing here? You weren't at the wedding. I would have seen you.'

'I need to speak to you,' she said. 'Can you give me a moment?'

'Yes, of course,' he said. 'Just let me put this away.' He was hanging the chasuble he had worn in a large cupboard packed with other vestments.

'David,' she said, holding out her hands.

He was filled with a most overwhelming urge to take her in his arms and comfort her. He even took a step towards her. But before he took another one – finding the strength from somewhere

– he went and sat down on a carved chair, one of a pair given to the church in memory of Canon Jones's predecessor. He put his head in his hands for a moment. Get thee behind me. When he looked up Chloe was staring at him in dismay.

'Sit down,' he said, rubbing his eyes. 'Tell me what's upset you.'

'Oh, I . . .' Chloe was beside herself with need. She yearned, like a child, for a physical expression of his sympathy. She had wanted him to make it all right for her at whatever cost.

'Is it your mother?' he asked.

'Yes.' Chloe sat down. 'You knew?'

He nodded. 'Was it a shock?'

The sight of her in such deep distress moved him horribly. It was as well he was sitting at some distance from her, otherwise he might have been tempted to try and touch her and that, as he knew, would have been fatal. But as he listened to her talking a strange thing began to happen to him. He became aware that he was praying and that his prayer was heard. This consciousness of a response both calmed and strengthened him in his appalling weakness. She was like the butterfly he had tenderly released earlier from its prison of bars. Somehow or other, it was his task to enable Chloe to face the problems of her own world, to strengthen her as she faced the need to acknowledge evil and to learn to forgive the casualties and ugliness of compromise. Somewhere, he remembered reading, someone had written that the Crucifixion had taken place on a dungheap. The world was a dungheap, full of stink and corruption. Chloe, locked into a fantasy of childhood, wanted it to be a Paradise garden.

'I feel as if everything I believed in has broken,' said Chloe. 'I don't know if you can understand that.' Tears were running down her cheeks. 'It makes everything seem a lie. I wish she hadn't told me. I didn't want to know. I didn't ask to know. It makes me wonder if she ever loved me at all, or if that was a pretence like her loving Daddy was a pretence.'

'She does love you, Chloe, she always did. She loves your father too, in her way. Perhaps she shouldn't have told you, but we all have to grow up sometime, Chloe, and learn to face things.'

'I don't want to face things. I can't cope with it. I just want everything to go on as it used to.'

'It can't do that,' he said gently, 'much as we would like it to.'

'Why?'

'Because the world is a harsh, terrible place. You have to learn to face reality without being turned to stone by it. You can't always run away back into the safety of childhood. The child in us never dies, but neither does it develop. It will always be a child, but it isn't equipped to fight the world, the flesh and the devil. That requires another aspect of our character to develop and that's what's happening to you. You're trying to grow up.'

'Thanks a lot.'

'Most people never manage it,' he said patiently.

'How long will it take?'

He smiled. 'I don't know.'

'Because I'm so bloody tired,' said Chloe. 'I feel ground down. I've been like this for ages. How much longer?'

'It will pass,' he said.

'Why do people always say that to you when you're in agony? Do you think Christ had someone whispering in his ear, "Don't worry, my dear, it'll pass"?'

'But it will,' he said. 'Darkness into light. C.S. Lewis said somewhere that if you love anything your heart will certainly be wrung and possibly broken. He said the only place outside Heaven you can be safe from the dangers and perturbations of love is Hell. You can't protect yourself, Chloe. You have to take risks and you have to learn to forgive.'

CHAPTER 25

Rupert's lawyer was called Jonathan Sturt. Like Charles Digard (with whom he played golf at weekends), he had an office in Lincoln's Inn and charged £250 an hour for his advice.

'You saw the letter from Digard,' he said to Rupert. 'All the usual stuff. Maintenance, capital settlement, details of shares, income, Lloyd's income, you know the form. What do you want me to do about it?'

'Nothing,' said Rupert, lighting a cigarette. 'What I want from you is advice on how to get my wife to let me come home.'

'You're going for a reconciliation?' Sturt raised his brows and pushed a piece of hair back. He had dark, quite long, rather greasy hair, like an actor in a Coward play, which he wore smoothed over the top of his head.

'Thanks,' he said, accepting a cigarette from Rupert who lit it for him, noticing Sturt's dirty fingernails.

'I must say I'm glad to hear you're trying to patch things up. Much the best way, really.'

Rupert laughed. 'It means you won't make so much money out of me,' he said.

'My dear Ru, we're not *all* about screwing you down, y'know. Besides, I had my whack out of you over Marcia.'

'You can say that again.' Ru blew smoke down his nostrils and looked round Sturt's comfortably appointed office.

'Is Chloe having it off with anyone else, or is she reasonably open to the idea of your return?'

'There's no one else as far as I know,' said Ru, 'but you know what women are like. Let 'em off the leash and they're at it.'

Sturt laughed. 'Reconciliation would be a much better bet for you, I agree. Digard smells blood in the air. He'll want bonemarrow: big capital settlement including the house, bags of maintenance, you name it.'

'The cleaners,' pronounced Ru, nodding. 'I thought so. She was cagey with me when the subject came up.'

'Didn't you have someone else?' asked Sturt. 'You'll need to clean up your act if you're to go back.'

'Oh, there was,' said Ru hastily, 'but . . . well, you know . . .' He shrugged. 'It didn't work out, one of those things. Prefer my wife, really.'

'That's the stuff,' said Sturt approvingly. 'You'll save yourself a fortune.' He thought for a minute, then said: 'Best way, in my view, to get a woman to come round is to buy her presents. Send flowers, buy the kids things they've always wanted and haven't been allowed. Bribery all round, that's my view. Flowers work magic on women. I've never understood it, but that's what they like. Move house, buy her an Aga, take her on holiday . . .'

'Steady on,' said Ru. 'Agas cost thousands.'

'So do I,' said Sturt. 'So does Charlie Digard. Has to keep himself in those fancy suits. Anyway, don't be stingy, old boy. Chloe's a nice kid. Worth the investment, I should say.'

'You're right,' said Ru. 'Of course.'

'In the meantime,' said Sturt, 'I'll hedge, shall I? I'll write Charlie a little billet doux telling him to hold his horses.'

'Excellent,' said Ru, rising. 'Thanks so much, old chap. I'll speak to you shortly when I've organized my campaign.'

'Best of British,' said Sturt. 'I know you're doing the right thing. How are the kids?'

'Fine,' said Ru. 'It would be best for them, too.'

'Oh, absolutely! No doubt about that. Children need fathers, that's my slogan.'

'How's it going, darling?' asked Pete, stopping by Lucy's desk.

'How's what going? Work or me?'

'You.' .

'All right.'

'What have you decided to do?'

'Have it.'

'Brave girl.'

'I don't believe in abortion. I couldn't have one. I'd never forgive myself.'

'Quite,' said Pete. 'I hope you know what you're letting yourself in for, sweetie. Babies are hell on wheels. I won't be understanding if it's not well or you want to go to speech day.'

'Yes, you will,' said Lucy, 'particularly as I'm going to ask you to be a godfather.'

'Oh, darling,' said Pete archly. 'I'm no guide for innocent youth. I mean look at my life. I might corrupt it,' he said, 'lead it astray, give it the wrong ideas.'

'I'll risk it,' said Lucy.

'What about its papa? Does he know of this?'

'I'm having dinner with him this evening,' said Lucy.

'Are you back together?'

'No.' She shook her head. 'It was all I could do to get to see him this evening. I leave messages, but he doesn't reply.'

'Nice fellow,' said Pete. 'Make sure he's aware of his obligations.'

'I intend to.'

'That's my girl.' Pete dropped a kiss on the top of Lucy's head. 'Must fly,' he said. 'Good luck, darling.'

Ru was late. They had arranged to meet in a restaurant in Park Walk at eight and it was now half past. Lucy twiddled her glass of mineral water, met the waiter's eye for the umpteenth time and wondered where the hell Ru had got to. It was too humiliating to be kept waiting like this. She tried not to remember the beginning of their affair, when it had been she who would arrive late from the office to find Ru sitting at his ease at the bar reading the paper or chatting to the barman.

'Sorry to have kept you,' said Ru, appearing out of apparently nowhere, pulling back a chair. He was wearing a new suit and seemed glossy and pleased with himself.

'I've been waiting hours,' said Lucy. 'What kept you?'

'The traffic is frightful. There was an accident on the Embankment. Have you got a drink?'

'I have, but I'd love another.'

'What is it? Vodka, gin?'

'It's water,' said Lucy. 'I'm not drinking at the moment.'

'Oh, right.' He glanced at her and then at the waiter. 'A large whisky and soda, no ice, and another glass of mineral water for the lady.

'Well, how are you?' he asked jovially, when the waiter had gone, leaving them the menus.

'All right,' said Lucy. 'I'd been wondering the same about you.'

215

'Jolly good,' said Ru, lighting a cigarette.

'I haven't seen you for weeks,' said Lucy. 'I've left messages with Andrew galore.'

'Yes, he said.'

'You could have replied,' Lucy said.

'Well, here I am,' he said, looking up briefly from the menu. 'What's the problem?'

'I don't think I heard you,' said Lucy.

'I'm going to have the stuffed mushrooms. They do them awfully well here, lots of garlic.'

'Ru,' said Lucy, 'I'm trying to talk to you.'

'Talk away.' Ru whisked off his glasses which he was vain about being seeing in and took a large mouthful of his drink.

'I'm going to have the baby,' said Lucy.

'I don't think that's a very good idea,' he said, as if they were discussing some risky insurance project.

'What do you suggest, then?'

'I thought you said you were going to have an abortion.'

'I never said any such thing. I'm a Roman Catholic amongst other things. I don't believe in abortion.'

'Listen, Lucy,' said Ru, lowering his voice. 'I don't want another child. I have enough problems as it is.'

'You can't force me,' said Lucy. 'I want this child, Ru. I want it badly.'

'Look,' he said, 'you're upset, you're overwrought; I am prepared to pay for it, if that's the problem, and a holiday for you too so you can recover.'

He clearly thought he was being exceedingly generous.

'I can't believe I'm hearing this,' said Lucy. 'Do you really think you can just wipe the slate clean like that, remove a life because it's inconvenient, because it doesn't happen to fit your game plan?'

'I was trying to help you,' said Ru, draining his glass, 'but you're making it rather difficult for me.'

'*I'm* making it difficult?'

Lucy turned her head away in disbelief. She was rarely angry, but she was perilously close to losing her temper with him. Thus was how Chloe must have felt on those nights she had described to Lucy, waiting and waiting for him to come home. And then

when he did he would pretend not to know why she was so angry
and upset. 'He's brilliant at not listening,' Chloe had said more
than once. 'He switches off. It's like dealing with a robot.'

'Would you like some wine?' he asked, whilst the waiter
hovered with the bottle of the something expensive Ru had
ordered.

'No, thanks.'

'It's a joint responsibility,' Lucy said when the waiter had
gone. 'I shall expect you to contribute towards the baby's
welfare.'

'Nonsense,' said Ru. 'You foisted this child on me. We didn't
discuss it. I've made a generous offer to you in order that you
can have an abortion which you would have no difficulty in
obtaining at your age and in your circumstances.'

'I see,' said Lucy. 'You've got it all worked out, haven't you? I
suppose you're going back to Chloe.'

'The matter is under discussion,' said Ru, who always became
pompous when he was irritated or rattled.

'Does she know about the baby?'

'Yes, she does,' lied Ru. 'She agrees with me that it would be
absurd for you to have it.'

'I see,' said Lucy, getting up. She was trying to be calm, but
she had to stuff her hands in her pocket to stop them shaking. Ru
didn't seem to be particularly surprised that she was going. He
didn't even bother to get up.

'You are leaving?' said the waiter, coming up in alarm.

'I'm afraid so,' said Lucy.

She looked over her shoulder at Ru who was examining the
menu with great interest.

'Good night Ru,' she said, but he didn't seem to hear her.

'You look tired, Chloe,' said Fanny. 'Are you still having trouble
sleeping?'

'Among other things,' said Chloe. 'I'm exhausted.' She actually
felt she was losing her grip. The other night she had found herself
in the kitchen shaking, as if she were in the middle of an
earthquake.

Fanny waited.

'Something happened,' said Chloe, 'when I went down to see

my mother a couple of weeks ago, and I can't stop thinking about it. It alters everything. You look back on your childhood, on whatever happy memories you have, as your foundation stone. Then suddenly someone comes along and says, "Oh no, it wasn't like that at all, it was like this"; and then nothing is what you think it is after that. You can't trust anything. Everything is in a state of flux. I don't know who to believe, or what to believe, or where to turn.'

'What exactly did happen?' asked Fanny, making a note on her clipboard before laying it down on the floor beside her chair.

'It's to do with my mother,' said Chloe. 'She wanted to tell me the truth about herself. In the war, when my father was a prisoner of the Japanese, she had an affair with a Dutch officer who had been sent to convalesce at Fordingbridge. The castle had been turned into a nursing home, you see.'

When Fanny nodded, Chloe continued: 'The affair was serious. She loved this man very much, so she said. Then she got herself pregnant. Of course there was no way she could foist the child on my father because he wasn't there, so she decided to have the baby – in Scotland – and give him up for adoption.' She stopped, and blew her nose with one of Fanny's endless supply of coloured paper handkerchiefs.

'It's all right, Chloe,' said Fanny, 'take your time over this. I can see it's important.'

Chloe blew her nose again.

'She never told anyone – other than one old friend, now dead – and the man in question vanished, the little shit. She assumed he had been killed. He was on special operations, I don't know what exactly, then the other day, a few weeks ago – I'm not quite sure of the timing – he got in touch again, saying he wanted to come and see her, asking questions about the baby . . .'

'And you never had an inkling?'

'My parents had a perfect marriage,' said Chloe. 'Or,' she added, 'at least that's how it seemed. I wanted to believe in it, so I suppose I overlooked things that didn't fit. It's as if you can know things and not know them at the same time. Does that sound crazy?'

'Not at all.'

'I knew and I didn't know some things weren't right between them . . . my father's mistress, for instance. But at the same time I'm a perfectionist, like my mother, and I wanted to believe what I saw. I like everything neat and tidy. Then again, I wanted my mother to stop being so wonderful and perfect so she could try and understand my confusion over Rupert and *sympathize* with my broken heart. I don't think she dared to too much . . . because it stirred her own repressed feelings. She just said, "Go. Divorce him. Start a new life." It didn't seem so easy to me. Now I don't know who the hell to trust or what I should do . . . Her life, *her* fucking awful problems seem to have run into mine. I'm so upset, Fanny, I know I'm ranting.'

'It must have been a terrible shock for you,' said Fanny. 'You must feel hurt and betrayed and angry too.'

'I do. It's the hypocrisy of it I can't bear.'

'And your father doesn't have any idea?'

'None.'

'Can you talk to him at all – about Rupert, for instance? Ask for his advice?'

'He's not the kind of man you can discuss things with.'

'Why not?'

'He just isn't,' said Chloe. 'I've never really talked to him. If you met him you'd see why. He's incredibly distant, the sort of person who stonewalls all discussion of feelings.'

'Do you think that's because he feels very intensely – like you, perhaps?'

'I don't know,' said Chloe, genuinely surprised. 'I'd always assumed it was because he didn't have any feelings much. He's always been very . . .'

'Very what?'

'Detached.'

'How are things with Rupert?'

'Oh, Rupert,' said Chloe evasively. 'Um . . . a bit better, in fact . . .' She looked down at her hands.

Fanny waited.

'He . . . I think . . . he wants us to get back together again. He bought me a new handbag, and he keeps sending flowers. It's rather sweet, really.' Chloe glanced at Fanny to see how she was taking this, but Fanny's face, as usual, betrayed no trace of what she was really thinking.

'So Rupert buying presents for you makes you feel well-disposed towards him?'

'It's not only the presents,' said Chloe hastily. 'I really do think he's making an effort towards me.' The more she said this, the more she found she could believe in it. She desperately wanted to believe in something. She dismissed the faint dissenting voice that told her Ru wanted to keep her in place like a butterfly with a pin through its heart.

'One of the times you were here recently,' said Fanny, 'we talked of the need to reward the kindness and understanding of others.'

'Oh, that was about David,' said Chloe, who cringed every time she thought of how she had exposed her disgusting neediness to him. In her present mood, she had no wish to be reminded of how mixed her feelings about everything were.

'You're not trying to reward Rupert, are you?'

'For what? He is my husband, for better or for worse.'

'Are you going back to Rupert, Chloe?'

Chloe reminded her of a deer or some creature so terrified out of its wits by a predator that it was about to run straight into the trap it had avoided earlier.

'I don't know,' said Chloe. 'He'd like me to.' Someone wanted her. In the confusion of feelings welling up inside her, that seemed enough. Someone, anyone.

'What about the girl, your friend?'

'I think it's over,' said Chloe. 'He's not seeing her any more.'

'How do you feel about that?'

'I try not to think about it,' said Chloe, untruthfully. Her sense of triumph over Lucy was mingled with an odd kind of jealousy, and a sense of loss. What had it achieved? Zero.

'Things are moving very quickly for you, Chloe,' said Fanny as the hour drew to a close. 'Other people seem to be making the running for you. I just want you to be aware that things can also go at your pace.'

'Thank you,' said Chloe. Nice thought, she said to herself, sweet idea, but completely untrue. She had spent her whole life adjusting her footwork to other people's pace. The idea of doing what she wanted seemed impossibly remote, particularly as she had no idea what it was.

CHAPTER 26

'What'll you have?' Maria asked Frances, looking up from her menu. They had taken to lunching together whenever they could. And their favourite restaurant was a dimly lit tiny French bistro tucked away in a back street the other side of the river.

'Watercress soup,' said Frances, 'then vegetarian lasagne.'

'I'll have the same,' said Maria. 'Let's be crazy and order some wine.'

'I won't have any,' said Frances. 'I've got a seminar this afternoon.'

'Oh? What on?'

'The demonization of women . . . aggressive patriarchal attitudes after the Reformation. I want to get as far as the Shakers if I can.'

'Sounds great,' said Maria, 'really interesting. I adore the Shakers. Ann Lee is my hero.' She paused. 'Did you know there's talk of axing your job?'

'No.'

'Departmental cuts. Apparently, our lords and masters consider it inappropriate that there should be a lecturer in women's studies in an art college.'

'I get plenty of kids of both sexes attending,' said Frances hotly, her earrings swinging. 'The boys are more feminist than the girls sometimes. I can't believe this.'

'It's the narrow view,' said Maria, putting her warm strong hand on top of Frances's. 'Galloping Thatcherism. It's like galloping consumption in the nineteenth century.'

'I haven't heard anything,' said Frances, gently removing her hand. She was increasingly scared by what she seemed to be getting herself into with Maria. It was like being wooed by a handsome prince with a woman's intuition; and those few stolen kisses had inflamed her more than she cared to admit, but at the same time what Tanya had said to her made her ashamed of herself. For the first time, she began to consider if Tanya was right. Was she justified in being so angry with David for not understanding her point of view? Perhaps she hadn't tried hard enough to understand him; she had simply got into the habit of being angry with him as, once upon a time, she had been in the habit of loving him. Since that day when Maria had come to the vicarage she had been very careful with him, picking her way round him. They hadn't discussed his exit, and by tacit consent they only discussed everyday practicalities, but she had become aware that the animosity he had felt towards her had gone.

He had taken to spending as much time as he could alone in his study. One day when she had gone in to look for a book she needed she had found him sitting at his desk with his head in his hands. When he looked up at her it was with a kind of raking glance that seemed to see straight to the heart. She had said something and apologized for interrupting, and when she was searching on the shelves for the book she could feel him watching her although he said nothing. The change seemed to have occurred when he came back from his wedding that Saturday afternoon strangely calm and somehow ordered. She didn't know what had happened, or indeed if anything had happened, but when he had taken Mass he had seemed almost exalted. She had not seen him like this since they had been very much younger and very much happier.

'If they do it now they can get away with paying you the minimum redundancy money,' said Maria, 'because you haven't been here very long. They are complete bastards.'

After the waiter brought Maria's glass of wine, she said: 'I want you to know something, Frances. I'm going back to the States.'

Frances was startled. 'How long have you known this?'

'Only a little while,' said Maria. 'My appartment is sublet, but the lease is coming up. I'm going home with Tashie.'

'Will you get her in?'

'Oh yeah, no problem. She was born in the States. I made sure of that. She has an American passport.'

'What about Viva?'

'I haven't told her.'

'I see.'

'Things have been ...' Maria hesitated ... 'very difficult

between us for a few weeks, since she walked out that day. We're not even sharing a room at the moment.'

'When will you tell her?'

'This is what I can't quite figure out.'

'Why?'

'Because I wanted to talk with you first. I wanted you to know the first; when I heard the gossip about your job being axed, I figured now was the moment. You see, I wanted to ask you to come with me.'

Frances closed her eyes. Everything was moving too quickly for her. She had been paid an enormous compliment, the greatest compliment human beings could pay one another, but that was only one aspect of this multi-faceted situation.

'I have to think this through,' said Frances. 'It is not a clear-cut issue for me. I have to consider David and the kids. He'd lose his job if I left him.'

'I know.' Maria drank some wine. Frances noticed a tiny drop of red wine at the corner of her mouth like a spot of blood. 'But that's not really your problem, is it? I mean, you have your life to lead too. It's obvious your relationship is in shreds.'

Frances raised her eyebrows. 'That doesn't mean I can just walk out on him. I have thought about it, before I met you. I'm sure you can appreciate that.'

'Sure,' said Maria.

'And there's Tanya and Kitty to think of. They're happy here.'

'I'm telling you how I feel, Frances.'

'But what about Viva?'

'I told you,' said Maria impatiently, 'we're not even sharing a room. We hardly talk. The atmosphere is terrible.'

'Perhaps she's waiting for you to make a move.'

'That's just it,' said Maria, 'she's got this incredible victim mentality. It's what Woody Allen calls passive aggression.'

'I think you should talk to her honestly,' said Frances, playing for time.

'You're accusing me of what?'

'I'm not accusing you, Maria. I'm saying I think you owe it to Viva to share your feelings with her. I should do the same with David. I'm not being honest with him either.'

'So I'm dishonest, is that what you're saying?'

'You don't have to be aggressive with me,' said Frances, 'I'm listening to you.'

'So I'm dishonest and aggressive. Thanks a lot, Frances. I thought we were friends, I thought we were more than friends, actually.'

'I thought we were friends too,' said Frances, 'but I don't want to be pushed around because I'm not doing what you want me to do.'

'Oh, right,' said Maria hotly. 'Anything else while you're about it?'

Her hair, untidily pinned up as usual, appeared to bristle with electricity.

'Maria,' said Frances, 'I don't know what's happening with you today.'

'You don't? I tell you I wanna be with you, expecting some response, and what do I get?' She mimicked Frances's voice: '"I think you should talk to her honestly." This is about us, Frances, not about Viva, not about David, but us. Our future together.'

Maria drained the rest of her glass of wine.

'I sure as hell wonder what's going on with you,' she said. 'You've been flirting with me since the day I met you, but when I want to make an honest statement you draw back. You're cautious, you don't know, you need to talk to your husband. You straights are all the same. You think because I'm gay it's not for real, it's kind of like a toy emotion, something for kids, something to play with. Well, that's not true. It's real, it hurts. You're cold, Frances, you're self-centred. You take what you want and leave the rest. That's very predatory,' she added, emphasizing each syllable.

'I'm sorry you feel like that,' said Frances coolly as their soup arrived, 'but I don't think that because you're gay you don't have feelings. I resent that very much. All my adult life I've supported gay rights.'

'Rights aren't feelings,' said Maria, taking some bread. 'Unless you're gay you don't know how it feels.'

'That's like saying you shouldn't buy a poppy to support the disabled victims of war because you weren't there yourself and you can't understand.'

'For fuck's sake, Frances, don't patronize me.'

'Are you about to get your period?'

'How like a man! No, as a matter of fact, I'm not.'

'Haven't you left it a bit late to hand in your notice?' said Frances to change the subject.

'Oh, they'll love it,' said Maria. 'It'll save them having to make me redundant.'

'Were they going to?'

'Probably.'

'I'm sorry you're so angry.'

'I'm giving myself permission to be angry,' said Maria tightly. 'It'll pass.'

But halfway through her soup, she said, 'Look, I can't stand this. I'm going. I need some space. See you around, kid.'

'OK,' said Frances. 'I'll call you.'

'It would be better if I called you,' said Maria, who liked to be in charge. 'I don't want to upset Viva,' she said. 'She's already upset enough as it is.'

When she went home after her lunch with Frances. Maria found Viva in the kitchen. She was baking cakes and at the same time making a casserole for supper. The kitchen was full of the comforting smell of baking and other aromatic and pungent smells. The radio was on, the kitchen curtains, a brave gingham that Viva had found somewhere, moved slightly in the breeze.

'Hi,' said Maria, banging the door to behind her and slinging her satchel on a chair. 'Smells good. What're you doin'?'

'Cakes,' said Viva, 'sponges and some biscuits for Tashie.'

She turned round as Maria came in and smiled nervously. She was wearing a sleeveless check dress with a long, loose cheesecloth waistcoat over the top and was barefoot. Her mushroom-coloured hair had come loose at the back. She looked slightly dishevelled and incredibly pretty.

'Love your dress,' said Maria, 'you look great.'

'Do I?' Viva stared down at herself as if she had forgotten what she was wearing.

'C'm here, kid,' said Maria.

Viva did not move. 'What?'

'Whadya mean "what"? I'm your lover, I wanna hold you.'

Viva edged her way around the scrubbed pine table towards Maria.

'You look like you're going to the scaffold,' said Maria, putting her hands on Viva's bare arms. 'I'm not going to eat you,' she said.

'You're not?'

'Well, I just might,' said Maria, pushing back a piece of hair that had fallen across her lover's face. 'What, kid? What is it?'

'Nothing,' said Viva, bowing her head submissively.

'You're really unhappy, aren't you?'

'Why?'

'It's OK,' said Maria, 'really, really OK. We're going to make it through this.'

'Tashie told me you are going back to the States.'

'Yeah, we are. We all are.'

'But I thought ... Frances ... you and she ... Look, I'm going to roll a joint,' said Viva, opening a drawer in the table. 'We have to talk,' she said.

'I know.'

'You do? You seemed so angry, I thought you wouldn't want to talk.'

'Well,' said Maria, taking a drag, 'we have to share with each other somehow, yeah?'

'I was thinking of leaving,' said Viva. 'I met some people at the Bull, travellers. They're going towards Hereford somewhere to stop a road and they said I could go with them.'

'Is that all?' asked Maria sternly. 'How would you manage to paint on the road? No studio, no space, cramped into some truck or other?'

'I'd manage,' said Viva simply. 'I managed before I met you.' She paused, took a drag for courage and said, 'I thought you and Frances had something together.'

'No, no.' Maria shook her head. She never accepted a rejection from anybody. Never had, never would. Rejection made her want to vomit.

'We were just friends,' she said, 'nothing more than that.'

'Then what has been wrong?'

226

'Job worries, nothing for you to concern yourself about, sweetheart.' Maria touched Viva's face with her warm, strong hand. 'Nothing at all. It's all over now anyway. All over now,' she repeated as Viva snuggled into her lap.

CHAPTER 27

David saw Marjorie dead-heading roses inside her little walled garden before she saw him. She had left the door open, held back by a cascade of ivy; it was odd that she had done that. He had never known her do it before. It was almost, he felt, as if she had given up guarding her sanctuary which seemed, if correct, a strange and rather disturbing assumption. From a distance, he thought, what she was doing appeared so perfectly appropriate: a good-looking gentlewoman in a straw hat snipping away at what he now knew was 'Zéphirine Drouhin', and placing some of the flowers in her basket. It was some weeks since he had been up here. He had wanted to let her make up her own mind about what to do, although he hoped she would forbid the man in question to come and see her. It seemed to him enormously indulgent to want to try and mend things when it was far, far too late. Damage limitation was the thing now; if not Chloe, then Guy. It also applied to his own marriage, he felt. He had so, so nearly wronged Chloe, so very nearly ruined her trust in anything, that he felt fantastically humble and grateful for the split second his last vestiges of self-control had granted him: the moment when he had drawn back, the moment when he knew that there was a central strand in every life, a story, destiny, fate, whatever one wanted to call it, that dictated there was this choice or that. *And that it mattered.* Hell was not knowing whether things mattered or not, or at least that was one aspect of it.

'Hello,' he called, raising a hand in greeting.

Marjorie paused, then straightened up.

'David,' she said. 'What a long time it seems.' She smiled. 'It isn't so long, is it?'

'A few weeks.'

'You've been avoiding me,' she said, half banteringly.

'Not really,' he answered lightly. He thought she was thinner, lighter, altogether more delicate-looking even than normal.

'Well, I don't know,' she said sighing, looking down at her trug of roses and then at the secateurs in her hand. 'I don't know anything any more. Have you seen Chloe? *She's* definitely avoid-ing me.'

'Shall we sit down?' he said, indicating the bench in the arbour that was painted a very, very dark green to blend unobtrusively into the background.

'All right.'

When they were seated, he said, 'She came to see me that afternoon . . . after you'd told her about everything.'

'I thought she might have done.' She touched her cheek under her hat.

'It came as a tremendous shock to her,' he said. 'But it might be what she needs, it might be the spur she's been searching for.'

'Spur?'

'She has to grow up,' said David. 'It hasn't quite happened, I don't think.'

'I haven't let her,' said Marjorie. 'I'm to blame. I let her believe in me. I hid the rest from her. My wickedness. My sorrow. When she sees those things in me now she's shattered. And of course Rupert is greatly to blame. He's deliberately suppressed her development by tyrannizing the fearful childish elements in her. I do hope she has the strength to leave him.'

'You mean she can't quite put it all together.'

'To Chloe, people are either good or bad. She can't cope with the fact that we're all a mixture of both. She can't cope with her own darkness, let alone mine.'

'It's a challenge,' said David. 'A test. She'll either pass or fail. I think she'll pass, myself. I have great faith in her.'

'How very Greek,' said Marjorie thoughtfully. 'A test, indeed.' After a minute, she said, 'And if your theory of a test is right, then what is mine?'

'Only you know that.'

'Don't dodge, David. I want to know what you think.'

'You must protect Guy,' he said. 'He mustn't know. Have you written yet?'

'No, but I'm about to. I had to have time to think it over, you were right. Will you stay to lunch?'

'That's very kind, but I must get back. Frances is at home today working and I promised to be there.'

'Oh?'

'Yes.' He nodded.

'That's very good of you.'

'No, no,' he said, shaking his head. 'I want to. Things haven't been –'

'I understand,' said Marjorie. 'But thank you for coming.'

She looked up at him and on impulse he bent down and kissed her smooth cheek.

When he glanced back, she was still sitting where he had left her with her hands in her lap.

'I'm afraid,' said Guy into the receiver, 'that I can't come this afternoon.'

'I'm sorry to hear that, darling,' said Marion. 'Any particular reason?'

Guy hesitated. 'I've just got things to do,' he said reluctantly.

'Oh?'

But when Guy did not respond, she said, 'What things, as a matter of interest?'

'Oh, you know . . .'

'Don't you want to see me?'

'I do, but . . .'

'It's Marjorie, I suppose, isn't it?'

'Um . . .'

'Go on, admit it.'

'She's not awfully well,' said Guy.

'She looked perfectly splendid when I saw her earlier.'

'Well, she isn't,' said Guy, tiring of the conversation. 'I owe it to her to be round and about when she's not quite the thing.'

'And what do you think you owe me?'

'I was not aware that I owed you anything,' said Guy.

'I was not aware,' mimicked Marion, and then put the phone down at the other end.

'Bloody rude,' said Guy into the receiver, before replacing it.

'You haven't eaten your lunch' said Guy, clearing plates on to the sideboard for Mrs B.

'Not awfully hungry, in fact.'

'Not even for calves' liver? Used to be your favourite.'

'I know. It's delicious.'

230

'But you must eat,' insisted Guy, investigating the puddings, 'otherwise you'll fade away. God knows you're thin enough as it is. Have some rhubarb fool.'

'Just a little,' said Marjorie, in order to keep him quiet.

'Cream?'

'A dab.'

'Here you are.'

Guy tenderly put a plate in front of Marjorie. Her thinness and fragility worried him. She had walked indoors with him and when he had taken her arm she had seemed like a bird drifting along. His heart had given the most terrible lurch when he had contemplated, even for a second, life without her. She had always been here. In the war that had comforted him, when everything else, including the Almighty, seemed to have failed him. Knowing she was there. Knowing she would keep everything ticking, knowing he could rely on her. It was the knowledge and then the memory of that that had prevented him from leaving her for the one woman who had come near her in his affections, the woman who might have borne him a son.

'What's that noise?' asked Marjorie, picking up her spoon and then putting it down again.

The sound of raised voices came from the hall.

'What's going on?' demanded Guy, as the door opened and Marion came in unannounced, followed by a distraught Mrs Bosworth, still in her apron.

'I tried to stop her,' she declared, 'but she wouldn't listen.'

'All right, Mrs B,' said Marjorie, 'don't worry. You go back and deal with whatever it was you were doing. We'll see to this.'

Marion was as drunk as a skunk.

'A little lunch à *deux*,' she said, 'how nice. Is there room for one more?'

'No, there isn't,' said Guy. 'What do you think you're doing here?'

'Come to see lover-boy,' said Marion. 'Did you know he was my lover?' she said to Marjorie. 'Tuesday's his day, but he can't come today because he's bizzeee.' She shrieked with laughter.

'Get out,' said Guy. 'Get out or I'll throw you out.'

'Tuesday's his day,' said Marion, paying no attention to Guy.

She was swaying to and fro. 'Little glass of wine, then beddybyes. Then Guysie Buysie gets dressed and goes back up —'

'Get out of here, Marion,' said Marjorie calmly. 'You're behaving in the most disgusting way.'

'He's a lousy screw,' said Marion, 'Just thought you ought to know.' She staggered towards the door, and then, leaving it open, stumbled across the hall and out.

After her departure there was a silence. Marjorie stubbed out one cigarette and lit another. Guy stood at the sideboard with his back to her, his head hung.

'I'm most awfully sorry,' he said, without looking round.

'Ghastly woman,' said Marjorie. 'Would you refill my glass?' Of course.'

Guy took the decanter and refilled Marjorie's glass and then his own.

'I think we should clear some of the hostas by the pond,' said Marjorie. 'They're taking over. We need more variety; I was wondering about Japanese irises, masses of loosestrife or something, to ginger it up. What do you think?'

'Absolutely right. Same thought had occurred to me.'

'And it occurred to me that some *Astilbe* would be attractive there. I particularly adore that flame-red. I was thinking about it in bed this morning. It might be rather bold with purple irises, or it might be vulgar.'

'No, no,' said Guy. 'Good idea . . . excellent.' He drained his glass and squared his shoulders. 'When you're ready, my dear,' he said.

Afterwards, when they had made their progress round the gardens and lingered long by the pond, Marjorie went indoors to her office and sat down at her writing table. Her secretary had been in and cleared things, everything was orderly, just as she liked it. Hubert's letter was in a gardening book on the fourth shelf down. She got it out and reread it and then, having done that, put it away again in a different place. She sat for a moment thinking, and then began to write. She would tell him the child had died prematurely but that he should come and see *her*. She thought of what David had said that morning about things being a test. If he was right, then she, unlike her daughter, would fail.

But she was too angry to care. She knew she shouldn't do what she was doing, but she did it anyway.

She had put the letter in its envelope and was writing the address when Guy came in.

'All right, are you?'

'Yes, thank you.'

'Who're you writing to?' He peered at the address. 'That the chap who wants to come for a return bash?'

'That's right. Would you be a darling and pop it in the post for me?'

'I'll do it now if you like.'

'Don't make a special thing of it.'

'I've got to go into the town anyway. Nero's gone lame again.'

'Poor darling.'

'What'll you do now, more letters?'

'I should think so.'

'Sure you're all right?'

'Absolutely sure, thank you.'

'Well then, I'll see you later.'

'See you later.'

Guy looked at Marjorie with admiration. What a woman she was! Who else could have behaved with such dignity and yet not blamed him, not set up a-wailing and a-bawling. Bloody Marion. Well, that was that. Shame in some ways. Bad habits catch up with one. She would have to get off the bottle. Stupid bloody woman.

When Guy had gone, Marjorie began another letter, this time to Chloe, but before she had got very far she tore the page in half and threw it in her wastepaper basket. Why bother? Chloe would blunder along whatever she, Marjorie, advised her to do; in fact, it was probably better to say nothing for fear Chloe would do the opposite of what she advised her to do. She sat at her desk thinking that everything seemed to be falling to pieces around her; the façade that she had carefully constructed for so long seemed to have suddenly crumbled, revealing the botched job beneath: first Chloe, then her, then Guy. Would they ever be able to face one another as what they were rather than what they liked others to believe? Probably not. She was too old now,

233

too old to change. She felt tired, so terribly tired. It was anger that made one so exhausted. Keeping one's composure was absolutely shattering. Of course one had known about Marion, but one didn't want it thrust in one's face; that was what hurt. Some people just didn't know how to behave and ruined it for everyone else. It was a question of breeding, really. And greed, of course. Guy had allowed something to get out of hand and it was both foolish and selfish of him. It had hurt her so much to have that woman bursting into her dining room and making a scene ... Everything seemed to have got out of control lately. It frightened her rather. She went slowly and rather dreamily into the drawing room and sat down in the chair covered in that parrot chintz that Guy's mother had been so fond of. After a moment, she dozed off.

CHAPTER 28

'I feel as if I've been taken for a ride,' said Frances angrily. 'When you hired me you didn't say there was a possibility of the job collapsing so quickly. You should have mentioned your underfunding problems.'

'Believe me, Frances,' said Norman scratching his beard nervously, 'believe me, I didn't know either. This bombshell's just been dropped on us. I'd love you to stay. I'm completely in favour of women's studies myself and I know the kids have enjoyed the lectures. They've been reelly popular. The Dean of Studies is very grateful to you, you know. I've been told to offer you the most generous terms possible.'

'It would be much better,' said Frances, 'if you made an effort to find out how I can be kept on.'

The thought of unemployment terrified her, of being nothing but herself, or, worse, the vicar's wife, open to every Tom, Dick and Harry who wanted a slice of her time for some useless committee, leaving her no choice in the matter: the church fete, the Sunday School, the WI; work was a way of beating her husband, of keeping him in his place. With a slight shock she realized how angry she was with him for forcing her constantly, as she saw it, to have to assert herself all these years.

'I'm reelly sorry, Frances,' Norman was saying, 'reelly reelly sorry. We very much value your contribution to our community here, but I'll see what I can do, leave it with me. There may be some way round this. I'll have another word with the Dean of Studies.'

As Frances rose to go he said, 'I'm reelly sorry we're losing Maria. You know about that, of course?'

He raised his brown, doggy eyes to Frances's face.

'Of course.'

Since their lunch they had tended to avoid one another. Once or twice when she had been fetching Kitty from school Frances had seen Viva, or Maria and Viva together. The second time they had been holding hands. Frances, watching them, had felt her heart sink. For a second she was not aware that she was

235

jealous, then the knowledge broke over her like a great wave. She realized she had been infatuated with Maria and that she missed the excitement and tension she had felt in her presence. Maria was the sort of person who made everything an adventure. Everything was fresh in her hands, new, challenging.

'It's quite something,' Norman continued, 'to be taking a kid back to New York, but I can see this place is too much of a cultural backwater for someone like Maria. She has to be centre stage, but her lesbian studies group will be sorry to lose her. She's a bit of a cult figure here, is our Maria.'

'Yes, I know,' said Frances, staring down at her hands. 'She has incredible energy. It draws people towards her like a magnet.'

'What will you do now, Frances?' asked Norman. It had not been lost on the staff room that there was a little frisson between those two, but Maria was like that. She had an appetite for people.

'Look for another job, I suppose,' said Frances, without enthusiasm.

'Not thinking of joining the priesthood?' said Norman.

'I think one of us is enough, thank you.'

'Well, I can't see you being just the vicar's wife,' said Norman. 'You should write a book, Frances, you write very well.'

'I don't want to write a book,' said Frances. 'I want to teach. See what you can do, Norman, won't you?'

'Could I have a word Mrs Doughty?' asked Kitty's teacher, Miss Davis, coming down the steps when she saw Frances.

'Now?'

'If you wouldn't mind. Kitty is classroom monitor this week. She's tidying up the classroom, she won't be along for a minute.'

'What is it?'

'Let's go in here,' said Miss Davis, opening the door of an empty classroom. She let Frances go ahead, then followed her in and perched herself on the edge of a desk. 'Sit down,' she said smiling. 'Kitty's been upset in school several times lately. Crying in the locker rooms, not wanting to eat her lunch. But she won't tell me what's wrong and I didn't want to ask Tanya as I felt that wouldn't be fair either to Kitty or to you.'

236

'Well,' said Frances heaving a sigh, 'I'll be honest with you. There's been a lot of tension at home. We're going through problems, my husband's job, my job . . .'

'I'm sorry,' said Miss Davis, who was young and dark and competent. 'I didn't mean to upset you, it's just that I felt I ought to ask.'

'You're not upsetting me,' said Frances, sniffing, 'it's me. I've had the sack from the art college. I really loved my work there.'

'I know,' said Miss·Davis kindly. 'Sense of identity is very important.'

'That's it,' said Frances, mopping her eyes. 'I feel like I've had a limb cut off. But look,' she said after a minute, 'let's get back to Kitty. There are tensions at home, things we need to sort out. I feel terrible about Kitty. Tanya told me she was crying at night and I didn't pay much attention.'

'I'd better get back to the door. Come along when you're ready. I'll keep Kitty there until you come.'

'I'm all right,' said Frances. 'I'm ready now. What do you think I should do about this?'

'Just be with her when you can,' said Miss Davis. 'Don't feel bad. Guilt makes the mea culpa stuff worse and improves nothing. Kitty's a wonderful girl, she's bright and nice, she'll get over it. I wanted to get a vague idea of what's going on. It must be hell being a vicar's wife,' she said sympathetically, 'even worse than being a teacher. Oh look, there she is now.'

'Hi, Frances,' said Kitty, 'what've you been doing?'

'Since when did you call me "Frances"?'

'Tashie calls Maria "Maria" so I· thought I'd call you "Frances".'

'I'd rather you didn't,' said Frances.

'Why?'

'Because I don't feel like your mother when you do, I feel like someone else.'

'Sorry,' said Kitty. 'Can you carry this?' She handed Frances her violin. 'Why were you seeing Miss Davis?'

'She's worried about you,' said Frances. 'She says you cry in school and won't each your lunch.'

'Oh.' Kitty was downcast.

'What is it, Kit Kat?'

237

'Nothing.' Kitty shrugged. 'Silly old Davy doesn't know any-thing. Where's the car?'

'Over there.' Frances pointed. 'Do you want fish and chips or something?'

'No, thanks.'

'But you love fish and chips!'

'You can't afford it,' said Kitty. 'I don't want you to waste your money.'

'What do you mean?' Frances put her hand on Kitty's shoulder.

'Nothing,' said Kitty stubbornly. 'Let's go home, please.'

After supper Frances went into David's study where, as usual, he was talking on the telephone.

'Who was that?' she asked, when he put the receiver down.

'Hang on,' he said, picking it up again as the telephone began to ring.

Frances went to the window whilst she waited for him to finish and looked out over the vicarage garden. In Canon Jones's day, as she was constantly being reminded, the lawn had been cut twice a week and the borders were of prize-winning standard, let alone the vegetable patch where the Canon had grown marrows the size of torpedoes. David had managed to make some inroads into the jungle: the grass was cut and, from a distance, the borders looked all right, although close to they were still badly choked with weeds and rank grasses. She wondered in a bitter sort of way if that might not be rather a good metaphor for their marriage. Behind her, she could hear David discussing some new parish group with someone, probably a member of the PCC.

When he had finished, she turned to him and said, 'I think we have to talk. Will you put the answering machine on?'

He did as she asked, without demur. 'Fire away,' he said, making a note on his pad before looking up.

'I've lost my job,' she said.

'I'm sorry. That must have been a blow.'

'I think I want a separation, David.'

'You've just lost your job and you want a separation. Why now?' Then he said, 'Is it something to do with that woman, Marion, no . . . Maria?'

238

'Not exactly,' she said, with uncharacteristic hesitation. 'It is connected to her. I'm trying to be honest with you,' she continued, as he began to interrupt, 'but it's more to do with the fact that I can't go on having to resist you, resist your job all the time. Without a job of my own, I feel utterly invalid, utterly defenceless in relation to you. That can't be right.'

'No, it can't be,' he said quietly, surprising her. 'Not in the way you seem to mean; implying that I want to wound you in some way. That is what you're saying, isn't it?'

'Yes . . . it does seem to be.'

'If I said the last thing in the world I wanted to do was to wound you, would you believe me?'

'I don't know.' She went and sat down opposite him. 'I only know that I don't want to end up just being the wretched vicar's wife, your sidekick.'

'You're not,' he said, 'you never were, not remotely.'

'Then why do I feel that?'

'I haven't helped,' he said. 'I made it worse. But I want to help you now.'

Frances looked at him, then she put her forehead in her hand and began to cry.

'Frances,' he said. 'Frances.'

'What?'

'I want to help you. Let me help you.'

He got up, went round his desk and put his arms awkwardly around her. He was unused to holding her and it showed. He was full of remorse for her unhappiness.

'You don't have to resist me,' he said tenderly. Her whole body felt hard with tension like a bundle of old iron girders.

'We have to talk,' she said. 'I feel so terrible inside. Kitty's teacher says she's unhappy at school and I feel so awful. Tanya told me Kitty was crying at night and I ignored her, ignored it all, just did what I wanted to do. I'm so sorry, David, so, so sorry . . .'

He smoothed her hair, her poor tortured hair, and stroked her exhausted face.

'It's all right,' he said, 'It's all right. We'll work something out.'

'You're different,' she said, after some seconds had passed. 'You've changed. Something's happened to you.'

'Yes,' he said, 'it has. I can pray again.'

'What do you mean?'

'I haven't been able to. Not for ages. Months and months, even longer.'

'Why didn't you tell me?'

'We haven't been telling each other things, though. Not for a long time.'

'No, that is true. When did it happen?'

He told her.

'Was Chloe another of your favourites?'

'Yes.'

'Oh.' She seemed rather floored by his admission. But then she startled him by saying, 'I'm not surprised really. She's wonderfully pliable – not like me – and so vulnerable.'

'That's what Tessa said. She gave me such a dressing down.' He remembered what his sister had said about romantic love and how she no longer believed in it. It was certainly an odd thing, so painful, so devastating, like a nasty virus.

'Good for Tessa,' said Frances. Then she added, 'I'm not angry, David, not any more.'

'Neither am I,' he said. But he knew he had to hang on his prayer like a man might hang on a rope picking his way up some perilous defile.

'I think I was jealous,' she said, 'jealous of you. Jealous of something I already had . . . why, I don't know.'

'I think I understand,' he said.

'Do you?'

'I want to,' he said, 'more than anything.'

Kitty had thrown off the teeshirt which doubled as a nightie and one bare, smooth shoulder protruded above the sheet. She muttered something as Frances bent over her and her eyelids fluttered, then opened.

'Mum,' she said.

'Just checking on you,' murmured Frances, stroking Kitty's cheek. 'Go back to sleep now.'

'OK.' Obediently, Kitty turned on her side.

Frances knelt down beside her. 'No tears?'

'No.' Kitty shook her head.

'If you want me in the night, come and wake me. I mean it.'

'OK,' said Kitty. Then she said, 'Is Dad here?'

'Making tea in the kitchen.'

'Are you going to bed now?'

'In a minute.'

As Frances made to get up, Kitty took her wrist in a vice-like grip. 'You won't leave me, will you?'

'Never,' said Frances. 'It's all right. Go to sleep.'

Chloe met her father coming out of Agnew's in Old Bond Street. She had been to the Royal Academy to look at some pictures and was on her way back up Bond Street to John Lewis where she had to get some new aertex shirts for James, who seemed to have grown about six inches in the last few months. If she'd been looking where she was going, which she wasn't, she would have avoided him. She had been suffering from a violent antipathy to both her parents in recent weeks.

'Hello Dad' she said, stopping in consternation.

He was wearing a linen suit and a panama hat and looked very dapper indeed.

'Ah, Chloe. I tried to ring you but your damned machine cut in. So I left it.'

'Why? I mean did you?' Her father had never to her knowledge rung her London number. She was surprised he even knew what it was.

'I told you. I wanted to see you. Worried about your mother. She frets because you don't come down.'

Chloe gazed at her father in silence.

'So,' he said, evidently registering that all was not quite as it should be but without the least desire to find out why (women's stuff), 'I've bought her a picture. Come and tell me if you think it's her.'

It was amazing, Chloe thought. If one didn't know better, one would say without hesitation that here was a devoted spouse shopping to comfort his ailing but equally devoted wife. It was amazing how people bought things for one another when they wished to disguise something: possessions were certainly splendid objects to paper over the cracks with. Buying things for people was considered the highest form of esteem; it roused the child in one, the part of one that never gave up expecting it to be Christmas morning or hoping a cheque would fall out of every envelope. Ru had been buying things for her lately, a deluge of presents from flowers to the offer to have the kitchen completely redone which she didn't think in the least necessary. A part of her, about Miranda's age, liked it very much, but another voice that would not be silent said he was buying her favours because he was re-establishing his hold over her. Each present was another chain binding her to her marriage vows.

'It's lovely,' said Chloe, standing in front of a small line drawing of a horse by Crawhall. 'Essence of horse,' she said.

'Eh?' exclaimed Guy. 'Like it, do you? If you like it, I'll go and pay for it . . . What about a spot of lunch,' he said, coming back from the desk. 'Are you busy?'

'No,' said Chloe, 'no, I'm not.' But she wasn't sure she wanted to have lunch with her father. She felt he wanted something from her. His awkward fumbling eagerness to seek her opinion rang an alarm bell. She preferred his usual taciturnity.

'I've got a table at the club,' said Guy. 'I was going to see Harkness, but he's ill, poor devil.'

'So I'll do instead, will I?'

'Eh, what?' He blinked at her, as if it had suddenly dawned on him that she might be taking the mick. 'Come along,' he said, setting off at a brisk pace. He led the way out of the gallery without looking to see if she was following.

'I hear Rupert has come back,' said Guy, when they were seated at a table in the In and Out. 'I think it's a jolly good thing he has,' he added, taking the wine list from the waitress. The only real trouble with Rupert was that he was the man from nowhere. One shouldn't marry out of one's own caste, that was Guy's view.

'Do you?' asked Chloe.

'Of course I do. He is your husband and the father of your children.' He continued examine the wine list as he spoke. 'I know he's made a few silly mistakes, but men are like that, my dear, and you might as well get used to the fact.'

'Some women are like that too,' said Chloe.

'What's that? Women? Well . . . yes.' He peered at her, wondering if Marjorie had said anything. But then, he thought, Marjorie would *never* say anything. What could she mean, tiresome girl?

'Tell me what you're going to eat and then I'll choose the wine.'

'Potted shrimps, then lamb.'

'That's the stuff,' said Guy. 'I like a girl who can make up her mind. And at least you'll eat your lunch, unlike your mother who just picks at everything pretending to eat. She thinks I don't notice, but I do.'

'You're very fond of her, aren't you?'

'What's that? Fond of your mother? Of course I am! Always have been. Mad about her.'

'You take my breath away,' said Chloe.

'Why do you say that?' Guy shook his head. 'What's the matter with you today? Shall I order some bottled water?'

'If you like.'

'How's James?'

'Absolutely fine,' said Chloe. 'And so is Miranda.'

After a minute she said, 'Do you regret not having a son?'

He hesitated. 'Nothing much I could do about it, was there? We can't order these things. What a silly question.'

'At least I was clever enough to have a boy,' said Chloe.

'Cleverness has got nothing to do with it.'

'Only teasing.'

Her father had surrounded himself with a kind of membrane, a one-way filter, where he could look out at the world but the world could not look at him. It was extraordinary how he managed to get away with it. She thought she might try another taboo subject.

'Do you ever think about the war?' she asked him.

'Never.'

'Why not?'

'Over and done with, long ago.'

'Not necessarily.'

'Why?' he asked, a fraction too quickly. 'What do you mean?'

'Things don't go away just because they happened more than ten years ago.'

'Don't know what you mean,' said Guy, buttering his roll. 'You're just like you were when you were a child. Always asking questions. Too many questions.'

'I try and answer my children when they ask questions.'

'Generation gap,' said Guy. 'Parents are the slaves of their children now. Quite wrong in my view.'

'What if Mamma had an affair? How would you deal with that?'

'My dear girl, are you ill? Your mother is the most loyal woman in the world. You seem over excited, perhaps you should get a tranquilizer.'

'You make me sound like a horse,' said Chloe.

'Nonsense. Now eat up your lunch and stop asking so many damn questions.'

Two days later, Rupert stopped off at an address in Fenchurch Street on his way home. It was after six-thirty, so he left the car on a yellow line and went up the dingy staircase that was like something out of a Raymond Chandler thriller. On the second floor, a frosted glass door bore the legend 'Merton Surveillance', and in smaller print underneath it said, 'Incorporating Newman & Digby Detective Agency, Est. 1923'.

'Ah, Mr Durrell,' said the receptionist. 'Go on in. Mr Merton is expecting you.'

'Sit down, Mr Durrell,' said Dave Merton, who had his back to the door as Rupert came in. He was rummaging in a tin filing cabinet. 'Here we are,' he said, sitting down on a swivel chair. A heavy man in a cheap dark suit without a tie; bags under his eyes, lard-coloured skin; too many long nights staking out a job, too much bad food. The wastepaper basket was stacked with hamburger cartons and empty drink cans.

'Nothing much to report. You go, she takes kids to school, sometimes she goes for a walk in the park alone afterwards. Home again. Tennis with a girlfriend, Sainsbury's; only one lunch with a gentleman a couple of days ago.' He read from his report:

'"Subject was walking up Old Bond Street when she met elderly gentleman coming out of T. Agnew & Sons, Art Dealers. Gent in cream suit, panama hat, brown Oxford shoes; subject and gentleman —"'

'It was Guy,' interrupted Rupert. 'Her father,' he added, seeing Merton's expression.

'Oh, well that's all right, isn't it? That's it then. She's clean, Mr Durrell, clean as a whistle. A virtuous wife.'

'Yes, all right,' said Ru, getting up. 'I'll take the papers, if I may. How much do I owe you?'

'Petra will settle up with you,' said Dave Merton, leaning across his desk to shake hands. 'Any time we can be of further use, please don't hesitate to let us know, Mr Durrell.'

CHAPTER 29

He knew her writing, although he hadn't seen it for half a century. The sight of it on the envelope had given him a fright and set his wretched heart somersaulting and making strange plunges in his chest like an aircraft that had got out of control. She had a large, black definite hand and used what looked like the same blue envelopes and writing paper that he remembered from the dark days of fifty years ago. The news of the premature death of the child made him terribly sad. Somehow, he discovered, he had half hoped that his son was walking about on the earth, under the same sun, the same moon; and yet he knew it was horribly selfish. How could she have managed, poor Marjorie, particularly in those days? He read the letter again, and discovered a terrible envy of the husband, Guy, whom he had never known. Guy who could see her every day, talk to her, watch her beauty. He had been fond of Eva, his wife, but he had not loved her in the way he had loved Marjorie; poor Eva, he had never been able to do much for her in the way of providing the kind of sheltered life Marjorie had led. Everyone went on and on about how much the world had changed and it had, of course it had, but in some ways it was still remarkably the same as it had been. People in England of Marjorie's class – and his own – lived on in their beautiful houses, tended their beautiful gardens, went up to town and stayed in their clubs, spent money in Harrods, popped over to Paris. They just kept quiet about having money or pretended, like Marjorie so cleverly had, that success was new to them, a ploy which appealed to an increasingly envious and proletarian world.

Hubert went out for a walk in the grounds of the house, now a public park. Young couples with small children in pushchairs strolled by the newly cleaned-up lake. A small boy fed the ducks with bread from a bag whilst his parents looked on indulgently. Hubert watched them and smiled and nodded when they looked round at him. In another life his own son would have swum in this lake, as he had done as a boy, or floated for hours in summer evenings in the old rowing boat, long since vanished. He sighed and turned away.

In the evening, the priest came to watch television. Hubert showed him the letter.

'What are you going to do?' asked Father Ignatius, handing it back and looking worried.

'Go and see her,' said Hubert, making a little gesture with his hands.

'Is that wise, do you think?'

'It was you who encouraged me to write,' said Hubert.

'I know it was. I hope I was right,' said the priest. 'I've had second thoughts about it.'

'Well, it's bit late for that now. Why? What second thoughts?'

'I suppose I thought it might have been better to let sleeping dogs lie. It is a long time ago, after all.'

'It is and it isn't,' said Hubert firmly. He also thought how he had detected her yearning for him between the lines of her letter. 'Anyway, I'll have to go now. She's expecting me and not to go would be worse than to go.'

CHAPTER 30

'Here's Daddy!' shrieked Miranda, who had been watching for him out of her bedroom window. 'Daddy, Daddy, Daddy!'

She ran out into the hall and opened the door.

'Hello, my darling,' said Rupert, in his big bear voice, bending down to pick her up. 'How's Daddy's little princess, then?'

'Have you got me a present?' squealed Miranda.

'Not today, my darling.' Ru laughed heartily. 'Not today. Maybe tomorrow.'

'Hi, Dad,' said James, leaning over the banisters. 'Can you come and help me with my maths? I can't do it.'

'In a minute, when I've kissed Mummy,' said Ru.

'Hello,' said Chloe, coming out of the sitting room where she had been reading the newspaper whilst she waited for Ru. Now he was back again she found herself locked once more into the habit of waiting for him and wondering where he was.

'Telephone,' said James.

'I'll get it,' said Chloe, going down the passage into the kitchen.

'Chloe?' It was Piers.

'Hello, Piers, how are you?'

'Great, thanks. How are *you*, more to the point?'

'OK.'

'Mum tells me Dad has come home again.'

'That's right.'

'Well, you're a fool to have him back,' said Piers. 'You know what he's like. He plays around with people's lives and doesn't care. Don't say I didn't warn you.'

'Thanks a bunch, Piers,' said Chloe, 'but what's the point of telling me that now?'

'Just warning you,' said Piers. 'Don't say I didn't warn you.'

'I won't.'

'Is Dad around?'

'I'll get him for you.'

*

At about ten-thirty Ru came into the kitchen and said to Chloe, who was making Miranda's lunch box, 'Are you coming up?'

'In a minute,' said Chloe, shutting the fridge door with her foot.

'I'll wait for you,' said Ru.

'You don't have to.'

'It's OK.'

'Please, Ru. I'll be up in a minute.'

'You say that every night.'

He took the half bottle of red wine that was standing on the table, got a glass and poured himself yet more wine.

'Haven't you had enough?' said Chloe, glancing at him.

'It's only a glass of wine,' he said. 'Have another yourself.'

'No, thanks. I don't want to be hungover in the morning.'

'Go on,' he said, reaching shakily for another glass. 'It'll loosen you up.'

'I don't want to be loosened up.'

'Come on, Chloe, I'm trying to be friendly.'

Chloe began to scour a saucepan.

'Come on,' said Ru, coming behind her and putting his arms around her. 'Come on. Let's go to bed.'

'I'm coming,' she said angrily. 'Just give me a minute.'

'You don't fancy me any more, do you?'

'Yes, I do,' said Chloe, 'but I don't when you're pissed.'

'I'm not pissed,' said Ru. 'This is nothing. What've we had? A few glasses of wine, that's all. Come on,' he said once more, putting his hand on her breast.

Chloe took a deep breath and tried to keep calm. 'You go,' she said. 'I'm coming up right now.'

It depressed her to see how quickly their marriage had fallen back into its old pattern. She found it difficult to relish the thought of sleeping with her husband unless she was drunk and she was certainly not drunk enough tonight. His touch made her shudder, his breath made her turn her face away, his technique was the same old channel ferry stuff – she wondered what Lucy had made of that – roll on, roll off. For all his antics with girls, Ru was a lousy lover. She did her best not to analyse the feelings that had driven her back to this barren imprisonment with a man she could no longer respect and did not love, the feelings of insecurity that chained her like a hamster to her treadmill.

When Rupert had finished, he fell asleep at once. He always did that. Chloe lay staring into the half dark in a state of feverish tension. She envisaged her life stretching ahead: how could she spend the next thirty or forty or even, God forbid, the next fifty years with this man? The thought horrified her and she pushed it away, but it returned again and again. Rupert had begun to snore. She raised herself on one elbow and looked at him with a mixture of pity and dislike.

'Ru?' she said, shaking him.

He stopped snoring for a moment and then began again.

'Ru?'

'Yeah?'

He opened his eyes and closed them quickly.

'I can't bear it,' she said.

There was no reply. Shortly, the snoring began again.

'Well, Chloe,' said Fanny the next morning, crossing her elegant legs. 'This is our last meeting for a while. How do you feel about that?'

'OK,' said Chloe, shrugging her shoulders.

Fanny was silent. She held a mug of herb tea in her hands and the steam drifted past her face like mist. 'Do you mind my going away?' said Fanny after there had been rather a long silence.

'Well, you have to have a holiday, don't you?'

'Yes,' Fanny smiled. 'But that wasn't what I asked you. I asked you if you minded.'

'How can I mind?' said Chloe impatiently. 'It's too bad if I mind, isn't it? I don't know why you ask.'

'I want you to see that it does matter if you mind,' said Fanny quietly.

'But it won't stop you going away,' said Chloe. 'Will it?'

'Would you like me not to be going away?'

'I don't know. Yes,' said Chloe. 'But why do you ask? It doesn't matter what I feel.'

Fanny reached behind her and passed the box of coloured tissues to Chloe. 'It does matter, Chloe. This is what I am trying to get you to see. Your feelings are valid and should be respected.'

'Nobody else thinks that,' said Chloe. 'They walk all over me.'

'They?'

'My father and mother. Rupert.'

'Go on.'

'We've been over this,' said Chloe, suddenly angry. 'We go over and over it and I still feel terrible. I'm right back where I started with Rupert as well.'

'Do you mind about that?'

'Terribly. I mind terribly. He's moved in again. I didn't really want him to, but it happened anyway, like everything else. I sometimes feel my whole life has consisted of people doing things to me: giving birth to me, educating me, marrying me, making me pregnant . . .'

'Couldn't you have said no to him?'

'The thing is, Fanny,' said Chloe slowly, 'that a part of me did want him to come back. When my mother laid her burden on me, I felt terrible, terribly insecure, as if whichever way I looked something sinister lay in wait for me.'

'The devil you know, in other words.'

'Yes.' Chloe nodded.

Fanny thought for a moment. 'What does Rupert represent to you?'

'Safety,' said Chloe automatically. 'He seemed to me to be the epitome of reliability when I met him, when I was younger, but he turned out to be anything but.'

'Is he, in any way, like your father?'

'They're very alike,' said Chloe. 'I was looking for a father figure . . . that's what you wanted me to realize, wasn't it? Father figures are, by definition, safe people, kind people, people who protect us, but what if one's own version is not like that? – My father figure is cynical and self-regarding, capable of love, but not always wanting all the responsibilities . . . each man, my father, Rupert, appears to be something he is not. Neither of them listens to a word I say. It's like a series of mirrors: husband reflects father who reflects mother's father and so on. It's rather frightening.'

She sat with this thought for a moment.

'What I want to say to you, Chloe,' said Fanny, 'is that you are free. I want you to think about yourself this summer, your own freedom, the responsibility you bear to yourself. You don't

have to ask permission,' she said, 'to have your feelings. Give
yourself permission. When you do that, you take responsibility
for your own life. You are valid. Remember that.'

'Darling,' said Lucy's mother, Charmian, when the waiter had
finished seating her, 'you look frightful. Anything the matter?'

'You always were tactful,' said Lucy crossly. 'Why? Should
there be?'

Charmian was staying at Claridges as she usually did and had
summoned Lucy to lunch 'for a little gossip', as she put it, which
was her idea of a mother/daughter relationship. Once or twice a
year Lucy endured Charmian, usually in the dining rooms of
the more expensive hotels, where, between the excessive atten-
tions of waiters, Charmian would give a brittle résumé of her
exhausting life.

'No, no,' said Charmian lightly, touching her ash-blonde helmet
of hair, 'I know you're a working gel and all that. How's biz?'

'We're doing all right,' said Lucy.

'And Mike? How's he?'

'Pete, you mean. He's fine.'

'*Dear* Pete,' said Charmian, unruffled, 'he always was a stal-
wart. Is he still with that divine-looking man?'

'Yes,' said Lucy, affecting to study the menu.

'Have a drink,' said Charmian. 'I'm going to have a g and t.'

'No thanks,' said Lucy. 'Some mineral water will do fine.'

'Not like you to be so dull.'

'I'm pregnant,' said Lucy, not looking up. 'That's why I'm
not drinking.'

'My God, I'll be a grandmother!' said Charmian in dismay.
'That makes me sound so *ancient*.'

'You are ancient,' said Lucy cruelly.

'Oh, you are unkind.' Charmian put a manicured hand to her
smoothed face as if to check it was still there. She had had a little
nip and a tuck in January and had thought she was looking
rather marvellous. Children adored to trip one up, little beasts.
Of course Lucy had always been jealous of her looks.

'Who's the lucky man, darling? I mean when's the wedding?
I'll have to get a new outfit ... I saw the most divine suit in
Caroline Charles this morning.'

'Rupert Durrell is the father, if that's what you mean.'

'Rupert? Chloe's husband?'

'Yes.'

'But is he going to marry you?'

'He's gone back to Chloe.'

'I always thought he was a bit of a swine,' said Charmian, reaching into her bag and getting out a compact and her lipstick which she applied as if she were alone in her own bathroom, making odd movements with her lips.

'I thought you liked him,' said Lucy.

'Terrible wandering hand trouble,' said Charmian. 'You'd be sitting one away from him at dinner and you'd still find his paw on your knee.'

'How's Heinrich?' asked Lucy pointedly.

'He's on a tennis course at the moment with the most wonderful man, darling, you'd adore him. It would be so marvellous if you could come and stay so we could help you.'

'I have a job to go to,' said Lucy, 'but thanks for the offer.'

'You're definitely going through with it?'

'Yes.'

'Well, I have to admire your courage, darling. It'll ruin your figure, of course. I hope you're seeing your dentist regularly as well. My teeth went into holes like crochet when I was having you in spite of calcium supplements. I must say I do think Rupert is a shit. Make sure he pays up, won't you? I can give you the number of a very good lawyer.'

'Who?' asked Lucy.

'Laura Grove, an absolute killer apparently. Very good on women's things. You mustn't be soft on him. I don't see why men should always get away with it.'

'Neither do I,' said Lucy.

Some days after Marjorie had handed Guy the letter to Hubert to post, she woke in the night from a terrible dream. Hubert had come and she had seen him, but she had not been able to speak to him. She had opened her mouth and all the wrong sounds had come out, animal sounds. Hubert hovered at her door and then turned to go . . .

She woke, hearing herself making strange noises, and discov-

ered that she was weeping. She sat up in bed and switched on
her light. Her little travelling clock, a wedding present from
Guy, said it was three a.m.

I might have known, she thought. Three a.m. was the terrible dead hour when all one's persecuting thoughts rose like
steam from the unconscious. She was struck once more by the
terrible atmosphere of the dream which was followed by an
absolute conviction that Hubert must not come here. I must
write at once, she thought, and then it occurred to her that
perhaps she could telephone him. But that in itself seemed a
monumental thing, something too nerve-racking to contemplate. The sound of his voice might completely ruin her. She
felt tears in her throat again and suppressed them firmly. If
she wrote now it would be fine. He would probably only just
have received her other letter and, after all, he would (she was
sure of this) contact her to confirm his travel arrangements
and to see if they were suitable. Of course he would do that.
All right, she said to herself, it's all right. Tears threatened her
these days at every juncture. It must be old age, she thought
to herself, lighting a cigarette and taking a swig from the flask
she kept on her bedside table for emergencies along with writing paper, envelopes, stamps, bottled water, fruit, books, magazines and innumerable other indispensable items.

She began to write a letter to Hubert, explaining why he
should not come, but she suddenly felt so sleepy that she folded it
inside the book she was reading, and turned out the light.

In the morning, when Guy came in as usual with her breakfast,
she was still asleep which was most unlike her. Guy put the
tray down on the table by the window and went over to where
Marjorie lay. Looking down at her sleeping face, he was struck
by her pallor.

'Marjorie,' he said, 'wake up, my darling, I've brought your
breakfast.'

Marjorie opened her eyes.

'Oh, darling,' she said, 'how terribly sweet of –'

But, attempting to sit up, she found she couldn't finish the
sentence. The words seemed somehow to run together in her
head; she was aware of a terrible pain in her arm as if someone

had lanced her just above the elbow, then everything went darkish, as if the room had suddenly filled up with black pigment.

CHAPTER 31

'Hello, Chloe.'

David put his head round the door of Marjorie's room, where Chloe had been sitting with her mother reading to her.

She had been taken into the hospital at Wayemouth and then removed again, as soon as it was possible, by Guy. Damn hell-hole, he called it. He engaged a Scottish nurse called Miss Innes to look after her and then returned to his gardening with a vengeance. He had a new plan afoot for an arboretum, between the existing wood above the ruins and the road that ran round behind, and he would spend hours there with McCormack talking about drainage and the pH value of the soil; soothing topics that took his mind off the agony of Marjorie's illness. Seeing her like that roused the most unbearable pity in him. She was going to die and he couldn't bear it. Couldn't bloody well bear it. So he planted trees instead.

'Hello.' Chloe got up with the book still in her hand.

'I don't want to disturb you,' he said. 'How is she?'

'Much the same.'

Marjorie was able to sit up but she could not feed herself. Someone else had to do that; sometimes Guy, sometimes Chloe, who could see that it was agony for her father. Marjorie couldn't speak either, although it was clear that she knew what she wanted and could understand things. The interpretation of her needs was the most difficult thing and there were times when she wept with frustration.

Chloe went to the window which looked out over the parterre toward the mystery of the ruins. The most beautiful room, the most beautiful view. In the very far distance the hills were a smudgy blue/purple. She listened to David having one of those absurdly embarrassing conversations which was all one could do with her mother these days, like something from Playschool, which was why she preferred to read to her. She wondered with a sudden revulsion if he would pray over her and give her communion, busy playing God again with those powerful tools at his disposal. She sighed and ran her hands through her hair, which she always did when she was anxious.

When David had finished, he got up and said to Chloe, 'Come outside for a minute. I want to talk to you.'

She looked round from the window and shook her head slightly.

Marjorie had dozed off. She did this now; little snatches of sleep here and there.

'Please,' he said.

'Say whatever it is here,' said Chloe. 'It won't make any difference to her.'

'I'd rather not.'

'Oh, all right,' said Chloe, 'but I don't want to be long. I promised Miss Innes I wouldn't leave her,' she lied.

'She's asleep. She won't notice.'

'Well then?' she said, in the gloom of the corridor outside.

'You're angry with me,' he said.

'No.'

'Chloe, be honest.'

'What's the point? You play games with people. You're like my husband, my parents. You're all the bloody same. You can't trust anyone.'

'I'm sorry.'

'I was vulnerable and then left dangling. Told to grow up, all that patronizing crap, when you —'

'I know,' he said. 'You are right. I'm sorry.'

'What a mess,' said Chloe. 'What a fucking awful mess. I almost feel this illness is another of my mother's schemes to make me feel bad. And that's such a terrible thing to say.' She put her hand over her mouth.

'I understand,' he said. 'She didn't have to tell you.'

'No, she didn't, but nevertheless she did. And now I know.'

'Are you with your husband again?'

'Yes.'

He looked at her.

'And it's awful. It's not going to work. I can't stay, but I can't seem to go. I don't know what to do.'

She broke down in sobs and he put his arms around her.

257

'I don't know what to do,' she said. 'Sometimes I just want to die.'

'No, you don't. You've got everything to live for.'

'*Don't* say that.' She shook herself free of him. 'Everyone says it: "Oh, Chloe, you've got everything to live for, you have such a wonderful life . . ." Nobody understands that you can't feel your life; you just want someone to accept how it is now for you. Everyone moralizes, or preaches at you, or takes the high ground and you're left floundering . . .'

'It will change,' he said.

'How do you know?'

'From my own experience.'

'You're so certain,' she said. 'Don't I make you angry, don't you want to punish me for my rudeness?'

'No, I don't. And you punish yourself more effectively than anyone.'

'I do, don't I? But I feel what's happened to her' – she jerked her head in the direction of the bedroom door – 'is my fault. I brought it on her by being angry with her.'

'That is pure nonsense.'

'Did she write to him? I've looked' – her voice dropped to a whisper – 'but I can't find any evidence one way or another. I don't think Pa knows, but he's beside himself with misery anyway. He cries about her. I can't stand it. Oh Christ, here's the old dragon . . .'

Sounds of Miss Innes clumping up the staircase.

'You go now,' she said, 'otherwise Miss Thing will start to wonder.'

'I'll be back tomorrow,' he said.

'OK.' Chloe wiped her nose with her sleeve. 'All right then. And David . . .'

'What?'

'Thanks.'

He shrugged and turned away.

Chloe went into her mother's room and found that she was still asleep.

She sent Miss Innes away.

'It was terribly inconsiderate of you to do this,' she said, when they were alone.

Behind her, the door opened. It was Guy come for his before-luncheon drink with Marjorie.

'How is she?' he asked.

'Much the same,' said Chloe stonily, stepping back from the bedside. 'Asleep now.'

'David was here?'

'Yes.'

'I must say he's been frightfully good to her.'

'I know he has. He has great gifts spiritually speaking.'

Guy glanced at his daughter, unsure, as usual, what she was getting at. She seemed to have changed recently and become rather bitter and cross, or at least she was with him. Snapped whenever he opened his mouth. Probably different with Doughty, who was young and glamorous.

'I'm going to stay for lunch,' Guy said, bending to kiss Marjorie who opened her eyes. 'Hello, my darling, here I am, come to have lunch with you. My favourite time of the day. Mrs Bos has made that pea and lettuce soup you like so much. There, there, don't cry. Your speech will come back. What is it, my love? Tell me.'

Guy looked behind him and saw Chloe still standing there.

'No need to hang around,' he said. 'I can deal with this.'

'Is that what I was doing?'

'I must be alone with her,' he said pathetically.

'When it's too late.'

'It's not too late,' he cried. 'It's not! Don't say that! You're upsetting her. She's crying.'

'She's crying with frustration, not sorrow,' said Chloe. 'Because there are things she should tell you and she can't.'

'You're cruel,' he said. 'A cruel woman. Go away and leave me alone with your mother.'

'I despise you both,' said Chloe. 'Do you know that?'

For a second she toyed with the idea of breaking him completely with her knowledge, but her mother made a convulsive noise that distracted her.

'Go and ring the doctor,' Guy said. 'I'm worried.'

'She's all right,' said Chloe, but when he looked round, she said, 'Don't worry, I'm going.'

And the moment passed.

*

259

When she had gone, Guy said, 'If you understand me, close your eyes and open them.'

Marjorie closed her eyes and opened them.

With a handkerchief, he gently dabbed away her tears.

'I want you to know,' he said, 'that I love you. I always did love you and I always will love you, irrespective of anything or anyone else. Show that you understand.'

She did, but the tears began to flow again.

'What is it?' he asked sorrowfully. 'I wish I knew. It's the same thing that's been on your mind for some time, isn't it? You see, I'm getting good at reading your mind now. I'm sorry I betrayed you,' he said, 'but you always were the one. Can you understand that?'

Again she did.

'When I was away, during those terrible years, I always thought of you here. That comforted me so much. To know you were here, looking after everything, taking care of the old place. Sometimes the thought of you was the only thing that kept me going.'

Guy broke down and wept himself.

And outside the not-quite-closed door Chloe listened.

'I tried never to think about those times,' he went on, after some more interminable seconds had passed, 'but they haunted my dreams. You can't know how tormented I felt. But I came back here and we did the garden together, and we were so happy, making something together. I hoped for a son, but of course that was not to be . . . and then you had Chloe . . . and you were so happy. She's turned against me now, she's so bitter, but you'll forgive me, won't you, my darling? Say you'll forgive me.'

A pause.

'Please don't die, Marjorie,' the awful grieving voice went on, 'please don't die, don't go away into a place where I can't find you. I don't know what I'll do without you . . .'

A couple of nights later Chloe woke suddenly, but she did not know what had woken her. When she was on her own at Fordingbridge, she slept in her old room amongst the relics of her childhood: the same bed, the same books in the bookcase, the copy of Fra Anglico's Annunciation on the wall: the angel bestowing the lily upon the Virgin that she had looked at a thousand times without really noticing.

There was one thought in her mind: I can't go on. The room seemed timeless, suffocating, endless. She had got away only to return into the powerlessness of childhood. What had seemed a way forwards was only a loop back. She had gone nowhere. She got out of bed and looked for a cigarette, found one and lit it. After two puffs, she put it out in a saucer. She paced up and down sweating. Her hands were shaking. She realized she wanted to die. And when she had thought that, she knew she had to talk to someone. But who? Everyone she had once trusted had betrayed her: her husband, her best friend, her parents. She went downstairs, taking the back stairs, and made her way in the half dark into her mother's work room, where the gardening books were kept.

She dialled Fanny's number in London, but of course . . . of course . . . Fanny was away. Always away when you needed them. She lit another cigarette and dialled David's number at the vicarage. The luminous face of her watch said it was two a.m. *He'll kill you*, said a voice. *And if he doesn't, the bitch wife will. There are some nice sharp knives in the kitchen; that one with the serrated edge would do* . . .

'Hello,' said a woman's voice. Frances. 'Fordingbridge Vicarage, Frances Doughty speaking. Who is it, please?' Rather brisk for someone who must have been asleep.

'Who is it?' the voice repeated into the silence.

'It's Chloe.'

'Chloe! Is it your mother?'

'No. It's me. I feel terrible. I can't go on . . .' She began to cry. 'It sounds stupid I know, but I can't –'

'It's all right, Chloe, I understand,' said Frances gently. 'You're at the end of your tether, aren't you?'

'I just can't . . .'

'I know, I know. It's all right. Do you want to come and talk about it here?'

'I can't . . . I can't bother you. I'm sorry –'

'You're not bothering us. Hang on a moment, don't go away.' She said something in a low voice to David, who was obviously beside her, then she said to Chloe, 'Are you dressed?'

'No.'

'Get dressed, then wait inside the door. He'll be along in five minutes. Have you got that?'

'Yes.' She replaced the receiver. Tears were pouring down her cheeks in a waterfall.

He had a rug with him which he wrapped her in like an invalid, then he drove her down the hill. Frances was in the kitchen making tea.

'Chloe,' she said, and went over and put her arms around her.

'I don't know why you're doing this,' said Chloe. 'I should be able to cope, but I can't ... I have all the equipment to cope and I just –'

'Shh,' said Frances. 'It's quite all right not to be able to handle things. You did the most sensible thing by ringing us. Asking for help is incredibly difficult when you feel like I think you feel.'

'I feel awful,' said Chloe, sitting down, 'but I'm so sorry to disturb you.'

'Don't be,' said David, lighting a cigarette and handing it to her. 'That's what we're here for – to be disturbed.'

'Everything just came together,' said Chloe. 'I woke up and I felt as if my head was breaking apart. There's been so much to deal with.'

'This business about your mother's been especially distressing,' said David, lighting a cigarette for himself, 'on top of everything else. I told Frances,' he said. 'I hope you don't mind. She'd never repeat it.'

'It's all right,' said Chloe. 'I don't mind. It's as though the foundations of my world have given way.'

'I know,' said Frances. 'Then freefall sets in. You don't know which way up you are.'

'Will it right itself?'

'Inevitably. But you mustn't hurry it.'

'No.'

'It's all right to be in a mess,' said Frances. 'It's all right to be in pain, to be afraid. You can be all those things: They won't destroy you, even though they feel as if they will.'

'They are destroying me,' said Chloe.

'No, they aren't. You're here, aren't you? It didn't happen, did it?'

'No.' Chloe looked at her. 'But I'm frightened it will again.'

'I don't think it will,' said Frances. 'I think this is it. But things will have to change. You might find you have to live in some different way, some more truthful way.'

'Frances,' said David warningly. Until now he had watched his wife handling the situation brilliantly, far better than he could have done. She seemed to know instinctively that Chloe need acknowledgement and acceptance of her pain. She didn't want to be diverted from it. At long last, she was ready to face it head on.

'No,' said Chloe, 'she's right. My marriage is over and done with. It's poisoning me; but it's not just what I want, there are the children too.'

'I know,' said Frances. 'But every situation is different. Remember that. And you have been living on your own with them. It won't be incredibly different.'

'I suppose not.'

'And we're here, right behind you.'

'I've no idea what I've done to deserve this,' said Chloe.

'You don't *have* to deserve anything to be helped,' said Frances, 'that's the whole point.'

The Bishop's study was lined with watercolours of India that his mother had done when his father was DC in Rajputana. There was an oil painting of his father in an elaborate gold frame, some heavy oak furniture that came with the job and glass-fronted bookcases that had followed the Bishop everywhere, even under an alien sun. It was an imposing room, David thought, on being shown in. Exactly as it ought to be.

'How's my poor old friend Marjorie Jessop?' asked the Bishop, sitting down in one of two chairs under a window. He didn't believe in conducting interviews from behind a desk.

'Much the same since her stroke,' said David. 'She can't talk, but I think she can understand what is said although sometimes it's hard to be sure. She's been a tremendous support to me since I arrived in Fordingbridge,' he added. 'I'm very grateful to her.'

'Marvellous woman,' said the Bishop, 'and an incredible

gardener. I'm always astounded by the garden at Fordingbridge Castle. It takes your breath, doesn't it? How are you finding things at Fordingbridge? Canon Jones was much loved, rather a hard act to follow I should think.'

'It's been fine,' said David. 'I have a very nice, very supportive PCC and I think I've managed to blend in locally without too much difficulty.'

'How are your wife's discussion groups going down?' asked the Bishop, looking amused.

'Quite well, I think. People certainly go to them. She's full of ideas, Frances, always has been. I sometimes think she's been rather hampered by my vocation.'

'I hear she's lost her job at Wayemouth College of Art,' said the Bishop. 'I'm sorry about that.

'It was a blow to her.'

'And to your fiscal situation, no doubt.'

'That too, of course.' David looked up. 'We have been having other problems,' he said, 'marriage problems. That's why I wanted to see you, really.'

'Moving's always unsettling, and job changes – job losses – don't help.'

'No, they don't, but the problems existed before that.'

'Of course they did. I know these things don't blow up overnight. Do you want to tell me about them?'

David told him what had happened over the last year or so. Then he said, 'I realized I'd treated her very badly, very unjustly, in some ways. I suddenly saw it.' He thought of that afternoon when Chloe had come to see him and of how he had been aware that he could pray again, that providential moment when everything had begun to move and to change; of how he had been given strength to resist temptation.

'That's the reason I'm here,' he said. 'I think my marriage is much better now, so much better, in fact, that I want to importune you on behalf of my wife. Is there anything you could do to employ her as a kind of spokeswoman for the diocese on various subjects? She's a very good talker, very persuasive.'

'You mean you want me to provide some extra scaffolding for your marriage?' said the Bishop.

'In a nutshell, yes.'

'Well, it's funny you should ask that question,' the Bishop said, 'because we've been thinking we want to set up a new post for someone to deal with women's affairs within the diocese – a paid post – to air the issues of the ordination of women, the plight of the single mother, getting mothers back into church, that sort of thing.'

'It's right up her street,' said David. 'It might have been made for her.'

'I think she had better come and see me,' said the Bishop, 'but I won't tell her you had anything to do with it.'

'Thank you,' said David. 'I'm very grateful.'

CHAPTER 32

The priest drove him to the airport, checked in his luggage for him and saw him as far as Customs where he stood waving on the other side like an illustration from some moral text for our times, Hubert thought. The angel sends the errant mortal off to make good, except that, in this case, the angel was rather worried about the mortal and whether he was doing the right thing, but Hubert had overruled him in order to suppress his own anxiety. Setting off on a long journey into one's own past was enough to be going on with. He had to stick to his own conviction that he was doing the right thing. The priest had said, 'You should have let her know you were coming,' and Hubert had replied, 'I did, I wrote, although I haven't heard anything.'

'You should have telephoned,' said the priest.

'I couldn't do that,' said Hubert. 'You don't understand.'

He allowed his conviction to sustain him through the unutterable frightfulness of the airport lounge, the aircraft itself (hateful little aluminium tube held up only, Hubert was sure, by God's goodness) the desiccated and dreadful items that passed for food, the synthetic smiles of the stewardesses.

England, or at least what he could see of it from the taxi on the way up the motorway, looked tiny, smug, green, suburban, lush. He was ravished by the foliage, the abundance of pretty buildings that had survived the Modernists (concrete nightmare of totalitarianism), and astonished by the number of shiny, new cars.

He had booked himself into a hotel in Dover Street, a small establishment he was pleased to find still in existence, for a night or two, for he wanted to renew his love affair with London before he went to Fordingbridge. A porter greeted him, took his luggage up, explained where everything was and went away again. The day's papers sat on a table in the sitting room. Hubert read them hungrily. He had forgotten the pleasures of the English press and was astonished after so long at the freedom with which everybody criticized each other and the government. He went into the bathroom and, by mistake, caught a glimpse of himself in the mirror over the basin as he was washing his hands. An old man with thick white hair and a ruggedly lined face stared shockingly back at him. It was almost, he thought, as if he had expected this voyage of return to make the youth he had once been out of him. He had been so reckless with Marjorie, so cruel in a way, but the spirit of carpe diem had informed everything in those days. He wanted to ask her forgiveness.

On Saturday morning, Rupert packed the two children into his car and set off for Fordingbridge. It was the first time he had been back since he and Chloe had got together again. Ru enjoyed Fordingbridge. Old Guy was a bit of a fart, but he had liked Marjorie and he had been hurt by her rejection of him during the time he and Chloe had been separated. He half felt her stroke was just retribution for her bad treatment of him, but on the whole he was sorry the old trout was laid low. Chloe had been terribly upset but he had been able to make some headway with her by suggesting that she should go down there and he would follow at the weekend with the children.

Ru was not given to introspection. He thought it rather a waste of time. Something happened, one reacted in one way or another and that was that. He had heard nothing from Lucy since he had bought her dinner and she had so rudely walked out, but he didn't think about her very much. It was over. He was back with Chloe. Lucy must take her chance. When he thought of his marriage to Chloe, which he did from time to time, he reckoned its chances as good. Chloe was difficult and childish in many ways, but she had taken him back and that was a good thing. It would be more difficult for her to push him out next time – if, of course, there was a next time, but that was something Ru didn't bother to contemplate. It wasn't his fault he was so attractive to women. If anyone had asked him if he was happily married he would immediately have answered, 'Yes. Very.'

'I brought your post,' he said to Chloe as they walked round the garden with the children running about behind, dodging in and out of the trees.

'Anything interesting?'

'I didn't really look,' he said, 'but I don't think so. A few bills, circulars, general rubbish.'

Chloe took the bundle of envelopes and opened a large, thick one that contained an invitation of some kind.

'Oh, Patrick Churchill,' the said. 'An invitation to his show. What a lovely painting.'

'Who's Patrick Churchill?' asked Ru suspiciously.

'Someone we met by mistake.'

'Who's "we"?'

'Me and the children,' said Chloe. 'He's a painter. Have a look.'

Ru glanced at the invitation and handed it back.

'Thanks for bringing this,' Chloe said, thinking about seeing Patrick again. 'How have the children been this week?'

'Fine. As good as gold. I took them to school every morning. I think they rather liked that,' he added proudly.

'I'm sure they did,' said Chloe, trying not to sound sarcastic. 'How is your mother?'

'Pretty awful,' said Chloe. 'You can see her in a minute.'

'No rush,' said Rupert, who had a horror of illness of any kind. 'She probably won't recognize me.'

'Of course she will,' said Chloe, 'she's not completely gaga. It's just that she can't speak, poor darling, and when she does, it comes out in a kind of giant garble. It's very frustrating.'

'Who the hell is that?' Said Rupert proprietorially as a man appeared from the direction of the ruins. He was wearing a cheap-looking pale grey suit which had some thread in it that seemed to shimmer in the sunlight. His shoes were grey too, with strange soles that looked as if they were made from recycled tank tyres, but in spite of the clothes he was tall and good-looking with a great shock of white hair.

'I haven't a clue,' said Chloe, but even as she said it she knew at once who it was. 'Hold on,' she said. 'I'll go and ask him what he wants.'

'I'll throw him out, if you like,' said Rupert. 'It's not even an open day today, is it?'

'No, it's not,' said Chloe, 'but there's no need for aggression. He's obviously foreign or something.'

'Appalling suit,' murmured Ru. 'I wonder where you buy suits like that?'

'Stay there,' said Chloe impatiently.

'Hello,' she said, approaching the stranger. The children, thank God, had vanished somewhere.

'Hello.' He raised a hand. 'You must forgive me. I came the back way. I remembered it from the war.'

'You were here during the war?'

'Forgive me,' he repeated, 'for my bad manners. My name is Hubert van der Meulen. I was a convalescent here during the war when your mother was running the castle as a nursing home.'

'How do you know she's my mother?'

'My dear,' he said, 'there's no doubt whose child you are. You are quite as beautiful as your mother.' He bowed charmingly. 'I wrote to her some time ago asking if I could come and see her, you see. She replied and said yes, I could. I wrote again telling her when I would like to come, but I heard nothing in reply. I should have telephoned, but instead I have turned up out of the blue.'

He spoke perfect unaccented English with just the faintest hint of foreignness in the formality of his speech.

'I do know who you are, as a matter of fact,' said Chloe staring at him.

'You do?'

'She told me you had written. I think she was rather upset by your letter.'

'I was worried she might be. But she did write back, you know, telling me to come.'

He searched her face, as if wondering how much she knew.

'She isn't well,' said Chloe. 'I don't think she's been herself for ages. She's had a stroke.'

This man's son was her half-brother. It seemed too enormous a fact to contemplate.

'What's going on?' asked Ru, coming to join them. 'Everything all right?' he asked Chloe.

'This is Hubert van der Meulen,' said Chloe, 'an old friend of my mother's. I was telling him what's been going on.'

'She's terribly unwell,' said Rupert, taking charge. 'It's not a very good moment.'

He could see that Chloe was upset by something, but he couldn't figure out what.

'But I've come all the way from Germany,' said Hubert. 'May I not have a glimpse of her?'

'I really don't think –' said Ru.

'It's all right, Ru,' said Chloe. 'I'll take him up. I think he should see Mamma.'

She took him into her mother's study first, before she led him upstairs.

'Sit down,' she said, indicating a chair. She herself sat with her back to her mother's pretty roll-top desk. 'Does my father know you are coming?'

'I don't know.'

'Why did you write?'

'I saw her on television. It roused . . . such memories in me. I have never forgotten your mother.'

'But fifty years,' said Chloe. 'That's pushing it a bit, isn't it?'

'I'm sorry you're so angry,' he said. 'I'm very, very sorry. I came to ask her forgiveness after all this time, for the harm I did her.'

Chloe looked at him.

'It wasn't intentional,' he said. 'Falling in love with someone is not intentional.'

'What about the rest of it?'

'The rest? I'm sorry,' he said. 'I don't follow.'

It dawned on Chloe that he did not know about his child. Her mother must have lied to him, for whatever reason.

'May I see the letter she sent you?'

He looked at her before replying, 'I'd rather you didn't.'

'Please,' said Chloe, holding out her hand, certain somehow that he would have brought it with him.

'If you must,' he said, taking it out of the inside pocket of his jacket. 'It's not a pretty story. She was pregnant when I had to go.'

'I know,' said Chloe. 'She told me everything not long before she had her stroke. She can't speak,' she said.

'I'm so sorry. So very, very sorry.'

Chloe, without saying anything, took the letter and read it. When she had done so, she folded it up and replaced it in its envelope.

'Stay here,' she said, rising to her feet. 'I'll go and tell her you're here, then I'll come down and fetch you. My father knows nothing of this,' she added.

'I understand.'

Chloe went slowly up the stairs. As she did so, her father appeared at the top looking dishevelled and unshaven.

'I was coming down to see about some lunch,' he said, as they stopped level with one another. Chloe could see he had been crying. Her mother's illness had broken his heart. She suddenly felt terrible pity for him, more pity than she ever thought she could feel. She knew then that she would never tell him what she knew. Her mother's secret had become hers. The pieces of the past must lie where they had fallen like the broken statuary of some forgotten empire. It was over.

'Is she awake?' she asked.

'Yes.'

He put his hand up and chucked her under the chin, a hopeless gesture, being about a quarter of a century late, but one which she understood nevertheless.

'There's someone in her study who wants to see her,' she said quickly, 'someone from the war.'

'Oh, yes.' Guy straightened his shoulders. 'She mentioned he might come. He ought to stay to lunch, I suppose.'

'Yes, I suppose he should,' said Chloe reflectively. 'Can he see Mamma? What do you think?'

'Of course he can. Quack says stimulation's the thing. Don't leave them to vegetate.' He sounded more like his normal self.

'I'll go and tell her, then,' said Chloe. 'Perhaps you'd bring him up.'

'Only a few minutes,' said Guy to Hubert outside Marjorie's door. 'She tires very easily. You'll have lunch with us, of course.'

'I hope it's no trouble.'

'No trouble. Glad to have you here. She can't speak,' he added in a low voice, 'but she likes to be talked to. She can understand some things, although not all. Come, I'll take you in.'

She lay on her pillows like a doll, very white, very fragile. Her eyes were closed.

'Marjorie,' said Hubert, taking her hand.

She opened her eyes and looked at him.

'I got your letter,' he said.

'Dad,' said Chloe, putting her head round the door, 'can I ask you something?'

'Excuse me,' said Guy, getting up and going out. 'Back in a tick.'

'I wanted to say sorry,' said Hubert when Guy had gone, taking her poor hand in both his. 'I loved you very much.'

He raised her hand to his lips and kissed it.

Marjorie closed her eyes, and when he spoke again she did not open them, but her hand lay in his as fragile as a bird.

'She drops off like that,' said Guy, coming back, 'mid-sentence. Quite normal, the quack says. Thanks for coming anyway. Come down and have a drink.'

On the stairs he said to Hubert, 'Best wife a man could have,' and his voice broke a bit as he said it.

'She was wonderful to us all,' said Hubert, a little shakily to match. 'Quite wonderful. We revered her, you know. We thought of her when we got into a sticky patch.'

'What happened to you?'

'Oh.' Hubert shrugged his shoulders. 'Nothing very much. Back into France, worked with the Resistance, captured, camp, that sort of thing.' He put his hand over his eyes for a moment.

'Me too,' said Guy. 'I must have been away when you were here.'

He might have been on holiday, the way he said it so lightly.

'You were,' said Hubert, nodding. 'She talked about you all the time,' he said, 'worried herself sick. Work helped her. She had such a great abundance of energy.'

'Marvellous woman,' said Guy, walking slowly down the stairs under the portrait of the hanging judge in his periwig.

'The very best. I am privileged to have seen her once more.' Hubert paused. 'Tell me,' he said. 'Is Babs still alive?'

'You knew Babs, did you?'

'Oh, just a very little,' said Hubert.

'Babs was always a bad girl,' said Guy knowingly. 'Dead now, I'm sorry to say, dead these many years. Gave poor old Archie the run around before he was killed.'

'Yes, she was rather a handful,' said Hubert. 'I'm sorry she's dead. I was hoping perhaps —'

'Well, these things happen. Now come and have that drink,' said Guy briskly, 'then I can show you the garden if you like.'

'Perhaps your daughter would join us?'

'Yes, yes, I'm sure she'd be delighted,' said Guy. 'She's acting chatelaine now, now poor old Marjorie's —'

'Yes, yes, of course,' said Hubert hastily as they went down the front stairs under the portraits he remembered so well.

'Who was that chap?' asked Rupert after lunch, as he walked to the ruins with Chloe. Guy had driven Hubert to the station in Wayemouth. 'He seemed a bit ... I don't know ... a bit familiar.'

'He's a friend of Mamma's,' said Chloe, who had decided that now was the moment to say what she wanted to say to Rupert, what indeed she had to say. 'I told you — and you must have gathered from what we talked about at lunch — that he was here in the war when Dad was a p. o. w. He wanted to come back and have a look.'

'I bet he was up to no good,' said Ru. 'He seemed to know an awful lot about the place and about your mother.'

'They were friends,' said Chloe. 'And anyway, lots of people know a lot about her.' It was amazing, she thought, how people who were normally very dense about their fellow humans could suddenly hit on something with absolute accuracy.

'Ru,' she said, 'sit down a minute.' There was an old stone bench inside the entrance to this place where the contemplative could sit and ponder.

'Why? I thought we were going on a bit.'

'I want a divorce,' she said.

'But we've just joined up again. I don't understand.'

'It's not going to work.'

'But it *is* working.'

Chloe shook her head. However long it took, she was absolutely and implacably determined on her course. This knowledge of what she wanted gave her courage.

'Please,' he said, 'please don't do this.' He fell on his knees

273

on the turf in front of her. 'Please,' he said. 'I want to be with my children.'

'You should have thought of that,' said Chloe. 'You really should. It's too late. It was too late before, but I didn't know it.'

'Someone's been poisoning your mind against me,' said Ru. 'I bet it's that damned shrink you've been seeing.'

'No, it isn't,' said Chloe. 'This is my decision.'

'I'll make it impossible for you,' he said. 'I'll fight you every step of the way. I'll apply for custody of the children.'

'You won't get it,' said Chloe, who was trembling, as every woman trembles at the thought of her children being taken from her.

'I'll tell the court you're unstable,' said Ru, getting up. 'I'll tell them about your temper and your bouts of –'

'Stop this. It's pointless.'

'You won't get away with it.'

'You're behaving like a little boy, Ru,' said Chloe. 'Grow up, for God's sake. Admit defeat.'

'Never,' said Ru. 'You'll never get away with it.'

'Yes, I will,' said Chloe.

'Why're you doing this to me?' said Ru, changing tack suddenly and becoming a whipped spaniel again. 'Why? We have everything anyone could want. Lovely home, cars, holidays, beautiful children . . .'

'You don't understand, do you? We have no love, no trust, no respect. We have nothing that really matters.'

'But I love you.'

'You don't. You regard me as an object, a possession, a useful handle. I'm not, Ru. I'm a human being.'

'I'll reform,' said Ru wildly. 'I'll change. I'll do whatever you want me to do.'

'You won't,' said Chloe. 'It's no good. You're too old to change.'

'Give me a chance.'

'It's too late, Ru,' Chloe said, standing up. 'I'm terribly sorry, but it is. And nothing will change my mind.'

'Bitch,' said Ru. 'Lying, conniving bitch.'

He flung off into the garden somewhere. A little later, Chloe heard the sound of a lawnmower. Ru, no doubt, mowing her down this time. She was in the firing line now, not Marcia, and she shuddered, remembering the campaign of hatred he had waged against his first wife. She sent a prayer into the ether for strength and resolution and courage.

CHAPTER 33

The following week Chloe went to London to go to Patrick Churchill's show which was being held in a gallery in Cork Street. She had decided to keep the children with her at Fordingbridge, as it was so near the end of term, and was slightly surprised when Ru did not object. Clearly, claiming custody was one thing, actually looking after children quite another.

A uniformed flunkey opened the door for her and asked her to sign her name in the visitors' book, which she duly did. On the line above she saw Lucy's familiar signature. She debated whether or not she should bolt, but then decided to press on. She had a sneaking desire to meet Patrick Churchill again and to see what his work was like.

'Hello,' said Patrick, who was standing at the bottom of the stairs. 'I hoped you'd come. I was sorry to hear your mother was so ill.'

'Yes, poor thing,' said Chloe. 'I'm just escaping for a —'

She broke off, having caught sight of Lucy.

'What is it?' asked Patrick, following her gaze.

'Someone I know,' said Chloe. 'The woman who borrowed my husband, in fact.'

'Has she returned him?'

'He returned himself,' said Chloe, 'but it's over. We've parted. Or at least I have. He keeps trying to come back.'

'Poor you.'

'I'll cope,' said Chloe. 'I'm getting used to it. Excuse me a minute.'

She went over to where Lucy was standing talking to a man in a crumpled linen suit. She looked tired, Chloe thought, and rather fat. Quite unlike her normal self.

'I didn't expect to find you here,' she said.

'Nor I you. I'm sure you don't want to talk to me, but I think you should know I'm pregnant.'

'Who's the lucky man?'

'Your husband,' said Lucy. 'Didn't he tell you?'

'It must have slipped his mind.'

'Is that all you have to say?'

'What do you expect me to say?' Well done, congratulations. Various clichés immediately presented themselves.

'I don't know,' said Lucy. 'I just don't know. I must go.' She put her glass down and moved off.

Some nights after this Chloe was woken in her room on the nursery floor by her father in his blue and red striped pyjamas.

She was awake at once. 'What is it?'

'She's going,' said Guy. 'I want you to come and be with us.'

'Go down,' said Chloe. 'I'll follow. Have you rung David?'

'He's on his way.'

They sat, Chloe and her father, in the dim room, long after the priest and the doctor had been, long after the prayers for the dying had settled in the air around them. They each held a hand. And sat and waited as the dawn came up, and the garden, magnificent in its summer plumage, sprang out of the dark. Birdsong and the trembling light hopefulness of a summer's morning anticipating the sun.

On her pillow, Marjorie's breathing turned the last corner.

'Open the window,' said Chloe. 'Let her go.'

Out over all the beauty she had created.

Mrs Bos put Marjorie into a grand evening dress she had ordered from Worth years and years before. It was made of sea-coloured silk taffeta and had long heavy sleeves encrusted with tiny glass beads. Her hair was in its usual pleat. She looked beautiful and peaceful.

'There she is,' said Guy, taking Chloe's hand.

Chloe looked down at that lovely familiar face.

'She loved you very much,' he said. 'So do I.'

'I know you do,' Chloe answered. She could only guess what it had cost him to say that. Guy who never discussed his feelings.

'Do you want a moment alone with her?'

'Would that be all right?'

'Of course.'

When he had gone out of the room, Chloe bent over and kissed her mother's cold face.

'Your secrets are safe with me,' she said. 'God speed, darling, wherever you are.'

EPILOGUE

On a day in early November, Chloe turned left off the coast road where a signpost said 'Port David'. A storm was brewing, according to the weather forecast. As she drove into the tiny fishing port, the waves were breaking so violently in the harbour that the spray from them could seen in misty spirals above the rooftops.

She parked in the car park by the harbour and got out, buttoning up her coat and pulling down her woolly hat. She walked a little way along the sea, marvelling at the power of the waves and the chill, sad cries of gulls gusting in the wind like scraps of paper. There was nobody about.

She thought of her mother coming here during those long-ago days of the war to have the child, and of how she must have felt with her husband a prisoner and her lover vanished into the darkness of war. Amongst her mother's copious papers had been a letter from Babs written with gossipy lightness in a code they had obviously worked out between them: 'I thought you'd like to know,' she said, 'that Kirsty's new baby boy is thriving. He's the centre of attention, a great cause for joy. It's been a marvellous thing for the family. I know this will please you.'

In the bar of the hotel, a middle-aged man in a big fisherman's sweater leaned his elbows on the counter. He was telling a story in a low voice to the barman and they were both laughing. He was tall and handsome with a beaky nose and had a great shock of white hair. They both looked up when Chloe came in.

'What can I get you?' said the barman politely. 'Terrible day.'

'A small whisky, please,' said Chloe, meeting the eye of the man in the sweater.

At that moment, the door opened and a boy of fourteen or so came in. He was the exact replica of the man in the sweater, tall and angular with the same beaky nose, except his hair was jet black.

'Come on, Dad,' he said. 'Mum's doing her nut wonderin' where you'd got to.'

279

'Better go, Jock,' said the man in the sweater, putting his glass down.

'You know what women are like.'

Chloe went and sat by the fire and drank a little toast to her mother.